David Rollins is the bestselling author of *Ghost Watch*. He lives with his family in Sydney. As always, he's writing the next book.

If you want to know what's coming up next from David, go to his website, davidrollins.net, and sign up to the newsletter. There's a David Rollins fan site on Facebook and you can also follow him at twitter.com/DavidRollins1.

Also by David Rollins

GHOST WATCH

DAVID ROLLINS

CORVUS

First published in Australia in 2012 by Macmillan, an imprint of Pan Macmillan Pty Limited, 1 Market Street, Sydney.

Published in trade paperback in Great Britain in 2012 by Corvus, an imprint of Atlantic Books Ltd.

10 9 8 7 6 5 4 3 2 1

A CIP catalogue record for this book is available from the British Library.

Trade paperback ISBN: 978 0 85789 643 8
E-book ISBN: 978 0 85789 681 0

Printed and bound in Great Britain by the MPG Books Group.

Corvus
An imprint of Atlantic Books Ltd
Ormond House
26–27 Boswell Street
London
WC1N 3JZ

www.corvus-books.co.uk

One week ago

The man's battered head rolled from side to side with the motion of the boat. A sound escaped his throat but nothing else had a chance of freedom. Not out here. Not now.

Benicio von Weiss regarded the man at his feet and then upended the chilled bottle of Evian. He took a long drink, wiped his mouth with the back of his hand while the lavender sea rolled slow and languid beneath the white hull of the *Medusa*, the über-luxurious Mangusta 130, his toy du jour. Von Weiss's eyes moved on to survey the horizon and saw nothing but the crisp blue line where sea met sky and the small solitary green island of Queimada Grande. Brazil lay thirty-two kilometers to the west. Out to the east, six and half thousand kilometers of empty Atlantic Ocean stretching all the way to Africa.

A woman in a brief yellow bikini appeared in the doorway, distracting him. The sun had turned her hair gold and her skin bronze. She was tall and . . . accommodating.

'Come and watch,' he told her.

'No thanks,' she said, in passable Portuguese.

'Really, I insist.'

'Okay, if you insist.' The woman lowered her sunglasses onto her face and sat on the leather bench seat, her mood one of disinterest.

Von Weiss caught a glimpse of his own reflection in a smoked gray panel over her shoulder and liked what he saw: a muscular build, blond hair and a new nose and laser peel that made him look closer to thirty than forty. He admired himself some more, lingering on the image before returning to the immediate business. 'Maybe this will teach you a valuable lesson to take into your next life,' he said.

Semi-conscious, the man, whose name was Diogo 'Fruit Fly' Jaguaribe, barely responded.

'Having fingers that stick to other people's money can get you into trouble, eh?' Von Weiss bent down, lifted one of the man's destroyed hands to give it a final inspection and then squeezed the thumb and forefinger together, producing a gratifying flinch from his captive, accompanied by a groan, as the knuckles parted once more.

The woman in the bikini barely moved.

Medusa's tender, a white jet boat, maneuvered closer, its exhaust pipes gargling seawater. It gently nudged the mothership's transom and von Weiss gave his men the nod. They picked up Jaguaribe and dragged him across the gap between the two craft, timing the transfer between the peaks of the swell, before throwing him onto the other vessel's spotless teak floorboards.

'Julio!' von Weiss called out after taking another mouthful of Evian. Julio Salvadore, a heavy-set young man with a mean streak and a bright future, glanced up from the tender. Von Weiss twisted the top onto the plastic bottle and then tossed it underarm toward the smaller craft, an easy catch. 'We don't want our friend to die . . . of thirst.'

*

Salvadore gave von Weiss a grin. He had a good feeling in his balls – other people's pain always had that effect. 'Yes, O Magnifico.' He turned to the man behind the wheel. 'Go!' The jet boat leaped high out of the water as the throttles were opened and it accelerated toward the island, sixty meters away.

'Wake him!' Salvadore shouted over the roar of the wind and the engine.

A man who had been using Jaguaribe as a footstool pulled the captive to his knees and slapped him several times before throwing a cup of seawater from a bucket into his face. The shock of it brought the captive back to full consciousness and he blubbered several times, blowing water from his swollen, blood-encrusted lips. The jet boat slowed as it closed with the rock shelf protruding from the island.

Satisfied that Jaguaribe was in control of his wits, Salvadore gave the signal and the man was tossed overboard into the deep blue water. 'Swim, Fruit Fly!' Salvadore shouted as the man bobbed to the surface in a plume of silver bubbles, floundering and choking as he struggled to keep his head above water. 'Go! Swim!' he repeated and pointed in the direction of the island. Jaguaribe swam toward the boat, but when the craft reversed a few meters he seemed to understand the implication and began struggling to the shore, his injuries and shredded clothing hampering his movements.

Salvadore watched patiently. Eventually, a wave lifted the man and pushed him up onto the black and gray rock shelf, where he rolled and tumbled and got dragged back into the ocean by the backwash. The next wave deposited him higher, but not before pushing him through a patch of oysters that tore skin off his stomach and legs. Then somehow the man managed to get his limbs working and drag himself higher before collapsing onto the rocks.

'Closer,' Salvadore said and the boat surged forward. When it was just off the shelf, Salvadore took the half-bottle of Evian and tossed it high and far so that it landed among the smooth rounded rocks above Jaguaribe's head, causing half a dozen birds to leap screeching into the air.

*

Mucus and salt had gummed Jaguaribe's eyes closed. Partially blinded, he tried to crawl but even the smallest movement sent bolts of pain shooting through his body. His hands in particular were spheres of agony. Blood and salt glued the remains of his torn clothing to the flayed skin on his belly and legs. He shifted a foot and the clothing pulled

3

away from his raw wounds; the pain made him cry out. Tears welled in his eyes, loosening the mucus and allowing him to open them.

Birds were everywhere – darting through the air, rummaging in the bushes. Several were nesting on the ground in the dry scrub behind him. His head dropped. A half-full plastic bottle lay nearby. *Water.* Why had they left him with that? Jaguaribe was suddenly aware of his thirst. He licked his cracked lips and tasted salt and copper. He had to get to the bottle. Coming to his knees, he cried out again with the messages of pain the raw nerve endings sent to his brain. He tried to flex his wrecked fingers but they had swollen to the thickness of Cuban cigars. He reached for the Evian bottle and with great difficulty held it between his palms, using his teeth to remove the top, spitting it out. As he tilted his head back to drink, the bottle slipped from his mangled hands and rolled down the rock shelf and into the sea.

Jaguaribe swayed on the spot, not knowing what to do. He glanced at his wrist. His watch was gone, but the sun was heading toward the horizon. How long had he been lying there? His pants were wet. The smell . . . He'd urinated where he'd lain, above the waves.

They'd taken him aboard *Medusa* in the early hours of the morning, but this nightmare had begun much earlier than that. It had started when they'd dragged him from the bed of his favorite whore, his exhausted member still clasped within the warmth of her hand. The beating had started out on the road and continued in the back of the truck as it had sped through the streets of Rio. The serious abuse had begun in von Weiss's mansion, in the cellar where the walls were lined with bottles of wine, the atmosphere controlled so that it was unnaturally cool and dry. It was also soundproof. Reeling from all the beatings, Jaguaribe had watched with morbid interest as they'd placed pencils between his fingers. Why were they doing that? he'd asked himself. The question had been answered when they'd then squeezed his fingers together until the joints had separated one at a time. When they were done with his fingers and the screaming had subsided, they'd worked on his knuckles. And when they'd finished with those, they'd gone back to his fingers, this time with a hammer, smashing them one by one.

Some time later they'd thrown him into the trunk of a car and driven for over an hour. The fact that they had not asked any questions frightened him. It was as if they were sure of his guilt. But he'd done nothing – nothing he could think of – that warranted this treatment. At dawn they had pulled him from the darkness of the trunk and he'd found himself in the forecourt of a house he recognized. It was von Weiss's house on the beach at Angra dos Reis, a holiday town down the coast from Rio. Jaguaribe had seen pictures of this house, sleek and modern and worth millions. After dragging him inside, they'd then beaten him unconscious, and that's all he remembered.

Jaguaribe turned and saw that von Weiss's boat was close by, barely a hundred and fifty feet away across the water. Von Weiss himself was standing on the rear deck, watching him through binoculars. A woman was beside him. Where am I? Jaguaribe asked himself.

O Magnifico had the wrong man. He was being blamed for something done by someone else. Jaguaribe had not double-crossed him. The risks were too great, as his current situation proved.

A man joined von Weiss and the woman. It was that dangerous pig, Salvadore. There was a rifle cradled in his arms. Yes, he recognized it – how could he not? It was a British RPA 7.62mm sniper rifle – the urban model. Jaguaribe had bought it himself and had it dipped in eighteen-carat gold. A present for O Magnifico on the occasion of his birthday. The rifle flashed yellow in the afternoon sunlight.

*

Von Weiss held out his hand and Salvadore passed him the weapon. He dropped the magazine and checked that it was full before replacing it, pulling the bolt back and pushing it forward to chamber a round. He shouldered the weapon and then took a knee, resting the long golden barrel against a polished chrome cleat.

'Can you see any of your little friends, O Magnifico?' Salvadore asked.

Von Weiss scanned the bushes behind Jaguaribe. 'Ah, yes,' he said. 'There's one. It's time to get our little fly's feet moving.' He cocked his head briefly toward the woman. 'Watch this.'

Von Weiss took the rifle off safety and brought the telescopic sight's crosshairs onto the bridge of Jaguaribe's nose for a moment before shifting the fine black cross down and to the left. He held his breath and squeezed the trigger. There was a deafening crack as the rifle stock punched into his shoulder, and almost simultaneously an eruption of blood blossomed on Jaguaribe's upper arm.

Salvadore complimented him. 'Excellent shot, O Magnifico.'

'Can I go inside now?' the woman asked.

*

The force of the blow twisted Jaguaribe around violently. At the same instant a small bomb appeared to have gone off inside his arm, an explosion of flesh and blood. Shock paralyzed him for a handful of seconds, but then he clambered to his feet and staggered up the rock shelf, toward the low bushes where the birds were nesting and there was cover. There he sat for a full minute, behind the tree line, breathing heavily, his heart pounding, thorns in the soles of his bare feet. He tried to pluck them out but his wrecked fingers were useless. Von Weiss was an excellent marksman; if Benicio wanted him dead, then why was he still breathing? Wounding him had to have been the intention, Jaguaribe told himself. Which meant that perhaps he had not been brought here to die after all. Perhaps O Magnifico would send the boat for him and toast his bravery with a bottle of *cachaça*. Jaguaribe lifted his head above the bush to see what was going on out on the water, hoping to find the tender coming for him, his crimes, whatever they were, forgiven. But the small bay was empty, the tender still tethered behind the *Medusa*.

Jaguaribe saw von Weiss hand the rifle back to Salvadore, exchanging it for binoculars. And the flash of relief he'd felt only moments ago was gone, the dread rushing back. Von Weiss was watching him, waiting for *something*. But what? The pain in Jaguaribe's arm was beginning to bite. It mingled with the jagged signals from his destroyed hands, clouding his judgment. *What should I do?* He caught sight of a blood trail across the rocks. It led to him, he realized. The length of his arm was now bright red and slick with blood oozing from the torn flesh and dripping from his fingers. Two birds began pecking at his naked ankles and bare toes, squawking and flapping their wings. Jaguaribe had to move again, get away from the birds and the shore, away from the golden rifle, away from whatever it was that von Weiss was waiting and watching for. Jaguaribe had no idea what that might be, but he was terrified. He got up and stumbled through the bushes, which were low near the shoreline but thicker and taller as he penetrated them, climbing away from the shore.

Jaguaribe trampled several birds' nests before he found a trail and then he stopped, panting. A *trail*. It had to lead somewhere. He turned to look behind him. Between the leaves were now only glimpses of the sea sparkling through the gloom. He saw *Medusa* in one of those glimpses, von Weiss still standing there, watching.

Movement above distracted him and he glanced up. A small brown bird hopped along the branch and then flew away. Jaguaribe turned, took a step, and froze. Something moved under his foot. It writhed and jerked its small powerful body. He lifted his leg, slowly raising his foot, then jumped as the thing coiled and struck, its fangs punching into the fabric of his pants above his ankle. Jaguaribe kicked out his foot in midair and the snake – yes, it was *a snake*! – flew spinning into the bushes. Jaguaribe's heart pounded rapidly. Was the snake venomous? He closed his eyes and swallowed and wondered again, *Where am I?* But then suddenly he knew. Benicio's love of reptiles, the barren island in the middle of the ocean, the birds. Oh God, this was Queimada Grande. Jaguaribe screamed.

*

Von Weiss lowered the binoculars.

'Did you hear that, O Magnifico?'

Yes, he had seen Jaguaribe stop and then the sound of a man on the edge of madness had come a moment later, striking out over the water. Von Weiss brought the binoculars back to his eyes and spotted his soon-to-be-ex associate a moment later, running on the spot, turning one way and then the other, knowing that he was trapped. It was comical.

*

O Magnifico was crazy for snakes. He kept them as pets. Jaguaribe recalled being brought to this island once before, years ago, to collect specimens – a special kind of snake. It was small and golden in color. Von Weiss had said that it was the most lethal in the world, and that it was everywhere on Queimada Grande. Jaguaribe stumbled a few steps forward. There was a viper farther down the path, moving toward him. Another hung from a branch up in the tree, close to where he had seen the bird. He turned, and saw another viper drop from the branch of a nearby bush onto the trail right where he had been standing. It moved toward him, drawn to him.

There was nowhere to go. Jaguaribe backed away from the path. There was a flash of movement in the corner of his eye – golden lightning. A viper sank its fangs into the soft flesh of his cheek, then dropped to the ground, disappearing into the leaf litter. Jaguaribe shrieked. The poison – it was as if someone had whipped his face with a length of barbed wire. Running forward now, Jaguaribe brought his wrecked hands to his head, which was on fire, the venom moving through his blood vessels like boiling acid. He staggered, falling into a bush, and felt the needlepoints of another snake's fangs puncturing his lips. He screamed again. The pain, excruciating.

Jaguaribe's panic overwhelmed him. He crawled farther into the bushes, feeling as though his skin was being peeled away from his skull. A large snake dropped down from a low tree bough and sank its fangs into the soft padding around his waist. As he struggled to his feet it got caught up in his shirt and bit him over and over, emptying its venom glands into the flesh around his ribs.

When the poison hit his brain Jaguaribe dropped to his knees, the pain like slashing knives inside his head. In the small part of his mind still functioning, he was aware that he was shaking uncontrollably. And then the last vestige of consciousness that was Diogo Jaguaribe blew out like a small candle, leaving only nothingness.

*

'He didn't survive long,' said Salvadore, walking behind von Weiss up the track toward the body prostrate on the ground. The skin on the dead man's face was purple and the tongue swollen, filling his mouth.

'No,' von Weiss replied. 'Not long. Exciting, yes?' He glanced over his shoulder at Salvadore and snapped, 'Be careful! You nearly stepped on one!'

Salvadore hopped over the snake as it struck at his boot, its head glancing off the plastic. 'I am sorry, O Magnifico,' said Salvadore uneasily. The boss's passion for these vile creatures was something he found unsettling. It was an obsession, perhaps even a weakness. He pointed at the leaf litter just off the path. 'There's one there on the ground, see?'

Von Weiss deftly scooped the adolescent golden snake into the bend of the hook and deposited it in a bag.

And then the body on the ground moved.

'Did you see that? Is it possible he is not dead?' asked Salvadore, eyes wide.

Von Weiss lifted a corner of Jaguaribe's shirt with the hook, revealing half a dozen snakes coiled on the corpse's back, soaking up the remaining heat. Another viper made its way out from inside the dead man's pants. Salvadore shivered.

'They're pit vipers, drawn to warm blood. Nothing attracts them like the heat of live flesh,' said von Weiss, handing the sack to Salvadore. 'Hold this.' Von Weiss dropped two snakes into it.

'The Navy will find him,' Salvadore said. 'There will be an investigation.'

'We're taking him back with us. I would like to see what the venom does to muscle tissue.'

'Yes, O Magnifico,' said Salvadore, his skin crawling as he watched another snake wriggle its way out from inside Jaguaribe's pants.

Three days ago

As the crowd packing the theater applauded the lavish production, Alabama and several other girls made their way quickly to the back of the stage, deftly avoiding the many holes in the floor where other sets had their anchor points.

Alabama noticed that her nipples were standing out like pacifier teats. All the topless 'talls' had their headlights on tonight, she noticed. She didn't think anyone out in the audience would be concerned about it. Something must be in the air.

The costume Alabama wore for this scene was no more than a bikini bottom and a skimpy sarong open at the front, both items dripping with blue cut glass, green Swarovski crystal, and gold and silver sequins. And the headdress was enormous. She called it 'the dodo'. It weighed more than a large Thanksgiving turkey, was covered in more cut glass and Swarovski crystals, and sprouted alternating blue and black bands of ostrich feathers. The effort required to keep the dodo perched on her head kept her warm, and though Alabama knew how heavy it was, she was damned if the audience was going to be aware of the discipline it took to manage it.

Alabama was just over six feet tall with auburn hair, blue eyes, a perfect thirty-six-inch C-cup, and large, eye-catching pink nipples that were the envy of the other 'talls'. She'd come to Vegas three years ago from Omaha, looking for work as a dancer, which wasn't easy when you towered over almost everyone including most of the male partners. But employment had been found eventually, in the cast of the famous Donn Arden's Jubilee Showgirls, and she'd managed to hold on to it despite the competition from new girls turning up on a weekly basis hoping to break in.

Alabama hadn't intended to stay long. Her plan had been to get some experience and move on after a season or two. But that had all changed after she'd met Randy Sweetwater, a pilot just out of the Air Force, who'd been stationed at nearby Nellis Air Force Base. Meeting him had sealed her commitment to Vegas and the Showgirls – at least for the foreseeable future. They had planned for Randy to get a job with the airlines, but right now he was making incredible money ferrying private planes around the country, and sometimes to other parts of the world, for a local Las Vegas aviation broker.

When she reached the change rooms, heat laced with suggestions of physical exertion and lavender soap billowed from the doorway. One of the stagehands passed Alabama a bottle of water. 'Thanks,' she told him, taking a swig as two of the dressmakers lifted the dodo off her head so that she could enter the room. Most of the other topless talls were already sitting at their mirrors, touching up makeup, re-gluing an eyelash or two, gossiping, joking, hurrying through their between-scenes routines, preparing for the show's finale.

Alabama picked up a small battery-operated fan and held it in front of her face for a few moments before giving her underarms a turn. She took another long drink of water then changed out of her blue and green costume and into the briefest of bikinis covered almost entirely in white crystal and gold sequins, and a matching choker. The headdress that went with this ensemble was a yellow number and would be lowered onto her head and shoulders by three stagehands just prior to her appearance on stage.

'Three minutes!' called the stage manager.

''Bama, honey,' said Sugar, a black girl from New Orleans with a

11

Cajun father, 'a package come for y'all. It's at yo' station.' Sugar was new to the show and she was also currently the girl all the straight males in the cast were trying to screw. She was short by the talls' standards – barely five eleven – but her proportions were perfect and her glossy milk-coffee skin had the warm sheen of silk. Sugar swung her hips as she walked, which made her butt and breasts jiggle. Yep, thought Alabama, Sugar was ridiculously cute and deserved all the attention she got. The black girl glanced over her shoulder and caught Alabama admiring her, which caused a hint of mischief to raise the corners of Sugar's full lips. Alabama had joked with Randy that maybe *he* should be jealous of Sugar. He might come home one day and find the Cajun beauty in bed with her, taking his place. This conversation had ended up where talk like that usually did – with them fucking, the bedroom windows open to the desert heat, their sweat soaking the sheets and the taste of each other in their mouths. The memory of his last night before taking off for Australia came back to Alabama as she dressed, and a shiver ran up her back as a warm wetness bloomed between her legs.

'Is it hot in here?' she asked aloud, snatching up the fan for another cooling blast.

The package Sugar mentioned was indeed on her chair: a FedEx bag. Who would have sent it? Randy would still be in the air, so it couldn't be from him. Intriguing, she thought.

'Two minutes!' came the call.

Several of the girls left the room to get their headdresses fitted. Alabama glanced in the mirror. Her makeup was fine. You've got plenty of time, she told herself. Reaching for a pair of dressmaker's scissors, she sliced off one end of the bag and found a Styrofoam box inside. *Styrofoam?* Now even more curious, she cut the tape securing the lid on the box and opened it. *What the . . . ?* Dry-ice vapor surged out and rolled around the rim of the box, onto the seat of the chair and then onto the floor, and she felt the coldness of it on her feet and toes. Alabama turned the portable fan onto the box to clear away the white mist and get a better view of whatever was inside. A few chunks of dry ice sat on top of what appeared to be a sheet of clear plastic wrap frosted up with the cold.

Now running out of time, Alabama picked up the box and tipped it out on the floor. A black plastic container came out upside down, along with more chunks of dry ice. It was the sort of container steak or ground beef bought from the supermarket came packaged in. Was this some kind of practical joke? She turned the container over and wiped away the frost on the plastic, and a scream strangled in her throat. Inside the container was a human hand. On one of its fingers was an Air Force Academy ring. She recognized it. Randy's.

One

I stood in the doorway of the room I shared with two other agents at the Office of Special Investigations, Andrews Air Force Base in DC, both of whom were currently away working cases. No one had moved in to claim the space I'd vacated, so it was a time capsule of sorts. My chair was pushed up to the desk, which was spotlessly clean and tidy – so clean and tidy, in fact, that it looked like someone else's desk. On the wall was one of those gray felt-covered pin boards seen all around here. Typically, it was covered with notes pinned to other notes, several layers of paper: Post-its, bills of lading, consignment notes, printed-out emails, newspaper and magazine clippings, photographs and identikits. On this board, though, none of the papers was current or even relevant, all of them referring to cases long since concluded, favorably or otherwise. The board reminded me of a photo I saw in *Time* of the anonymous sheets of paper lying in a dust-blown Manhattan avenue the day the Towers came down.

Noticing a photo frame on my spotless desk, I wondered how it had found its way there. It showed my uncle and a few of his buddies standing around a 105mm battery in 'Nam in '71, shirts off, runt-like chests on display, shell casings scattered on the mud all around them. There was nothing else of a personal nature in the office, except for a half-size

15

promotional Redskins football on the floor. A stack of mail bound with a thick red elastic band was rolled beside the computer keyboard, just begging to be left unattended for another month or two. In front of the keyboard was a small stack of loose papers, a Post-it note with the words *Do these first* stuck on the top sheet.

I sighed. The hardest thing about leaving is coming back, even when the place you went to had folks shooting at you or trying to put you in the slammer. I pulled out the chair and sat. The sooner I could get a skin of mold growing on a half-empty mug of coffee or two the more comfortable I'd feel about sitting here.

I glanced at the stack of papers. The top one was a handwritten note on the commander's personal stationery, BRIGADIER GENERAL JAMES WYNNGATE embossed in black at the top of the page. In fountain pen he'd written, *Glad to have you back in the fold, Vin. The place would have been too quiet without you, going forward. And congratulations!*

Hmm . . . the boss liked it quiet, so maybe he wasn't altogether glad. And the congratulations bit – congrats for what, exactly? Beating the Article 128 charge – assault with a deadly weapon occasioning grievous bodily harm? That was last week's news. And surely it wasn't because I'd reached number twelve in *People* magazine's list of the 'World's Sexiest People', either, an achievement that had more to do with the PR machine of a certain celebrity whose ass I'd helped pull out of the fire than any genuine sexiness on my account.

I pushed the general's message to the side and moved on. Second note of the day answered one of the questions raised by the first. Here I was looking at a letter from the Secretary of the Air Force, officially inform-ing me that I'd won the Silver Star for bravery under fire in Afghanistan, and that the medal would be awarded in a month's time.

I put that letter aside too. Next on the stack was a third note from Wynngate, a copy of an all-staff email. The subject line read, *Guaranteeing positive outcomes during personal interactions going for-ward.* This, in fact, was far more like the sort of bonhomie I'd come to expect from the boss. The guy was a stickler for political correct-ness, applying it like a tourniquet around any 'personal interactions' here at Andrews, in the hope that they'd all turn gangrenous and drop off. General Wynngate was the master of bureau-babble, the mindless double-speak of the desk-bound management set. Mostly, no one had a clue what the guy was on about, which meant that he could never be accused of getting it wrong – probably an asset when you spent most of your time buddying up to folks on the Hill, which he did. Wynngate's sentences were as long as the human genome and just as complicated. It also struck me that he managed to work the phrase 'going forward' into just about everything. I reread the email: the general required everyone at OSI to do the accompanying test to determine each individual's strengths and weakness in the compatibility department, or something. I flicked over to the test, which was attached, and caught the words 'Myers-Briggs Type Indicator Assessment'.

'You done it yet?' Lieutenant Colonel Wayne asked, leaning on the doorjamb behind me.

I swung around. Arlen Wayne. I guess I'd call the guy my wingman. He was also my supervisor. A year ago we were both majors, but he'd since climbed a rung higher than me. And his reward was that he got to push even more paper around a desk. These days he was running a large chunk of the operation here at OSI HQ, Andrews Air Force Base. He was older than me by a couple of years, his brown hair starting to lighten at the temples and a few extra pounds gathering around his gut. Nothing a bottle of Just For Men and a week in the sack with a nymphomaniac wouldn't fix. 'Done what?' I asked him.

'The personality test.'

'Yep, scored a hundred percent.'

'It's not that kind of test, Vin. You don't *score* anything. There are no wrong answers.'

'Doesn't that mean there are no *right* answers? And if there are no right or wrong answers, wouldn't it also follow that said test is a complete waste of time?'

Arlen came in and took a chair belonging to one of the absent agents. 'We've all taken it. It's gonna tell the Man what pigeonhole you fit into.'

'Going forward,' I said.

'Going forward, what?'

'Forget it.'

'Y'know, Vin, I think you need to absquatulate.'

'Is that something you do one-handed?'

'No. *Absquatulate*,' he said. 'According to Google, absquatulate is the most ridiculous word in the English language. I looked it up. It means to run away, and it usually also means to take someone with you.'

'You feeling okay, bud?'

'Think about it at least. You're owed a few weeks. Afghanistan Command has released you back to OSI. You were off active duty for quite a while, pending the court martial, and your place at Security Ops there has been filled since you left. I know you'll be disappointed to hear that.'

'Heartbroken,' I said, mentally pumping my fist in the air at this news. I was over Afghanistan and I was thrilled to hear that the fucked-up joint was over me. I tapped the photo of my uncle. 'Where'd you find this?'

'In one of your drawers after you left. Thought it might add a little welcome-home warmth to the place,' he said, glancing around at the mostly bare walls.

'What's a type indicator?' I asked.

'You heard of Myers and Briggs?'

'Nope.'

'They were psychologists – a mother–daughter team. They developed a psychometric test to identify various personality types, based on theories proposed by psychiatrist Carl Jung. He—'

'Can you see my eyes glazing over?'

'You asked. The test is supposed to work out how you process the world around you. Myers and Briggs believed that there were four opposite pairs of psychological differences in people, or sixteen different psychological types – type indicators.'

'You're sounding like Wynngate.'

Arlen grinned. 'Maybe just take the test and we'll see what comes out.'

'Which pigeonhole do *you* belong in?'

'The general thinks that we'll all get on better and work more efficiently – you know, "enhance team dynamics" – if we understand each other's psychological differences.'

'Nuts.'

'It's called the modern workplace.'

'Again, what did the test reveal about *you*?' I asked.

'That I'm popular, easygoing and know how to get the best out of people,' said Arlen.

'So basically: nice guy, but a little sly.'

'It's going on the bottom of all my emails.'

'What is?'

'My type indicators are ENTP – extraversion, intuition, thinking, perception. The general wants everyone to put their type indicators on their emails so that the receiver knows what kind of person the sender is. Though in your case I think the word is already out.'

'Does this test have to be done now?'

'No hurry. Before you leave for the day will do.'

'Right.' I put it aside.

'Seriously, why don't you just take it easy for a couple of days?' said Arlen. 'You've been through a lot with the court martial.'

In fact, the wringer was what I'd just been through, and mostly because I was guilty of exactly what they said I'd done, which was pistol-whipping a Department of Defense contractor by the name of Beau Lockhart at a US training base in Rwanda. Worse, I'd entertained twenty witnesses while doing it. But the asshole deserved it, and luckily for me some photographic evidence of the contractor's involvement in murder and human trafficking came to light just in time to save me from doing eight years in Leavenworth with guys who get hard-ons looking at a hair-clogged drain hole. 'Which reminds me, how's the investigation into Lockhart coming along?'

'The prosecution's case is rock-solid. He'll go away for several lifetimes,' said Arlen, leaning down to pick up the Redskins football on the floor. He tossed it over. I caught it, lobbed it back.

'What about Charles White? Anything new on him?' White was Lockhart's gun-smuggling partner, providing the weapons for the bloodbath going on in a nasty little part of the eastern Congo. Arlen had debriefed me on the guy shortly after the conclusion of my court martial.

'Nothing I haven't already told you,' Arlen said, firing the ball back at me.

What he'd told me was that Charles White was former Marine Recon, honorably discharged three years ago with the rank of sergeant. He was then employed by FN Herstal and lasted six months there, after which he fell off the radar for a time. Interpol believed he was involved in the illegal weapons trade, which I could confirm. Arlen also told me that White had plenty of contacts within the US military, was believed to now be living in Rio de Janeiro and was moving around on false passports. 'What about the M16s with their numbers removed that we recovered from the Congo? Any news on them?'

'Other than they were manufactured by FN Herstal? Nothing, except that it suggests a possible connection to White, given that FN once employed him. As for the numbers, professionals removed them and we still don't even know what batch the rifles came from or what the manufacturing date was. For all we know they were pilfered right off the assembly line.'

'Is that what you think?'

'Right now, I'm not sure what I think. Some solid evidence would be handy.'

'Or even a lead, by the sound of things.' I tossed him the Redskins ball overhand, imparting a spin to it. Arlen caught it, and spun it right back. 'So what's the next move?'

'There isn't one,' he said.

'What do you mean?'

'We're off the case.'

I dropped the ball. 'Who says?'

'The DoD.'

'Why?'

'This one's too big for OSI – it goes across service lines and happened overseas.'

'When were you told to stand down?'

'An hour ago.'

'So who's on it?'

'CIA.'

'You're kidding,' I said.

'I wish I was.'

The Company shot itself in the foot so often it had no toes left. But aside from that, picking up the threads of that case was the only work I was interested in doing. 'So what now?'

'For you? We've got a couple of deserters from Lackland AFB to chase down. We think they're involved in the drug trade, possibly with a Mexican cartel. Thought you might like to take it on. Mexico . . . beaches . . .'

I flicked him the ball and sucked a little air between my front teeth.

Arlen shrugged at the lack of traction he seemed to be getting. 'We haven't had a chance to talk about the report. You've read it, right? You want to talk about it?'

'I read it. And let's skip it.'

'Okay . . .'

The report Arlen was referring to concerned the death of the late Special Agent Anna Masters. Masters and I had been close – partners and, well, *partners*. She died in a shootout. There was a lot of lead flying around at the time and some of it was mine. I'd gone a ways down the road thinking it was my bullet that killed her, but a forensic report just completed a week ago – many months after her death – confirmed otherwise. Whether it was my bullet or not, I'd always carry the guilt. She was gone. Nothing could change that.

'Vin, it's been eight months. Time to move on.'

I didn't respond. Arlen juggled the ball back and forth between his hands. 'You don't want to go to Mexico on a case? Your call, I can accept that. How about instead I make it easy and fill out a 988 for you? All you'd have to do is sign it.'

I nodded.

'Take some time, buddy,' he continued. 'You need it, *and* you deserve it.'

The 988, or more correctly the AFF 988, was the request leave/authorization form. I couldn't skip Dodge unless it was properly filled out and countersigned by my supervisor, which happened to be Lieutenant Colonel Arlen Wayne here. 'All right, you win. Put me down for a week or two,' I said.

'There you go . . . So, what you gonna do?'

Before she was killed, Anna had said she was headed to her sister's scuba-diving business in the West Indies. She'd told me she was leaving the Air Force to get her diving instructor's license and work on her all-over tan. The memory of that conversation came with a picture of her bronze body lying in the sunshine, naked. 'Maybe I'll go to the West Indies – get in some diving,' I said.

'The West Indies. That's not so far. Maybe I could come for a few days, stitch it onto a weekend.'

'Satchquatch.'

'Absquatulate.'

'Yeah, you need a holiday too,' I told him. 'Give all those paper cuts time to heal.'

Arlen managed a smile, but only just. 'Why don't I come over to your place later? We can talk about it and maybe go out for a drink.' He let the ball drop to the floor and tapped it into the corner with his toe. 'A new bar's opened over your way. They get a young crowd. Maybe we could go there and cut a couple out of the herd. What do you say, Hopalong?'

'Yee hah,' I said.

'Call you later,' he replied, leaving the room.

Hmm. The more I thought about it, the more I liked the idea of some time off. I folded the Myers-Briggs test and dropped it in the file, the round one on the floor under my desk.

'Vin, before you go . . .'

I glanced over my shoulder and saw Arlen's head around the corner of the door.

'The test. Do it.'

That's the trouble when you know someone well – they know you well right back. I gave a weary sigh, retrieved the forms from the trash, filled out the fields for my name and service details and then scanned the questions, all of which required a simple yes or no answer – questions like 'You feel involved watching TV soaps', 'You tend to be unbiased even if this might endanger your relationships with people', 'You spend your leisure time actively socializing with a group of people, attending parties and shopping', 'You tend to sympathize with other people', and so forth. Seriously, Wynngate had to be fucking kidding.

Two

St Barts was the name of the place in the West Indies. I checked it out online and liked what I saw. Blue water and white bikinis. I was on the edge of jumping in, the onscreen arrow poised over an orange button that pulsed 'Book now, Book now', when I heard a knock on the front door. I checked the time. Arlen wasn't due over for at least another half hour, unless he'd clocked off early. I got up, opened the door, and went into shock, paralyzed from the eyeballs down.

The person standing in front of me could not be real. Was I hallucinating? My heart thumped loudly from an unusual place, like it had taken up residence somewhere between my ears. This could not be possible, could it? I spent a bunch of pregnant seconds standing in the doorway questioning my memory – the Mexican standoff, the shootout, the funeral, the grief – because the woman framed in the doorway, with her dark chocolate hair, green eyes, the lips, I *knew* her. 'Anna?' I tried to get the word out but it got stuck somewhere in my throat like a cork pushed down into the neck of a wine bottle.

'You going to ask me in or should I just stand here for another minute looking at your open mouth?' she asked.

I let the door swing open. The apparition came in pulling a bright red overnight case behind her, a family-size bucket of KFC in her other hand. She was an inch shorter than I remembered and her scent . . . there were only echoes of familiarity with it.

'Jesus . . .' She turned, looking around the room. 'You honestly *live* here?'

A few things weren't marrying up as they should have, like her height and the perfume she used and that last comment. *This* Anna had never been to my place before. And then the clouds parted and I snapped out of it. 'Nice of you to call ahead, Marnie,' I managed to extract from my larynx.

'Well, we didn't part on the best of terms and I thought you'd tell me to get lost if I gave you advance warning.'

Actually, the language I'd have used for the terms we parted on might have been a little stronger than that. 'You look different' I said, changing the subject.

She took a length of hair and examined it up close, which made her briefly cross-eyed. 'I got sick of all the blonde jokes, so I went back to my normal color. Sorry if I startled you. Everyone's been telling me how much I look like . . . you know.'

Yeah, I knew. Marnie Masters was fifteen months younger than her sister, Anna. I wasn't in Marnie's good books. She blamed me for Anna's death, so that made two of us. When I last saw her, which was at the wake, she was crying, yelling at me to get lost while throwing plates, wine glasses and pastrami sandwiches in my direction – whatever came to hand. I'd slunk away and we hadn't spoken since.

'You look different too,' she said. 'Still got those rugged good looks, but . . .'

'Only they're getting more rugged.'

'You look – I don't know . . .'

I rubbed the bridge of my nose and felt the swelling beneath my fingertips. 'I've had a nose job since I last saw you.' I didn't think it worth mentioning that it had been performed by a truck's steering wheel in the Congo.

'I'd ask for a refund.' Marnie smiled. 'Anyway, I've had time to think through what happened. I came to realize that I owe you an apology.'

'Forget about it,' I said.

'No, hear me out. Anna *wanted* to be a cop. That was her dream, her choice. She knew it came with risks, and the risks added to the job satisfaction. I'm saying I know you didn't kill her, Vin. It just *happened*, just one of those things. I don't hold you responsible. I did, but now I don't. I shouldn't have said those things to you at the funeral.'

'I haven't eaten pastrami since.'

'I'm sorry. I was in shock. I loved my sister and she was gone and you were the only person I could blame. There was no one else closer to her than you.' She took a deep breath. 'I could have put all that in an email, but I thought I owed it to you to come here in person. I'm not proud of my last performance.'

I didn't know what to say. I was a little in shock myself. One minute I was surfing soft porn lying around on a beach on St Barts and the next I was looking at Anna reincarnated, full of forgiveness, a bucket of fried chicken in her hand. *Surreal* was the word that came to mind. I must have been looking at that bucket because she glanced down at it then lifted it onto the table.

'Don't worry,' she said. 'I'm not here to throw fried chicken at you.'

'That's a relief,' I said.

'Anna loved you, by the way. But you know that.'

I did know that.

She ran her fingers through chocolate-colored hair, then flicked her head a little to reposition the bangs. 'It's been a hell of a trip.' She took in my interior-decorating skills again. 'Who does a girl have to blow to get a drink around here?' Marnie might have looked like Anna, but she didn't talk like her.

'Well, *that* guy's not around, but I'll see what I can rustle up.' I headed for the kitchen. 'There's Jacks or single malt,' I said over my shoulder. 'I might have a couple of beers.'

'Beer, please,' she said.

I looked in the fridge and saw a pair of Heinekens, the right number. 'Glass?' I called out.

'Thanks.'

I took the tops off the bottles, delivered hers with the glass and then poured it for her.

'Friends?' she said, holding up the glass.

I clinked it with the bottle, said, 'Friends,' and took a swig.

'So, you really got a bit of a shock when you opened the door, right?'

I was going to say that I'd thought I was looking at a ghost, but I changed my mind. 'Yeah.'

'When we were in our teens people used to think Anna and I were twins.'

I could believe it. The similarity would once have been uncanny, but now it was spooky given that Anna was dead. I moved it along. 'Not that I believe in these things, but it's a coincidence that you should arrive just now.'

'Really? Why's that?'

I spun my laptop around and touched the space bar. The screen lit up showing a woman lying face down on white sand.

'Did I interrupt you in the middle of something?' she asked with a raised eyebrow.

I backspaced and the girl in the white bikini bottoms was now standing on the shoreline, her top around her neck, hanging in her cleavage.

Marnie sipped her beer. 'You were saying something about a coincidence?'

I skipped through another half dozen pages showing the white bikini girl in various semi-nude poses.

'I can come back, if you like?' Marnie said sarcastically. 'How long do you need? A minute or two?'

Finally, an image opened of the white prow of an old fishing boat against the blue of the sea and the sky.

'Hey, I know this website. That's home – St Barts. You were checking this out?' Marnie asked.

'I was about to book a trip, head over, get in some diving. That was Anna's plan. She was gonna come to St Barts and spend time with you. At the funeral, I never got around to telling you that.'

'I guess I never gave you the opportunity.'

27

No, she hadn't.

'It's kinda freaky that I should suddenly just turn up on your door-step then,' she added.

Like I was saying.

Another knock on the door. 'Excuse me,' I told her and opened up on Arlen armed with a six-pack of Heinekens. I was about to tell him to come on in when he said, 'Hey, Marnie,' pushed past me and went straight over to her. I stood back and watched as they air-kissed and embraced and asked each other how the other was, and so forth. I gathered that Arlen and Marnie had become Facebook friends since hitting it off at the wake, after I'd been given my marching orders.

Once the pleasantries were out of the way, along with a repeat of the conversation about how much Marnie now looked like a certain some-one else, Arlen went over more old ground about the trip to St Barts, which, if nothing else, at least confirmed that I wasn't making it all up, and also gave me the chance to relieve him of one of his beers.

Eventually, when Arlen realized that I was also in the room and stead-ily working my way through his booze, he excused himself to Marnie and presented me with the 988. 'This is filled out on my end and ready to go.'

Except that Marnie was here now and a big part of the reason for going on vacation was null and void. I checked over the form.

'Today you're on Air Force time,' my supervisor and closest pal said. 'Sign it and tomorrow you're on yours – do you good, buddy.' He picked up his beer. 'I was thinking we could take Marnie out for dinner, but I see you've already got it worked out.' He nodded at the bucket of KFC on the table.

I glanced at her. 'You want me to reheat?'

'Maybe you should sit down,' she said. 'Both of you.'

The way she said it told me that it wasn't because the chicken would need more than a minute or two in the microwave. In my job, when folks tell you to sit down it's usually because they're gonna tell you something that'll make you want to jump to your feet, but I took her advice and a chair, along with Arlen's last Heineken.

'So what's in the bucket, Marnie?' Arlen asked her.

Whatever it was, it wasn't hot. Now that I was looking at it more closely I saw condensation had formed on the sides. A droplet of water slid down into a small puddle that had formed around the base. Arlen sat and frowned at the bucket, waiting.

Marnie opened her mouth to speak, closed it, opened it again, then closed it. She didn't know where to start – that much was clear. 'This is complicated,' she finally managed to say.

'Just show us what you've got,' I suggested.

Marnie hesitated and then peeled the lid off the bucket. A white fog of dry-ice vapor rolled up like a smoke ring beneath the lid and climbed above the table, followed by a wave of the stuff pouring out over the sides. I had to admit I was intrigued. So was Arlen, leaning forward on the table, up on his elbows. Marnie's hand disappeared inside the bucket.

'Some days ago, a woman I have recently come to know received this,' she said, producing a plain white envelope. She handed it to me. It was cold and wisps of fog clung to the edges. I'd been expecting . . . Actually, I don't know what I'd been expecting once I knew a drumstick was unlikely, but an envelope wasn't it.

'Open it,' Marnie urged.

I did as she suggested and removed a sheet of paper. A line of default Microsoft Word black twelve-point Times New Roman type was printed on it. The line was italicized suggesting urgency and several words were in caps. The note read, *FAILING to come up with $15 MILLION will TRIGGER delivery of his HEAD. You have 20 days. You will be contacted. No police.*

And then Marnie lifted a human hand packed into a meat tray from the KFC bucket and placed it on the table.

Arlen's jaw hit the floor.

The sight of it caught me by surprise too, as well as giving me a flashback to a scene I witnessed in the Congo of a man kneeling in the mud, screaming, as soldiers hacked off both his hands with machetes.

'They run out of chicken?' I asked her.

Marnie wasn't amused.

I reached for the pen in Arlen's top pocket and poked the tray with it, positioning it so I could get a better look at the hand, condensation fogging the plastic wrap with each passing second. Through an oval window in the frost, I could see that the hand itself was greenish brown, the fingernails rimmed with dried blood. A gold ring dressed its squat pinky. 'So who's the woman who was sent this?'

'Her name's Alabama. She's a friend of Anna's. Or, rather, her boyfriend was,' Marnie said, looking away from the tray. She got up from the table and walked toward the kitchen, the sight of the severed hand obviously giving her some problems. 'She's a topless dancer in Vegas.'

This was getting more interesting with each passing second. It was also getting more confusing.

'We should call this in to the local PD,' Arlen decided.

'But the letter . . . it says no cops,' Marnie said.

'This is a matter for police,' he insisted.

I reread the note. Someone wanted money to supposedly stop a man being killed. Presumably the contact mentioned would specify the collection details. I wondered why the capital lettering on selected words. Maybe it was used merely for emphasis. 'Why don't you take us through the story from the beginning?'

'Do you mind covering *that* first?' she asked, her eyes flicking to the tray.

I considered whether to use something that wouldn't leave my DNA on it. The tray and its contents would end up as evidence in a case sooner or later, but Marnie had handled it and I guessed this Alabama person had, too; and I doubted that KFC had provided the original packaging. So I picked up the tray with my fingers and gave the hand a closer inspection through the window of frost, now starting to melt, before returning it to the Colonel's care.

Marnie relaxed a little once the lid was back in place. 'Alabama Thornton – she's a Vegas showgirl. Her boyfriend's ex–Air Force. That's his connection to Anna. According to Alabama, he met Anna in Germany, but I don't think Alabama and Anna ever met. Anyway, from what I can gather, the boyfriend mentioned Anna to Alabama at some stage. When *that* arrived,' Marnie said, motioning at the bucket, 'Alabama didn't want to involve the police, but she had to turn to someone so she called Anna. And along the way, Anna being my sister, Alabama was given my number. She called, and next thing I know I'm on a plane to Vegas, but I'm not Anna and I'm creeped out in a major way by dead things, let alone things chopped off people. I told Alabama about you, Vin, and that's why I'm here.'

To drag me into it. It was amazing how Marnie managed to get the whole tangled mess out in one clean breath. 'So you picked up the hand in Vegas?'

'Yes.'

'How'd you get it here?'

'I drove.'

'Long drive.'

'Especially with *that* riding in the passenger seat.'

'Whose idea was the KFC bucket?'

'Mine,' said Marnie with a shrug. 'Nothing more innocent than fried chicken.'

She'd brought the severed hand across several state lines, so I couldn't argue with her thinking. Driving wasn't a bad decision, either: airport cops get sensitive about dismembered limbs in the carry-on. But there was a time limit specified in the note – twenty days, and now at least four of them had been soaked up.

'What's Alabama's boyfriend's name?' I said.

'Randy – Randy Sweetwater.'

'So the hand belongs to Randy?' Arlen said.

'I doubt it,' I said.

'Alabama knows it's not his. She already told me that.'

Arlen took back his pen. 'Okay, but how do *you* know that, Vin?'

'Skin tone. It's dark – Mexican, perhaps – and Randy's a white guy.'

'And you know this because Mexicans don't call their kids Randy or have surnames like Sweetwater?'

'They're good reasons, but in this instance, no. Actually, I think I've met the guy.'

'You met him?'

'Depends on how many Randy Sweetwaters are kicking around out there, but I flew with one of them in Afghanistan. Hitched a ride in his C-17. While we were refueling at a forward operating base, he accidentally dropped some package being ferried around for a colonel and, wouldn't you know it, half a dozen bottles of Glenfiddich just fell out. Then Randy discovered a whole bunch of mechanical troubles that grounded the plane for several days. My kinda guy.'

'So this package just happened to be full of single malt?' Arlen said dubiously. 'Sounds like something *you'd* do.'

I grinned. 'Okay, officer, ya got me. Too bad the statute of limitations is up on this one. And anyway, smuggling booze into a Muslim country . . .' I shook my head and tsked. 'The colonel could have gotten into a lot of trouble.'

'So is he the guy or not?'

'The colonel?'

'Jesus, Vin.'

'Okay, okay . . . My memory's hazy on the details of the episode – understandably – but I do remember *this* Randy Sweetwater saying that he was about to go to Nellis AFB, which, as we all know, snuggles up to Vegas.'

'Sometimes I'm surprised you remember anything.'

That made two of us.

'So, assuming the Randy Sweetwater you met *is* Alabama's boyfriend,' said Arlen, 'and that this is not his hand, what's Alabama worried about?'

'Because Thing here is wearing Randy's academy ring,' I said, looking at Marnie. 'Right?'

'That's right,' she confirmed.

'Well, like I said, this is a police matter,' Arlen repeated.

'And what are we, chopped liver?'

He had a point, though. Randy was ex–Air Force, and the 'ex' bit took him beyond our frame of reference. Technically, we couldn't get involved. At least, not officially.

'What's Alabama expecting us to do?' I asked Marnie. 'What are *you* expecting us to do?' I sensed discomfort from Arlen that I was including him in 'us'.

'To help her, obviously. The ransom – she doesn't know what to do or who to turn to. And she doesn't have fifteen thousand, let alone fifteen million.'

In this instance help could mean anything, except maybe assisting Alabama with a loan application for the ransom money. 'And what about you?' I asked Marnie. 'What are *you* gonna do?'

'Me?' Marnie pointed at herself like I'd just accused her of something. 'I've done my bit throwing you the ball. I'm going home. I've got a diving business to run.' She looked at me and then at Arlen.

The initial Anna Effect experienced when I'd opened the door and seen her standing there had worn off. Marnie had Anna's eyes, hair and bone structure, and even the tone of her voice was similar, but in every other way she was the kid sister. Anna wouldn't have looked elsewhere to offload this. I reached across and again lifted Arlen's pen from his shirt pocket and signed the 988 with it. 'Sorry,' I told him.

'What for?'

'You're gonna have to absquatulate on your own.'

Three

I hitched a ride on the first plane heading for Vegas, a C-17 ferrying a load of practice missiles to Nellis. And five hours later, I was in the Nellis commissary buying an ice chest and freezer packs to go with it, condensation having terminally weakened the waxed paper seals on the KFC bucket. The amputated hand was in real danger of slipping out the side, and that would be tricky to explain. With Thing newly secured in a plastic ice chest, I caught a cab out past McCarran airport to Thrifty to pick up a rental. And half an hour after that I was driving down the Strip in the last of the early evening sunshine, the Ford Focus's AC wound to the stops yet barely able to penetrate the midsummer desert heat.

I drove nice and slow to soak up the sights. It'd been a few years since I'd visited Vegas, and while the town needed nighttime to show its true colors, there was a feeling of urgency in the air that reminded me of someone drowning. Maybe the global downturn had hit the place harder than anyone liked to admit. The guys on the sidewalk handing out calling cards for the hookers were going at it in broad daylight, scooting from prospect to prospect like rats on a foundering ship hunting for an exit. Several glossy new buildings stood vacant, others looked a little tired – none more so than Bally's, 'the home of Donn

Arden's Jubilee Showgirls', as the posters up and down the Strip called the show. Bally's was a refurbished seventies tower which, I'd learned when I'd booked a room online, was once the MGM Grand before it caught fire. In fact, looking at it on screen, if Bally's were a dancer, I'd be hoping her clothes would be staying on.

From what I could tell from the advertising, the Jubilee girls were old Vegas – all poise and sequins and makeup and feathers. Their antecedents would have danced for Sammy Davis Jr and Ol' Blue Eyes. Today, however, out on the Strip, the advertising for Jubilee was engaged in a running battle with posters for joints where the girls danced in people's laps. Without seeing what the Showgirls had to offer, I didn't like their chances of routing the competition.

My cell rang. It was Arlen. I put him on speaker. 'Hey, s'up?'

'Your friend, Randy. Seems he checked out with a BCD.'

BCD – a bad conduct discharge. 'What were the circumstances?' I asked, surprised.

'Cloudy. "Conduct unbecoming" is what the file says. There was a court martial. I talked to the JAG and his defense counsel. There was a suspicion he was acting as a courier service in Afghanistan – hashish.'

That didn't sound like the Randy I knew, but then I probably didn't know him all that well. 'Was Anna involved?' If Sweetwater was in trouble he'd have called her, wouldn't he?

'First thing I checked. Anna's name doesn't come up in any of the records, and JAG has no recollection that she was ever called.'

Somehow, that was important. I didn't want Anna messed up in this in any way. 'Were the charges proved?' I asked.

'The BCD was the result of a plea bargain.'

'How'd he swing that?'

'The evidence went missing.'

Sure it did.

'He pleaded guilty to possession but without intent to distribute.'

I couldn't help but smile. Randy was lucky. He could've done hard time.

'Maybe it's not relevant, but I thought you should know,' said Arlen.

'Thanks,' I told him.

'So what are you doing?'

'Driving down the Strip, looking for my hotel.'

'Put ten bucks in a slot for me. Oh, and I'm acting on the advice I gave you.'

'Which was?'

'Take a vacation. Marnie invited me over.'

'You're going to St Barts?'

'Yeah . . . Look, if you've got any problems with that, let me know, because if you do I'll—'

'No problem my end,' I said. 'Knock yourself out, bud.'

'You sure?'

'I'm sure.'

'Cool. Hey, before I forget, your test result came back in.'

'What test?'

'Your Myers-Briggs test.'

'Did I pass?'

'No passes or fails, remember? You're supposed to go through the results with a specialist, but, in short, your type indicators are ESFJ. Do you want to know what that means?'

'That I'm good with the ladies?'

'Dream on. Extroverted, sensing, feeling, judging – ESFJ. I'll make sure the initials go on the bottom of your emails.'

'Tell me you don't actually believe in this shit?' I asked him.

'Depends who's asking. If it's Wynngate, it's genius.'

'Who am I supposed to get on with best?'

'Other ESFJs.'

'And who should I avoid?'

'ENTPs.'

'Aren't you one of those?'

'Yep.'

'I rest my case.' The driveway entrance to Bally's was coming up. 'Hey, gotta go. When you come up for air in St Barts, gimme a call.'

'Roger that.'

I hit the end button, went up the ramp and found a space in the parking lot. Eventually, I made my way to reception and stood in line behind buffalo-sized people moseying toward the counter. The air hummed with the sound of musical bells and magical twinkles rising from the slots down in the pit.

After checking in, I took the ice chest and carry-on, wheeled over to the counter selling seats to the evening's Showgirls performance, and bought my seat from an uninterested black guy who conducted the transaction without eye contact. I still had plenty of time to freshen up before the show so I took myself up to my room out on the end of a dark two-hundred-yard-long tunnel on the twentieth floor. Opening the drapes I discovered that I had an aerial view of 'Paris', its pool occupying the area around the base of the Eiffel Tower. The place was packed, the countless lounge chairs still occupied, the desert heat ignoring the fact that the sun was below the horizon. Waitresses in bikinis worked the couches, shuttling drinks and snacks. Ah, Vegas . . .

I took a shower and dressed conservative – jeans, desert boots and a navy shirt. If I hurried, I still had time before the show to indulge in Vegas's other main attraction: the buffet, the place where the buffaloes roam. I was on vacation after all, and seriously underweight compared to the rest of the herd. When I couldn't possibly fit in another complete four-course meal, I lumbered over to the Jubilee theater at Bally's.

When I arrived, the tiered theater, which probably sat around seven hundred, was close to full. Frankly, I was surprised. Maybe old-style Vegas was the new black. I found my seat, close to the front and in the center, as the lights went down and the music welled up. The curtain opened on a guy in a tuxedo singing a song about 'hundreds of girls', who then began to appear wearing almost nothing, and all of it sparkling. I wondered which one was Alabama. Pretty much all I knew about her was that she danced topless, narrowing it down to about half the field. The show rolled on into a Samson and Delilah number, about a guy whose girlfriend cuts his hair off, which I just knew was a euphemism for his balls, followed by a number where the girls sank the *Titanic* under several tons of rhinestones. The finale saw the cast all gliding down a giant glittering staircase balancing ornaments the size of Chewbacca on their heads. I liked the costumes and I liked the breasts even better, especially when they were coming down those steps. There was a feverish round of applause, which died out pretty quick.

The theater evacuated fast, the patrons eager to leave and get back to the slots. I was almost last out, and loitered around the side entrance. Ten minutes later, a tall woman in gray sweatpants and an old sweat top, wearing outrageously heavy makeup and her hair pulled back in a net, appeared outside the entrance and scanned the area like she was expecting to see someone. Me, I figured. I walked over and introduced myself.

'Alabama Thornton?' I said. 'Vin Cooper.'

'Vin, hi. So great to meet you. You got here fast.' She was all smiles and gave me a long slender hand to shake. I must have been frowning at her because she suddenly became self-conscious. 'Oh, excuse the makeup. It looks weird off stage, I know.'

I gave a shrug like it was no big deal, but she was right. Her false eyelashes were long enough to sweep the floor, and a thick black line was drawn under each eye as well as above those lashes. The rouge on her cheeks was heavy, as was the fire engine–red lipstick she wore. On stage and under bright lights the effect was glamorous. Up close, she looked like Chucky.

'I don't want to talk here,' she said. 'You wanna come backstage?'

'Sure,' I said.

'We're not supposed to bring people back. If anyone asks, you're with management. Act like you own the place.'

'I can give you incompetent arrogance. That do?'

'Perfect.'

Four

I followed Alabama to an unmarked brown steel door with a combination lock. She tapped in the code, leaned into it with her shoulder, and we entered a brightly lit corridor that sloped down toward a flight of stairs and another door with NO ENTRY painted on it. Alabama ignored the instruction and pushed through. Another corridor opened out at right angles on either side behind it. This one was busy with men and women going back and forth, some chatting and joking, others deep in conversation or carrying costumes or tools, and others wearing makeup that singled them out as dancers. No one asked who I was or what I was doing there. Seal's version of 'My Vision' came from a room with a sign over the door that read DRESSING ROOM I. We headed for it. The music underscored the sound of women laughing and chatting within.

'Everyone decent?' Alabama called out before entering.

'Hang on,' came the reply.

'This is the topless talls' dressing room,' said Alabama, pausing at the doorway. I must have given her a look, because she translated, 'The girls are tall, and they're topless.'

'Right,' I said. Another tough day at the office for Special Agent Cooper.

'Okay . . .' a woman called from inside.

Alabama motioned for me to follow her in. The room was filled with sequined costumes and feather boas and fishnet stockings and makeup and hatter's heads topped with headpieces and plenty of other items of clothing that I couldn't identify, most of it covered in colored cut glass and sequins. A number of mirrors rimmed with warm yellow lights were set up round the walls. Most of the mirrors were adorned with photos of boyfriends or husbands, I supposed – a couple had snaps of young children – as well as news clippings and show reviews. There were books and magazines and iPods and hair dryers and portable fans and various items of makeup at each station, and the air smelled vaguely of warm soap. Around half the mirrors had their lights turned off, which suggested that the women who sat at them had already gone home. There were still plenty of showgirls in the room though, sitting at their stations taking off makeup or organizing their lives into overnight bags. Everyone was chatting over each other. One or two women smiled at me, but mostly I was ignored. The women who were standing were indeed very tall but, disappointingly, not a single one was topless.

Alabama went to a mirror at the end of one wall. Her station was no different from any of the others. A photo of a Siamese cat was tucked into the frame around her mirror and below it were two pictures of a guy I recognized. Randy. In one he was dressed in a flight suit, standing on the flight line, a C-17 behind him. In the other he and Alabama were cheek-to-cheek, Randy's arm extended in front of them – one of those photos couples take when there's no one else around to get the shot. In the background was the Statue of Liberty.

'Nice-looking cat,' I said.

'That's Fluffy. She's our baby.'

Fluffy?

'Was your obstetrician surprised?' Even though you know it's the wrong time and place, some questions just have to be asked.

'I'm sorry?'

'I know Randy. Met him once,' I said, getting things back on track. I reached for the photo. 'Do you mind?'

'Please, go right ahead.'

I took the photo of Randy and the C-17 off the mirror for closer inspection. I'd seen thousands of photos like this over the years – guys with their planes. This one was taken in Afghanistan – Bagram, perhaps. It might even have been the plane I hitched a ride in.

'So, you met Randy . . . ?'

'In Afghanistan, before he came to Nellis. He's one of the good guys.'

Hope lit up her face. 'I'm sure he's okay. I'd know if he was in trouble. I'd feel it.'

I suspected that, even though she knew the hand wasn't her boyfriend's, the facts that it was wearing his ring and accompanied by a ransom note were more reliable indicators on the trouble scale. And they were saying that, no matter what her feelings told her, the shit was up to Randy's nostrils.

'Hey, I know who you are now,' said Alabama, studying my face. 'You were in the Congo, right? There was a court case and you got off. I don't watch the news – too depressing – but I sometimes read *People*. A couple of the girls buy it. That was you, wasn't it?'

'No,' I said. I'd been trying hard to forget the place.

'Yes it was,' she insisted. 'I was only reading about it the other day. Small world, isn't it? I mean, Marnie told me that you and Anna were . . .' Alabama didn't finish the sentence. She cleared her throat and began again. 'Even though I never met her, I was sad when I heard about, you know, what happened . . . Randy talked about Anna – they were good friends. We exchanged Christmas cards.'

Really? First I knew about that. 'Do you know how Randy and Anna met?' I asked.

Maybe it was the way I put the question, or maybe it was the way a woman's mind worked, because the answer began with a reassurance. 'Hey, don't worry. They weren't, like, *lovers* or anything. Randy did a tour at Ramstein. His car was stolen, used in a hit and run. There was a lot of crap with the local authorities. Anna did all the liaison work with the police, and they became friends. Randy told me about it when I found a

Christmas card she'd sent him, a photo of her wearing reindeer antlers. She was pretty and I – well, I guess I pulled the jealous female routine.' I remembered the Anna-wearing-reindeer-antlers card. I received the same one. 'Randy set me straight, gave me the background and told me if he was ever in trouble with the law, Anna Masters would be the first person he'd turn to.'

I took another look at Randy's photo. Yeah, small world.

'Thanks for stepping in, Vin – you didn't have to.'

'I haven't done anything yet.'

'I guess not.' She managed a wan smile. 'You mind if I take my face off while we talk?'

I motioned at her to go right ahead and sat at the next mirror over while Alabama peeled those brooms off her eyelids. She put them in a box with a clear top, then snatched some wipes from out of a plastic container and went to work on her face.

'Where's the . . . you know . . . ?' she asked.

'You mean, Thing?'

It took a few seconds. 'Oh, *Thing* – as in the Addams Family? Yeah, I guess that's funny.' She wasn't laughing.

'I brought it back with me. You need to turn it over to Vegas PD.'

She stopped wiping her cheeks. Her forehead was lined with concern. 'But the note says . . .'

'I know what it says, but that's what you have to do. I'll be there with you to make the report – I've got a contact. We want their forensics people to have a good look at it.'

'That makes me nervous.'

'We've got no choice, and there's a chance the FBI will become involved.'

'The FBI? Why?'

'They get brought in if a crime has been committed that crosses state lines. It's nothing to worry about. It's just the way the turf is divided up.' One of those tough questions I had to ask was up next and I wondered how she was going to take it. 'Was Randy involved in anything illegal that you know of?'

Alabama shook her head and turned to face me. 'No. No way. Randy's a straight shooter.'

As reactions went, it was a good one. I believed that she believed her lover was squeaky clean, but that didn't mean he was. Show me a relationship with no secrets and I'll show you a unicorn. 'And the ring. You're sure it's his?' I asked.

'Well, his name's engraved inside the band, along with "Class of '96".' She shrugged. 'That's exactly as I remember it . . .'

'You checked it?'

Her nose wrinkled. 'I picked at it with a chopstick. I . . . I had to.'

I was vaguely surprised that she'd had the nerve. Maybe Alabama was tougher than she looked.

The expression on her face morphed into one of hope, the possibility that it might have been a forgery evidently not having occurred to her before. 'You think the ring could be a fake?' she asked.

'Don't know, and that's why we need a competent forensics report – if only to eliminate angles.' Thing had been bouncing around for over four days now, mostly in his chicken bucket. The police weren't going to be overjoyed about that – the time factor. Trails would have gone cold.

'If it's not genuine then that might explain something,' she said, wiping her nose and leaning towards the mirror for a closer inspection.

'What's that?'

'Randy works for an aircraft sales company. At this moment, he's supposed to be delivering a plane to Australia.'

'Really? You know that for sure?' The Randy I knew was a good pilot, but not good enough to be in two places at once.

'I guess . . . That's what he told me he was doing.'

The makeup on her face was now transferred to a pile of dirty brown and black wipes on the bench in front of her. Alabama removed the hairnet and shook out her hair, running her long fingers through it. Thick and auburn, it fell down around her shoulders with a gentle wave. At least Randy was lucky in love – Alabama was a knockout punch, her eyes a soft blue-gray, cheekbones high, heart-shaped lips and smooth clear skin that glowed with all the rubbing.

'Has he called since he left?' I asked her.

'From LA – that's where he said he was. He told me he was about to depart for Hawaii. That was over a week ago. Hasn't called since, which is unusual. He's normally pretty good about that – staying in touch. I've left him a dozen messages . . .' Those lines returned to her forehead and her eyes moistened.

'What's the name of the company he works for?'

Alabama reached into a bag hooked over the side of her chair and produced a purse from which she pulled a deck of business cards. 'Nevada Aircraft Brokers,' she said, shuffling through them. She took a card, eventually, and held it toward me between long index and middle fingers. 'The guy to speak to is Ty Morrow. He's the boss.'

I repeated the name to myself, to plant it in my memory, and took the card. 'You still got the packaging the hand arrived in?' I asked her.

'Yes, I kept it in case it was important.'

'Mind if I take a look?'

She bent down, glanced under the bench, then reached out with her foot and scooped back a FedEx-branded box. She handed it to me and I checked it over, moving it around with a makeup pencil. There was nothing to see with the naked eye, other than the consignment note taped to it. The sender was an illegible scribble with an address in Rio de Janeiro. I wrote down what I could make out. The FBI was firming as a certainty. 'Vegas PD will want this packaging, too,' I said.

'Okay.'

'You got something I can put it in?'

She opened a drawer under the bench and pulled out a large Bally's branded paper bag and held it open while I placed the box inside it. 'Where are you staying?'

'Here – at Bally's.'

'Can you give me a minute?' she asked. 'I'm just going to change.'

'You want me to leave?' I prepared to stand.

'No, I'll just go round the corner.' She motioned at an island of shelving stuffed with feathers and sequined fabrics that ran down the center of the room and divided it in half.

I sat back down and took the opportunity to give Randy's card the once-over. It was plain gloss white with the words NEVADA AIRCRAFT BROKERS in dark blue and, below them, a set of gold wings with the initials NAB in the center. Under that was Randy's name and his title: Pilot. Also included were phone, cell and fax numbers as well as email, website and street addresses. The card was blank on the flipside. I scribbled Morrow's name on it with the makeup pencil and pocketed it. To pass the time, I opened the Bally's bag and had another look at the packaging, thinking about what had arrived in it. I wondered who it belonged to and whether the right hand knew what the left hand was doing – hanging out with a topless dancer in Vegas. I also wondered how it came to be wearing Randy's academy ring (assuming it wasn't a copy), when, according to Alabama, Randy was supposedly airborne on the other side of the world. And how did Rio de Janeiro figure in all of this?

'Excuse me,' said an unfamiliar voice, interrupting my thoughts. I looked up at a milk-coffee-colored woman wearing a black G-string so skimpy it could've been a shoelace. She stood beside me, tall and slim and sweet smelling, her bare breasts full and firm and crowned with generous dark-chocolate nipples. Leaning over me, one of those breasts brushing my shoulder, she reached languidly for a hair dryer on the bench. My mouth went dry and I nearly choked on my tongue. Little Coop woke up and sprang out of bed, causing me to shift in my seat.

'Thanks,' she said, sauntering away.

Alabama reappeared from around the island, now dressed in jeans and a blue cotton top, and not nearly as happy as I was.

'Some of us are goin' out for a bite t'eat, 'Bama,' said the black woman. Her weight shifted to one hip and Alabama's hair dryer dangled by its cord from her fingers. 'Maybe you an' your frien' wanna join us.'

'We'll call you.' Alabama frowned at me and said, 'Shall we go?'

'With her?' I gestured at the topless tall. 'To eat?'

'No.' Alabama picked up her shoulder bag and the Bally's bag with the FedEx packaging inside and headed for the door. I had no choice but to follow. I glanced back in the direction I'd seen the black woman heading. She was now sitting at a mirror and I caught her reflection smiling at me. There was all kinds of trouble in that smile.

A short walk later, Alabama and I left the theater area and entered the lobby. 'You want to ask me about Sugar, don't you?' Alabama said as we joined the throng of midnight gamblers moving between Bally's and Paris.

'Sugar?'

'The black woman: Sugar. Not a stage name either. It's on her driver's license. I'm only asking because you're a man and therefore susceptible. Hell, even *I'm* susceptible to Sugar.'

The thought of Alabama and Sugar rolling around in a clinch was something I was prepared to consider favorably, as was my mischievous little buddy who lived in his own cloistered world down below.

'Everyone wants to fuck Sugar. She's usually happy to oblige. I'm pretty sure she wants to fuck you.'

'Me?' I asked.

'Why not? She wants to take everything she thinks is mine, and you're with me, so . . . Perhaps she has something against me. I think she fucked Randy.'

I sensed that I was getting in the middle of something with sharp nails. Whatever, there seemed to be a lot of fucking going on here.

'It'll come with obligations, though,' she continued.

'What will?'

'Doing Sugar.'

'Okay,' I said, as if taking this on board. The truth was that it had been well over eight months since I'd been with anyone, which was plenty long enough for even muscle memory to have amnesia, despite Little Coop's antics.

'I need a drink. You mind coming with me?' she asked.

I still had questions and, I had to admit, one of them was the name of a half-decent bar. 'Sure,' I said.

Alabama led the way to the main exit. The guy managing the forecourt said hello to her and immediately took us to the head of the queue for cabs like we were Bally's royalty. 'Where are we going?' I asked. There were plenty of places to drink at Bally's.

'Away from here. This is where I work.' The forecourt guy closed her cab door after she palmed him a tip. 'Caesars,' she told the driver.

Outside, the Vegas Strip was just coming into its stride, the sidewalks packed, the neon adding a few degrees to global warming.

'Tell me more about Randy's job,' I said.

'He ferries aircraft around the country, mostly. Sometimes he goes away for a few days, interstate. Occasionally he flies to other countries. This is his first trip to Australia.'

'What about Nevada Aircraft Brokers? Did Randy talk much about his job there?' I took out the card she'd given me.

'He's a pilot – he loves flying, but sometimes the hours get him down.'

I turned the card over. 'And what about his boss, Ty Morrow?'

Alabama's phone rang. She cut the caller off, but then the cell rang again and this time she answered it. From what I could gather it was a girlfriend, the conversation small talk. Alabama rolled her eyes for my benefit like she wasn't particularly interested but had to make out that she was. Her phone beeped with a couple of incoming texts. AT&T central.

By the time she was off the phone, we'd pulled into Caesars. I followed her through the casino, heading for the Forum shops, according to signs. Our destination was a place called Shadow Bar. Lined up outside the door was a queue, another one that didn't seem to apply to us, as Alabama went up to the guy managing it, a black body builder in a black Lycra top with a secret service–style earpiece in his ear, and kissed him on the cheek. Inside, the place was popular but not overpopulated. The barkeeps, mostly Jake Gyllenhaal look-alikes, were finishing a show, flipping bottles, juggling glasses, spinning around, somersaulting. They should have no trouble putting a couple of rocks in a glass, I figured. Once they stopped dancing and started serving, the music selection slowed and the navy-blue silhouette of a woman appeared on each of the pink video screens up behind the bar and began moving to the beat, slow and sensuous. The dancing turned the mood-o-meter to erotic, as did Alabama's nemesis, Sugar, who I was surprised to see was now also here. She'd changed into a black ultra-mini to go with her shoelace. The dress was a knockout – fitted and cut high at the front, but with a low back, rows of polished stones around the hemline. She swayed a little to the music as she talked to some college types at the bar, occasionally emulating the moves of the women behind the screens. She glanced at Alabama and blew her a kiss. Or maybe it was meant for me. Little Coop thought it was meant for him. Several other women seemed to be with Sugar, all of them tall. Topless talls, I guessed, though they were currently covered. Alabama didn't seem too pleased to see her bosom buddies, even though I'd gathered from the behavior of the muscle at the door that this was a current favorite watering hole among them.

'Can I buy you a drink?' Alabama asked as she claimed a booth well away from her fellow dancers. 'The least I can do . . .'

'Sure. Glen Keith with rocks if they've got it, Maker's Mark if they don't.'

'Back in a second,' she said, and went over to Sugar and pulled her aside. The black woman rested her hand in the small of Alabama's back while they talked, and let it drop six inches or so. Alabama didn't seem to mind, smiling, engaged. In fact, it looked to me like the two were extra-specially good pals.

'No Glen Keith, I'm afraid,' said Alabama when she returned from the bar with two drinks, one of which was nuclear-waste-lime in color. 'So I got you Maker's.'

For a moment there I'd thought maybe the Green Lantern thing had my name on it. I breathed a quiet sigh of relief, said thanks and accepted the bourbon. 'I thought you and Sugar didn't get on.'

'We don't,' Alabama replied, sipping her Three Mile Island or whatever. 'You mean our little girl-hug a moment ago? We've got a love–hate thing.'

'Have you been with her?' I asked.

Alabama hesitated then said, 'That's a pretty direct question.'

'Got a direct answer?'

'Why's it important for you to know?'

'I don't know what is and isn't important at the moment.'

Another pause. Alabama sipped her drink. 'Yes. Twice.'

'Has Randy?'

'I don't know for sure, but Sugar was interested. And she is persistent.'

Glancing over at Sugar, I saw she had her arm around a woman and was laughing at something being whispered in her ear by one of the men in her orbit. She seemed the type that could get anything, and anyone, she wanted.

I pulled the business card from my pocket and changed the subject. 'Let's talk about the company Randy works for, about his boss.'

Alabama was shaking her head slowly. 'Randy hasn't said much of anything about either, except that there are always plenty of planes around, which he likes, of course. I've been out there a few times to pick him up after work.'

'Have you met Morrow?' I asked her.

'We haven't been formally introduced, but I know what he looks like.'

I looked at Alabama hard. She was undoubtedly hot, but she also seemed pretty clingy. Was she too clingy? Was it possible Randy had had enough and posted the hand himself to throw his needy girl-friend off the scent? Maybe Randy was just across town, living it up, now free to sleep with women who had cellulite, cankles or less than perfect breasts. 'Is it possible,' I asked her, 'Randy staged his own disappearance?'

'What? No! Why would he do that?'

'People do,' I said. 'It's not uncommon.' Was I being unnecessarily cruel putting this thought in Alabama's head, that maybe she was into Randy more than he was into her? Perhaps, but it did seem to me that two and two were adding up to three and a half here. I ran through the factors in my head:

1. It obviously wasn't Randy's hand.
2. Someone had quite possibly managed to get hold of Randy's ring.
3. Randy was supposedly flying a plane to Australia, which, last

time I looked, was a long way from the FedEx box's origin in Rio de Janeiro.

3.5. Randy's ring was placed on Thing's finger and, just in case any-one had any doubts about his health prospects, a ransom note had been included.

My problem was that I had plenty of doubts. This business had the whiff of a hoax about it. If so, was Alabama in on it? And if she was, why? 'Do you know whether Randy has an insurance policy?' I asked her, probing this notion.

'He's a flyer, so I'd say he would.'

'You haven't seen it?'

'No.'

'He hasn't discussed it with you?'

'No.'

'Who might the beneficiaries be?'

'No idea.' Alabama seemed agitated. Maybe our conversation wasn't heading in the direction she'd hoped. 'You really think something else is going on here, don't you? And you think it has something to do with me.'

Alabama was quite possibly on the level about what she did and didn't know. And her concern could easily be genuine fear for her miss-ing lover's safety, rather than the fact that I was rubbing her the wrong way. Nevertheless, I still had a test I wanted to put her through. 'Did Randy tell you that he was running drugs back in Afghanistan?'

She froze, but recovered quickly and looked me dead in the eye. 'He wasn't. That was a lie. I thought you said he was one of the good guys, that you were his friend.' She gathered her things.

I'd told her that I'd met him. I hadn't said we'd graduated to friend sta-tus. 'He was court-martialed,' I continued. 'The charges were serious.'

'And they were dismissed,' she said.

'The Air Force still kicked him out.'

'Okay, I think we're done here.' Alabama began to get up. 'I'll send you a check for your expenses.'

Alabama was a dancer, not an actress, so I was prepared to believe that *she* believed Randy was innocent of drug running. 'Relax,' I said. 'Sit down.'

'Stick it where the sun don't shine, buddy.'

'The story is loaded with inconsistencies. I just wanted to assure myself that . . .'

'That I'm not one of your inconsistencies.'

I shrugged. 'Yeah.'

'Call me when you're sure,' she said.

'As far as I can see, no crime has been committed here,' I said as she turned to go.

That stopped her. 'What?'

'Okay, it might be illegal to courier amputated limbs around the country without a permit or some such, but, aside from that, where's the crime?'

She stared at me, confused.

'Look at it this way: the hand – it isn't Randy's, so we can reasonably conclude that he still probably has both of his. Also, there's no concrete proof that the ring is his – even the engraving could be copied, and as far as we know he's safely cruising along at thirty thousand somewhere over the Pacific. Bottom line, how do we know beyond any doubt that he's being held captive?'

'There's the ransom note.'

'It says you're going to hear about where to take the money. Have the kidnappers got back to you?'

'No.'

The note stated that Alabama would be contacted, but no such contact had been made. It had been close to five days now since she received the parcel.

'What do you think that means?' she asked.

'I don't know. Maybe they lost your number.'

'What?'

'Silence doesn't serve the hostage-takers' agenda. What do they hope to gain with no further contact?' And while I was on the subject of things I didn't know, what was the significance of having twenty days to pay the ransom in the first place? Why not seven days, or three days, or twenty-four hours to come up with the money? In my experience, kidnappers gave their victims less time rather than more to produce the cash. It didn't suit the perpetrators' reasons for committing the crime to allow authorities the time to track them down and stomp on their asses before they'd split with the dough. Maybe Randy was already dead. Even if he was, that wouldn't stop the hostage-takers' attempts to extract a pile of cash from Alabama with assurances that it would be in exchange for his life. Kidnappers demanding large sums of money didn't usually play fair. No, at the moment I had no idea what the lack of contact might mean. Or pretty much anything else connected with this case.

'When exactly did you last see Randy?' I asked her, going back over some details.

'Nine days ago.'

'So four days before the package arrived.'

She nodded. 'Yes, he left on a Sunday – that would make it the twelfth.'

'Was the fifth the day Randy left for Australia?'

'Yes.'

'And you received the package the following Thursday?'

'Yes.' Twenty days time from that Thursday would be Wednesday the fifth. I made a note of the date.

'Who else knows about the package, aside from Marnie?'

'As far as I know, only you.'

'And you say you've been in contact with Nevada Aircraft Brokers?'

'Yeah, pretty much every day since . . . since the package arrived. I've been asking them to tell Randy to call me.'

'You didn't say anything about the ransom angle?'

'The note said no police. Letting Randy's boss in on it, the police would've been called for sure.'

'And do you know if Randy's checked in with them at all while he's been en route?'

'They said they haven't heard from him. But they also said they're not expecting him to contact them until he lands in Darwin.'

'Any problems with the flight that they know of?'

'I didn't ask them that, not exactly, but they know I'm stressed about it. They'd have told me if they were worried.'

'When's he expected in Darwin?'

'Any time now. What do we do next?' she asked.

I figured I could just hang around playing the slots and wait for Randy to show up, but that probably wasn't what Alabama had in mind. 'We could take the severed hand to the metro police.'

'I could have done that.'

'Why didn't you?'

'I really don't know. I thought there might be a better option – you, I guess.' Her body language suggested having me here was no longer anything to break out the band for. I heard her phone buzz. She checked the caller ID on screen, got excited and plucked it up off the table. I went back to watching the shadow girls working the screens, and Sugar working the floor.

'What?' I heard Alabama say, suddenly in shock. 'Oh my God . . . Yes, yes, of course . . .'

'What's up?' I asked when she ended the call.

She looked at me, her eyes bathed in tears. 'That was Ty Morrow. It's Randy . . . Darwin expected him two hours ago but he hasn't turned up. They think he crashed at sea.'

Five

I called Morrow back. The guy told me the police had been notified, along with the Federal Aviation Administration and the National Transportation Safety Bureau. Beyond that, he said, nothing could be done – not until morning. It was late – or, rather, early – by the time we left Shadow Bar. The place was closed to the public at two a.m., but management kept it open for Alabama and a couple of her close friends from Bally's. I also stayed back in case I was needed – I wasn't.

Nevertheless, it was almost three a.m. by the time I hailed a cab for Alabama and her friends, who she'd asked to stay over at her place to keep her company. I flagged down another cab for myself, and a yellow and green Prius pulled to the sidewalk. As I opened the door, a woman slid in ahead of me to claim the back seat. I stood there holding the door, working up to being indignant.

'You goin' my way, honey?' called a voice from inside.

There weren't many ways to go in Vegas, so there was a good chance I just might be. I bent down to say sure and noticed the black dress with the polished stones around the hemline. Sugar.

'It's Vin, right?' she asked when I hesitated.

'Yeah,' I said and got in.

She held out her hand. 'Sugar.'

'I know,' I told her. 'We've met already, at Bally's, in the change room. You might not remember.' Her fingers were long and slender, the fingernails real and painted a soft pink, her skin warm, moisturized and fragrant.

'Sure I remember. But we never exchanged names, so it ain't official. An' y'all have seen me naked, so y'all have me at a disadvantage.'

I had, and I'd like to again.

The driver was getting edgy sitting in traffic, banking it up. 'We headin' somewheres, folks?' he asked, half turning in his seat.

'Where you goin'?' Sugar asked me.

'Bally's.'

'What do you know, me too. Bally's, please,' she said to the driver, then to me: 'You're stayin' there, ain't you? I heard you say something about it to 'Bama.'

'Yes.'

'You a frien' of hers?'

'I'm helping her out with a problem.'

'You're from back East. I can tell by yo' accent. That's a long way to come. Must be a big problem she got.' Sugar shifted in her seat, uncrossed her leg one way and recrossed it the other, her body curling like smoke, her perfume fresh and imported. She smiled at me, eyes set to bedroom mode. 'I think I'm gonna like you. 'Bama has good taste.' Something amused her. 'I sure liked the taste of Randy.' She licked her lips. There was no mistaking her meaning.

My collar felt tight. The driver was somehow managing to avoid colliding with other vehicles, despite the fact that his eyes were superglued to the rear-view mirror.

'I spoke with one of the girls about half an hour ago,' Sugar continued. 'She said somethin' had happened and that 'Bama was upset. Somethin' about Randy.'

'You'll have to ask Alabama,' I said.

Sugar smiled at me, her lips parting, one eyebrow arched. One leg rubbed against the other. If I'd been required to say anything more at that moment, I probably would have stuttered.

'Yes, good idea. I'll do that,' she continued. 'So, the important question is, how long will y'all be stayin' in Vegas?'

A thud followed by a lift under the cab's front wheels told me we'd hit the ramp leading up to Bally's forecourt.

'Until I leave,' I said, more cryptically than I'd intended.

'Well, obviously.' Sugar did that uncrossing thing again with her legs, preparing to get out, the cab coming to a stop. 'Sounds like longer than a day or two, at least.'

'Who knows,' I said. The meter said eight bucks. I gave the driver twelve and asked for a receipt.

'Maybe we could have a drink. You got a card?' she asked me.

I handed one over and she held it up to the light. 'So, Mr Special Agent, y'all have come all the way from Andrews Air Force Base, Washington DC. What's so *special* about you?'

'I'll tell you some other time, perhaps. You probably want to get to bed before the sun rises.' That's what I wanted to say, but what came out was, 'Umm . . . er . . .' followed by a croaky kind of swallowing sound that ended in a squeak.

'Can I borrow your pen, please, honey?' Sugar asked the driver.

The way the guy looked at her told me he'd have been prepared to hand over his Prius.

She made a slow circular motion at me with the pen. I got the message and turned around. She rested the card on my shoulder and wrote on it. Then she whispered in my ear, 'Use it, don't lose it,' and let the card flutter into my lap. 'Goodnight,' she said, her door opening.

''Night,' I replied to her bare, smooth back. I fumbled for the card when she was gone. A phone number, ending with an exclamation mark, was penned on the flipside.

Once she'd disappeared from view, and time and space returned to normal, the driver twisted around in his seat and said, 'So who's a lucky motherfucker?'

*

The street Alabama and Randy lived on was in Summerlin, a suburb twelve miles northwest of the Strip. The street itself seemed, at best, semi-occupied. Every third house or so was on the market, a faded 'For Sale' sign out front with a bleached photo of a smiling agent looking more like a ghost. The front yards of these unsold houses were mostly mini dustbowls of dead plant life and brown grass, the houses looking as discarded and dried out as shed rattlesnake skins. Alabama and Randy's place was in the middle of a small green belt of occupancy, a little island holding out against the rising tide of foreclosure. A sprinkler system soaked the green lawn of the house next door, a miniature rainbow hanging over a flowerbed bursting with purple and red flowers.

I got out of the rental and went up the short path to the stairs to Randy and Alabama's veranda. My knuckles were poised to rap on the front door when it opened and Alabama appeared. She didn't say a word. I caught a glimpse of her eyes as she walked out and made for the car. They were red-rimmed behind a pair of large black sunglasses that took up half her face. Despite the sunglasses, or maybe even because of them, she looked haggard, as much as someone like Alabama could look haggard. I figured she hadn't slept much, if at all, and if she had it was probably in the old blue jeans and faded Giants t-shirt she was wearing. A red Caesars ball cap completed her ensemble for the morning's unpleasantness. For me, it was jeans, a plain white tee and runners. I opened the car door for her and she slid in, still without saying a word.

Shortly thereafter we pulled into the lot outside Nevada Aircraft Brokers. Two vehicles were parked outside. They had a federal look about them, that is to say tired and worn out. Alabama didn't comment on their presence, perhaps because I'd already briefed her on what to expect as we drove there. Keeping us company on the rear passenger seat was the small ice chest and a Bally's branded bag.

I parked beside a white Ford Explorer with darkened windows and an FAA sticker on the rear bumper, and got out. The desert heat was thick with the smell of kerosene and burned aviation jet fuel. Three hundred yards over on the active runway, a United Airlines 767 lifted its chin and strained for height, its engines grinding through the heat of the morning. I collected the ice chest and bag off the rear seat – I didn't want the hand fricasseed in the oven the rental would soon become in the morning sun.

Nevada Aircraft Brokers was housed in a large white modular building, gold heat-reflecting film on its windows and front double doors. Behind the flat-roofed box, beyond a mesh fence topped with razor wire, several white executive jets gleamed on the ramp. Alabama and I walked toward the building's gold-filmed front door just as a man and woman opened it, both in their early thirties, slightly overweight and dressed in a hundred percent polyester. The two walked out, not in any particular hurry, and headed for the Ford Explorer with the FAA decal. The guy smiled at Alabama; the woman gave her a frown. Nothing unusual in Alabama's universe, I figured.

On the other side of those gold doors the temperature dropped into the low twenties. We stepped into a waiting room that took up half the width of the building, a white Laminex reception desk at one end occupied by a large older woman with brassy hair, and down the other end a frosted glass wall with a door. Behind the woman hung framed photos of executive jets like the ones outside, the pilots visible in their cockpit windows. There was a leather couch to sit on and a low coffee table in front of it scattered with assorted financial and aircraft magazines and newspapers. A coffee machine and a water cooler stood in one corner, and a slot machine held down the one opposite; SLEEPING BEAUTY said the colorful lettering on it. Now that I thought about it, there was a musical hum in the air, sprinkled with what I supposed were meant to be magical bells, the same sound I'd heard dominating the reception foyer at Bally's. A pictorial showed Sleeping Beauty herself comatose on a bed, Prince Charming coming through the window behind her. From the looks of it, Ms Beauty was in for either some morning glory or a rude awakening, depending on how she felt about strangers in her bedroom. The slot took quarters for a chance at winning a cool hundred-thousand-dollar jackpot. I had some change in my pocket – maybe later, on our way out.

The receptionist peeked at us over bifocals, her eyes small in the expanse of heavily made-up flesh around them, like marbles pushed into dough. Chubby gold-ringed fingers paused over a keyboard. She touched a mole on her cheek like it was a button that would switch on recognition, but doing so failed to help her penetrate Alabama's cunning disguise of sunglasses and ball cap. 'Can I help you folks at all?'

'Special Agent Vin Cooper, here to see Ty Morrow,' I said, placing the bag and esky down and my card on her desk, the gold leaf on the embossed OSI agent badge a nice match for the windows. 'And this is Randy Sweetwater's partner,' I said.

'Oh, *Alabama*! Is that you, honey? I didn't recognize you with those glasses on.'

Why did I ever doubt how Clark Kent got away with it?

'Hello, Carol,' said Alabama, taking off the sunglasses, revealing red eyes above deep black, sleep-deprived shadows.

'Oh, you poor thing,' said Carol. 'Can I get you something, honey? A cup of coffee? Water?'

'No thanks, really . . .'

'Well, whatever you need, just ask. Mr Morrow is busy with some folks. Shouldn't be long now.'

Carol seemed uncomfortable. I wondered whether it was because we chose to remain standing or the fact that neither Alabama nor I appeared at all interested in playing slots. Whatever, after a few moments she got up, went to the door in the frosted glass wall, opened it and popped her head around the corner. I heard her murmur something in a low voice before turning and informing us that Ty would just be a minute.

Less than a minute later, dark shapes appeared in the frosted glass and the door swung open. Two men in suits that were coffee-stain brown came out. NTSB, I figured, given the authorities Morrow said he'd notified. They turned and said words like 'thanks' and 'we'll be in touch' to a short guy in his late fifties wearing polished black shoes, navy-blue suit pants, a pale blue shirt and pink striped tie, loosened at the collar. Had to be Ty Morrow. He looked well kept, like he rolled in money on a regular basis. His tan face glowed with a laser-burnished gloss, and his shaped and dyed black eyebrows sat above light gray eyes that matched the professionally layered silver hair swept back behind his ears. The guy had country club written all over him. But, like they say – mustn't judge.

'Alabama,' he said, putting an arm around her shoulder. 'I'm *soooo* sorry.'

This apology seemed to confirm Alabama's worst fears and her hand went to cover her eyes as her face crumpled.

'Agent Cooper,' Morrow said, offering a quick handshake as he ushered Alabama into the meeting room. Morrow was Texan, longhorn cows in his drawl. 'Good of y'all both to come on over.'

He guided Alabama into one of the expensive-looking aluminum and black mesh chairs arrayed around a table, the top of which had been made to look like the skin of an airplane – white, powder-coated and riveted aluminum – the winged NAB logo in the center. I took the chair beside her and put the ice chest and bag on the floor. Morrow sat opposite, hands clasped together in front of him.

'So, what's the latest from the authorities?' I asked.

'Nothing new, I'm afraid,' Morrow said. 'Randy departed Henderson International slightly ahead of schedule, after taking the required break. He was vectored into the airway, cleared to twenty thousand feet. Local air traffic control handed him on to the flight information region for southwest vectors, and he flew on his way. He made all the scheduled stops on his flight plan, as well as all mandatory radio calls, and no problems were reported. Everything was normal until he failed to make the appropriate radio calls approaching Darwin. I received notice that he was missing late yesterday.' Morrow glanced at Alabama. 'Ah'm sorry, honey,' he said again.

'He make *any* calls in that sector?' I asked.

'No. The standard ones departing Henderson Field in the Solomons, but nothing after that.'

'No Mayday call?'

'No.'

'He didn't phone me from Hawaii or anywhere,' said Alabama, blowing her nose with a tissue, her face red, her eyes redder. 'He *always* phones me.'

'There's a search underway,' said Morrow.

I didn't ask where they were searching. Haystacks didn't get much bigger than the Pacific. Ask Amelia Earhart.

'Randy was a great guy and a hell of a pilot,' Morrow continued, issuing the last rites.

'What kind of plane was he flying?' I asked.

'A Hawker Beechcraft Super King Air 350.' He opened up a folder, took out a color photo and passed it to me. 'That's the actual aircraft. Eighteen months old. Practically new. The type has an unbeatable reputation for reliability.'

A reputation Randy had just dented. I glanced at the photo. The King Air was a large, sleek-looking twin turboprop with a T-tail. Windows down its side indicated that it could take maybe a dozen passengers. 'What's the range of a plane like this?' I asked.

'That's a 350ER – ER for extended range. Two thousand two hundred nautical miles, plus reserve. He also carried an internal bladder in case of headwinds. The leg from LAX to Hawaii was right on the aircraft's range.'

'So fuel was going to be tight.'

'Randy's problem wasn't going to be fuel, it was boredom. The King Air's no jet. He was in the air a lotta hours.'

I had nowhere to go, but then I wasn't an experienced aircraft accident investigator. The flight had originated on US soil, which meant the NTSB would be putting this one under its microscope.

Morrow made a huffing sound, an ironic smile on his lips. 'What's up?' I asked him.

'I was going to send someone else. Randy wanted the job, practically begged me for it. Said he'd never been to Australia before.'

Alabama bit a knuckle.

'How many hops did he have to make?' I asked.

'Quite a few. He was going to do it over an eight- to ten-day period, depending on the weather. Flying conditions were good, by the way.'

'Did he have a co-pilot?'

'No, flew solo.'

'Long solo flight.'

'Randy had the option of taking a co-pilot, but he chose to go it alone. As I said, boredom was going to be an issue.'

'Any idea what might have happened?'

Morrow shook his head. 'None whatsoever.'

Alabama had recovered a little composure. I stopped asking questions so that she could ask a few of her own.

Morrow beat her to it. 'So you're OSI?' he said, my card in his fingers.

I nodded.

'Local? From Nellis?'

'No, out from DC.'

'Randy was a civilian – no longer Air Force. Are you on this official-like?'

'No. Just a friend of the family's. Have the authorities told you what happens next?'

Morrow dropped my card in his folder. 'They said all we can do is wait, see what the search turns up.'

'I know Randy's alive,' said Alabama. 'I can feel it.'

Morrow gave her a pitying smile. 'I'm sorry, honey,' he said, clearly not a believer in Alabama's instincts.

'I'd *know* if Randy was gone,' she said, bolder this time, assured by her own conviction. 'Is there a chance he could have had some trouble and put down near an island somewhere?'

'I guess anything's possible, but . . .' The look he gave us said there was more chance of relieving Sleeping Beauty out in reception of her jackpot.

'What about the plane's electronic locator beacon?' I asked.

'It had one. As far as I know, it didn't light up.'

'Isn't that unusual?'

He shrugged. 'ELBs are electronic gadgets – they can fail like any other electronic gadget. There'll be an investigation. All we can do is wait and see.'

I leaned down, picked up the ice chest and put it on the table. Time to let Randy's boss know that there might be more to the disappearance of his aircraft than he or the authorities thought.

'What you got there?' Morrow asked, half a smile lifting part of his face.

'Several days after your King Air departed LAX, Ms Thornton here received this.' I opened the chest and turned it around.

Morrow leaned forward and peered inside. 'Jesus Christ!' he exclaimed, that tan of his appearing more like badly applied makeup as the blood drained from his cheeks.

'This is what brought me to Vegas,' I said. 'After we leave your office, we're taking it to the metro PD. If you look carefully, you can see an Air Force Academy ring on its pinky that we believe belonged to Randy. The package also came with a greeting card asking for a ransom in exchange for Randy's life.'

Morrow sat back in his seat, mouth open and probably dry. 'Jesus,' he repeated, whispering it the second time around. The guy was in a state of shock. Perhaps giving him a peek at Thing was a little on the melodramatic side, but he had to know that there might be another angle being played here. 'Is that Randy's . . . you know . . . his . . .' Morrow asked, voice cracking.

'His hand?' I said. 'No, but you can see the problem, right? Alabama here was understandably concerned when she received this home delivery, but reassured because, one, this wasn't Randy's hand and, two, he was supposedly flying a plane to Australia. But now the place she thought he was safely tucked away in – your King Air – has disappeared.'

Morrow's face had gone a splotchy white.

'Are you okay, sir?' I asked. I didn't want the guy having a heart attack.

'If Sweetwater's not in that plane, the . . . the damn insurance company won't pay out,' Morrow stuttered under his breath, the full force of the implications suddenly hitting him in his wallet.

And those who say you shouldn't prejudge just don't know shit from ice cream.

*

I called ahead and asked Detective Sergeant Ike Bozey to meet Alabama and me at the desk sergeant's area and escort us through. I wasn't keen on getting searched. I could warn the guy at the x-ray station that there was an amputated human hand on my person, but police I had no connection with were likely to get jumpy about this and I had no desire to be forced onto the floor at the point of a quivering Glock.

'Hey, Cooper,' said Bozey in a voice full of gravel. 'Good to meet you. And this is Alabama, right?'

Alabama waved.

'Coming through,' said the detective sergeant, beckoning at us to come past the usual search procedures. 'These people are my guests,' he announced loudly.

'On your head be it, Bozey,' the desk sergeant called out, making a note.

'Get a dick in your ear, fatso,' Bozey replied loudly. The sergeant he was referring to was on the skinny side of scrawny, his neck filling his shirt like a straw fills a glass.

'Fuck you,' came back at him.

In an aside, Bozey said, 'He's married to my sister . . . Makes for an interesting Thanksgiving.'

Alabama and I fell in behind the detective sergeant, a former light-heavyweight boxer who walked like one. The guy also came with a heavy New York accent and buzz-cut brown hair, tending to gray. A wide scar was clearly visible meandering over the crown of his skull. He'd taken a bullet there that, according to Arlen, had exposed a part of his brain. It happened the day he took on five thugs attempting to sexually assault a fifteen-year-old girl in broad daylight, after dragging her into a back alleyway. One of the perps had fired a .38 at Bozey, the slug digging out a piece of his skull, but the guy had kept on fighting, even madder. Three of the five perps ran off after Bozey had knocked the other two out cold. When the cops turned up they found him sitting on one of the alleged attackers, trying to fit the pieces of bone back into the hole in his own head. When Bozey finally got out of hospital, he joined New York's finest, only to quit a couple of years later to move west with his sister. Vegas was the place he decided to put down roots, after she met and married – the desk sergeant, I assumed – and Bozey joined the force again.

We rounded the corner. 'Arlen said I should lend you every assistance. So, here I am, lending.' We came around another corner and this time the hallway broadened into open-plan office space populated by a mixture of uniformed and plainclothes police. The sound of computer keyboard clatter dominated, punctuated by several phones that rang and rang and rang.

'How do you know Arlen?' I asked him.

'Can't say,' he said.

'Why not?'

''Cause it happened here in Vegas, and there are rules.'

'I'll ask him.'

'Won't do you no good.'

We arrived at a cubicle-sized space that reminded me of my office at Andrews: gray partitions and one entire face covered with papers and photos and sticky notes and maps, some of them hand-drawn. It felt like home.

'I hear you work at Bally's,' Bozey said to Alabama.

'That's right,' she told him as he pulled in a chair for her to sit on.

'That's a good clean show.'

'Yes, it is.'

'And that's a damn shame,' he said, giving her a grin full of mischief. He cleared his throat and took a seat. 'Now, what can I do for you folks?'

'Arlen told you nothing?' I asked.

'Not a word, except that you was family.'

'That mean you're gonna start calling me names?' I asked.

He grinned. 'Maybe.'

'Okay, well, Alabama received this in a FedEx box,' I said, handing over the ice chest.

'Do I want to know what's in here before I lift the lid?' he asked.

'It's a body part,' I warned him.

Bozey opened it, took a peek inside, sucked his lips into a seam and raised an eyebrow. 'Right,' he said.

'There's a note.' I took the letter, now protected in a clear plastic ziplock, from the Bally's bag and passed it to him.

'When did this arrive?' he asked, reading it through the plastic.

'Getting on for six days ago,' I said.

'That's not helpful. Six days lost, fourteen to go, according to this. Why not bring it in sooner?'

'I was scared,' Alabama admitted. 'If I contacted the police and the kidnappers found out . . .'

'Doll, these people don't want you contacting the police because *they're* scared. They're scared there'll be no payday; they're scared their asses will get stomped on by law enforcement; they're scared they'll spend the best part of the rest of their lives eating someone else's dick in Club Fed . . . Sorry, just don't get me started.'

'Any other hot buttons we should know about?' I said.

'I'll tell you after you push 'em. Has any further contact been made?'

'No,' said Alabama. 'And this is not Randy's hand.'

I took it from there and filled Bozey in on what we knew – that perhaps the ring was the boyfriend's and that, at the time his kidnappers claimed they were sawing pieces off him, he was supposedly flying a plane to Australia. I then told him the news we'd received last night: that Randy's plane had gone missing and was now presumed crashed in the Pacific, somewhere between the Solomon Islands and Darwin.

'Could be an elaborate con gone wrong,' the detective concluded without hesitation. 'What's the ransom?'

'Fifteen million,' I said.

'And you don't got it,' he remarked, looking at Alabama.

'On what we make at Showgirls?'

Bozey shrugged. 'Honestly? Not a lot of what you're saying makes much sense to me. But until something else turns up, I can see pretty clearly that you do have one small problem.'

'To go with the big ones,' I said.

'Yeah. As far as we know, this hand could have come from a university cadaver. My problem is, well, I can't see where the crime has been committed – nothing I can investigate, anyway.'

'I figured as much,' I said.

'Then how can I be of assistance?'

'CSI – forensics. Put the hand through the wringer. It might turn up something to go on. There's also the note.' I motioned at the Bally's bag. 'And in here is most of the original packaging everything came in.'

The sergeant rubbed his chin. 'I don't know . . . Vegas is a pretty busy port of call, forensically speaking, and we don't have a lot of those kinds of resources to splash around here.'

'Oh, sure you do,' I said. 'I've seen the TV show.'

Six

Alabama said she was tired so, as there was nothing more we could move on, I drove her home to Summerlin with a promise to call if anything else turned up, then took myself back to my hotel for a swim.

It was maybe a hundred and ten in the shade down in the pool area, the place surrounded by glass buildings focusing the sun's rays like a magnifying glass picking out bugs. In the pool it was virtually standing room only, packed with college kids come to Vegas to get drunk, get laid, lose all their money and go home with sunburn, a hangover and a misspelled tattoo across their backs – the usual.

A loud alcohol-fueled bikini contest was coming to a conclusion, the music and the bar pumping, as I wandered around the crowded sunbaking area in search of an empty sun lounge. A leggy black college kid was showing the crowd her moves, egged on by the DJ. The masses in the pool applauded when she gave her hips a workout. And when she turned, bent over and wiggled her money-maker at the audience, it rewarded her with waves of hoots and applause. Up next, a large white woman in a high-cut green one-piece costume with deep scallops out of the sides, her ample upper thighs the shape of ice-cream cones and just as dimpled. She didn't seem to care though, and moved as dirty as any woman I've ever seen, which seduced roars of approval from the spectators. A woman in her early twenties won the contest when her tiny gold bikini top suffered a wardrobe malfunction, something I firmly believe everyone except network executives appreciates.

I circumnavigated the pool area twice before finding a sun lounge in the process of being vacated. A woman in a Bally's shorts-and-tee ensemble came and took my drink order, while I waited for a heavily tattooed jock to pack up and leave. It had been a while since my bare skin received a dose of sun, and I had a bunch of reasonably new scars that were still pink, so I figured I had maybe half an hour before I got second-degree burns. I stripped off my top and rolled it into a headrest then lay face down. The sun's heat immediately went to work on my back and I exhaled loudly, feeling relaxed, on vacation at last.

I'd only drifted off to sleep for maybe five minutes when a cold shock between the shoulder blades woke me with a start. I looked up, ready to get all indignant, and saw that it was Sugar. She was standing beside me, her shadow across my face, the sun a corona behind her head, a cheeky smile on her lips. A Heineken, my Heineken I supposed, hung from her hand and swung beside her leg. She held it out to me. 'This yours, I think.'

'Thanks.' I rolled onto my side, propped my head on my hand. Her bikini was a knitted orange number. It didn't hide much, and what it did I'd pretty much seen already. She wore heels, slip-ons, which made her look taller and maybe just a little hotter, if that were possible. A multicolored canvas satchel hung casually off a shoulder.

'You bin banged up some, ain't you.' She leaned a little toward me, peering at my body over the top of her Ray-Ban Aviators. 'You bin in a car accident o' somethin'?'

Or something probably covered it best. The last few years had left their marks – several bullet wounds and nicks, a little shrapnel mauling here and there, some barbed-wire tears, a few stitches. I could remember when, where and how I'd received each and every one, but that was a private litany I wasn't prepared to share poolside. 'Yep,' I said, keeping it loose.

'Hey, is 'Bama okay? I heard Randy's in some kinda trouble.'

'You've got a lot of interest in Alabama and Randy.'

She smiled. 'You jealous?'

I parried her smile with one of my own. My beer was looking neglected, so I took a moment to give it some attention. Sugar began digging around inside her bag. 'The sun gonna turn you into a crawfish. You want some cream on?'

I thought about saying no, but only for the nanosecond it took to change my mind. 'Thanks,' I said and rolled onto my stomach.

'Move over a little.'

I wriggled across and she sat beside me on the sun lounge. Looking under my arm I saw her knitted bikini bottom wedged against my hip. Seconds later I heard the splodge of the lotion squirting from the bottle, and a cold wetness on my back. I smelled piña colada. Her hands went to work immediately, moving the lotion around in circles.

'Must have been some car accident,' she said as her fingers slid over a knot of scar tissue on my shoulder blade where a 9mm slug had left in a hurry. Little Coop woke up, stretched out, and wondered if some piña colada might possibly be coming his way too.

'A few of the girls are sayin' somethin' came for 'Bama in a FedEx box.'

'Really,' I said, adding nothing.

'A body part – Randy's.'

'I don't think—'

'His penis.'

That one caught me off guard. I twisted around and looked at her. 'I can promise you that nothing cut from Randy has been received by Alabama, unless she took delivery of it within the last two hours and she's neglected to tell me about it.'

'Is that the truth? 'Cause somethin' came for her, somethin' sick. One of the girls caught a glimpse of it. 'Bama's upset an' then you arrive, a secret agent . . .'

'*Special* agent – I'm just a cop.'

'Okay, but you a cop that's come all the way from Washington.'

'Just a friend of the family lending a hand.' I allowed myself a smirk at that, and went back to getting myself sun-blocked.

'Sure you are.'

'That's the truth.' Interesting how rumors grow. Maybe the super fertilizer on this one had been what one of the girls had caught sight of – perhaps one of Thing's fingers.

'Were you gonna call me?' she asked, changing tack.

'Haven't had the time to give it much thought.'

Sugar responded to this nonchalance by giving me a stinging slap on the back of the leg. 'Then I would have called *you*.'

'Why?'

'Why what?'

'Why would you have called me?' That was a genuine question. Sugar played in a different league table. I was still wondering why she gave me her phone number in the first place. Why would a woman like this be interested in a lowly paid public servant from out of town with a busted nose and a cheap room in a three-star hotel? Come to think of it, why was she giving me the current poolside attention? 'A little down to the left,' I told her, milking it before she realized she could have her pick of half a dozen jocks in the vicinity leering at her.

'I like you. You're a real man.'

'Like Randy.'

Her hands hesitated. 'Yeah, like Randy.'

'Have you ever had sex with Randy?'

Another hesitation. 'The *questions* you ask. Now, I'm gonna put some cream on your legs,' she said, kneading my shoulders. 'You gonna fry, you.'

'Have you?' I persisted. 'How about with Alabama?'

Slap number two.

I gave my shoulders the barest of shrugs. A few seconds later I heard the bottle squirt and felt the cold wetness of the lotion on the back of my legs. Her hands went to work, working it around, the amplitude of movement quickly taking in ankle to upper thigh. Little Coop was close to panting. I tried not to think about it, bending my thoughts in another direction. There was some kind of triangle between Alabama, Randy and Sugar which Alabama readily admitted to. She found the Cajun woman attractive, an attraction that seemed to be mutual. Somehow Randy was also involved, but on what level? Where did he fit into it? 'Why are you so interested in Randy?' I asked her.

It took her a few moments to find an answer. ''Cause he's dangerous an', for me, danger is an aphrodisiac. I like fast cars, motorcycles, speedboats – anything with an engine. I like men and I like men who like women. There ain't nothin' wrong with that, is there?'

The brains of the operation in my shorts was applauding. 'Did you know Randy when he was in the Air Force?' I asked.

'No. I wasn't workin' in Vegas then.'

'But you've met him plenty of times since he left the Air Force.'

'Sometimes, not so many. He has an interestin' job, flyin' airplanes all round the world.'

'And planes have *very big engines*,' I said.

'Yes they do,' she giggled. 'Maybe that's why I'm interested in him.'

'How do you pay your mechanic when you get your car engine serviced?'

Slap number three, though it was more playful than the first two. 'All these scars are tellin' me you're dangerous too. I was right about you, wasn' I? You know, I think I like scars now.'

I'd have happily done without them and the things that had left them on my skin.

'*Phew!* All this work is makin' me hot,' she continued. 'I'm gonna swim. You wanna come?'

'Won't swimming wash the cream off?'

'It's waterproof, silly.' She stood, slipped out of her heels, dropped her sunglasses onto her bag, and took a few steps to the side of the pool. Several guys dangling their legs in the water nudged their buddies and motioned at her. The bikini pageant would have been no contest with Sugar in the line-up. Her ass was generous but tight and rode high on long, straight athletic legs. Her waist was also incredibly narrow but her shoulders were wide and strong. She turned sideways and beckoned me to hurry up. Her breasts, firm and buoyant, did likewise. It was going to be potentially embarrassing getting into the pool, Little Coop having turned my trunks into a teepee. But I sat up anyway and wriggled down to the end of the chair, saving at least one step out in the open, and giving myself the opportunity to get Mr Embarrassing down below better organized. I stood, walked quickly to the pool and jumped in, going under immediately and putting in a few strokes. The water was tepid, but still refreshing. When I came up I scoped around for Sugar, but she'd disappeared. I swam underwater to the edge, turned, spread my arms wide, gripped the side of the pool and leaned back against it. I was slippery due to all the lotion, but I wasn't complaining. And Sugar would find me. I put my head back, closed my eyes and enjoyed the heat of the sun on my face.

'Where'd you get to?' I heard Sugar say.

I put my head down and opened my eyes. She had her back to me and was speaking over her shoulder, wading slowly closer in reverse, entering my personal space. Before I knew what I was doing I lowered an arm and put it around her waist, and stroked my hand against her flat stomach. She immediately pressed in closer, took my hand and guided it down inside her bikini bottom. She then squeezed my fingers into the lips of her vulva and pressed them up against her clitoris, which was hard and distended, her lips slippery and warm.

She put her head back on my shoulder and whispered, 'Oh, you've found it. Have you ever done it in public?'

There were people all around us. 'Not this public.'

As I said this, her free hand worked its way inside my shorts and found what it was looking for. She held me between her fingers and began sliding them up and down the length of my shaft, stopping occasionally to rub the head with her forefinger. She was right about the sunburn lotion being waterproof.

'Try not to make it too obvious, handsome,' she said in my ear as she moved against my fingers, which she was holding inside her.

I swallowed and tried not to squeak.

A college girl up on her boyfriend's shoulders glanced across at me. I gave her a smile, trying to look like I hadn't just been busted with my hand in the cookie jar. Or whatever. Did she know what was going on? She leaned down and said something to her mount and he threw his head back and laughed.

Sugar's breathing quickened and I heard her moan, her lips against my ear. I felt her body shudder and go rigid suddenly. She crossed her legs, which forced my fingers up hard against her pelvic bone.

When she relaxed a little I said, 'That was quick,' and tried not to gasp as she did that thing again with her forefinger.

'My body is good to me,' she said dreamily, her head resting on my shoulder. 'I can sneeze at will, too.' She murmured, 'Let me know when you're gonna come.'

With her own needs taken care of, Sugar put a little more concentrated effort into the operation behind her back. The DJ over at the bar goosed the volume on a new Fiddy Cent number and most of the folks in the pool started bumping and grinding, covering my own movement, which was becoming a little involuntary. I tapped on her shoulder, and said urgently, 'Letting you know . . .'

'I thought so. A woman can tell.'

Sugar put in a few more strokes before turning and sliding below the surface of the water. She took me in her mouth and cupped my aching balls as things began to pump. I felt the action of her tongue as she swallowed a couple of times before letting me go, the water against my skin suddenly cooler than her mouth, and my eyes rolled back in my head.

Sugar surfaced slowly, a smile on her lips as she stroked the skin behind my balls. She wiped the water from her eyes and then kissed me on the mouth, her breath smelling vaguely of coconut and starch.

'A protein shake,' she giggled, then ran her tongue around her lips and added, 'There's lunch taken care of.'

'How'd you even manage that under water?'

'Practice. An' . . .' She pinched her nose between thumb and forefinger to demonstrate the secret.

'Cooper,' I heard a voice say behind me. 'That you?'

Sugar shifted her focus, smiled her dreamy smile and said, 'Hi, 'Bama. Hey, why don't you come on in, join the fun. There's always room for one more. We can order some drinks, have us a party.'

'Hello, Sugar.'

Shit, Alabama . . . I felt a pang of guilt about what had just happened. I turned and the woman was standing behind me looking kinda . . . was it angry? Disappointed? How long had she been there? What had she seen? Did I really care? I knew how she felt about Sugar so, yeah, maybe I did care.

'You mind if Mr Cooper and I talk in private for just a minute?' Alabama asked Sugar, a firm no-nonsense tone in her voice.

'Sure, why not? You look nice, 'Bama.'

She did. Her hair was up in a ponytail and she wore a floral-pattern cotton sundress, the hemline riding somewhere up around Canada. White sandals were on her tan feet, the straps lined with rhinestones – what else.

'I'll see you later,' said Sugar, kissing me on the cheek. She waved to us both and swam off.

I lifted myself out of the pool, the concrete scorching hot against the palms of my hands.

'Can I get you folks a drink?' asked a waitress who materialized beside us.

I could use something. I checked with Alabama. She was wringing her hands and perhaps that look on her face was anxiety and nothing to do with what she might have seen happening in the pool.

'You okay?' I asked her. 'Can we get out of the sun?' she said, and headed for the bar without looking back. 'Scotch – a double – no ice,' she told the barkeep when she arrived.

He lifted an eyebrow at me. 'Same, with rocks,' I said.

'They've found him.' Alabama took off her sunglasses, her eyes red and raw – worse than I remembered from the morning.

I didn't need to ask who, so I asked where.

'His plane . . . it crashed in Australia, after all. Came down in some swamp. Morrow called me half an hour ago. He got a call from the FAA.'

I pulled my phone and saw there were two missed calls – from Morrow and Alabama. I had to ask the painful question. 'Was his body found with the plane?'

'No.' Alabama upended her glass and drank the scotch in a single gulp. She put the glass on the counter and gestured for another. 'No body.'

My cell started ringing. The window told me it was a local Vegas number. I excused myself and answered it.

'Cooper? Bozey,' said the voice in the speaker.

'Hey.' I walked a little away from the bar.

'Just letting you know I got a call from the FAA about your friend Sweetwater.'

I was wondering how the FAA knew who to call when Bozey added, 'I'd only just gotten off the phone to aviation authorities, following up on the inquiries arising from the meeting with you and Alabama.'

'Just heard the news myself,' I said. 'No body, apparently.'

'No. A place called Darwin's the nearest city. The local PD is out looking. Tricky countryside.'

'A swamp, I heard.'

'A wildlife sanctuary.'

'What sort of wildlife they got there? Koala bears?'

'Didn't ask. Anyway, I'll keep you posted if anything else turns up.'

The line went dead. I turned back to the bar in time to see Alabama throwing her head back, downing a scotch. Assuming it was another double, that would make it half a dozen shots in less than five minutes.

'Vegas PD heard,' I told her.

'He's still alive. I know it.'

I nodded, not as convinced as she was about that. And given her level of anxiety, maybe she wasn't so sure either.

'He could have crawled away, got lost or something.' Alabama's speech was starting to slur, along with her reason.

I ordered another scotch for myself and a club soda for her. My confidence that I would be able to see this through to some kind of positive conclusion was fading fast. Randy was down in a swamp eight thousand miles away, surrounded by wild koalas, and I had no doubt that he was dead, or about to be, which also meant that the mystery around the severed hand and the ransom was moot. There wasn't a lot I could do to help, except maybe pay the bar bill. I put some cash on the counter.

Alabama wrapped a hand around the club soda that had appeared on the bar. 'I saw you and Sugar, y'know,' she said, her eyes flat.

I swallowed. Guilty.

'I knew she'd get to you. Men are so *stupid*.'

That was a hard one to argue with.

'Did she ask you about Randy and me while she was doing you?'

Her mouth was under water at the time, and otherwise too engaged to ask questions, but I knew what she meant. 'No, she didn't,' I lied.

'Bullshit.' Alabama looked at her half-glass of club soda and then back at me. Maybe she was considering whether or not to throw it over me. She put the glass down heavily on the counter, spilling some of its contents. 'I can't blame you. I'd just love to know what it is about me that makes her so competitive. And you should ask yourself – why you?'

'Why me?'

'Well, you're not exactly her type. No offense, but she likes pretty boys with money.'

'None taken.' I didn't tell her Sugar thought I had a big motor.

Alabama's eyes crossed momentarily, as if she was grappling with a puzzle. 'You're no oil painting, Cooper,' she said, in case I'd misunderstood.

I'd asked myself the same question Alabama was asking: why me? Maybe I shouldn't have been satisfied with the answer Sugar had provided.

'Thanks for nothing, Cooper,' she said suddenly and walked off a little unsteadily into the hot sun.

The barman took our glasses, wiped the counter and shook his head at me, unimpressed. I countered his look with a mind-your-own-business-pal look of my own, and went back to the pool. A half-hearted attempt to find Sugar failed. She was nowhere around. I'd had enough sun so I picked up my things and handed my lounge chair over to a college girl hovering nearby.

*

There was a flight back East at seven forty-five the following morning, so I booked it. Nothing more could be done for Alabama, not by me at least, and the scene at the bar left me with the feeling that my welcome was worn out anyway. I decided to avoid the morning panic and check out that evening. There was no queue at reception so I went straight up to the clerk behind the computer, gave her my room number, answered the usual questions about the minibar and so forth, and listened to the beguiling magical bells of a bank of Sleeping Beauties down in the pit while she tallied my account. After reviewing a few forms and clattering away on the keyboard, she announced, 'It's already been settled, sir.'

'The bill?'

'Yep, you're all square.'

'Who paid it?'

'Ms Alabama Thornton.'

'Thanks,' I said. I pulled out my cell and dialed my benefactor's number as I drifted toward the dormitory of Sleeping Beauties. 'Alabama, it's Cooper.'

'Hello.'

'I just went to pay my hotel bill but you beat me to it. You didn't need to do that.' Silence. 'Alabama?'

'Yes, I did. You didn't need to come here. You felt obliged.' The tightness in her voice told me she'd been doing plenty more crying.

'I was happy to help out.'

'It's over. Randy's gone. You're . . . you're free to go.'

I hadn't realized there was a lock on the door. 'Okay, but let me buy you dinner, at least.'

'I have a show to do tonight. Another time.' Her tone suggested another time might well be when folks were ice skating in hell.

'I wish it could have worked out different,' I said.

'Me too.'

Silence.

'Okay, well – goodbye,' I said, not a lot more to say.

'Sugar has split.'

'I'm sorry?'

'Sugar. She up and left – back to wherever it was she came from in the first place. Handed in her notice this afternoon; didn't give a reason. Maybe when she heard about Randy, that he was . . . she just . . . I suppose she just lost interest.'

Was Randy's death the motivation for Sugar's departure? Maybe it was. The news of the crash had been made public after my rubdown in the pool. Sugar certainly hadn't mentioned anything about leaving. 'If there's something I can do for you, Alabama, just let me know.'

'I will,' she said. 'And thanks – I mean that.' There was a change in her tone that told me she did in fact mean it this time around. 'What are you going to do? Stay in Vegas?'

'No, think I'll head home tomorrow.'

'If you want to see a show, I can get free tickets to Celine Dion . . .'

Celine Dion? 'Thanks. Think I'll pass,' I said. 'I'm just gonna hang around the pit here at Bally's, drink too much and lose all my money.'

There was a pause. I imagined a smile flickering briefly on Alabama's lips.

'Hey, if you're ever in DC, look me up,' I said.

'I will, Vin . . . Bye.'

The call ended. I hooked the cell under my chin, retrieved from my wallet the card Sugar had given me. I dialed and an automated voice answered: 'The number you have reached is not in service. Please check the number and dial again.'

I took the advice but got the same result. Sugar's phone number was a dead end. Maybe it had never been connected. I hadn't dialed it before now so I couldn't be sure either way, not without getting official about it. I gave a mental shrug. Sugar didn't strike me as the reliable type. Maybe that's what she did – blew in, blew a lucky special agent when she could find one, and blew out. I went to the machine that turns Ben

Franklin into Abe Lincolns, stuffed the wad of cash in my pocket and went off to play the slots via the bar for a single malt.

The Sleeping Beauties were calling me, those magical bells a seductive lure. The theme here was that Ms Beauty was waiting for Prince Charming to come along and roll a row of kisses so that she could be awakened from her slumber and, presumably, shower the lucky royal with riches. Those magic-dust twinkles I'd been hearing almost everywhere since I arrived greeted my bills as the slot gobbled them up. I won fifty-five bucks and lost ninety. Maybe I wasn't charming enough. It took me another six hours and a forgotten number of single malts to lose the four hundred I had in my pocket. I was hunting for a Ulysses S. Grant – I was sure I still had one on me – when fingers grabbed my arm and spun me around. It was Alabama, I think. I peered at her through my Glen Keith glasses. Yes, it was her. I recognized those red eyes.

'Been looking for you. You're drunk,' she said.

'An' you're Ala . . . Alababama,' I slurred. 'Whuz up?'

'They found Randy.'

'What time's it?' I squinted at my Seiko.

'One in the morning. I got a call from your police friend a couple of hours ago. He left a message.'

I took out my cell, which had inadvertently been switched to mute. There were three missed calls, one from Bozey several hours ago and two recent ones from Alabama. There was also a text from the detective. I read the message. *Sweetwater fnd. Not good. Call me 2mara.*

'They want me to go to Australia and . . . and . . .' She brought her hand to her face and cried behind it. I did my best to sober up while she got herself under control. 'They want me to go and identify the remains.'

Remains. Bozey was right – not good.

The news had sobered me up a little. She leaned forward against me. I put my arms around her, her face hot and wet against my neck, and rubbed her back gently. 'Can you go?' she asked.

'Go where?'

'I can't do it. I don't want to go; don't want to see him. I'll pay your expenses. Please, can you go?'

To Australia? 'What about relatives, next of kin?' I asked.

'Randy didn't have any. He was alone in the world.' I felt her body shudder, wracked with mostly silent sobs.

So the guy was like me: no living relatives. That wasn't so tragic, and there were advantages – no awkward Christmases, no irrelevant birthday presents to buy or receive or regift.

'I want to remember him the way he was. You met him. *You* can sign the forms.'

I wasn't so keen, and I wasn't so sure my signature would be accepted, not being Randy's spouse or next of kin. Did he have any tattoos or scars? And Darwin was halfway to the moon.

'Please . . .'

Seven

I went straight from Darwin International Airport to the office of the coroner, Jim Hunt, a big tired-looking guy with thick gray hair parted low on the side of his head. He wore tan Hush Puppies with knee-length off-white socks, brown dress shorts, a pink shirt and purple tie, and had a face that reminded me of one of those Chinese dogs with excess rolls of skin. He leaned forward in his chair and passed the photographs to me over his lunch, a large hamburger with enough cholesterol dripping from the bite he'd taken out of it to block a storm water drain. A blob of egg yolk had collected in a corner of his lips – a snack for later, maybe. The photos showed a couple of sharks lying on the heavy wooden slats of a pier, one two-thirds the size of the other, like it might be the larger one's kid brother. Both had their undersides slit open from anus to chin. Spilling from the slits onto the slats were the sharks' insides. Clearly visible in the larger one's viscera was a human buttock and thigh, and among large sausages of guts pulled from the smaller one was a hand attached to an arm, the glint of a steel watchband on its wrist.

'You're a hundred percent sure you got Randy Sweetwater there?' I asked, flicking through the photos. I didn't know Randy well enough to positively identify his butt cheek.

'When you get people in like this – as I'm sure you know, Mr Cooper – identification becomes a bit of a work in progress,' Hunt answered. 'Though, at the moment, there's enough for me to at least *believe* that those bits and pieces there are your man. Had Randy Sweetwater's wallet on him for starters. We're waiting on a DNA profile and prints from the man's former employer to make a positive ID.' By 'former employer' he meant the USAF, where it was standard practice to keep DNA and fingerprints on file in the event that an aircrew ended up a smear.

'In the meantime, you could provide us with an idea of his height and weight. Might as well start with the basics.' He slid a pad and pen across the desk toward me. I jotted down my best estimate. Hunt opened a drawer and brought out a large brown envelope, which he upturned. A chrome pilot's watch, a Breitling with a black face, slid out of the envelope onto the desk, along with a black leather wallet.

The watch's second hand was working. I picked it up, turned it over and read the inscription, *Anything, Anywhere, Anytime* – it was the motto of the 17th Airlift Squadron, Randy's outfit back when I'd met him. Now that I saw it up close, I remembered the watch being on his wrist back in Afghanistan – he'd just bought it and his co-pilot believed it was a fake. It was still ticking so maybe it was the genuine article after all. I opened the wallet. Through the plastic I could see the photo on a Nevada driver's license. The face was blank, emotionless, but it was clearly Randy's blank and emotionless face.

'Bull sharks – buggers'll eat anything,' said Hunt. 'Once found a steam iron and ironing board inside one of 'em. Only thing missing was the bloody Chinaman.' He rewarded himself with a chuckle. 'There's only one thing more savage than a bull shark and that's a salty.'

'What's a salty?' I asked him.

'Saltwater croc. Fucken sharks are good-natured compared to those bastards. That your bloke's watch?'

I said I believed it was and explained the significance of the inscription.

'Any tattoos, scars, birthmarks?' Hunt asked.

'He had a tattoo – Air Force wings. Here,' I said, showing him the area, on the arm under the bicep. Unfortunately, that was one of the bits of Randy still missing.

Hunt took the photos of the remains, examined them at close range, picking a pair of glasses up off the table and putting a lens between his eye and the photo. 'Let's wait for the formal identification then, eh?'

'What about getting a look at the wreckage?'

'Yes, well, as I said on the phone when you called ahead, that might prove a bit difficult – it's a fair way out in the bush. Anyway, Detective Inspector Grubb can fill you in on all that. And maybe after you're done, you might like to join Grubby and me at the pub for a little ice-cold refreshment, eh?'

'Sure,' I said, standing. I'd come a long way on Alabama's credit card, and I couldn't exactly call it quits after a glance at a few photos and lunch with a head on it.

A fly buzzed around the burger. Hunt brushed it aside, eased himself up and out of his chair and held out a hand. 'You know where you're going?'

I remembered the address. 'Seventy-one Smith Street.'

'Just two minutes' walk up the road, mate. That's what we like about Darwin: everything's just up the road – or down it.'

The formalities concluded, I picked up my bag and left.

Down on the street it seemed to me that the only folks going about their business in the growing mid-morning heat were seniors on electronic scooters and young moms pushing strollers. Take away those moms and I could have been somewhere in Florida in winter. The Aussies called Darwin a capital city but it felt more like a large Gulf vacation town to me. There were too many trees, the pace was too relaxed, and there weren't enough frowns on the faces of the people walking around for this to qualify as a capital city.

Continuing the Gulf theme, Darwin's shores were lapped by water, in this instance the Timor Sea, the ditch that kept Australia and Indonesia apart. It was also the final stretch of water over which Randy had had to fly before making landfall, having navigated a distance of roughly eighty-eight hundred miles. And that was Randy's problem: 'roughly' wasn't quite good enough. His flight plan set out a journey of 8823 miles – LA, Hawaii, Kiribati, the Solomons, Darwin – but he'd fallen short, apparently coming down in a remote shark-infested tributary 344 miles east of Darwin airport's runway threshold markers.

I counted down the street numbers till I stood in front of Darwin police headquarters, 71 Smith Street, half a dozen stories of Lego prefab opposite a building that appeared to be a cross between a barn and a collection of large croquet hoops – the Darwin Memorial Uniting Church, so a sign said. I went into the police building, showed my ID to the security on the ground floor bench and was buzzed up to the office of Detective Inspector Gary Grubb.

A few minutes later, I came around a corridor corner to find myself beckoned into an office by a large guy with a red beard whose shorts were being pushed down off his hips by a fifty-five-gallon drum tucked under his shirt.

'Cooper – you found us. This way, mate, this way . . .' The hand that shook mine was the size of a clutch plate, and just as hard. The skin on his nose was pitted and pepperoni red. The guy had suffered badly from acne as a kid: a multitude of crescent-shaped depressions on his cheek and neck looked like someone had dug their nails repeatedly into his skin. I pulled out my credentials again; before I could show them, he clapped me on the back like we'd had some good times back in the day, and said, 'Forget the fucken formalities, mate. You wouldn't'a made it this far if you weren't who you said you were. Jim called ahead. Problems with the remains, I hear – not enough of them for a formal ID.'

I went inside and put my bag on the floor. Grubb's office was cooler than the corridor outside. Located on the corner of the floor, it was lit from two sides, the green waters of Darwin harbor clearly visible out the windows.

The phone on the desk rang. The DI picked it up and after a moment said, 'Yeah, mate, send 'er up.' He re-cradled the handset and excused himself. 'Make yourself at home, mate. Got company.' He stepped back out into the corridor, leaving the door ajar.

I took the opportunity to scope the office, get my bearings. On one wall was a gray pin board just like the ones back in my office and Bozey's office, similarly covered in notes and printouts and mug shots of the usual resentful faces. Sharing the wall were large maps of the Northern Territory and the Darwin city area. Tucked into one corner was a personal collection of photos that mostly showed the DI on the back of a boat named *The Office*, holding up a variety of impressively huge fish by their silver gills. Among the images were shots of dead black hogs the size of horses, their tongues lolling in the dirt, small dogs with wide heads standing around the carcasses, grinning. The DI again featured prominently – him and his buddies, I guessed, leaning on the beasts, rifles in the crooks of elbows, grinning like the dogs. I looked closer and recognized Jim Hunt, the coroner, in several scenes.

'Come in, come in. Join the party,' I heard the DI say. The door swung open and a woman entered, the compact sparrow type: blonde shoulder-length hair parted a little off-center, maybe a hundred and fifteen pounds, fair skin, blue eyes, no makeup and around thirty years of age. She wore navy-blue slacks, a loose-fitting cream-colored shirt, flats on her feet: the churchgoer type. Maybe she was lost, looking for the building across the street. We shook. Her hand was tiny and clammy. The *nervous* churchgoer type.

'Investigator Kim Petinski,' she said, introducing herself. 'US National Transportation Safety Board.'

That surprised me: the NTSB, here already? 'Vin Cooper,' I said.

The pause told me she was looking for more than a name, a hint DI Grubb also picked up on. 'Mr Cooper's here to identify the remains,' he said, filling the gap.

'Oh, so you're related to the deceased?' she asked, a blonde eyebrow just a little arched.

'No. We served together.'

'Don't you have to be a relative for formal identification purposes?'

'Friend of the family,' I replied.

'I thought the deceased had no family.'

When Petinski said 'I', it came out 'ah'. '*Ah* thought the deceased had no family.' A Texan, maybe, come straight from Houston. And on the way she'd done her homework, checked the records. She was looking at me, smiling a smile – if I wasn't mistaken – that wanted to know why I was taking up her valuable time.

'I've been asked to be here on behalf of Randy's girlfriend,' I informed her.

'His girlfriend?'

'Okay, *de facto*, if that helps.'

'Would anyone like coffee or tea?' Grubb asked.

'Thanks, but no thanks,' said Petinski. I copied that.

Nothing to do, the DI shrugged and eased into the chair behind his desk, and let the conversation between Petinski and me continue.

'So, you said you served together?' Petinski asked.

'Air Force.'

'Of the United States?'

'Who else's?'

The woman smiled again. Seemed to me she did that when she wasn't pleased. 'You retired?' she asked.

'Nope.'

'If you don't mind my asking, what's your unit?'

I was close to minding, not being a fan of the game of twenty questions unless I'm the one asking, but I played along for the sake of civility. 'OSI.'

The investigator set her head on a tilt. 'What did you say your name was?'

'Cooper.'

'Cooper . . . Cooper . . . Hey, I remember you.'

She had me at a disadvantage there. I couldn't recall her at all, but I could have been drunk at the time.

'Haven't I read about you? Yeah, you were in the Congo with . . .' she clicked her fingers to jog her memory, but it only wanted to be partially jogged, '. . . with those two entertainers. Didn't you make some list in *People* magazine?'

Maybe I should start wearing sunglasses and a ball cap.

She turned to Grubb and said, 'Y'know, Mr Cooper here is famous.'

'Famous? Then you'd better bloody well sign something for me. How about those identification papers for Sweetwater's remains?' He chuckled politely, unsure about whether or not there was tension in the room that required relieving. I had to admit, I was wondering the same thing, the polite interrogation giving me the impression that I was somehow stepping on Ms Petinski's petite toes.

'You been to see the coroner?' I asked her.

'My next stop. You have, obviously.'

'Yeah. I wouldn't hurry. There's not much to see, remains-wise.'

'I'm actually more interested in surveying the wreckage. Speaking of which,' she turned to Grubb, 'we still good to go have a look at it, Inspector?'

'Not a problem,' he said, relieved that the pissing contest between the two foreigners in his office seemed to be over. 'The fishermen who caught the sharks also found the wreckage.'

'Can we drive there?' she asked.

'I wouldn't recommend it.' He got up out of his chair and went to the territory map. 'Came down here, near Elcho Island. Mightn't look far on the map but it's around eight hundred kays or so.' He tapped the spot. He was right, it didn't look far at all – less than a couple of inches, max. 'I've been contacted by the ATSB,' the DI informed us. 'They've got a team on the way, so they reckon.'

'The ATSB?' I asked.

'Australian Transport Safety Bureau,' Petinski said.

'Local version of you?'

She nodded.

The DI was about to add something further when his phone rang again. 'Excuse me,' he said, lifting the receiver. 'Detective Inspector Grubb. Yep . . . Uh-huh, uh-huh . . . No worries, give us ten minutes, eh?' The crow's-feet of his smile migrated north to become frown lines on his forehead. Looked like bad news. 'Something's come up,' he said to Petinski and me, putting his hand over the mouthpiece.

*

Two unmarked police cruisers were already on the scene, as were two plain white vans and a vehicle with the word CORONER in large lettering down the side. Jim Hunt was talking to several men in blue undershirts, shorts and flip-flops, accompanied by a pair of khaki-uniformed police. A well-used blue and white fishing trawler with a rusting A-frame behind the superstructure was lashed against the concrete pier, pushing gently against half a dozen rubber sausages with the rhythm of the calm green sea.

DI Grubb parked behind the marked police car, and we all got out into the heat of bright tropical sunshine. Jim Hunt, hands on his hips, glanced over at us and gave his buddy a friendly nod. As we came closer, I could see a man and a woman in forensics overalls, as well as another male–female team from the coroner's office – pathologists, probably – in the back of the trawler, all wearing rubber gloves on their hands. The female from forensics was taking photos.

Grubb and Hunt exchanged brief pleasantries, which slid naturally into the introductions, Petinski not having met the coroner. When they were done, Grubb asked his buddy, 'So, what we got here, mate?' The DI already knew, having spoken with Hunt on his phone, but the beginning was a good place to start.

'Catch of the day,' the coroner replied with a wry twist of his lips, the egg he'd been saving no longer hanging in the corner. Then to me, he said, 'Never know, mate, might get those papers signed after all, eh?'

I gave his optimism a brief smile.

We crossed the pier to the trawler as the forensics and pathologists on board were packing their respective gear into cases. In the back of the boat was a shark, a good ten to twelve feet in length, gray to black and broad across the back like a heavyweight boxer, lying in a pool of blood and seawater gently sliding back and forth with the motion of the boat. A badly mangled leg with deep puncture wounds, a Rockport shoe on the foot, extended from its bloody mouth. The shark's belly was slit open, the viscera pulled out. Among the rolls of gut and intestines was part of a human head, including a cheek and an ear, attached to the shoulder by a flap of skin and a couple of tendons. The arm, with hand attached, all of it punctured like the leg, was joined to the shoulder, as were maybe three ribs, which were, in turn, clinging to a length of spine. A blue cotton shirt turned partially black with blood was tangled up with the body parts. This didn't look anything like the Randy Sweetwater I'd shared a drink with in Afghanistan.

Two of the fishermen – the men in the undershirts and shorts – joined us as the forensic and pathologist teams began the grisly job of transferring the remains into large ice buckets.

'Caught her thirteen kays north'a Maningrida,' said the stockier of the two men, the tips missing from all four fingers on his right hand down to the first knuckle.

The taller of the two, a native guy with orange hair and a face as black as a bottomless well, nodded.

'When'dja find out what the bastard had for tea, Clock?' Grubb asked, producing a pad and taking notes. Petinski took out a notebook herself and likewise started jotting.

I watched the forensics and pathologists juggle the slippery remains into the ice bins and glanced at Petinski. She was craning her neck to get a look at what was going on – pretty interested in the remains after all.

'Just bin telling yer mate over there,' the fisherman called Clock said, nodding at one of the uniforms. 'Pulled 'er out of the chilli bin thirty kays north, t' give 'er time t' thaw before we docked, 'n saw the cunt had spewed a fucken foot. Surprised the shit out of us. We opened 'er up and what you see's what we found. Called youse blokes straight after that.'

The leg and shoe went in one ice bin, the remains of the head and body, along with his shirt, in the other.

'More sharks in the area where you hooked him?' Grubb asked.

'Fucken millions.'

'Stroke of luck hooking this one.'

'Reckon,' Clock said with a snort. 'Heard a rumor some blacks jagged a couple of bulls further east. Body parts in those bastards too, I heard.'

'Nah,' said Grubb. 'Bullshit.'

The fisherman nodded. 'How long you blokes gonna be, d'y'reckon? William and I got a shitload of fish t' get t' market.'

William agreed, 'Yeah, shitload, mate,' and gestured toward the buildings at the end of the pier, DARWIN FISH MARKETS painted on the side of one of them in peeling black lettering.

'Jim?' Grubb pointed at the shark. 'Ya done?'

Hunt massaged his chin. 'Got pictures, plenty of teeth and jaw measurements: not much more of interest here for me.'

'She's all yours, mate.' Grubb motioned at the gutted shark. 'Not gonna find 'er in me sushi, am I?'

'Nah. Gonna sell 'er to the sport fishers and the tourists – bait.'

'Where do I reach ya if we got more questions?'

Clock gave Grubb their details.

'So, Mr Cooper,' said Hunt, making his way toward me. 'Lemme get these remains back to the bench – see what they tell us. There's more to go on, but not much more, so I reckon we're still gonna be waiting for that DNA screen. We can lift some prints from the hand we've recovered. That might speed things up for us. Who knows, eh? I got your number . . . Where you staying while you're in town?'

'The A-Star.'

The look on his face suggested I'd be more comfortable in a dumpster. 'Round here, we call that the A-Soll,' he said drily. 'And Ms Petinski? You're at . . . ?'

'The Crowne Plaza.'

'Nice.' He took notes while I wondered what could be so bad about the A-Star, aside from the fact that it was cheap and had an unfortunate name. I hadn't checked in yet.

'Not sure what your movements are,' the coroner said, speaking to both of us when he stopped scribbling on his pad, 'but if you could hang around for twenty-four hours or so, I might have something for you.'

'I need to get a look at that wreckage as soon as possible,' Petinski insisted to Grubb. 'Today, even.'

'Well, it's on the cards, I s'pose, but only if I can tee up some transport.'

Grubb rubbed the bottom of his nose with his forefinger. 'Drop ya back at your hotels, if y'like, and give y'a call later.'

'Okay, good,' said Petinski. She examined her notes. 'Um . . . Clock. Was that his first or last name? For the report.'

'Neither. His name's Clock 'cause he's got one fucken hand shorter than th'other.'

I smiled. Petinski frowned.

'Happened five or six years back,' Grubb continued. 'Hooked something big. Took him by surprise. Got tangled in the line. Next thing he knew he was looking at his fingers on the deck.'

We all stepped back up onto the pier, except for Clock and his mate, who both disappeared into the wheelhouse. An unmarked van driven by Jim Hunt's pathologists scribed a slow one-eighty and motored off toward the fish markets, trailing one of the cruisers.

The detective inspector drove us back to our respective hotels and provided a potted history of the city along the way. He told us that in February 1942 the same Imperial Japanese naval fleet that smashed Pearl Harbor turned up and dropped even more bombs on Darwin than it did on Pearl. This slid into a story about how, on Christmas Eve 1974, a cyclone by the name of Tracy came along and completely flattened the place. 'Darwin's like a plantar wart,' he said as he pulled into the crumbling asphalt forecourt of the A-Star. 'Rip the bugger out and it pops up again, bigger and better. Well, this is you, Mr Cooper.'

From the street, my hotel appeared to be an old-fashioned three-story motel, the kind with low ceilings, rumbling air-conditioning and athlete's foot in the shower recesses. Sitting in the front passenger seat, Petinski turned and gave me an attempt at a smile, then turned back, keen to get moving no doubt to four-star Crowne Plaza–land. I got out of the vehicle and pulled my bag from the rear seat.

Grubb waved vaguely out his open window as his vehicle crept forward, crunching on the loose gravel.

I made my way to reception where an unshaven old guy in shorts and a pajama top was sitting behind the desk, eating a toasted sandwich, watching dog racing, a cigarette smoldering in an ashtray made from half a mother-of-pearl shell. He ignored me until the race was finished, and then he ignored me some more.

'Got a minute, Mac?' I finally said.

'Yeah, yeah, keep ya shirt on,' he replied.

'I've got a room booked.'

'Smoking? Non-smoking?'

'Non-smoking.'

'Name,' he said, turning from the TV to face the computer screen.

I gave him my details and credit card and filled in the usual form. In return he gave me an old brass key attached by string to a length of dirty plywood, the room number burned into it with a soldering iron. I found the room on the second story of the main wing facing the street. Inside I was greeted by two narrow single beds, an old-style TV, an old bar fridge with a motor chewing on its bearings, and a smell somewhere between mothballs and old mattress. I checked out.

*

Heading onto the tenth-floor pool terrace, I could see the Timor Sea sparkling emerald green beneath a tropical blue sky. I opened the door and a hotel staff member asked which lounge chair I'd care to occupy and inquired about my needs drinks-wise. This was more like it. I chose a vacant chair beside a trim blonde in a silver bikini lying on her front, reading some report opened out on the floor tiles, one smooth leg bent at right angles and her foot doing languid circles in midair above her ass.

'A Heineken, please,' I told the guy. 'Wait a moment,' I said, changing my mind. 'What's Darwin's favorite beer? Whatever you guys drink here, I'll have one of those.' Being on the far side of the world, I told myself, I should take the opportunity to soak up some local culture. And Aussie beer – at least so the Aussies claim – is the world's best. The guy took my room number and scooted on back in the direction of the bar.

'Cooper . . . ?'

The trim blonde in the silver bikini lying beside me closed the report, rolled over and turned into Petinski.

'Hey,' I said, as surprised as she was – more, perhaps.

'What are you doing here?' she asked, sitting up. 'What about the A-Star?' She hurriedly threw on a robe like I'd just caught her nude, the Plaza's logo on its top pocket. 'Aren't you staying *there?*'

'Not anymore.'

'Why not?' she said, apparently annoyed.

'Because I like Darwin and I want to keep on liking it.' I lay back and closed my eyes and felt the sun's warmth wash over my skin. From Petinski's huffy attitude I gathered she thought I was invading her personal space. I waited a minute before opening an eye and when I did I caught her staring at me – or, more accurately, at those scars of mine. She turned away suddenly and fumbled with her gear, packing up.

Squaring my face to the sun, I said, 'Stick around, why don't you? Let's talk about what we've got here. There's more to this Sweetwater thing than either of us realize.' I wasn't on a case, not officially. But what would it hurt to share, especially now that I'd seen what Petinski looked like without any clothes on, more or less. Okay, so I have shallow moments, and this was one of them. She was a petite Barbie doll: slender legs and hips, and breasts that belonged on a bigger model. It was the kind of mismatch that argues with the atheist in me that there really is a god.

'You've, um, collected a few scars,' she said. 'Look, I . . . I didn't mean to stare.'

'Forget it.' I was tempted to tell her to take off her robe, lie back and let me even the score with a little staring of my own, but this was a moment of moral superiority. They happen so rarely, I didn't want to blow it.

'You've been shot?'

I grunted.

'What's that like, to be shot?'

Petinski. If there was a question on her mind she was going to ask it. To her abruptness, I could add bluntness. Abrupt and blunt. Fun combination. 'It hurts,' I said. In truth, the moment of being shot, at least in my case, wasn't so bad. The adrenalin surge took away most of the immediate pain. But the recovery was always a bitch. It went on and on, a long and arduous journey with plenty of rehab. And when a bullet passes through, even if nothing important gets hit, it takes something indefinable with it that you never get back.

'You don't like answering questions,' she said.

'Do you?'

'No.'

'You like asking them, though, don't you?'

'And you don't?'

I grinned. 'Well I'm glad we sorted that out.'

I detected a more relaxed Petinski, confirmed when she slipped the robe off her shoulders, deciding to stay. She lay down on the chair and presented her magnificent lungs to the sun. I thought about the last time I was poolside – at Bally's with Sugar. 'Hey, don't suppose you got any sun cream on you?' I asked on the off chance.

'Sorry.'

I gave a mental shrug. Didn't hurt to ask, right?

'You've got a shark's tooth around your neck,' she said without looking over.

'From a great white.'

'It's big.'

'Uh-huh.'

'Is it significant?'

'A memento from a past case.'

'You know much about sharks?'

'I know they've got teeth,' I said.

She glanced at me then looked away, no doubt stunned at the depth of my general knowledge.

The pool attendant came back with an enormous half-gallon-sized brown bottle with a frosted glass on a silver tray. 'Beer, the way we like it in Darwin.' He grinned. 'We don't care about the brand, sir, just as long as there's plenty of it. Just let me know when you want another.'

Once the attendant was gone, Petinski asked, 'So, what do you know about Randy Sweetwater?' Her head was back, arms along the armrests, a shapely leg bent, nice and relaxed at last.

I poured myself a glass and drank half. 'What if that wasn't Randy they pulled from the shark's gullet?'

'Who else is it going to be?'

'Beats me.'

'You don't think it's Sweetwater they found?'

'I don't know,' I repeated.

'What are you *really* doing here, Mr Cooper?'

'I told you already. And you can call me Vin.'

'I'd prefer to keep it formal, Mr Cooper, if you don't mind.'

'Why would I mind? At least lose the mister. You're making me sound fifty.'

She gave a shrug that said 'whatever'.

'Can I get you a drink? A scotch, maybe?' I asked her.

'I don't drink.'

Of course she didn't. 'What, *never*?'

'Rarely.' Big sigh. 'Oh, all right. Maybe I'll have a diet soda. A Coke. Thanks.'

I signaled and the attendant guy came over. I ordered the soda and some nuts. When he was out of earshot, I said, 'Around a week ago, the woman I work for, Randy's de facto, took delivery of an amputated human hand. It was FedExed to her from an address in Rio. Randy's Air Force Academy ring was on its finger and it arrived with a ransom note demanding fifteen million bucks.'

Petinski sat up like someone had just plugged her toes into a wall socket. 'What? You're kidding.'

I told her I wasn't. Meanwhile I was having my own problems digesting what I'd seen being scooped into the ice buckets. Alabama was waiting back in Vegas to hear from me, and I'd have to give her a call soon to bring her up to speed. The trouble was that I couldn't give her any kind of satisfactory answer to the question uppermost in her mind: was the dead guy I came all the way here to identify her boyfriend, or not? If the meat found inside those sharks was indeed Randy Sweetwater, then that might be something she wouldn't want to hear. Alternatively, if the remains weren't Randy's, did that mean the folks who mail body parts really were holding him hostage in Rio? Either way, things didn't look good for Randy. He was either already chewed up, or about to be sawed up.

Meanwhile, the nuts arrived along with Petinski's Coke. I signed and handed the investigator her drink just as a black man in a khaki policeman's uniform pushed through the door between the elevator and the terrace and walked toward us. He didn't look like he was here for a swim or a beer.

'Ms Petinski,' the uniform said. 'Detective Inspector Grubb wants you to come with me. He also suggests that you bring a change of underwear.' He looked at me. 'Are you Mr Cooper, by any chance?'

I gave him a nod.

'Aren't you staying at the A-Star? I was going there next.'

Eight

Without headsets the flight from Darwin was noisy as well as being cramped and dull: two hours of looking at pretty much nothing except the occasional herd of cattle or kangaroo or dolphin pod out the tiny porthole beside my shoulder as we flew low across the top end of Australia. Finally, the Cessna dipped its wing over the blue sea as it lightened to green, and the droning engine note changed. In the front passenger seat, Grubb turned and pointed down at the ground, following this with the thumbs-up sign as we crossed a white-and-black-sand beach of an island that was tinder-dry khaki-colored scrub over red earth. Elcho Island. Petinski struggled forward, craned her neck and looked past me out the window, then wedged herself back into her default position, a cross between aloof and snooty, and continued staring at pretty much nothing except the back of Grubb's head.

The pilot flew over the corrugated metal roofs of the settlement called – if I heard it right – Galiwinku. Grubb had already briefed us on the place before departure. It was home to the largest indigenous community in this part of the world, known as Arnhem Land. It was also home to Senior Constable David Nolngu, sitting behind us in the back seat, whom the detective inspector had borrowed from another department to act as our guide and effectively get us a free pass into the community, access to which was apparently limited and subject to all kinds of formal requests to public servants who always said no.

The Cessna banked again several times to line up the runway, then dived steeply down, flaps extended. Something didn't feel right. Maybe it was our speed. The pilot pulled the nose up a little, goosed the throttle, and we roared along, tracking the strip at about tree height. I understood the problem when I pressed my nose up against the porthole and saw maybe fifty kangaroos scattering helter-skelter across the dusty runway below us, in a panic to avoid being chopped into pet food. The pilot was just clearing the decks. Another circuit of the runway and we landed, bouncing a couple of times on the undulating surface lined with kangaroos staring blankly at us, and finally taxied up to an aluminum-clad shed servicing another light aircraft similar to the one we'd arrived in.

'How was that, mate?' Grubb asked as we climbed out of the winged sardine can.

I opened my mouth to clear the ringing out of my ears. 'Can't wait to do it all again,' I said, brushing a fly out of my face while trying to adopt the über-casualness of the Australians.

'There a restroom nearby?' Petinski asked, scanning the area.

Grubb consulted with SC Nolngu and then said, 'Sorry, luv, not here. Plenty of bushes, though.' Black flies were at the corners of his mouth, a couple making a play for his nostrils. 'Is it urgent?' He brushed at his face.

'I'm okay,' she replied.

I waved at half a dozen of the critters myself, my hand hitting several on the way through, something that didn't seem to discourage them at all.

'The flies are bad,' said Petinski, stating the obvious.

The senior constable produced a tube of insect repellent and handed it to her.

'In this part of the world, we got two seasons,' Grubb remarked. 'Dry season and fly season. This is nothing – hardly any of the buggers around at the moment.'

Petinski squeezed some repellent into the palm of her hand then passed me the tube. The back of Nolngu's khaki shirt was covered in moving black dots.

An old Toyota SUV drove out from behind the maintenance shed and came to a stop in front of us, an Aboriginal man at the wheel. Nolngu raised his hand and smiled broadly, approaching the car. A hand came out the window and patted the senior on the back. Nolngu opened the rear passenger door and gestured at us to climb in. 'This is Robert. He's my brother.'

Robert turned and flashed us a startlingly wide grin as we took our seats. We made our own introductions as the pilot and SC Nolngu pulled gear from the underside of the Cessna and transferred it to the Toyota's roof racks.

'Only an hour of daylight left,' said Grubb. 'So we're going to stay here overnight and get up at sparrow's tomorrow.'

'Sparrow's?' Petinski inquired.

'Sparrow's fart, luv. Means fucken early.'

The Toyota moved off with a jerk, bumped over some ruts and rattled down a road of red dust. The homes – the handful I saw – were small with simple gable roofs and deep verandas all the way around. None had gardens or lawns. Mostly they were set on hard-packed red dirt, a layer of red dust over everything. I wasn't sure whether the place was dirt poor or the people just lived simply. The only white folk around were in the vehicle with me. Kids seemed happy enough though, and I saw groups of them chasing each other, fighting with sticks, playing in and around an abandoned rusted-out vehicle sitting in the dirt on bare axles. Small groups of adults sat in the shade here and there and talked, mostly ignoring us as we drove by sending up a wall of red dust that drifted across toward them. There were no shops, at least not on this road.

'I bet the A-Star chain has a hotel here,' I said, leaning forward.

'No hotels, no pubs. But they got a footy club,' Grubb replied over his shoulder. 'That's where we're staying.'

'No pubs? No bars?' A cold shiver ran through me.

'This is a dry community. No alcohol allowed. Causes problems. No gasoline, either, for the same reason. Cars here run on stuff called Opal – you can't get hooked on it.'

I didn't know anything about Australian Aborigines – the indigenous people – other than that they'd been in this country a very long time and were supposedly masters at living off the land; at least, they were when they lived on it. My guess was that the European Johnny-come-latelies had changed the rules of survival too fast for the locals to catch up. If so, the story had a familiar ring to it.

I sat back as we drove past two old women in colorful summer dresses that fit them like only hand-me-downs can. First one woman and then the other looked up and waved at us. David Nolngu waved back, hand out the window, as we motored by and bathed them in dust.

A few minutes on down the road, we pulled up to the footy club, a cinderblock bunker beside an oval playing field. The windows had been removed, leaving black holes in the brick. We parked, got out, and I helped the Nolngus pull the gear, packed into a couple of sealed canoe-shaped tubes, off the roof racks. The DI opened one of the tubes, found a backpack, took out a roll of toilet paper and tossed it to Petinski.

'It's inside.' He gestured at the club.

'Thanks,' she replied, and walked hurriedly up to the building's open doorway.

'Gonna go with me brother,' said the senior constable. 'Bring back some tucker. All right, sir?' Nolngu talked fast, his lips barely moving. Make a hell of a ventriloquist if he could do that drinking a glass of water.

'No worries, mate,' Grubb told him. 'See yez later.'

The two brothers hopped back in the Toyota, and Grubb and I watched it disappear in a red dust cloud.

'Gimme a hand,' said the DI, putting the lid back on the tube and lifting the front end. We carried it up the steps and into the club. The space inside was littered with trash – paper, cans, containers, plastic and bottles, some of them smashed. The interior walls were covered in spray-painted black writing. I couldn't make out any of it, though

I gathered that someone was unhappy about something. Actually, having just driven along the outskirts of the settlement and seen the conditions there, I figured the unhappiness was probably about everything.

We set the tube down on the floor, a smooth concrete slab, and went back for the other. Setting it down, Grubb removed the lid. Inside were a number of items – sleeping bags, inflatable mattresses, a gas stove and various cooking and eating utensils. There were also two rifles, both with telescopic sights.

'That a Remington 710?' I asked.

'Yeah, a .300 Win Mag. That's mine. The old Brno 601 is Nolngu's.'

I was familiar with the Remington. There were photos in a drawer back home of my uncle holding one. The camera was close and he was looking over his shoulder into the lens, smiling. I never knew what happened to that gun. Maybe he pawned it.

The DI lifted the weapon out of the tube. It was probably the rifle featured in the hunting pictures on his office wall. It was well used, the look of an heirloom about it. He pulled back the bolt, showed me the empty chamber and the fact that the safety was on, and handed it over. Nice rig. The weight and balance felt about perfect. I took the cups off the sight, kept my forefinger outside the trigger guard and aimed out the window, at the sky. The .300 Winchester was a large bore round – 7.62 x 67mm – and it packed a kick.

'Expecting trouble?' I asked him.

'Keeps the salties honest.'

I handed the rifle back as Petinski came out with the toilet roll in hand, her face pale. She dropped the roll in the tube and said, 'Next time I'm going behind a bush.'

The Nolngus returned half an hour after sunset with a massive silver fish, already gutted and scaled. Robert cut steaks off it, which were thrown with some unidentified herbs into a large pan sitting on the gas burner, and within a few minutes half a dozen black men in shorts and t-shirts turned up to help us eat. They sat crouched on their haunches in a semicircle around the burner, smiling broadly, but there wasn't much dinner conversation to go with the best fish I'd ever eaten, at least not with Petinski and me. They didn't speak our language. Or maybe they did – we just couldn't understand it. Eventually, though, Senior Constable Nolngu introduced us to two of the men, who were somewhere between thirty and fifty, saying that they were the two who'd caught the original bull sharks from which the partial remains of the pilot had been pulled. Petinski and I both told them they'd done a great job, which seemed to trigger a flurry of amused discussion between them and the senior constable.

'They want me to tell you a joke,' said Nolngu when the exchanges had finished.

'Must be a good one,' I said, based on the fact that one of the men was already on his back, laughing.

'There are two sharks,' the senior began, 'a large father shark and his smaller son. They are swimming around and eventually come across some humans splashing about at a beach. "Let's go and eat them," says the son, who is ready to snatch a tasty-looking human. "No," says the father shark. "That is not the best way. Follow me and do as I do." The son follows his father, who rises to the surface so that his fin slices the air above the water. The humans scream. The father shark then rushes away and comes back, flicking his tail above the water. The son does as his father does. The humans are crying and wailing. Finally, the father shark races in, circles the humans and snatches one, shaking him hard so the water turns red. Later, after the father and son have had their fill of human and are swimming away, the young shark asks, "Father, why didn't we just go straight in and tear them all up? Why waste all that time going in and out?" The wise father shark says, "Because, son, they taste so much better when there's no shit left in them."'

I saw the punch line coming, but the way Nolngu told it was funny. The men all fell over, the sound of their cackling bouncing like stones off the cinderblock walls.

Petinski leaned close to me and whispered out the side of her mouth, 'What's so funny?'

I looked at her, the grin frozen on my face. Maybe Petinski had a no-humor policy to go with her no-drinking one. Fortunately, though, she had infeasibly large breasts with which to offset those deficiencies.

'There's a man torn to shreds, Cooper – someone you knew, for Christ's sake,' she reminded me.

She was probably right, but the times you don't feel you should laugh are, perversely, some of the times when you just can't seem to stop.

*

Robert Nolngu turned up with his Toyota at dawn and drove us through low, salt-battered bush five klicks or so to a boat ramp on the other side of the island. I'd slept okay, the hard floor agreeing with my back, though I sensed Petinski tossing and turning a few feet away. She sat beside me, looking the other way, silent. She hadn't said much to anyone since we arrived, preoccupied with the seriousness of the task at hand, I supposed.

My window was down, the rushing air cool, the flies still in bed as we broke through the scrub and the sand dunes and the sea opened out to a horizon edged with rose gold. I could see a large double-hulled fishing boat nosed up onto the sand; two men silhouetted by the predawn light were tending to its anchor. Robert plowed the Toyota down onto the beach, but didn't get far before it stopped with a jolt. One of the silhouettes acknowledged us with a quick wave.

We got out and walked toward the boat, and the man who'd waved jogged up and shook hands with Grubb. The guy was large, as well as being salt-, sun- and alcohol-damaged, with short gray hair and a puffy red face that reminded me of a blister about to burst. Grubb handled the introductions. The man's name was Ern. This was his boat, the words *Killing Spree* stenciled on the side in pink and silver lettering. The detective inspector was going to borrow it for the day, which Ern seemed more than fine with. I overheard several exchanges between the two pals; I gathered they were regular fishing buddies. Perhaps his photo was up on Grubb's wall along with the coroner's.

Within minutes the DI was behind the wheel, opening the throttles on the two massive outboards hung off the back of the boat, and we accelerated toward the horizon just as the top of the sun winked above the edge of the world.

'How far?' I shouted above the engine and wind noise, the boat leaping over the lines of swell.

'Bit more than an hour,' Grubb shouted back.

On the other side of the DI, Senior Constable Nolngu gazed out across the water, dark eyes hidden in the deep shadows under his brow.

I glanced behind to watch the shoreline recede, a white gouge in the blue water churned by the Johnsons. A few fishing rods placed in holders along the boat's gunnels whipped back and forth a little in the wind. A couple of crab pots and a hand net occupied some deck space. Petinski sat in a chair facing the receding shore, a waterproof jacket done up tight to keep out the morning chill and sea spray, her hair contained under a blue NTSB ball cap. She seemed lost in her own world. I worked my way back and sat beside her.

'Be there in an hour,' I said.

She gave almost no response other than the barest nod. I wondered what the Myers-Briggs type indicators for Ice Maiden were.

*

The boat surged forward briefly, picked up by its stern wave after Grubb cut the throttles. We'd been motoring south for at least half an hour, heading for the mouth of a dark green estuary. The banks on either side, lined with mangroves that appeared to float on the water, were gradually converging at a point somewhere before us. Black birds squawked into the sky, disturbed by the burble of the outboards.

Dead ahead, a large fish leaped clear of the water, disturbing the glassy surface.

'Get 'im on the way back, Senior,' the DI told Nolngu as the widening rings it left behind disappeared beneath our bow.

More birds, large white ones with long black legs, took to the sky in a panic above the mangroves. The place wasn't used to humans. Or maybe it was and knew what to expect. The water soon lost its clarity and became a murky green, the air thick with insects as the banks closed in on either side.

We puttered through a one-eighty-degree bend, the river continuing to narrow and the hum of insects competing with the noise of our outboards. The boat got hung up on the bottom momentarily, clouds of billowing black mud rising to the surface behind our stern.

'Shallow here,' said Grubb. 'Three feet, maybe less.' He operated a control and the motors angled back, changing the exhaust note from muted burble to a throaty growl.

Petinski slapped at her neck, and Nolngu passed the insect repellent back to her. 'Sand flies,' he said. 'Bad fellas.'

Petinski squeezed a long worm of the thick, foul-smelling repellent into the palm of her hand, passed me the tube, and started applying the worm to her exposed skin. Apart from the insects, the landscape seemed pretty benign. I hadn't seen any salties, sharks or boogie men.

'Nice country,' I said to Grubb as I rubbed some repellent into my forearms.

'Yeah, and it'll bite you on the arse if you're not careful, as your pilot mate found out,' he said. He turned to Nolngu. 'Senior, take the wheel. Let's drift a little.'

Nolngu slid into the DI's place behind the controls and cut the throttle to idle as Grubb stepped back toward the stern. He lifted one of the rods out of its holder and unhooked the lure.

'A bibbed minnow,' he informed me, holding the bright silver lure with three hook clusters in front of his eyes. 'Barras love 'em.'

'Barras?'

'Barramundi. Gorgeous fish.'

Killing Spree had come almost to a stop. The DI cast out toward the shade beneath the mangroves, plonked the lure in a hole just in front of them, and then reeled it in. Nothing. He cast out to the same place a second time. Nothing. He went for third time lucky and, as I was starting to wonder what point he was hoping to make, the rod jerked violently. Grubb whipped it back and began reeling in.

'*Yeah . . .*' he said, straining. 'Fucken monster.'

The rod bent into an inverted U. Petinski came and leaned against the gunnel to get a better look. Grubb brought the fish alongside, its silver flanks flashing in the sunlight beneath the surface of the water.

'You need the net?' I looked down at it. The fish was seriously big.

But then a shadow stole over it like an eclipse on fast forward. A thrash and the silver was gone. Grubb grinned and lifted what was left of the fish out of the water, dropping a big head attached to some guts onto the deck.

'What happened?' Petinski asked.

'Bull shark, luv,' Grubb replied. He unhooked the head and tossed it overboard. Something moved just below the surface and took it. 'Water like this is perfect for the buggers – shallow and shitty.' He signaled to Nolngu, who put the engines into gear so that we idled forward. 'Only a couple of feet deep here, but that's all they need. And then, as I said, there are the fucken salties.' He motioned at a tree trunk floating in the water over toward the opposite bank. On cue, the thing suddenly grew a tail, propelled itself forward and then slid below the surface. 'Not so nice country.'

Okay, point made.

'Boss,' said Nolngu. He motioned ahead, another bend in the river approaching. A chunk seemed to have been taken unnaturally out of the wall of mangroves where the SC was pointing. Behind it was a rise in the ground – a hill about a hundred and fifty feet high, the only one I could see anywhere. The something unusual was halfway up the hill. It was white, and far too large to be a bird.

'There,' said Petinski, pointing.

The object was a wing partially obscured by the bush. The angle changed as we closed the gap and most of the rest of the broken aircraft came into view, lower down the hill slope.

'No fire,' I overheard Petinski say, commenting to herself.

A thin screen of mangroves lined the curve in the river, a mudflat behind them. Grubb steered for it and brought the Johnsons farther out of the shallow water, the exhaust note amplified by the natural amphitheater caused by the river bend. The hulls kissed the mud then, grounded more firmly, nosed straight into the mangroves. Nolngu climbed up onto the side of the boat with the Brno in one hand, and moved forward to a hatch. He pulled out an anchor, threw it onto the mud, and then jumped down after it, disappearing from view until I saw him lugging the anchor up the mudflats toward more solid ground lined with scrub, tugging occasionally on the attached rope, slipping once or twice in the mud.

Grubb came back and extracted the Remington from the opened tube. 'Saltie tracks further up,' he explained, pointing to a stretch of the mudflat twenty yards away and loading a magazine from his hunting vest.

'You look worried,' I said.

'Nah, just cautious. Worry is the look I get when I'm firing repeatedly at point-blank range at the fuckers but the slugs don't seem to make any difference. The crocs round here are fucken dinosaurs. The cunts don't feel pain. The big ones are extra mean and unpredictable. They'll jump right out of the water if they think they can get you.'

Hmm. The water was particularly murky here – black lagoon murky. Any kind of creature could live down there, and probably did.

'Shall we, y'know, get off?' I suggested, a little less cool about it than I intended.

'Yeah. Move up the beach quickly,' Grubb advised. 'Away from the water's edge.'

I had no intention of hanging around collecting shells. I shouldered a pack with built-in camelback. Petinski likewise had her gear and water supply in a pack slung over her shoulder.

'Let's go,' she said.

Grubb eyed the water behind our boat, standing his ground like he was covering our retreat. I climbed up onto the hull, went to the bow and jumped. My boots disappeared into the soft mud, which made farting sounds as I pulled one foot then the other clear of it, using the anchor line for support. When I reached the scrub, I stopped to catch my breath and sucked in some insects along with the oxygen, swarms of them buzzing furiously around my head. Gagging, I spat the things out. Ahead, Nolngu materialized from behind a screen of scrub and waved at me to come toward him. Easier said than done. The ground stopped being mud and had turned into a bed of rotting desiccated bush. Something snapped dully under my next footfall and I sank up to my knee in the bed of powdered twigs.

'Can I get past?' said Petinski impatiently as she pushed on by, stepping lightly on the rotting vegetation.

I dragged myself up and out of the decaying ground one step at a time and eventually found solid footing, my shirt and hat soaked with sweat, the repellent stinging my eyeballs. I drank a mouthful of warm water from the camelback, spat some into my hands and rinsed my eyes. Petinski and Nolngu had gone on ahead, tired of waiting. I caught up with them standing among the buckled, twisted remains of a largish twin turboprop Beech Super King Air spread around the side of the hill. The plane was broken into half a dozen large pieces, the T-tail ripped off the fuselage along with one complete wing, the fuse itself broken into three. Bits of gnarled aluminum skin and hunks of foam insulation and wiring were scattered everywhere. Petinski had a Canon in her hands, and she began photographing everything. Grubb came through the scrub behind us, the Remington slung over his shoulder.

'Shit,' was all he said, looking around, taking in the destruction.

I caught up with Petinski as she climbed the hill to get a view looking down on the wreckage. 'Hey, I've been meaning to ask you,' I said when she stopped climbing. Petinski ignored me and kept taking photos. 'Where's your team?' It had gradually dawned on me. Would Uncle Sam send her all the way down here by herself to investigate the accident?

'What team?'

'The Aussies are sending a team. But the NTSB has sent just you. You don't even have a partner. You must have a partner.'

'I work on my own.'

'What sort of Myers-Briggs indicators do I need to win that jackpot?'

Petinski stopped clicking away with her Canon to scowl at me. 'Can I do my job here? *Please?*'

'And what is your job, exactly?'

'You're watching me do it. Now, if you don't mind . . .'

'Seriously, who gets to work on their own?'

She kept up the scowl. 'I'm the advance party, making initial observations before adverse weather sets in – document the scene, take photos. Working on my own, I can move faster. Be nimble, flexible.'

'Right.'

'The NTSB has some more investigators joining the Australian team. Teams take time to organize.'

'Okay.'

'Now, can I get back to work?'

'Who's stopping you?'

Petinski's eyes flashed a couple of shades of blue at me, changing color the way a squid does when it's angry, before returning to her viewfinder.

'So what do you see?' I asked her.

'Cooper . . .'

'Just asking.'

'You're not a good advertisement for partnership, you know that?' Petinski swept the wreckage with her camera several times. 'Okay, well, what I'm seeing that I *think* might be significant . . . the landing gear is up but the flaps are down. And see the engine on that wing?' She gestured with her camera at the buckled stub of riveted aluminum still attached to the fuselage. 'The propeller's feathered. Same as the prop on the other engine. That says to me that Randy had no power but had enough time to get set up for a dead-stick landing. He made a decision to put it down here, rather than on dry land. I have no idea why he didn't make a Mayday call. Maybe he did, but it wasn't picked up. This aircraft had VHF and UHF radios, so I don't know why it wouldn't have been. Maybe by the time he got around to it he was too low. Looking at the physical evidence, he obviously tried to land on the river, gear up. But he might have misjudged it, maybe came in a little fast, skipped off the water like a stone, hit the mangroves followed by the trees and the hill.'

I took in the scene, looking back toward the river. The mangroves and trees were damaged pretty much in a line that joined up with the dark green river beyond. Petinski's hypothesis fit. 'And the cause?' I asked.

'That's why they're sending in that team you're so hot for.' Petinski brought the Canon back to her eye, peeled off a bunch of shots. 'I'll give you an educated guess when I've finished nosing around, okay? And *please* don't touch anything. Think of this as a crime scene. Now, if you don't mind . . .'

I could take a hint. We went our separate ways, Petinski continuing up her own ass, me down the hill toward the broken fuselage. The nose was punched in on the co-pilot's side. Randy was lucky to have walked away from this one – albeit briefly. I stepped between the separated tubular sections of the fuselage, the one just behind the flight deck, the two sections still joined by umbilical cords of wiring, cables and hydraulic lines. The air smelled vaguely of jet fuel. I could see the backs of the pilot and co-pilot seats. Flies buzzed in the air, interested in black coagulated blood spatter on the smashed instrument panel and a splash of it on the shoulder area of the co-pilot's seat.

Petinski arrived, ducked around me, stepped up inside the area behind the seats, and snapped away with her camera. Somewhere along the way, she'd put on a pair of rubber surgical gloves. Her camera dangled around her neck while she slipped blue crime-scene covers over her boots.

'When you said don't touch anything, I didn't realize trampling was okay,' I said.

'I'm trained for this – are you?' She climbed over the console between the seats and disappeared from view.

'What do you see?' I asked her.

'Nothing.'

Abrupt, blunt, aloof, snooty, humorless, uncommunicative ice maiden.

'This crate equipped with black boxes?' I asked her.

'Has a cockpit voice recorder as standard. Flight data recorder was an option and the registered owner has informed us that the option wasn't installed.'

'That's Ty Morrow.'

'Mr Morrow, yes.'

'The recorder in the tail?'

'That's where they always are.'

'You wanna go get it?' I asked her.

'No, I'm not touching it.'

'You don't want to get a photo of it, for the album maybe?'

'Busy here, Cooper.'

I looked back toward the rear. More wires, cabling, crushed and twisted metal. Lashed against the side of the fuselage was a life raft canister, mandatory equipment for over-water flights. It could've transported the pilot safely down the river, and the survival gear that came with it would've come in handy too.

'See any personal effects up there – a suitcase or sausage bag?' I asked. 'Randy would've had a change of clothes with him, toiletries.'

'No.'

I supposed he could have taken his things with him when he left the scene. Maybe there was a bull shark swimming around, about to shit a Samsonite. The blood spatter indicated injury. Maybe the pilot had a head wound and he was dazed, disoriented, which might have explained why he didn't use the raft. Whatever the reason, he'd wandered down to the water and decided to swim for it. Bad decision.

'Bingo,' said Petinski.

'What you got?'

She held up a large document wallet then unzipped it, examined the contents.

'And?'

'Passport, FAA security pass, FAA license. All in the name of Randy Sweetwater. The photos are consistent. They're Randy's.'

'Or forgeries,' I suggested. Petinski didn't respond to that. Assuming they weren't, the documents said Randy was behind the wheel. Was it unusual that he would leave the scene of the crash with his clothes but not his ID? Maybe. People often behaved irrationally under intense stress. I once pulled a woman from a house fire who wouldn't leave because she couldn't find a pair of socks in her washing basket to put on.

Looking around, I noticed a collection of magazines wedged in the space between the pilot seat and fuselage, jammed there by an aluminum rib bent out of shape. I reached forward and, working them up and down, eventually pulled them free. Six glossy magazines. 'Hey, Petinski, you found any moisturizer up there?' I said, flicking through them.

'What?'

'Moisturizer. You found any?'

'No.'

'How about tissues?'

She popped her head up, curious. I showed her the magazines, which brought on a look of supreme distaste.

'Inflight entertainment,' I said. 'I don't recognize the language, although *her* I understand in any language.' I held up a spread of a naked black woman doing the splits; she reminded me a little of Sugar if I looked at the page with a squint.

'Show me that,' Petinski demanded, climbing back over the center console. I handed over the mag and she examined the spread intently.

'Something wrong?' I asked. There seemed to be.

'This . . . this woman here. Her name's Emanuel. She's an Olympic gymnast, or was. Brazilian.' Petinski shook her head, disappointed. 'Mani . . . She was a finalist in the uneven bars.'

'You sound like you know her,' I said, having difficulty hiding the sloppy grin spreading across my face.

'*Knew* her. I was on the US team.'

'You were an Olympic gymnast?' That explained her body type, at least from the waist down.

'My specialty was the floor. Rolled my ankle in a warm-up session the first day of competition. And that was the end of me.' She shook her head with dismay, apparently as much at seeing a fellow champion gymnast plying a new trade as at the memory of her own career. 'Mani was good.'

'She still is, in a bad kinda way, if you know what I mean.'

Petinski did, and she wasn't impressed. 'Where'd you find this?' she snapped. 'I told you not to touch anything!'

I showed her. Botox wouldn't have budged the frown on her face. 'Did Randy speak Portuguese?' she asked.

'No, as far as I know he didn't. Though I'm sure that if he did, he wouldn't have brought those along to *read*. Hence my question about the moisturizer.'

Petinski pursed her lips. 'You're disgusting.'

'And you've got nice-looking friends.'

'Just because these magazines are here,' she said, 'doesn't mean Randy brought them on board. As he didn't speak Portuguese, that suggests to me a previous pilot or passenger left them behind.'

A reasonable assumption, but it was also not impossible that, despite the presence of his FAA license and so forth, perhaps Randy wasn't the pilot at all and that someone else was, a Brazilian maybe, who brought the pornos along to help pass the time. *Un*reasonable, it seemed to me, was Petinski gravitating to a particular view about it while so readily excluding other likely theories along the way.

'I'm taking them back with me,' I said, holding my hand out, wiggling my fingers, gesturing at her to hand them over.

'Why?'

'Because it's a long trip.'

Nine

A thin female pathologist with gothic makeup and lank purple hair accompanied Coroner Jim Hunt. Detective Inspector Grubb, Petinski and I stood on the opposite side of the stainless-steel dissection table and all of us were staring at what was laid out on it: a small portion of skull and spine, a few ribs, a butt cheek and scrotum, some thigh, and an arm with hand attached.

'He's not your bloke,' said Hunt.

'You're sure about that?' Grubb asked.

'Yep.'

'You still don't have his records,' said Petinski.

'No, but you and Vin both said Sweetwater was a little over six feet two inches.'

I nodded.

Petinski nodded.

'This fella's a short arse,' Hunt continued. 'Five eight in his socks.'

Hmm. I stared at the remains. This didn't come as such a surprise after the contradictory items we'd found in the plane wreck, but it did raise a bunch of questions, such as how someone who wasn't Randy Sweetwater came to have Randy's watch, wallet and documentation. Why had he taken Randy's place in the King Air's pilot seat? Had it

115

been done under duress? And was the plane's crash due to random accidental factors, or was it somehow brought down with intent, linked in
some way to Randy, the severed hand and the ransom note – some kind
of botched cover-up, maybe? I didn't have any answers and if Petinski
did, she was reluctant to confide. Still, I could now inform Alabama
that her boyfriend hadn't become an entrée – at least not down here
in a northern Australian swamp. And the focus would again return
to Thing, the ring and the ransom note FedExed from an address in
Brazil. Was Randy Sweetwater still alive and kicking? Maybe he was,
and maybe he wasn't. It was hard to deny though that there were pieces
of body claiming to be Randy Sweetwater scattered all over the planet,
and none of them appeared to fit together.

The fingertips of the hand attached to the arm on the pathology
table were inked blue-black. 'Where've you sent the prints?' I asked.

'The United States Department of Defense,' said Hunt.

'You mind forwarding a set to my boss?' I wrote Arlen's email address
at Andrews AFB on the back of my OSI card.

The coroner took the card and examined it under his bifocals. 'No
problem.'

'And to my office, please,' said Petinski.

Jim Hunt assured us that the detailed forensic analysis of the remains
would also be sent to both our respective offices, and then the meeting concluded. Hunt brought his hands together and gave them a rub.
'Who's coming to the pub? Grubby?'

'Jeez, is it that late?' The DI glanced at his watch. 'Bloody oath.'

It was ten-thirty in the morning.

'Kim? Vin?' he asked.

'Sure,' I said. 'I'm on vacation.'

Petinski waved him away. 'Love to, but I have to write up a report.'

Love to? Seemed to me Petinski was keen to exit the immediate area
forthwith.

'When are you leaving?' I asked her.

'Soon,' she said.

'When, exactly?'

She drew a deep breath. 'One a.m.'

'Qantas to LAX. We must be on the same flight. Maybe we can get our seating changed – sit together?'

'Maybe.' She managed to make it sound like, 'I'll scream if they try.'

'Come for a Diet Coke.'

'Can't, sorry. I have to make some calls. And I wasn't lying about the report. I want to write it up here in case I have questions.'

Questions were *all* I had. Now that there was some closure on these remains, I also had a call to make to Alabama.

Petinski gave Hunt, Grubb, the Goth and me a curt goodbye, and walked out the door. I watched her go and thought: an abrupt, blunt, aloof, snooty, humorless, uncommunicative, teetotaling, former Olympic ice maiden . . . with hot friends who did porn. The universe does love balance.

*

It was on the approach to LAX that I found myself waking up beside Petinski in economy, a deep-vein-thrombosis leg stocking balled up and stuffed in my mouth.

'You were snoring,' she said as I pulled the thing out hand over hand like I was part of some magician's act. I thanked her for her understanding and drank a bottle of water to wash away the taste of cotton.

'You talk in your sleep, you know that?' she said eventually, after we'd landed and were taxiing to the jetway.

'Did I say anything sensible?'

'What do you think?' she answered out the corner of her mouth, no eye contact. 'You did say something about coincidences, and that you didn't believe in them. You were talking very loud and acting out, pushing the coincidences away – at least, I think that's what you were doing. The flight attendant and I had to restrain you. What were you drinking?'

'I've been drinking?' I said. I gave the back of my neck a one-handed massage. It felt like someone had worked over my cerebellum with a blunt instrument. Those Aussies sure were a thirsty bunch.

Petinski pursed her lips and fussed with some personal effects, keen to get up and out, the conga line down the aisle finally starting to shuffle.

I pushed myself out of the seat and stood up, swaying a little.

'If you're looking for your bag, it's in the overhead locker,' Petinski said, nodding in the general direction. 'So, you don't believe in coincidences?'

If I wasn't feeling like something had coughed me up, then I could have given her an eloquent lecture on this belief system of mine. But instead I collected my bag and concentrated on not hurling.

'Coincidence is God's way of remaining anonymous, you know,' she persisted.

'And I don't believe in him, either,' I managed to say. 'Unless I'm in a fix.'

'You always so sure of yourself, Cooper?' she asked me as I moved forward. I didn't answer. All I was sure of was that if she didn't stop talking then I really was going to heave. Maybe she knew that and was just having fun. Wait, I'd already established that Petinski had no sense of humor. I concentrated on the guy in front of me, and moved forward when he did.

Petinski and I got separated from each other at customs and immigration and I didn't get the opportunity to say goodbye, not officially, but I was feeling way too seedy to care. I had half an hour to make the connecting flight to Vegas, so I stopped off at the head, donated the contents of my stomach, and swore I wouldn't drink again – at least not till the next time I drank. I bought another bottle of water and some breath mints and made the Continental flight as the last of the passengers were checking through the gate. I sat in an aisle seat, kept my head down, and snoozed away the short flight to McCarran. Things looked brighter with the extra sleep and I managed to get in a few pleasant thoughts about the pool area at Bally's before I heard a familiar voice behind me as I stepped from the Boeing's hatch into the jetway.

'I thought you were going back home to DC.' It was Petinski. She sped up and fell into step beside me.

I shook my head. 'No. Some unfinished business.'

'The severed hand, the ransom note?'

'Something like that,' I said. In fact, my intention was just to give Alabama the courtesy of a face-to-face report on what I'd seen in Australia, and officially come off the tit of her Visa card.

'Staying in town long?' Petinski asked.

'Long enough to lose a little more cash to Sleeping Beauty.'

'Who?'

'Friend of mine,' I said. 'I'll be heading back East tomorrow. You?'

'Not sure.'

Sure she wasn't sure. 'You're gonna pay Ty Morrow a visit at Nevada Aircraft Brokers, aren't you?'

'I think I told you – I've got some questions. Hey, I'm glad you're feeling better,' she said, deflecting, as she stopped at the escalator. 'That's all you took with you, right?' She motioned at the overnight bag by my side.

'Yep.'

'Well, I guess you don't take a hair dryer when you travel. I have to go and collect my baggage.' A smile sputtered across her face like sparks that failed to light a fire, and she held out her hand to shake. A delicate hand with slender fingers – clipped nails, no rings. All business. 'Goodbye, Cooper.'

'Petinski.' Unlike the first time we shook, this time her grip was warm, dry and firm. Somewhere along the way she'd changed into clean work clothes – black slacks and a blue and white casual shirt, both fitted. She stepped onto the escalator and I watched her descend. Her hips were narrow, but perfectly in proportion to her legs and tiny waist. She was, well, built like a gymnast. I asked myself whether she could do the splits like her friend Emanuel.

Bells chimed electronically through a thin rattle of coinage. I turned and walked past a bank of slots in the center of the wide corridor. They formed an island on which a handful of departing vacationers were temporarily marooned while Vegas siphoned off the last of their money.

I made a beeline for the cab rank and gave the driver the address for Nevada Aircraft Brokers over on the other side of McCarran. Petinski wasn't the only one who had questions for Morrow. And, as I had no luggage to collect, maybe I'd get there before her.

A short while later, my cab pulled into the forecourt outside the familiar white box with its gold windows. I paid the driver. A new black pickup with heavily tinted windows and big chrome wheels was parked by the front door, opened out, oddly, to let in the morning heat. Something felt different about the place. I stood with my overnight bag in the parking area and wondered what it was. A sheet of paper wafted out the open front door. Through the mesh cyclone fence cordoning off the ramp from the public, I saw a guy run to a small twin-engine plane, climb up onto the wing and jump in. A vehicle turned into the forecourt behind me and parked – a beige Ford Focus. Petinski got out. She'd made it here quicker than I expected. Must have had a rental ready and waiting. She and her frown stormed toward me.

'What are you doing here, Cooper?' she demanded. 'I thought you were done.'

'Satisfying my curiosity.'

'And who's paying for it now?'

An aircraft engine chugged, coughed then fired into life nearby, followed by a second engine. The plane on the ramp.

'I'm here on my own time – just interested.' I was interested because Randy Sweetwater was a guy I'd shared a laugh or two with in a war zone, over a crate of a superior officer's illegal single malt, and bonds like that run deep.

Two Latino types in boots, shorts, tattoos, undershirts and tightly plaited hair appeared in the doorway carrying Sleeping Beauty between them. They heaved the slot up onto the pickup's bed. An air of panic: that's what was different about this place now.

'You wanna continue this later?' I suggested. 'I've got a feeling we should maybe go in and see what's up before the whole place gets hauled away.'

Petinski was about to say something but changed her mind and gave a curt nod instead. We squeezed behind the pickup as it inched forward and went in through the open door behind it. The reception area was empty this time, having lost its couch, cappuccino machine and the aforementioned slot. Shouting was coming through the walls and glass of the boardroom, and I could see darkened areas where several parties were standing and pointing at each other as they argued. While I could make out the details of the conversation and the names mentioned, none of it meant anything to me, other than I had no doubt that the tension had been triggered by Randy Sweetwater's disappearance and the events linked to the crash in northern Australia. I was nosing around the reception desk awash with papers and folders for a bell or buzzer with which to announce our presence when the door to the boardroom swung open. Carol the receptionist came out, looking a little disheveled and distressed, strands of brassy hair escaping from the bun on top of her head and her tan caftan rumpled and askew.

'Yes?' she said.

Petinski said, 'Investigator Kim Petinski from the National Transport Safety Bureau and Special Agent Cooper, Air Force Office of Special Investigations, here to see Mr Ty Morrow.'

From the look of horror on Carol's face Petinski might as well have said, 'This lizard and I are from outer space and we've come to conduct experiments on your unanesthetized body. You must accompany us immediately before we decide to probe you here and now.'

My cell buzzed against my leg to let me know that I'd just received a text. I ignored it.

The loose skin quivered under Carol's chin, her mouth moving a couple of times without sound coming out. She swallowed, her throat working up and down like a pump action chambering a round. When her voice box finally kicked in, she said, 'I'm sorry, but Mr Morrow . . . Mr Morrow has gone.'

'Gone where?' Petinski asked.

'We think he just . . . we think he just left.'

'Left to go where?'

'I . . . we . . . No one knows. Everyone's wondering what's going on.'

'You've got no idea?' Petinski said.

'Last night, around six-thirty, Mr Morrow received a phone call. It made him nervous as hell. Next thing I know he's taking files, shredding papers. Then he . . . he jumped into a Citation and just, you know, took off.'

I glanced at Petinski.

'Can you give me the aircraft's registration?' she asked.

'Yes, certainly.' Carol riffled through paperwork on her desk, then provided Petinski with the numbers and letters.

'Carol, I'm going to have to ask you to touch nothing, okay?' Petinski said. 'Do you have a key for your filing cabinets?'

'Yes.'

'Then I want you to lock them and give me the keys.'

It appeared that Carol was about to protest this, but her objection was quickly wrestled to the ground and hogtied by common sense. She opened a drawer, took out some keys on a ring, secured the cabinets behind her and put the keys on her desk.

Petinski scooped them up and pocketed them. 'Thank you. Now, please turn off the computer and write down any user names and passwords.'

'Before you do that, Carol, can you print out the flight plan submitted to the FAA by Randy Sweetwater?' I interrupted.

'Yes,' said Petinski, hurriedly chipping in. 'If you wouldn't mind.'

Carol nodded, her hands shaking.

'Hey, it's okay,' I reassured her. It probably wasn't, but I doubted any of it would touch her, at least in a legal sense.

The boardroom door opened. A middle-aged man walked out wearing khaki work clothes and black boots. His head was down. He glanced at us when he stopped at Carol's desk. The way he was dressed suggested that he could be the company's licensed aircraft mechanic.

'Excuse me,' I said to him. 'You the crew chief round here?'

'Who wants to know?'

I showed him my ID, as did Petinski. 'What's your name?' I asked.

'Dewy Baker.'

'Your boss left in a hurry, Dewy. Got any idea why?'

'Yeah – money.'

'You don't know that,' said Carol.

Dewy ignored her.

'Money?' Petinski echoed.

'The Super King Air was worth seven big ones and the person sup-posed to be flying her wasn't at the controls, right?'

Petinski nodded.

'That means the insurance company won't pay out. Morrow didn't own the plane. And the boss didn't have a lazy seven mill clogging up his bank account. Like everyone else in this game, he's in it on a wing and a prayer – literally.'

'If you want me, I'll be out back,' Carol said, departing angrily through the door in the partition behind her desk.

'Anyone else leave in a hurry?' I asked.

'You're referring to Stu Forrest, my two-eye-cee, who took off in the twin just before you got here?'

'Where'd he take off to?'

'Don't know, but I'd put money on Mexico. Sell the plane, live in a beach shack . . .'

'You got its registration numbers handy?'

The mechanic reeled them off from memory. Petinski took them down and asked, 'Why'd he go?'

'Don't know that, either. For what it's worth, Stu was the King Air's crew chief.'

'Did anyone witness the King Air's departure?' I asked. So far, we hadn't placed Randy at the controls when he left.

'No one except Stu. The takeoff was at three-thirty a.m.'

'Why so early?'

'Avoid the early-morning traffic out of LAX.'

'The NTSB investigation team following up, and probably the FAA, will want to talk with you. You'll make yourself available.'

'Do I got a choice?'

'No.'

'I have to get another job – got kids, two ex-wives, three cats.'

'No one's stopping you,' said Petinski. 'Just make sure your contact details are up to date, don't take anything when you go, and don't leave the country.'

He nodded, dug his hands deep in his pockets, picked up a folder from Carol's desk.

'Maybe you should leave that,' said Petinski.

He shrugged, put it down and trudged off out the back door.

Petinski asked, 'You got any connections with local law enforcement in this town, Cooper? We need this place locked down.'

'Why?'

'Because it's going to take me an hour at least to work up the affidavit, find the judge on call in this town and get the warrant issued. I need someone in uniform here while I go off and do all that – unless you want to hang around and wave that pay check you got from your topless dancer friend as your legal authority.' Petinski was getting more agitated by the minute. She wrung her tiny hands.

'What's going on your affidavit? You got grounds? It mightn't have been in Morrow's interest for that plane to go down, but a desire to avoid creditors doesn't look like probable cause to me.'

Petinski lost patience. 'Look, if I have to get this place sealed up on a freakin' building violation, then that's what I'll do. You want to find out what happened to Sweetwater same as me, and *my* intuition tells me this is the rock to look under.'

'You're federal. Why don't you call in Homeland Security?'

'Cooper, we – or rather *I* – need someone here *now*.'

She was right about HS. Before doing anything, those guys would first set up a task force, otherwise known as a committee, and we both knew how fast *they* moved. 'You seem pretty tense about this, Petinski.'

'I take my job seriously.'

As far as I could tell, Petinski took everything seriously. 'You might want to see if your FAA pals know where Morrow took off to. Same for Forrest. Check their flight plans.'

'I know what to do, okay?'

I shrugged.

'What about getting this place closed up? Can you help, or not?'

I retrieved my cell. 'As you ask so nicely, I do happen to know someone local.' The screen told me I had a text each from Arlen and Alabama, as well as a voice message from a number I didn't recognize. They could wait. I extracted Ike Bozey's number from the phone's memory and dialed. 'Detective Sergeant Bozey?' I asked when the call went through.

'Speaking.'

'Vin Cooper.'

'Hey, Cooper. You're a mind reader. Called you half an hour ago. Spoke with Arlen. Welcome home. How was Australia?'

'Hungry. That place eats people.'

'Hey, I heard you didn't find your guy?'

'No.'

'Long way to go for no.'

Maybe, but it was the best answer for Alabama. It meant she could continue to believe in that feeling she had about her boyfriend being out there somewhere, breathing, all his bits still attached. 'We need a little assistance. Wondered if you could help us out.'

'Who's us? You including that cute showgirl pal of yours?'

'No, an investigator from the NTSB.'

'Whadaya need?'

'We need premises at McCarran sealed, pending a federal warrant.'

'Why?'

'To stop any more evidence here flying away before the NTSB team looking into the plane crash arrives.' I gave him a brief rundown.

'The federal courthouse is down on South Las Vegas Boulevard, near the old casinos. You could get it done in an hour or two.'

'Yeah, but in the meantime we're gonna need someone to babysit the place.'

'See what I can do. Should be able to get a black and white over there within the next ten to fifteen. That suit your schedule, Cooper?'

I crooked the cell phone under my cheek and signaled ten minutes to Petinski, who nodded. 'Yep, that's good for us,' I told him.

'Any pal of Arlen's . . .'

I gave him the address. 'Say, while I got you – the amputated hand. Anything come through from pathology?'

'You *have* been watching too much TV, Cooper. I doubt it's even made their to-do list yet. I'll go talk with them, see if leaning on 'em will speed things up.'

'Thanks,' I said.

'Don't thank me. Leaning on them usually makes them go slower. Stay in touch.'

I said I would and the line went dead. Petinski's hands were on her hips, scoping the room like she was wondering what to do next. 'When did you call Morrow?' I asked her.

'Excuse me?'

'In the coroner's office back in Darwin, you said you had some calls to make. Was one of them to Morrow?'

'What?'

'Simple question, Petinski. What time did you call him?'

'Look—'

'What time?'

'Around eleven.'

'Eleven a.m. in Darwin, six-thirty p.m. in Vegas. You talked to Morrow and within minutes he's shredding documents.'

'No, I—'

'You tell him the dead pilot who flew his wrecked King Air wasn't Sweetwater?'

Her blue eyes flashed, did that squid thing. 'Yes.'

'Why the hurry?'

'Did you call your topless dancer client?' she asked, fighting back.

'I got around to it eventually, but that's what I was being paid to do – identify the remains and notify her. I'm still not clear on what it is *you* do?'

Petinski took a deep breath. 'Okay, calling Morrow was a mistake,' she admitted. 'I should've had someone arrive here with the news and the warrant at the same time.'

Imagine that – a mistake. Petinski was human after all.

'Excuse me, Mr Cooper?' It was Carol. She'd reappeared with a wad of paperwork, which she handed me. 'A copy of Mr Sweetwater's flight plan.'

I thanked her and opened it up, Petinski looking on.

'LAS, LAX, OGG, CXI, FUN, HIR, POM, DRW,' the investigator said. 'McCarran, Los Angeles, Kahului, Kiribati, Tuvalu, Honiara, Port Moresby, Darwin.'

'No wonder he took so much reading material,' I said.

'Randy flew to LAX, gave his wallet, watch, license and other ID to the Brazilian stand-in, who took it on from there,' said Petinski.

'How do you know that?' I asked.

'I don't – not for sure. But that would work.'

'You don't know if Randy gave up the pilot seat willingly.'

'No, but LAX is way bigger than any of the other airports in the flight plan. You could do a lot of things at LAX and no one would know or care. On Kiribati, for instance, you're going to be the center of attention. If it happened, it happened at LAX.'

'So then, by that reasoning, he *could* have been shanghaied in LAX, his documents stolen and so forth.'

'Okay,' said Petinski reluctantly, a little annoyed. 'Yes, that's possible. It just doesn't feel like that's what has happened here. But I can't explain why.'

Maybe she'd been reading tea leaves. The cell buzzed in my pocket again, reminding me about those unchecked messages.

Two uniform cops walked in through the front door. I'd hung up on Bozey maybe five minutes ago. These guys should deliver pizza. The uniforms checked out the room, thumbs hooked into their utility belts, looking around to see what was what. Petinski motioned that she was going to have a word with them. I nodded okay and took the opportunity to check my cell. There was the voice message from the blocked number. I hit the button and listened to Bozey asking whether I was back in the country yet and how it all went. Old news. I touched the text from Arlen. It read, *St Barts. Amazing place. So is Marnie. Am here*

two more days. You're still on vacation – come on over. Marnie has friends.
The message concluded with a smiley face. There was a photo attached.
I opened it and felt my heart stop. Like I said, Marnie was the spitting image of Anna, and here she was practically falling out of a tiny
emerald-green bikini. Arlen had his arm around her tan shoulder, his
hand an inch from a breast. He looked a lot older than her – a bit of a
gut, lecherous. He should be wearing a raincoat. St Barts was the one
place I *wouldn't* want to be.

I put the photo out of my head and opened the text from Alabama.
The message said, *Come over. I have others*. Another photo attachment.
I opened it up. The lighting wasn't great unless you wanted it intimate.
I recognized Ty Morrow. He was with a woman, having dinner. She was
plenty younger than he was so maybe the lighting was just how he
liked it. Aside from being young, the woman was also attractive and . . .
familiar. The dots took some seconds to connect, the angle on the girl
a less-than-ideal rear three-quarter view. Jesus, was that . . . ? It was:
Sugar. Ty Morrow and Sugar. *Together?* There was a time and a date on
the photo. It was shot at 0210 this morning, which meant that it was
taken some time *after* Morrow supposedly flew off into the sunset.

Ten

With the uniforms in place, Petinski left NAB to work on her affidavit and chase down the local judge. I kept the photo of Morrow and Sugar to myself and went in the opposite direction, taking a cab to Alabama's home at Summerlin. Whatever was going on with Randy Sweetwater, it was a universe expanding way beyond Thing in its KFC bucket: new connections were still being made, new trails heading down unexplored paths. There was the dead pilot from Brazil who spoke Portuguese and flew halfway around the world on Randy's photo IDs; Stu Forrest high-tailing it from NAB; and now Sugar and Ty Morrow, Randy's boss, caught cozying up together. I knew Sugar got around, but what were the odds of those two randomly hooking up? I wondered what the core inside this boil was all about – a ransom, an insurance fraud, a con gone wrong, or something else entirely? This was a different experience for me – watching events unfold as an interested spectator rather than being the special agent in charge and personally having to lance the sucker. If I'd never met Sweetwater and had no connection with the guy, this would almost be pure entertainment.

My cell rang: Petinski.

'Cooper,' I said.

'Dewy Baker was on the money,' she said. 'Stu Forrest is on his way to Acapulco.'

'Can we stop him?'

'Provided he sticks to his flight plan. Otherwise, no. If he's got something to hide, he's gone. He's supposed to stop at Tucson, Arizona, to refuel, but he could divert and go anywhere. We'll see what turns up in the next hour or so when he's due to land there. You'll never guess where Morrow has gone.'

'He didn't leave town,' I said.

'How'd you know?'

'My client spotted him early this morning.'

'And when did *you* know that, Cooper?'

The cab pulled up outside Alabama's home. 'Gotta go. Call you back,' I said.

'Coop—'

I hit the off button and set the ring tone to mute. A curtain flickered in a window and then the front door opened. Alabama came out onto the front porch in a purple satin halter top tied tight around her flat midriff, fitted cream-colored hot pants cut extra hot, bare feet and her hair worn in a high ponytail. Okay, so I notice details like these . . . She leaned against one of the veranda's roof supports, a drink in hand. I waved at her while I counted out some bills. The cab driver was more interested in watching her than he was in collecting the fare, which I completely understood.

'Tall, ain't she,' the driver commented.

'Yeah,' I said.

He didn't count the bills when I placed them in his open hand, just stuffed them in a pouch with his mouth slightly slack, which surprised me. I thought cab drivers in this town would've seen it all – one of the few perks of driving a cab in Vegas.

Alabama went inside when she saw me get out of the cab, and left the front door ajar. Being on staff, I figured I wouldn't be required to knock.

'Leave the door open,' she called out from somewhere inside. 'Need some air in here.'

I found her perched on a stool behind an oldish Mac desktop.

'When did you get in?' she asked.

'With the sunrise.'

'Good flight?'

'Great,' I said, happy to skip the details.

'Vin, I know I said this when you called, but going to Darwin for me, waiting to see whether those remains were Randy's or not. Jesus, I . . . I couldn't have faced it.'

'That's what employees are for,' I told her. 'Do I get a bonus?'

'No.'

'Well, then let's have a look at those photos, shall we?'

'Thanks, Vin.'

'So . . . you said you had some other photos?'

She turned around to face the Mac, tapped a key and the screen lit up. They were already loaded, three shots of Sugar and Morrow – one of which I'd already seen – sitting opposite each other at a table for two.

'What are you drinking?' I asked.

Fluffy the cat wrapped its tail around my leg, then ran off to chase a shadow.

'Orange juice.' She shrugged apologetically. 'It's the morning. Help yourself.'

'Feels like evening to me.' I passed on the juice offer. 'Were you the photographer?'

'No, one of the girls from work took them. She emailed the shots to me this morning.'

'Why'd she do that?'

'Because I've been asking around – seeing if anyone has seen Sugar. They were taken at a place called the Green Room.'

'What's that?'

'A swingers' club.'

'As in keys-in-the-bowl kind of swingers?'

'Anyone can go there. It's no big deal.'

I wasn't making one. If it exists, it exists in Vegas, Vegas being that

131

kind of town, but she was missing the point. 'Do you think they were there to be seen, or to hide out?'

'The Green Room's not exactly the Hard Rock Café. They wouldn't have gone there to put themselves on display.' She put her glass down. 'Morrow and Sugar meeting up,' she continued. 'That *means* something, doesn't it?'

'That they swing?' I said.

'You know what I mean, Cooper. It can't be a coincidence, can it?'

'Hmm, coincidences,' I said.

'What does "Hmm, coincidences" mean?'

'It means that Sugar and Morrow knew each other. It probably also means Sugar's interest in you and Randy had something to do with Morrow. And I guess it could also mean that the severed hand you received purporting to be Randy's is connected somehow to a woman you worked with, and to Randy's employer.'

The muscles in Alabama's throat moved up and down and her eyes went hot and wet as she also stopped believing in coincidences. She wiped away the tears before they had a chance to fall, using her palms and then the backs of her hands. 'Fucking bitch . . .'

'I'll get Bozey to put an all points out on both of them, have 'em brought in for questioning.' Even as I said it, I knew the chances of finding them were slim. I'd be surprised if Morrow was still in the vicinity. Maybe the meeting with Sugar was the reason he came back. Perhaps he came back *for* Sugar – to take her somewhere. Whatever the reason, I doubted he'd be hanging around. But there was always luck, and occasionally it was the good kind. I put in a call to Bozey, got the detective's voicemail and left him a message to call back.

The leather couch I was sitting on was new and expensive. A couple of ceiling fans rotated slowly overhead, pushing the air around, evaporating the sweat on my head and under my shirt. The room was pleasant, a mix of male and female. Two people lived here who enjoyed full lives and had an easy accommodation with each other. There were photos of Alabama and Randy together, sharing wall space with photos of Alabama's girlfriends and Randy's buddies. Large, original, brightly colored works of modern art also dominated. Objects collected from Randy's various tours were displayed – pottery, figurines, rugs. Two vases of flowers further brightened the place, and the air smelled vaguely of jasmine and money. Given Alabama's comments about her Showgirls salary, I had to assume that Randy was well paid.

'Tell me about Australia,' Alabama said, getting up off the stool and sitting on a leather chair opposite me, folding a leg beneath her, holding her glass in both hands.

I gave her a rundown: the discovery of the first set of remains, followed by the second set hooked by the two fishermen. I then described the trip to Elcho Island and the wreckage we searched in the shark-infested estuary. I concluded with the discovery that had stumped both Petinski and me: 'In the cockpit, we found Randy's passport, FAA license and security pass, as well as his logbook.'

She scowled at me, questions etched in the lines on her forehead.

'The items were either flawless copies or the originals. The NTSB is checking on that now, along with the FAA and Homeland Security. And if they're originals, then they were either stolen from Randy or he gave them to the pilot, or to someone who passed them on to the pilot.'

'Why would Randy give them away?' she asked.

'Your guess is as good as mine.' That little Department of Speculation was a thirty-story building full of options and variables. I looked around the room again. 'Summerlin's a good neighborhood.'

'It's okay.'

'And it's a nice place you got here.'

Alabama glared at me. 'Are you going to ask me how much Randy earns?'

'How much did Randy earn?'

'I've told you already. He wasn't into anything illegal.'

'How much?'

'Check with NAB. One-fifty, plus bonuses.'

'Bonuses for what?'

'Beats me, Cooper. Flying planes?'

'If there's anything you think I should know, you need to come clean about it. Randy's life – and maybe yours, too – is about to be squashed between two glass slides and put under a microscope.'

'Look, if I had something to hide, why would I engage you to go all the way to Australia to identify Randy's remains?'

'Don't think I haven't asked myself that question.'

'You're not on the payroll anymore, Cooper,' she said. 'Maybe you should leave.' Alabama stood, went to the door and opened it wide, the dazzle from a summer's day in the desert almost blinding. I noticed her legs – hard not to. They were long, lean and toned. Dancer's legs. Maybe she could do the splits, too. I got up and walked toward her and the door and she stepped a little to the side to let me pass.

'And what about Randy?' she asked.

'What about him?' I was tempted to say that, like she just told me, I wasn't on the payroll, but I held off. Something undoubtedly odd was going on with Randy, but Alabama's reactions to the hard questions and her persistence to find the answers suggested that, whatever it was, she didn't know enough to leave it alone. 'There's the pathology report still to come on the amputated hand. Once that has come in, as well as the verdicts from the FAA and DHS on the documents purporting to be Randy's, we might know something more concrete.'

A wall of dry heat met me in the doorway. A dragonfly pulled to a stop in the shade beneath the awning, its beating wings glittering. I had no vehicle and there didn't appear to be any cabs out here cruising for fares.

'Hey, I'm sorry, Vin,' she said. 'This business is just messing with my head. I'll keep paying your expenses. If I don't have you looking into this, I don't have anyone.'

I hesitated, partially distracted by the dragonfly. It turned and zoomed off, away into the sunshine.

'You've come this far,' she continued. 'Please don't make me beg.'

I found her hand – it was still vaguely moist with her tears. I gave it a squeeze and went down the stairs. At the bottom, I called over my shoulder, 'Let you know when I hear something.'

'Vin.'

I stopped and looked back up at her.

'Thanks – for me, and for Randy too. You're a good friend. I . . . I mean that.' She glanced up and down the street. 'Hey, I forgot you came by cab. Can I drive you somewhere?'

'No, thanks. I could do with the exercise.'

'Midday in Las Vegas in summer ain't the best time to take it,' she cautioned.

It was baking hot, the overhead sun a white point like the tip of an oxy-acetylene torch, but what I needed was time to think and I had to do it away from Alabama and those legs of hers. 'Which way do I go? There a main road nearby?'

'Okay . . .' she said with a shrug suggesting that it was my funeral, and pointed down the road. 'Keep going till you see the golf course, then turn right. It's a twenty-minute walk.'

I went for ten minutes and made no progress on what might have happened to Randy Sweetwater, but I made leaps and bounds on the cab front, catching one that had just made a drop-off at the golf course.

'Where we going?' the driver asked.

'Bally's,' I told him.

'You seen the show there? The girls?'

'Yeah.'

'Shame. Could'a got you cheap tickets. How long you in town, buddy? Need some company?'

'You're not my type,' I said.

Checking the screen on my phone, I saw I'd missed three calls from Petinski, and one from Bozey. I flicked off the mute button and it rang immediately.

'Cooper,' I said.

'Don't hang up on me again, okay?' Petinski demanded.

'I'm headed back to Bally's. Wanna join me poolside? If we hurry we can catch the afternoon bikini contest. You can even enter it.'

'Are you trying to get *me* to hang up on *you*?'

'Am I that transparent?' I asked her.

'Cooper, I'm in Detective Sergeant Bozey's office. You and I are taking a conference call with your supervisor in twenty-five minutes and we've got a few things to talk about beforehand.'

'My supervisor?' *Arlen?*

'Yeah.' Petinski cut the call there, evening the score.

The driver stomped on the gas when we hit Summerlin Parkway. Arlen was supposed to be on St Barts with Marnie, but now suddenly he was back in DC, changed out of his board shorts and raincoat, with something to say to both Petinski and me, and maybe Bozey too. I had to admit I was intrigued.

'Been a change of plan, buddy,' I said, leaning forward. 'The police department down near McCarran.'

'Now that I think about it, you *look* like police.'

'What do police look like?'

He adjusted the mirror so I could see myself in it and said, 'A little like that.'

Eleven

'Hey, Cooper, how you doin', pal?' said Bozey, glancing up from his blotter.

'What kept you?' Petinski had her back to the window. Her voice sounded tense, the tone clipped. She checked her wristwatch and glanced at Bozey, some kind of signal.

He gave her a nod and said, 'Well, I gotta step out for a few minutes, go fight some crime. Make yourselves at home.'

'Great, where's the fridge?' I asked him.

The detective grinned and pointed at me, then closed the door behind him.

'Okay, Petinski,' I said. 'What's up?'

Her tiny frame was silhouetted against the sunshine streaming through the window, and behind her I could see the sprawl of McCarran International. Directly adjacent to the police department building, on the other side of a high fence topped with stainless-steel razor wire, was the area designated for helicopters where a large corporate gnat hovered blowing the beige-colored desert dust off the taxiway. If I squinted, a quarter mile or so beyond it I could spy the executive jet ramp area and the hangar used by Nevada Aircraft Brokers.

'There are a lot of people working on the King Air crash,' she said.

'So far, Petinski, all I've seen is an army of one – you, always one step ahead of the vast resources of the NTSB supposedly rushing in to fill the vacuum behind you.'

The investigator walked around Bozey's desk and sat in one of the chairs reserved for visitors. 'That's a fair call,' she said. 'You're going to have to trust me.'

'Lucky for you I'm the trusting type, as my personality type indicators will tell you.'

She failed to catch the ironic tone and instead jumped straight to saying, 'We've made progress. Sweetwater's place at the King Air's controls was switched with a stand-in at LAX. We think the switch was made voluntarily by Sweetwater and no coercion was involved.'

'You told me most of that already,' I reminded her. 'Only now you've got proof, right?'

'I'll get to that,' Petinski replied. 'Preliminary results are in on the investigation of the crash.'

'That was fast,' I said. According to my Seiko, our boots had been back on home soil barely ten hours.

'We're in a hurry.'

'Why are we in a hurry? And who is *we*, exactly?'

Petinski ignored the questions and that told me plenty right there. She pulled out an iPad and touched it up until she found what she wanted. 'These are the photos of the King Air's fuel gauges I took at the scene.' She handed me the device. 'This particular aircraft was fitted with the latest glass cockpit. It was equipped with both digital *and* the older-style analog gauges.'

'That so unusual? If I was flying solo across the Pacific in a slow mover, I'd want backup,' I said.

'Take a good look at the gauge.'

The photo was of an analog fuel gauge, glass face cracked and the needle stuck at about half full. Several photos to the left and right of this image showed other instruments, all of which displayed critical damage. I returned to the fuel gauge question. 'And then . . . ?' I said. Whatever the point was, I was missing it.

'There was no fuel in the tanks. Nothing. Not a drop. The pilot ditched on fumes, but that's not what the instrument says.'

'What was the digital instrument reading?'

'We don't know. There was no flight data recorder, and the fuel system's processing units were also destroyed in the crash, so we can't reconstruct with any certainty the information the pilot was getting. There's speculation, though, that the digital instrument might have been rigged to fail, so that all the pilot had to go on fuel-wise was the analog instrument you see there.'

'So you think the pilot believed he had plenty of gas up his sleeve when there was actually nothing left?' I said.

'Yes.'

I knew where Petinski was going with this – sabotage. But I wasn't seeing it, not yet. Fuel starvation through poor fuel load calculation was a common killer in civil aviation. Some people just forget to fill 'er up. 'And then . . . ?' I said.

'If you remember, Carol gave us a copy of the flight plan, which also included the fuel planning log, weather en route and so forth.'

I remembered.

'Moresby to Darwin was one of the shorter legs. And each leg required different combinations of fuel tanks to be filled to allow for the best flight characteristics. According to the fuel planning, the pilot should have had enough to reach Darwin with plenty in reserve. The fuel gauges were doctored to overread.'

'Who's we, again?' I asked.

'I said I'll get to that. We've modeled the fuel calculations with the aircraft's actual fuel burn recorded in the pilot's log, compared the performance achieved with the forecast weather conditions factored in, and then compared the outcomes with the actual weather conditions experienced.'

'You're losing me.'

'Too many three-syllable words?'

'I think you *want* me to get lost.'

'We reach an understanding at last, Cooper,' she said. 'The modeling tells us that, based on the forecast weather conditions, and with the actual fuel load in the King Air's tanks, it should've ditched at least two hundred miles *off* the coast of Australia. However, there was an unforecast tailwind of a hundred and ten miles per hour. It took the plane farther than expected – over dry land.'

'If it had ditched at sea, it never would've been found,' I said, some of the tumblers lining up for me. 'He'd be pronounced missing, presumed dead. Except that he's not, is he?'

'No. At least, we hope not.'

There was that *we* again. 'You going to tell me what's really going on here, Petinski – if that's what your real name is?'

'Stu Forrest, the NAB guy who took off in a hurry to Acapulco, did the fuel planning for the flight. He hasn't landed in Tucson, by the way. And, as you know, he can cross the Mexican border any number of places and evade detection.'

'Who exactly do you work for again?' I asked her.

'Maybe now might be the opportune time to bring your supervisor in on the conversation.' Petinski leaned across Bozey's desk and spun the computer monitor around one-eighty degrees. Arlen's face was on the screen.

'Hey, Vin,' he said. 'How do?'

'Colonel Wayne,' I replied, keeping it official. 'How long you been online, sir?'

'Just got here and Arlen will do fine, Vin. We're among friends.'

He could have fooled me. 'I thought you were in St Barts.'

'I was,' he said, rubbing the back of his neck. 'And I'd like to go back there once we're done here.'

'You got recalled because of this?'

'Because of what I'm about to tell you, yes.'

'Sounds serious. That was a hell of a nice bikini you left behind.'

'Tell me about it.'

Petinski sucked in a breath that sounded like, 'Can we please get the hell on with it?'

Arlen got the hint and cleared his throat. 'Vin, I've only just been brought in on this myself, so don't blame me for you being kept in the dark.'

'No promises,' I said.

'Off you go, Kim,' Arlen told her.

'My name *is* Kim Petinski but I'm not NTSB, though I was formerly with that organization. These days I'm with DCIS.'

The Defense Criminal Investigative Service. 'You're a spook.'

'Randy was my partner. He was working undercover at Nevada Aircraft Brokers. The Drug Enforcement Administration, under the Proceeds of Crime Act—'

'Sweetwater was also a spook?'

'DCIS,' said Petinski. 'Same as me.'

'So the discharge from the Air Force, the court martial, the plea bargain – that was part of his cover story?'

'What do you think?'

'What does Alabama know?'

'Nothing. As I was saying, the—'

'What am I doing here?' I asked.

'Can you let me finish?' said Petinski, the tiniest vertical stress line between her eyes.

I stretched my legs out in front of me and settled in for the long haul.

'As I was saying, Randy, my partner, was working undercover at NAB. The Drug Enforcement Administration, under the Proceeds of Crime Act, has impounded three out of nine aircraft sold by NAB over the last twelve months. Its biggest customer – through several dummy companies – happens to be a Brazilian crime baron wanted by the FBI, CIA, Interpol and half a dozen other organizations and governments for drug smuggling and illegal arms trading. Things got extra complicated when Randy somehow managed to infiltrate this crime boss's inner circle. From what we can piece together, we believe his cover was about to be blown unless he could be two places at once – create some internal confusion by flying that plane to Australia while also hanging out with this crime boss in Rio.'

'You lost track of your own partner. Is that what's going on here?' I said.

'Yes. Things were getting complicated.' She stood up and went to the window.

'DCIS couldn't run an egg and spoon race.'

'Don't confuse us with CIA.'

'I'm not – CIA hasn't learned how to tie its shoelaces, so it wouldn't even make the starting line.'

'Just like the OSI.'

'Oh, we can tie 'em just fine, or we could if our hands weren't tied behind our backs by agencies like yours.'

'Children – please,' said Arlen, interjecting. 'Vin, as of now, you're off vacation. You're working with Special Investigator Petinski as her partner.'

'Oh, c'mon . . .'

'It's been cleared all the way to the top.'

'Meaning Wynngate?'

'Yes.'

'Does the general know I'm an ESFJ – an extroverted, sensing, feeling, judgmental kinda guy? I mean, I'd have to know what Petinski is before I'm comfortable with it, going forward.'

'Vin, we both know you've got no say in this. And as for your Myers-Briggs profile, you ticked box A for every single question, so who knows what you are,' said Arlen.

'I've got a pretty good idea,' said Petinski.

'See,' Arlen concluded, 'Ms Petinski has figured you out all on her own. It's a perfect match.'

'I'm an ESTJ,' said Petinski. 'The T makes all the difference. He's oil, I'm water.'

'I get the picture,' said Arlen. 'Nevertheless . . .'

'Who was flying the plane?' I asked her. 'Who'd they cut out of those sharks?'

'One of ours,' said Petinski. 'Low level. A Brazilian native – an enabler with our South American desk.'

'And you didn't know that when you were in Australia?' I said.

'If I did, I wouldn't have needed to go there, would I?'

From memory, Petinski had been far from comfortable around the human morsels reclaimed from the Aussie wildlife. Now I understood why – she had a personal connection to them, believing the remains really could have been her partner. The discovery of Sweetwater's personal effects would have hardened up the identification of those remains, so the coroner's conclusion at the end of our stay about them *not* being Randy's must have taken her emotions on a rollercoaster ride.

Okay, so I found myself having some sympathy for Petinski's situation, but not enough to go quietly into partnership with her. 'The pilot was one of yours, but you didn't know it? Are you *sure* you're not CIA?'

Petinski flared. 'Sometimes when you're deep undercover, Cooper, you can't just pick up the phone. And I think you know what it's like to lose a partner, right?'

Raw heat bloomed in my face.

'Whoa, let's just back it off a notch or two,' Arlen said, and no one spoke for a few seconds.

'So, Vin,' he said quietly when he felt things had cooled a little, 'the name of this crime boss in Rio de Janeiro, one of the guys we want a piece of, is Falco White. His brother is one Charles White, the arms dealer you came up against in the Congo. You remember him?'

The name penetrated my anger. Charles White – big, black and dangerous – delivered US-made weapons and ammunition to all comers in the Congo, regardless of which side they were on, who then used them to kill and maim each other. Working with a few Special Forces soldiers, we'd managed to relieve White of enough arms to take on a company-sized force, freeing hostages being held for ransom. That was, in fact, my last case, the one that had ended with me up on a charge for assault with intent to cause grievous bodily harm. White had slipped through my fingers in the Congo, flying off in a chopper a few hours before the attack on the turds holding our hostages had been launched. I figured I had a score to settle with the guy. 'Yeah,' I said. 'He's a hard guy to forget.'

'The White brothers are working with an even bigger fish, a man by the name of Benicio von Weiss,' said Petinski.

'Never heard of him,' I said.

Petinski played with her iPad and handed it to me again. 'He's not exactly a public figure.'

I scrolled through half a dozen pictures of a man of around thirty-five to forty years of age, all pastel sweaters tied around his shoulders and boats and blond hair. 'What's this guy selling, besides poor color choices?' I asked.

'Among other things, the American weapons you found in Afghanistan and Africa – the ones with and without their numbers filed off,' said Arlen.

'This guy was responsible for them?'

'White's middle management. Von Weiss is your man,' Arlen confirmed.

'Vast caches of everything from M26 hand grenades and mortars to M16s and laser targeting systems are flooding the market,' added Petinski. 'We believe Benicio von Weiss is the guy masterminding the operation. He uses Falco and Charles White as intermediaries. Von Weiss is an arms dealer and one of the world's wealthiest men – certainly one of the top three wealthiest men in Brazil. He even runs the favela in Rio responsible for a big slice of the city's weapons and drug trade.'

'Favela – sounds like something you dip in guacamole,' I said.

I distinctly heard Petinski tsk. 'A favela is a slum.'

Arlen glanced at the investigator. 'Vin, you fell into this operation because of Anna's friendship with Randy,' he said. 'The Department of Defense took OSI off the case, but you've put us back in the game.'

'What game?' I asked.

'An organized crime ring operating within US bases is stealing arms for von Weiss and causing a lot of worldwide mayhem. We've got weapons in inventory that terrorists would love to get their hands on: Barrett rifles, Stingers – standoff weapons capable of bringing down aircraft.'

'So where does Sweetwater fit into all of this?'

'Kim?' said Arlen giving her the floor.

'As I've already told you, Cooper, Randy went undercover at NAB. We followed the ownership trail of those aircraft impounded by the DEA to companies owned by Falco and Charles White. Randy managed to get close to them, joined their organization, found the connection to Benicio von Weiss. And then, about three weeks ago, we lost him – lost Randy. We thought he'd surfaced, flying that King Air to Australia, but that turned out not to be the case. Somehow, he'd managed to make contact with the CIA operative and convince him to stand in on that flight to Australia.'

'He used him as a decoy?' asked Arlen. 'That's rough.'

Petinski pushed on. 'Cooper, it was only after you told me about the severed hand and ransom note business that another avenue of investigation opened up.'

'And which avenue is that?' I asked.

Petinski shifted a folder and picked up a number of pages stapled together, handing them to me. The letterhead informed me that the forensic lab of the Las Vegas Metropolitan Police had compiled it.

'You seen this?' I asked Arlen.

'I'm half an hour ahead of you,' he said, lifting his copy into view. 'But that's all.'

It was the report Bozey said would have to wait its turn in the queue. Someone had leaned on the system heavily to have our case jump to the head – the detective, I figured. I read through the report, taking it for a short walk around Bozey's office. It began with a bunch of disclaimers, which basically said the tests on the hand, note and packaging were incomplete and that more time was required to reach definitive conclusions on each item, and so forth. I flipped the page and read some more. In the limited time available most attention had thus far been given to examining Thing. The report said that the hand belonged to a male of mixed racial origin between the ages of forty and fifty. Every knuckle was separated, and all the fingers as well as the thumb had been broken. Badly bruised skin in the areas of the breaks indicated that the damage was done while the victim was alive.

Maybe the guy had won a few too many games of pool . . .

According to the report, the manner in which the bones in the wrist had been cut indicated that a surgical saw of the highest quality had been used to do the job. There was no vital reaction in the soft tissue around the cut at the time of the amputation – no bleeding – meaning that the hand was amputated post-mortem. Whoever he was, this guy had pissed someone off pretty bad. I turned another page and kept reading, and what I read made me read it again. A snake's fang had been found embedded in the webbing between the first and second finger. Toxicology tests revealed a lethal amount of snake venom in the blood. It was the view of the pathologist that snake venom had killed the man who belonged to the amputated hand. In fact, there was so much venom in the blood and tissue that the pathologist who performed the tests believed the victim had been bitten many times prior to death. DNA analysis of the venom revealed that it had come from one of the world's most lethal serpents, the golden lancehead viper, found exclusively on the island of Queimada Grande, which apparently lay off the coast of Brazil, not far from Rio de Janeiro.

Rio. Plenty of roads seemed to be leading there.

I flipped over another page and saw the subhead *Air Force Academy Ring*.

'I'll save you the trouble reading,' said Petinski. 'The ring's the real deal.'

'Randy's,' I said.

'No question.'

The following page dealt with the FedEx packaging. I skimmed the findings, which were no more or less disappointing than I thought they'd be. The paper, plastic and packing tape were all covered in fingerprints, hairs, skin cells and other biological material, but all of it was next to useless as evidence, or even identification. According to the analyst's assessment, the box had simply gone through countless hands and environments, and identifying which fingerprint, hair and/ or skin cells were salient to building a case was impossible. The FedEx box itself was standard issue and the address was not a house or apartment but a post office somewhere in Rio, at a place called Céu Cidade. Whoever posted the package could have driven across town to that post office. That lead was probably a dead end.

I dropped the paperwork back on the desk. 'So what does all this tell you?'

'Benicio von Weiss is a herpetologist, an expert on snakes. He's one of the world's foremost authorities on venomous South American vipers, and has written several definitive papers on the effects of venom on human flesh.'

'So he's an expert on snakes, and the guy missing a hand died from snakebite. What's the connection beyond the circumstantial one? And what's that got to do with Randy's ring?'

'You don't believe in coincidences, Cooper, so why don't *you* tell me what it means?'

'I'm just asking,' I said, opening my hands out, Mr Innocent.

Petinski's head was lowered, her eyes on me like a bull about to charge – a very small blonde bull that could possibly do the splits.

'C'mon,' I said. 'I'm the one who's blindfolded here. Just tell me what this is all about.'

'I can't give you the full picture, Cooper, not in the presence of the colonel, because he isn't cleared for it. This is as secret as it comes.'

'The lady speaks the truth, Vin,' Arlen confirmed.

I leaned back against the door. 'Then I'll take a down payment – tell me whatever you can in my supervisor's presence.'

'Okay, well . . .' she began, eyes flicking to Arlen and then back to me, 'as I said, Randy went undercover to keep an eye on Ty Morrow, who picked him up to fly guns and drugs out of South America, once Randy passed the audition. Randy flew legal for three months until the bad guys were happy. They stepped it up sharply after that – deliveries of weapons and drugs throughout South America, and sometimes also into North America. Randy finally came into contact with Mr Big – Benicio von Weiss – after more than fourteen months of flying, on a run to São Paulo, Brazil. He hit it off with the boss straight away. But then the DEA got too enthusiastic on a tip-off from Randy and raided a secret drugs-manufacturing plant in the north of Brazil, in concert with Brazilian government troops, and that set off alarm bells in von Weiss's camp. Von Weiss, or one of his people, figured that the leak could have come from limited sources, one of them being Randy. So they put a watch on him around the clock. We think Von Weiss ultimately decided not to wait till the songbird broke cover and had all suspects whacked simultaneously. We think Randy might have got word that he was a target at around the time he had to do the run to Australia. One of our people piloted that plane in Randy's stead to give him some breathing space, and you know the rest about that.'

'And Thing? The severed hand?' I asked.

'The theory is that Randy sent it.'

'Randy sent the hand?'

'That's what we think.'

'You *think*?'

'The fingerprints identify the hand as belonging to a low-level crook known to Brazilian authorities as Diogo Jaguaribe, alias "Fruit Fly".'

'Fruit Fly?'

'He's got sticky fingers, apparently. Money tends to disappear around him. Word in the favelas is that Jaguaribe was killed by von Weiss – stole some cash from the boss; Jaguaribe living up to his alias. Somehow, Randy came across his dismembered corpse. Maybe he was asked to dump it as some kind of test – we don't know for sure. But we are reasonably certain that he used the severed hand and his ring to send us a message . . .' Petinski hesitated.

'Which was?' I asked her.

'That he's still alive and in Rio. Using his academy ring authenticated the message, and the packaging gave us his location – Céu Cidade, the favela von Weiss runs.'

'Really?' I said. I wasn't sure I bought it. There'd have been less dramatic ways to get the message across, surely.

'We've been monitoring his girlfriend and—'

'Alabama?'

'Yes. And there have been no further communications. That's as much as I can say.'

'Why didn't Randy just post the hand to you?'

'I would have thought that was obvious, Cooper.'

'Help me out with it anyway.'

'I'm a federal agent. We don't know who we can trust so sending the hand to his stripper girlfriend was a safer option.'

'Alabama's not a stripper.'

'Then what is she?'

'A topless tall.'

'Whatever. Look, the obvious part of this is that if Randy thought he could FedEx me something and get away with it, I'm sure he'd have forwarded me a full debrief with all questions answered.'

'Arlen, for the record I want you to know that I'm not buying any of this.' It all smelt like it had been lying around in the sun too long. To Petinski I said, 'Why the trust issues with you being a fed? Why don't you just tell me what's really going on here?'

'We should give Bozey his office back,' Petinski answered, gathering up her iPad, iPhone and assorted papers.

'Hey, I'm *nowhere* near finished here. Just leaving the big picture aside for a moment, who cut off the hand with the high-quality surgical saw?' That seemed a little genteel to me, given the damage done to his fingers. Why not a machete, a large pair of bolt cutters, or even just an axe?

'The cutter would have been von Weiss.'

'You seem very certain about that.'

'Von Weiss wouldn't have been able to help himself. Studying the effects of venom on human flesh – that's his specialty. He'd have performed a complete professional autopsy on the corpse. No different than his father.'

'Who was his father?'

'Von Weiss claims to be the illegitimate son of Josef Mengele.'

The name rang a bell. 'The name rings a bell,' I said. 'Wasn't he some Nazi or other?'

'Mengele was a *Hauptsturmführer* in the Nazi SS and the chief medical officer at Birkenau. The inmates called him the Angel of Death. After the war, Mengele fled to South America and lived in Rio, Buenos Aires and Paraguay, and died in São Paulo, Brazil, in 1979. Mengele changed his name and went by Weiss, Rudolph Weiss. Benicio von Weiss literally means "son of Weiss".'

'Why'd they call the old man the Angel of Death?'

'Because he'd stand on the railway platform as the cattle cars arrived, survey the newcomers as they shuffled along, and with his arms out wide like an angel with its wings open he'd say, "Death to the left, life to the right." And then he'd perform medical experiments on the ones chosen to live. As I said – like father, like son.'

There was a soft tap on the door. 'You folks done?' came Bozey's impatient voice through the wood.

'Just a minute, Ike,' Petinski called out, and then turned back to the computer screen occupied by Arlen. 'I can't take this any further, Colonel, I'm sorry.'

'No problem,' said Arlen. 'Vin, this is where I turn and burn, buddy. Why don't you two go have some fun?'

'Thanks a whole bunch,' I said.

'Don't mention it.'

Twelve

Petinski sat behind the wheel of the rental and pulled a gadget from her bag. She ran it around the ignition and dash with the motor off, then repeated the performance with the motor running.

'A bit melodramatic, wouldn't you say?' I said.

Petinski put the bug sniffer away, selected drive and pointed the Focus toward the Las Vegas Boulevard exit. 'You know when I said this was beyond secret? The trade in stolen weapons is only a small part of it.'

I knew it. I looked across at her.

'Cooper, we've got an Empty Quiver situation.'

'What's that?'

My casual lack of understanding arced her up some.

'It's a missing nuke, for Christ's sake. So, no, I wouldn't say I'm being—'

'A what?!'

'You heard me.'

'What do you mean, *missing?*'

'What do you think it means?'

The investigator now had my fullest attention. The situation a lot of people had been dreading for a very long time appeared to be unfolding, only the scenario usually went that the nuke would originate from a leaky weapons storage depot in Siberia, or be provided by some North Korean crackpot, or built by a terrorist group. But this was *one of ours*; how was that even possible? Suddenly all the subterfuge seemed inadequate.

Petinski went for a break in the traffic and accelerated hard into the gap. 'It's a W80, part of our upgraded stockpile, a thermonuclear warhead with a variable yield of between five and one hundred and fifty kilotons of TNT. We think Benicio von Weiss obtained it through Falco and Charles White, who we now believe set up the operation to steal it, building on the contacts and systems they put in place over the years to pilfer small arms and other weapons from US bases.'

'How long's it been gone for?'

'We don't know for sure.'

'You mean, you don't know *at all*.'

The look on Petinski's face told me I was right. 'Up to six months,' she said.

'When did someone realize we were down a nuke?'

'Six weeks ago.'

'Where's it gone missing from?'

'Nellis, Area Two. Kirtland was also under a cloud for a while, as was Barksdale.'

'Under a cloud. Great metaphor. Does anyone have any idea where the weapon is?'

'No.'

'We don't know much, do we?'

'No.'

'Well, is it likely to go off in a US city?'

'The physics package cannot be detonated without codes, and they're impossible to crack.'

That just sounded too reassuring to be reassuring. I mean, was there such a thing as a code that couldn't be broken? 'Petinski, as you're in the driver's seat, you can take me to Summerlin.'

'Sorry, we're going to Nellis.'

'Sure, we can go to Nellis *after* I've paid Alabama a visit.'

'There's no point to that.'

'There's plenty of point.'

'It's not our priority.'

'It mightn't be yours, but it's top of mine.'

'You can't tell her anything.'

'I can inform her that her boyfriend's alive.'

'It's not a good idea, Cooper. We don't know who's watching.'

'As in ours, or theirs?'

Petinski wasn't forthcoming with an answer.

'Who *is* in on this wayward-nuke story, Petinski?'

'That's classified.'

'Does the Air Force know?'

'Classified.'

'In other words – no.' I already knew that Arlen was not included in the need-to-know. And his access was ordinarily much higher than mine.

'Listen, Cooper, stockpiled US thermonuclear weapons *can't* just disappear. I mean, can you imagine the panic if this gets out? If we can lose one, then why not a dozen or more, right? It will tell our enemies and our allies that our procedures and protocols are totally and completely broken. If this leaks, all kinds of doors within the Air Force will slam shut. No one will talk and tracks will be covered.'

'Not to mention asses.'

'The Department of Defense and DCIS have been looking into the theft of weapons from US bases for a couple of years now. We believed we were close, and then the hole in the W80 inventory was discovered. As soon as it came to light, all kinds of contingency plans went into effect, and all of them are as secret as you can get.'

'Great, only you don't know when the weapon went missing, how it was stolen, where it is now, or even where your undercover agent is.'

'I'll admit it looks bad.'

'And I thought you had no sense of humor.'

'It's not like *I* lost it.'

'No, but you're part of the bullshit.'

'And now you are too.'

'Would you mind turning this crate around and driving me to your partner's partner?' The turnoff flashed by. 'If you want my further cooperation, Petinski, that is not – repeat *not* – a multiple-choice question.'

*

Alabama's front door was closed, but I'd rung through to confirm that she was home and tell her I was coming over. Petinski pulled to the curb as Randy's girlfriend came out onto the porch and waved. Petinski sat and stared straight ahead as I got out of the car.

'Hey,' I called.

Alabama put her hand to her forehead, using it as a shield against the sun. 'Who's your friend?'

I heard Petinski come up behind me. 'This is Special Investigator Kim Petinski. She's also been working on Randy's disappearance.'

Petinski displayed her credentials without comment.

'Thank you so much for helping,' said Alabama.

Petinski gave her a fleeting smile.

'Another couple of agents came calling after you left, Vin,' Alabama continued. 'I thought they were FBI, but now I think about it, their IDs were more like yours.' She nodded at Petinski.

'What did they want to know?' I asked.

'Mostly stuff about Nevada Aircraft Brokers and what Randy did there. They didn't ask about the hand or the ransom note. Maybe they didn't know about that. They were polite. So far, the between-two-glass-slides thing you talked about hasn't been as bad as I thought it would be.'

Actually, given what I knew was going on in the background, I was surprised that the entire security machine of the United States hadn't descended on this street, locking it down, sealing it off and making Alabama a virtual prisoner. That told me the folks at the top who knew about the missing W80 were scared – so scared they were tip-toeing around the crisis, hoping the mess wouldn't literally blow up in their faces.

'So, any leads?' Alabama asked.

'You mind if we go inside?' I said. The slight breeze coming off the desert was superheated and dry, like it had stopped in a kiln to fire some pottery on the way over.

'Sure. Come on in. Can I get you a drink?'

'Just water would be fine,' Petinski replied, looking around the room.

Alabama went off into the adjoining kitchen. 'Vin, you?'

'Water too,' I called out. 'Though I'll take mine as ice. And if you could maybe just add some tomato juice, a shot of vodka and a dash of Tabasco . . .'

'Okay.'

Petinski glared at me. I knew what she was thinking – this was wrong, but I knew how to fix it. I called out, 'And if you've got a stick of celery to put in it, that'd be great.'

'Jesus, Cooper,' Petinski hissed. 'We're in a hurry here. You mind sticking to the rules? Don't make this more difficult than it has to be.'

'I'm allaying suspicion, Petinski. Just being my normal self. But perhaps you're right,' I told her and called out again, 'Maybe forget the celery if it's too much trouble.'

Alabama popped her head around the corner. 'No problem. With or without?'

'What do *you* think?' I asked Petinski.

Three hundred watts.

'Okay, with,' I said.

Moments later, Alabama appeared with a Bloody Mary in one hand and ice water in the other. Petinski and I relieved her of them. I crunched the end of the celery stick.

'So, the drink aside, Vin,' Alabama said, her eyes flicking between Petinski and me, 'this is looking a little official. Should I be worried?'

'No,' I said. 'The opposite, in fact.'

She seemed to relax when she heard that, and even attempted the shadow of a smile.

'Some information has come to light,' I said. 'I can't give you specifics, but we're as sure as we can be that Randy is still alive.'

'Oh my god.' Alabama sat heavily, her knees giving way. 'Look, I can't tell you how much . . . *Such* a relief. Thank you. How do you know?'

'We're not in a position to say,' I replied, doing the government sidestep.

'Who's we? You two?'

'The federal agency I work for,' said Petinski, backing up my sidestep with a little shuffle of her own.

'Which agency is that again?' Alabama asked.

I drank some of my Bloody Mary, then drank some more.

'Defense Criminal Investigative Service,' said Petinski.

'Where is he?'

'We can't say,' Petinski replied.

'When will I be able to see him?'

'I'm sorry but—'

'But that's classified, right?'

Petinski answered with a reluctant nod.

'You government shitheads play dice with people's lives.' Alabama's anger flushed into her cheeks, turning them red. 'It's like we're goddamn lab rats to you people.' She stood up and glared down at both of us, her hands flexing briefly into fists, little white and pink balls of frustration. 'You can go now. *Both* of you. Don't bother finishing the damn drinks.'

'Don't you feel better about that now, Petinski?' I said as we stepped down off the veranda. 'I know I do.'

My new partner didn't answer and went silently to the Chevrolet, aiming the alarm remote at it. I heard a *tweet* and she pulled the door open without a backward glance. No matter what Petinski thought, I had a duty to Alabama and to Randy and I felt that I'd discharged at least some of it.

When we were back in the car, I took a stab at deciphering the odd electricity in the air and said to Petinski, 'You knew about her, but she didn't know about you.'

Petinski snapped, 'That's none of your damn business, Cooper.'

Bullseye.

She started the car, signaled, and did a vicious U-turn. She said nothing for a few hundred yards or so. 'I was with Randy *before* Alabama. You happy now?'

'He leave you for Alabama?'

'No.'

I let that sit in the air.

'All right, there was overlap.' Petinski pulled to the side of the road, the Irish greenery of the golf course visible ahead. 'Randy cheated on me with that stripper, and it hurt. I wanted him to be punished. I thought maybe that wish had come true when he disappeared.'

'Alabama's not a stripper,' I said.

'So you keep saying. Whatever she is, I've hated her. I think I have that right.'

'You mind if I drive?' I asked her.

'Do whatever you like,' she told me, her meaning clear.

I leaned past her and removed the keys from the ignition in case she decided to drive off when I got out. I opened the door, went around to the driver's side and opened it. Petinski unwillingly got out and swapped sides. She stared out the window as we drove back toward town, Mandalay Bay on the Strip in the distance picking up the sun's afternoon rays and shining like a nugget of gold lying around for the taking.

'Y'know, Cooper, I don't care what you think of me or the organization I work for, and your interest in my love life is beyond trivial. You just wasted half an hour of precious time on that woman, and it's time we're running out of faster than you know.'

'Then why don't you tell me what I don't know?'

'The note that came with the severed hand – as I told you, DCIS believes that was a message from Randy to us, authentication confirmed by the presence of his academy ring.'

I still wasn't sure I bought that.

'You remember the ransom note verbatim?' she asked.

'Probably not.'

'"Failing to come up with $15 million will trigger delivery of his head. You have 20 days. You will be contacted. No police." Sound right?'

I nodded.

'My agency's interpretation is that, at the time the hand was received by the addressee, Randy believed the nuclear warhead would be delivered in twenty days time. By the calculations of my superiors, we've got nine days left.'

Was my chain being yanked here? 'Couldn't it also mean that failing to come up with fifteen big ones will result in Alabama receiving Randy's head in a couple of weeks, probably in a FedEx box?'

'Look at the language, Cooper. There's more to it than just a ransom note. The words FAILING, MILLION, TRIGGER and HEAD – all capped. Why do that?'

'Because the writer's shouting?'

Petinski pursed her lips. 'Randy and I had been working on the weapons being sold out the back door of certain Air Force and Army bases for around a year – it was Randy's first case with us. Then he went undercover at NAB. DoD believed a lot of stolen weapons were leaving the country packed into aircraft, Morrow's among others. This investigation was called Operation Roy Rogers. Randy and I shortened it, named it for Roy Rogers's horse, Trigger.'

'What about the other capped words in the note? What's their significance?'

'We believe they're capped so that "trigger" wouldn't stand out if the note and the package fell into the wrong hands.'

I'd found the wording and the use of caps unusual when I'd first laid eyes on the note. And 'trigger' was an odd word to use in the context of a ransom note. *Nine days and counting* . . . 'How would the device be "delivered"?' I asked putting a couple of air bunnies around the word.

'We're expecting the worst.'

'But you've already said detonation is impossible.'

'Whether it can or can't be detonated isn't the issue. Who's the weapon going to? A missing nuke in the hands of terrorists? We're talking the ultimate loose cannon.'

'What do White and von Weiss want?'

'Yeah, well, that's the other part of the problem, Cooper – no one's got the faintest idea.'

Thirteen

The Strip drew closer, its skyline rippling in the shimmering dry heat against the brown desert hills beyond.

'What exactly are we going to do at Nellis?' I asked Petinski. 'Your service record says that you have no experience with—'

'You been snooping around in my records?'

'Cooper, people so high up they carry their oxygen around in tanks have picked over every detail of your life to clear you for this. I just got the summary.'

'Who are you again?'

'As I was about to say, we're going to Area Two, Nellis, because you have no experience whatsoever with nuclear weapons handling procedures, and you need to see how that's done to know what we're up against. We have a rendezvous with the commanding officer of the 896th Munitions Squadron, Lieutenant Colonel Dade Challis. He's going to walk us through the weapons storage area.'

'That's nice of him.'

'No, it's procedure. The only place harder to get into than a nuclear WSA is the bunker where they keep our UFOs embedded in ice.'

'They embed UFOs in ice? Why do they do that?'

Petinski ignored me.

I shrugged and tapped the Air Force base into the Garmin and the voice told me to continue on ahead for another two hundred yards, and then turn right – drive time: twenty-seven minutes. I turned the voice off. Two females in the car telling me where to go was at least one too many.

'What's the present situation at Area Two?' I asked.

'DoD has eighteen personnel working undercover there at the moment. The surveillance op is fully compartmentalized. Each agent is working on his or her own, their presence and true identity unknown to the others. They've been secreted in place in both the conventional weapons storage and nuclear weapons storage facilities over the course of normal change of stations for the past three months. As people have moved on, ours have taken their place. We've got two majors, two captains, a lieutenant and assorted enlisted personnel holding down positions in everything from security to weapons maintenance.'

'Three months? You told me the authorities have only known about the missing nuke for six weeks.'

'Suspicions that something was seriously wrong have been around longer.'

'What can you tell me about the theft of conventional weapons?' I asked.

'Probably started the way these things always start – small. A handgun first, followed by a rifle, then a case of rifles, and so on. And then when no one was caught people got organized and the money rolled in and everyone turned greedy. From what we can ascertain, this has been going on for years at a number of installations.'

'How's it being pulled off?'

'The simplistic explanation, 'cause I barely understand it myself – everything in supply has a number and a barcode so it can be tracked through the system. But the system itself has somehow been manipulated and the inventory program tampered with. The way it's supposed to work is that, on the almost unheard-of occasion when a duplicate barcode or number is picked up, a simple notification is made and a new barcode and number are issued and registered on the system. It seems, though, that the duplication notifications have been switched off. A shipping container of rifles, for example, can be removed unde-tected because they carry numbers and barcodes identical to others in inventory. When the system can't pick up the duplication, the total vol-ume of rifles appears to remain the same even though the case is no longer on the floor. The numbers and barcodes of the missing weapons were simply double-counted without any alert.'

'Two rifles were counted as one,' I said to make sure I followed her, 'so that when the duplicated rifle was taken, as far as the system was aware the total numbers in inventory hadn't changed.'

'Exactly. In reality, only a small fraction of what's in inventory has been stolen. And we have so much scattered around the world that the pilfered items are rarely missed.'

'If their serial numbers are removed, when they do surface their point of origin can't be traced.'

'You got it.'

It was a clever scheme. I took the boulevard that wound around the back of the Strip and headed north-east, out to Nellis, driving on auto-pilot, listening to my own thoughts. Only a fraction of the items might have been stolen, but I'd seen what even small numbers of them could do in a place like the Democratic Republic of Congo, and the picture was far from pretty.

'DoD is quietly running a check on stores of all US military equip-ment, everything from M1 Abrams tanks to uniforms,' Petinski continued. 'As you can understand, it's a massive job. From what I've been briefed, it looks like whoever is tampering with the system has been working up to nukes, testing their own systems, going for bigger and bigger items.'

'I was at Incirlik last year,' I said. 'They lost ten F-16 engines. I remem-ber a captain in supply going nuts about 'em simply vanishing from the system. They found 'em a day later.'

'Sounds exactly like the kind of trial run I'm talking about.'

At the time, Anna and I were investigating a number of apparent serial killings that began with the US Air Attaché to Turkey. That had been her last case. I could picture her the day we walked into the warehouse at Incirlik, hunting for leads, the folks there searching high and low for their missing engines. On that day, Anna was alive, challenging, difficult. And a week later she was dead in my arms with a hole blown in her chest.

'Something wrong?' Petinski asked, looking at me.

I shut down the memory – I was getting better at doing that. 'Nothing. You mentioned Barksdale. That episode related to this one at all?' Barksdale was one of the bases involved in a mysterious incident back in '07 when six armed W80 nuclear warheads mounted on AGM-129 Tomahawk advanced cruise missiles were discovered on a B-52 headed for the Middle East. The missiles were spotted on the aircraft's wing pylons while it was sitting out in the open, unattended by its flight crew. Aside from the fact that the plane was carrying hot nukes, it had also carried them halfway across the United States over densely populated areas, a flight that was totally illegal.

'That's part of what we're here to find out,' said Petinski.

'Were you involved in that case?' I asked her.

'No, I was still in the NTSB at the time.'

'But you're aware of the details?'

'Of course.'

'What can you tell me about the subsequent investigation?'

'The easy questions were answered. The processes and procedures that allowed the Tomahawks to leave their igloos and get mounted onto the aircraft were found to be compromised.'

'You don't buy the conspiracy theories that the White House either secretly ordered their deployment, or some highly placed general ran amok?'

'No, and neither should you. So, do you know *anything* about nuclear weapons handling, Cooper?'

'I know that dropping them's probably not a good idea.' A road sign for Nellis flashed by. Two miles to the turnoff, confirmed by the Garmin.

She sighed. 'Jesus . . . Okay, then, from the beginning. If a nuclear warhead is to be installed on a missile or other delivery system, the procedures to be followed are designated "C2".' She delivered this little speech in the tone of a mother potty-training a three year old. 'Even if the weapon has to be moved, it's signed out of its bunker under a set of security measures called "Use Control", which are designed to prevent unlawful and unauthorized access. In other words, no matter what your intentions are, there's a strict nuclear weapons handling procedure that's rigorous and inflexible. On top of which are the Nuclear Management Information Systems that track the location of every nuclear warhead – and even individual bomb components – every second of its life from cradle to grave.'

'So our nuke's vanishing act can't be explained.'

'Exactly.'

'Any theories?'

'One. We believe that the weapon's barcode and number code could have been exchanged for something else less accountable – something there's plenty of, like a Humvee. It's impossible to even conceive of this happening, but it looks like the weapon has simply been walked out on a trolley under everyone's noses. The damn thing's small enough.'

'Who could have done the walking?'

'The specific personnel who've had access and the training have all been scrutinized and cleared.'

'How're they screened to get the job in the first place?'

'A battery of psych, loyalty and background checks conducted by us – the Defense Criminal Investigative Services. Every fiber of their being is verified red, white and blue before they're allowed anywhere near a nuke. And even then, no one is permitted to be alone with a war-head. Everyone – and I mean *everyone* – works in pairs.'

I signaled and turned behind a low brown-brick wall with the sign WELCOME TO NELLIS AFB, and motored slowly to the guardhouse. I lowered the window, showed my common access card. Petinski leaned across and did the same. The DoD security guy in a dark blue shirt with black sweat stains under his arms spent around 0.6 diligent seconds examin-ing our right to enter, then waved us through.

'Where to from here?' I asked.

'Area Two is a left turn on Ellsworth. Just follow it around behind the end of the runways.'

'What are their ideal personality type indicators – our nuclear bomb handlers?' I asked.

'I'm sorry?' Petinski asked, puzzled.

'Are they INTJs, ENFPs . . . ?'

'Still not with you, Cooper.'

'One of the questions in the Myers-Briggs test was, "You often think of mankind and its destiny." Would the ideal nuclear bomb babysitter answer yes or no to a question like that?'

'I don't know why you care either way, Cooper. You answered "A" to everything, remember?'

'They said there were no wrong answers, so what I put down didn't matter.'

'They told me that too, so I answered "B" to everything.'

'Really.'

'Of course. It was a nonsense test.'

Well, well . . . Petinski thumbing her nose at stupidity *and* we had something in common. That was right up there with the most surprising thing I'd heard all day, namely that someone had wandered off with a thermonuclear device tucked under their jacket.

'Something I keep asking myself about you, Petinski,' I said, looking at her with fresh eyes.

'And what's that?'

'Can you do the splits?'

'Cooper, this stream-of-consciousness thing you do. If we're going to work together, you'll have to turn it off.'

'And you'll have to find a sense of humor.'

'What do you mean? I've got a *great* sense of humor,' she said, sliding her ID wallet into a front pocket of her jeans.

'Shall we give it a test?'

'I'm game.'

'Okay, so why did God create the female orgasm?'

Petinski pursed her lips.

'So that women can moan even while they're enjoying themselves.'

More pursing.

'I rest my case,' I said.

'What's there to laugh at? That joke's not funny. None of your jokes are funny. You want me to fake it?'

'Now you're messing with me, right?'

Petinski was focused on a point somewhere ahead. I gave an internal shrug and concentrated on the driving; not that I had to. The landscape outside was a tan-colored lifeless desert cut by shallow dry gullies, the road through it smooth, hard and straight. Speaking of the outside temperature, the display on the rental's mirror indicated that it was a hundred and seventeen degrees, and an accompanying graphic of little flames licked the bases of the numbers in case I didn't know that a hundred and seventeen degrees was hot.

A couple of miles ahead, a shape appeared like a mirage out of the shimmering heat – a guardhouse. I figured the standard luscious pool of cool water surrounded by date palms was probably somewhere behind it.

'Who are we seeing again?' I asked Petinski.

'Lieutenant Colonel Dade Challis. He's the MUNS commander.'

'How long has he had his hand on the stick?'

'Sixteen months. Standard rotation is two years.'

Which meant that he'd be moving on to a staff job somewhere in eight months time if the brass considered that he'd discharged his duties well at the 896th. Given that there was a nuke gone missing on his watch, this colonel would be lucky not to find himself cleaning out gasoline storage tanks on Diego Garcia with his tongue.

'And what's our reason for being here?' If this whole situation was on the QT, we were going to need a cover.

'We're both about to be transferred to Air Force Materiel Command, the agency that conducts nuclear surety inspections. As Nellis has a perfect NSI record, we're here to see the best of the best in action. An indoctrination tour, basically.'

The road took us around the northern ends of the side-by-side runways. A single gray B-52 sat on the ramp, its wings drooping as though exhausted by the heat.

'What's Challis like?'

'The serious type, I believe.'

I'd met plenty of light colonels in my line of work and few of them I would describe as comedic. But did I want Red Buttons sitting on a stockpile of nuclear weapons?

'Does the colonel know he's down a warhead?' I asked.

'As I told you already, for the time being this is completely compart-mentalized. I don't know what he does and doesn't know, but we have to assume the worst.'

'That he could be in on it?'

'It's possible – given that he's been here as long as he has, he's not undercover, not one of us. And Cooper, use of deadly force has been authorized around these weapons and components, so be on your best behavior.'

'So no bomb jokes?'

'Cooper, *all* your jokes bomb.'

If I wasn't mistaken, my radar had just picked up some low-flying sarcasm. I glanced over at Petinski; sure enough, the corner of her mouth suggested the hint of a smirk. Maybe there was hope for the woman after all. Looking past her, out her window, a high double fence had come out to meet us and was now running parallel to the road. It was topped with razor wire and signs hung on it every fifty yards or so warned that more of that deadly force had been authorized against unlawful entrants. We were getting close to the mother of all WMDs. I had no doubt that there would be all manner of additional security systems attached to those fences: motion and vibration sensors, laser tracking sensors, multi-spectrum cameras and so forth.

The guard shack was a little more formidable than the one waving people through at the base's main gate. I counted five men and three women, all dressed in airman battle uniforms. Two tech sergeants out-side the glass-sided building carried M16s and wore M9 Beretta side arms. Two sergeants and a senior airman walked out of a side door, also armed, and trotted to a blue Explorer parked nearby.

I lowered the window and felt a blast of hot air on the side of my face. I handed the female staff sergeant my CAC card and OSI ID. Petinski handed me her credentials as well as a sheaf of paperwork to pass across for inspection. The top two letters I caught a glimpse of bore different logos – one from the Department of Energy, and the other from Air Force Materiel Command. The sergeant flicked through the paperwork, excused herself politely, asking us to wait, and took the bundle inside. I saw her pick up the phone and dial, then lift a couple of Petinski's referral letters and give them further inspection. She nodded a couple of times, put the phone down, and started making photocopies in triplicate.

From what Petinski had told me, I gathered that only a mushroom cloud was going to get more attention from the 896th than a letter of authority from the Air Force Materiel Command.

Fourteen

The staff sergeant appeared by my window and handed back all our details. On her head was a black beret bearing the unit patch of the 99th Security Forces Squadron, a black scorpion beneath crossed rifles with bayonets fixed. I don't like scorpions.

'Can you tell us where the squadron building is?' I asked.

'I'll do better than that, Agent Cooper,' she said. 'You'll be accompanied. It's the rules.'

Two senior airmen in ABUs and packing side arms came out of a door and approached my window. One of them, a fit-looking guy by the name of Gertrude with a bullet-shaped head, said, 'Please step out of the car, sir, ma'am.'

His buddy, a skinny, long-necked guy named Fryer, wanded us down and discovered that I had metal in my belt. It was made in China, so that was definitely a surprise. Petinski was clean. They then went over our vehicle, inspecting it inside and out.

'Find anything?'

Gertrude held up a quarter.

'Don't spend it all at once,' I told him.

He pressed it into my hand. 'Ready when you are, sir.'

Petinski and I got back in the car, the airmen taking the rear seats.

'Where are you going, sir?' asked Fryer.

'The commander's office,' Petinski answered.

'Well, keep on this road till you see three buildings arranged in a semicircle around a garden,' he said.

I motored slowly away, bringing the window up to keep the sauna out.

The garden turned out to be a clump of cacti with a few rocks, the buildings a little less inspiring than the landscaping. I parked us in the lot, an eighty-yard hike to the front door. As Petinski and I approached it with our armed escort, sweat beading at my hairline, the door to the building snapped open letting out a blast of cold air. It was held open by a senior master sergeant, 'Burton' on his nametag.

'Have a nice day, sir, ma'am,' said Gertrude as he handed us off to the sergeant.

'Senior Master Sergeant Burton, Squadron Superintendent,' said Sergeant Burton. 'Welcome to Area Two.'

The guy was sharply dressed in an airman battle uniform, the pixel pattern catching a sheen that suggested it had been heavily steam-ironed every day of its life. We walked through a foyer past framed photos of various aircraft, airborne and on the ground, armed with air-launched cruise missiles on pods under their wings. Among them was an illustrated unit patch of the 896th MUNS, a red-tipped missile hanging over the globe, beneath it the squadron's motto, 'Nothing less than perfection.' The red tip indicated that the missile carried a live nuke.

The sergeant led the way up two flights of stairs to the command section on the second floor populated by administrative personnel. The hallway ended in a set of glass double doors. Gold lettering on one of them read: 896TH MUNITIONS SQUADRON, and below that, LT. COL. DADE CHALLIS, COMMANDER. One of the doors was ajar, the colonel sitting behind his desk, tapping on a keyboard. He glanced up when he heard the knock, took the glasses off his nose and stood. He was a little over forty, six five and under a hundred and ninety pounds, with a lean face speckled with strawberry freckles which also dotted his thin lips. He looked the nervous type, deep lines across his high forehead. The guy's coloring was, in fact, Red Buttons, but any similarity with the comic appeared to end there.

'Thanks, Dan,' he said to Sergeant Burton, who was standing beside us in parade rest mode. 'Please,' he said, waving us in. 'Good to meet you, Investigator Petinski?' He glanced at me, then my partner, not sure who was who.

'Petinski, sir,' my colleague said, putting him straight, holding out her child-sized hand.

The colonel shook it and moved on to mine. 'The briefing room set up?' he asked the sergeant waiting at the door.

'Yes, sir.'

'Excellent.' All business, to Petinski and me he said, 'Care to follow me, please?' Picking up his hat and walking out, there was no question that we wouldn't.

The briefing room was a large office down the hallway. A young captain at the foot of a rectangular brown Laminex table snapped to attention when the colonel entered the room, and moved to a podium beside a screen built into the wall. The screen announced: *896th Munitions Squadron – Mission Briefing*, and in the lower right corner, *Capt. Reece Jones, 896 MUNS/CCE*.

The colonel assumed his seat at the head of the table. Petinski and I sat either side. Challis introduced the briefer without fanfare. 'My exec, Captain Jones. Let's get started, Reece.'

Jones followed orders. 'Ma'am, gentlemen,' he began, 'the following briefing is unclassified.'

A new slide flicked into place, a shot of the administration building that we were in. I already knew what it looked like and the photo didn't do it any favors.

'The mission of the 896th Munitions Squadron is to administer and manage one of the largest Air Force weapons stockpiles in the free world,' the captain continued. 'The area consists of seven hundred and sixty-five acres, seventy-five specialized munitions storage igloos, fifteen maintenance and support facilities, twenty-six miles of roadways and forty-four vehicles of various types. The unit stores, maintains, modifies and ships Priority A weapons and associated components.'

When the captain was still going thirty minutes later, I decided PowerPoint had reached WMD status.

Jones eventually finished up with, 'That concludes my briefing. Anyone have questions?'

I was prepared to shoot anyone who did.

Challis glanced at us. 'Thanks, Reece,' he said when he drew a blank, and stood. Petinski and I did likewise. 'Before we go and have a look around, there are some more details to take care off.' Sergeant Burton materialized out of thin air beside him. 'Dan, take our visitors next door to Security, get them legal for our purposes.' He handed the sergeant our documents. 'I'll be in my office when you're ready.'

Half an hour later, red 'Escort Required' badges dangling from our necks, Petinski and I were returned to the commander's office. Challis picked up his cap without preamble and headed for the door. 'We have a standard tour,' he said. 'But anything in particular you'd like to know?'

I was about to say something extremely clever related to missing nukes, like how difficult would it be to steal one, but decided against it. We both fell in behind the colonel as he fitted his cap onto his head, his bandy legs flapping around inside his ABUs as he strode down the corridor. 'In Area Two,' he began, 'we currently have eight hundred and fifteen gravity bombs of varying yields, mostly B61 warheads from our former bases in Europe, the ones we no longer occupy. We also supervise five hundred and eighty-four W80 warheads removed from deactivated air-launched cruise missiles. We maintain all these warheads so that they continue to remain as good as new. If the president needs a nuke or two, we've got 'em here, ready to spread the Stars and Stripes in ground or air-burst mode at a moment's notice.' The colonel pushed through the doors and strode into the bright Nevada blast furnace. 'Let's pick up our escort and get this show on the road.'

'Where are the igloos, sir?' I asked.

'Back behind the building, dug into the flint. Area Two is in fact the largest above-ground nuclear weapons storage facility in the world. Mind if we take my vehicle?' he asked, walking up to a white Lexus SUV. 'We could walk. Ain't far, but it's a mite warm.'

'No problem,' said Petinski. I didn't have one either.

The vehicle unlocked with a flash of its lights and Petinski opened the rear passenger door. I took the front and buckled up.

'So you're giving up police work for AFMC?' Challis asked me. 'We're a unit of theirs, y'know.'

'I didn't know, sir. At least, not before the briefing,' I said.

The colonel took a pair of reflective sunglasses hooked into the vehicle's sun visor and put them on. 'Mister, I'm sure that, like *I* do, you'll find it's a privilege to be working with our country's nuclear stockpile, keeping Uncle Sam's *cojones* primed and ready for action.' The colonel was looking forward over the top of the steering wheel, deadly serious, Petinski-like.

'Yes, sir,' I said. 'What about the maintenance on those *cojones*? Where does that happen?'

'Rest easy, Mr Cooper. The full tour is coming your way.'

The colonel turned into the driveway of a building with the words SECURITY FORCES painted in white lettering on a corner of the facility facing the road. We'd driven maybe a hundred and twenty yards from command HQ.

'This is us,' the commander said, killing the motor and removing his shades. He got out of the car, strode to the solid brown-painted door, and held it open for us. I followed Petinski inside. The immediate area was a small foyer with more framed photos – these ones showing multiple nuclear re-entry vehicles leaving trails of smoke as they burned through the atmosphere, heading for targets. A little scary. Beyond the foyer was a large open-plan office populated by men and women wearing ABUs, Berettas slung low on their thighs. A staff sergeant came to meet us, a black man the size of a plains buffalo, 'Sailor' on his nametag.

'Sir, ma'am, Airman Nagel and I will be your close escorts today,' Sailor informed us. He turned to the colonel. 'Will you vouch for the visitors, sir?'

'I will,' the colonel intoned officially.

The sergeant then asked for our IDs, which we gave him. He went back inside the office, made multiple Xerox copies of our details, then returned to his desk and made a phone call while examining our credentials. He seemed to be having a friendly chat with someone on the other end.

'How long will this take, sir?' I asked the colonel. It was well after three in the afternoon and we were still shuffling paper.

'As long as it takes. Security is the first and last thing we do here, Mr Cooper. Visitors are rare and never casual. *All* visits follow a strict routine. That's the way we roll here and the sergeant's just doing his job.'

A short, round, blonde female senior airman by the name of Nagel came toward us, a box the size and shape of a portable credit terminal in her hand. 'Can I have your forefinger, sir?' she asked me. 'Place it inside the opening, here.' She held the box toward me. There was indeed a hole in the front with the instruction *Place finger here* on a decal. I did as I was told and the senior airman nodded when the screen on top of the box lit up green with a tick and the word *Confirmed*.

The senior airman went through the same procedure with Petinski, thanked us, and went back to the open-plan section, plugged the unit into her desktop and settled down behind her screen.

'DNA check,' Challis explained. 'That's a scanner that reads the DNA in your perspiration and matches it against the DNA profile in your records. Fingerprints, even retinal scans, can be altered, but not your DNA codes.'

Sergeant Sailor returned with our red 'Escort Required' cards dangling from lanyards. 'Congratulations, sir, ma'am,' he told us. 'You are who you say you are. You must wear your badges clearly displayed here at all times. Without it, you will be detained, forcibly if necessary. Do not fail to comply with any order or instruction from your escort or security forces personnel or you will be detained, forcibly if necessary.'

I was starting to get the general idea, and put the lanyard back over my head. My card was identical to Petinski's, except for barcode numbers printed on a sticky label affixed to it.

'You have to swipe that everywhere you go here, Mr Cooper,' said Challis, 'so we can track your journey for future reference. Shall we do this, Sergeant?'

'Yes, sir,' said Sailor. Nagel came out to join us, planting a patrol cap on her head.

'What are you most interested in seeing?' asked the colonel.

'The storage igloos, sir,' Petinski said.

'You're in luck. That's our first stop.'

A couple of minutes later we were back in the SUV, the colonel reaching for his gun bull shades. An Explorer bobbed into the wing mirror, Sailor and Nagel on hand to apply some deadly force if we stepped out of line, or maybe told a bad joke. Half a mile later we stopped at another guard shack and had our passes checked – the colonel included – by more armed security personnel. Either side of the shack was a triple razor-wire fence, the space between each fence being a minefield, according to another sign, death guaranteed if a foot was put wrong. Driving deeper into this silent, ultra-secure area it was as if even sound was forbidden.

We motored slowly past a concrete bunker dug into the desert, a heavy brown steel door facing the access road, 'A 1001-12-2-24' painted on the door in large white lettering.

'A-structures are storage igloos,' the colonel said, before Petinski or I could ask. 'This is igloo number one. It has twelve vaults, two warheads per vault for a total of twenty-four. In this case the weapons are B61 3/4/10 gravity thermonuclear devices, each being 141.6 inches long, 13.3 inches in diameter and weighing approximately seven hundred and fifty pounds. Every weapon has a unique number that is tracked individually by our people in Munitions Control twenty-four-seven.'

'How many igloos?' I asked having forgotten the number he'd given us earlier.

'We had seventy-five, recently increased to ninety-two. Some of the larger ones have more than twenty vaults.'

'Can we inspect one?'

'There's nothing to see. Plus, those igloos maintain negative air pressure to keep out the dust, which is a problem, so we don't open them up unless we have to. But there are three W80s in for maintenance. You'll see that procedure presently. It's in the tour.'

'Who takes responsibility for weapons surety when a physics package is being maintained?' I asked.

'The buck stops with me, Mr Cooper,' said Challis. 'But daily briefings are held so that everyone is aware of the weapons coming and going. It's the munitions control room's responsibility to know where each weapon is every second of every minute of every day. No excuses.'

The colonel continued driving down the access road for another half a mile, past three more igloos, a couple of which were set back from the road and much bigger than igloo #A 1001. He then turned left and left again shortly after, so that we were headed back roughly in the direction of the HQ. The igloos on this return road were smaller and there were far more of them.

'The W80s are stored here,' said Challis. 'They're more compact than B61s; about the size and shape of one of those bulk milk cans folks in the country sometimes use as mailboxes. A few of these milk cans strategically placed and set to a variable yield of a hundred and fifty kilotons and you could probably blow California into the Pacific.'

The colonel looked at me, unsmiling. My nose was very big in those reflective sunglasses lenses. I didn't like it, almost as much as I didn't like that I couldn't tell what he was thinking behind them. We turned right and cruised by a parking area full of weapons trolleys, and then past another partially vacant lot where containers were stacked in neat rows. I glanced behind us. The Explorer with the extra security was bringing up the rear.

Shortly after another right-hand turn, which brought us back onto the road we drove in on, the colonel pulled into an area dominated by three low concrete bunkers and parked beside a collection of Air Force vehicles.

'This is a C-structure,' said Challis. 'Maintenance. Like the igloos, these structures are hardened. Their walls are twelve feet thick, and reinforced with reactive armor plating. They're secure against all comers, except perhaps a direct hit from a bunker buster with a megaton yield.'

'How about from someone with a front-door key, sir?' I said.

'Unlikely, Mr Cooper.'

We got out of the Lexus, Sailor and Nagel joining us. Challis led the way to the door, which was a solid heavy steel number with no handles, windows, visible hinges or even keyholes. The colonel punched a code into a keypad recessed into the concrete, swiped a card, then stood back to be examined by an array of surveillance cameras. A green light appeared over one of the cameras and the colonel punched in another code.

'Entry to this facility is managed not by the people inside it but by Munitions Control, which is in another part of the facility entirely. Swipe your cards, please.'

Petinski and I stepped forward and swiped, followed by Sailor and Nagel.

A red light above the door illuminated and began to revolve. A pneumatic hiss followed and the massively thick door, which resembled something from a bank vault, opened. The colonel motioned at Petinski and me to go inside. I followed the investigator into a chamber occupied by two armed senior airmen from 99th Security Forces Squadron, their hands resting on their side arms, which were slightly bigger pistols than the standard issue Beretta M9. Hard to see for sure, but they looked like old-school Colt .45s – my preferred handgun – and still in inventory for when you shot folks you wanted to stay shot.

'Good afternoon,' said the colonel.

'Afternoon, sir,' both airmen replied.

One of them stepped forward, tall and black, name of Arthurs according to his tag. 'Please remove the contents of all your pockets,' he said to Petinski and me. 'Remove any belts, jewelry, watches and so forth and place all of it in the trays provided. Also, remove your shoes and keep hold of them.'

The colonel didn't need to be told this and was already turning out his pockets and taking off his wristwatch. Sailor and Nagel withdrew a little to the wall behind us and rested their hands on their weapons – overwatch, in case I stepped out of line and maybe told the one about the chicken that crossed the road.

Arthurs's senior airman buddy, a young white guy with pallid sunken cheeks, wanded Petinski and got no reaction from the device. He gestured her to one side and gave me the treatment. No reaction. The colonel was up next and the wand picked up a paperclip in his breast pocket.

'Apologies,' he said, dropping it in a tray.

'Happens to the best of us, sir,' said Arthurs, straight-faced.

More code entering, card swiping and red flashing lights and another heavy door opened into a large garage-style area occupied by various machinery I couldn't identify on benchtops, a bomb trolley, and several large black Kevlar containers side by side on the concrete floor. Overhead was a medium-weight gantry crane. This could have been a machine shop for a high-end engineering firm.

The colonel led the way to a steel wall in which there was a line of slots at head height. 'Take a look,' he told us.

Petinski and I took a slot each. Through thick green-tinged glass I could see four people dressed in heavy coveralls working on what reminded me of that bulk milk can the colonel mentioned. It was secured on its side on a rig. The access hatch of the can had been removed, and one of the figures in coveralls reached inside the opening and extracted a sealed black box assembly attached to a wiring harness. The walls and ceiling of the room held more security cameras than the gaming pit at Caesars.

'What are they doing, sir?' asked Petinski.

'These W80s are part of a block which have already been refurbished. The technicians are checking that the weapons meet mandated standards upon receipt from the depot. From memory, the components to be verified on this particular warhead will be its signal generator and gas transfer system.'

'Right,' I said knowingly, only in truth I now had some sympathy for the woman I'd heard had been told by a motor mechanic that the halogen fluid in her headlights needed topping up. I went back to the nuke porn going on in my peep slot. The W80 really was small, maybe thirty inches in length with a diameter of around twelve inches. Yeah, a country mailbox-sized bulk milk can.

'How much does it weigh?' I asked the colonel.

'Two hundred and ninety pounds. It's a two-stage radiation implosion thermonuclear weapon. The bomb you see there was once loaded into a BGM-109 Tomahawk air-launched cruise missile. It would've been carried by a Buff.'

A Buff – short for big ugly fat fucker – was the Boeing B-52 Stratofortress bomber, the backbone of our nuclear detterence since its introduction to service in 1955 and still on the frontlines of freedom. The aircraft had all the beauty of a bull shark in a plastic wading pool.

'The Buff on the ramp got anything to do with Area Two?' I asked.

'No, there are Red Flag exercises starting here in a couple of days time. I'd say it has something to do with that,' said Challis.

'Presumably, sir, B-52s have crashed while carrying nuclear weapons over the years?' my partner asked.

'There have been plenty of B-52 incidents, but none involving the W80.'

'What about accidental detonation?' I asked.

'It's never happened. The W80 is as stable as they come. Loaded onto Tomahawks, unless you have the launch and release codes – that's four sets of codes changed on a daily basis, entered simultaneously by two different people into the launch console, which is only attached moments before launch – nothing will happen.'

'What about the high explosives that crush the plutonium core and detonate the bomb? Couldn't a fire set them off? Could one of those bombs be loaded, say, into an aircraft and used 9/11-style?'

'Hmm, imaginative, Mr Cooper,' said Challis. 'But the scenario you suggest wouldn't – *couldn't* – work. Let me give you a bit of background . . . The W80 is a Teller–Ulam design, named for Edward Teller and Stanislaw Ulam, who developed it for the United States back in '51. They created an infallible, elegant design where high-explosive lenses merely initiate the chain reaction in a first stage, which is itself really just the primer for the secondary stage. More specifically, the high-explosive lenses detonate and compress a core comprised of uranium-238, tritium gas and a hollow sphere of plutonium and uranium-235, so that a fission reaction results. It's this fission reaction that triggers the fusion reaction in the second stage – basically a plutonium sparkplug encased in lithium-6 deuteride and uranium-238 – by a process called radiation implosion.'

There was that word – trigger. I wondered whether I should be taking notes and whether I could ask him to start again at 'Hmm, imaginative . . .'

'In other words, the W80 is probably the safest bomb in our arsenal,' he continued. 'Getting back to those lenses around the first-stage core. They utilize IHE, or insensitive high explosives, which are highly resistant to cooking off in a fire, or detonation due to mechanical shock. They'll melt or burn before they explode. Only one person on earth can cause launch and detonation of that weapon, and that's the President of the United States.'

Ten minutes later, we were back in the colonel's SUV being tailed by Sailor and Nagel. And not long after that, after more code entering, card swiping and wanding, we were standing in another hardened bunker, Munitions Control – the 'nerve center', according to Challis – looking at enlisted folk at consoles quietly watching technicians maintaining weapons, or viewing the interiors of empty igloos where, as the colonel had correctly said, there was nothing to see. The order of the day seemed to be everyone watching everyone else, even though both the watchers and the watched had been especially verified loyal to the core.

After the quiet vigilance of Munitions Control, Colonel Challis drove Petinski and me back to the HQ building, wished us the best of luck in our new roles at Air Force Materiel Command, and turned us over to Jones for out-processing. After signing documents swearing never to reveal anything to anyone, anywhere, under any circumstances, unless we wanted to be sat on by the full weight of the Uniform Code of

Military Justice, our red badges were collected and Jones turned us over to Sergeant Burton, who escorted us in silence to our rental with Sailor and Nagel in tow.

Burton motioned Sailor into the back of our vehicle, and bid us good day. He then nodded at Nagel, and she tailed us back to the guard shack. After another search of our persons and the vehicle, which had been sitting outside the MUNS building all this time, we were free to leave, and a technical sergeant armed with an M4 carbine waved us through the shack and out into the main base area.

Leaving Area Two, I felt like I'd just come from a high-security prison where the world's most dangerous criminals had been doped to the eyeballs but could at any moment break through their torpor and erupt into unspeakable and unstoppable violence.

I shivered involuntarily even though the AC had yet to bring the car's interior temperature much below broil. 'Too early for a drink?' I asked Petinski.

'That was probably the creepiest experience of my life,' she said. 'The hair is still up on the back of my neck.'

'At least we know who our prime suspect is,' I said.

'Challis?' she asked.

'No, the President of the United States.'

*

'There's this little bar I know,' I said after driving a few moments in silence.

'If you mean Olds Bar, I don't think it's a good idea.' Petinski massaged the back of her neck. 'We need somewhere we can talk.'

The bar at Nellis was named for Robin Olds, a triple ace with sixteen kills collected during World War II and the Vietnam War. If the Air Force fighter jocks had a Mecca, Olds Bar was probably it. The place also had two other things going for it: they poured single malt there, and it was closer than any other bar. But maybe she was right – privacy was paramount. 'I know another place.'

'Is it a place we can talk?'

'As long as it doesn't get in the way.'

'Of what?'

'Of drinking.'

'You're in the driver's seat, Cooper.' Petinski rolled her head from side to side and repositioned the AC vent on her face.

This Area Two tour was all about making me realize fast that we were dealing with a conspiracy. The theft couldn't have been the work of a lone nutbag. It was a long-term operation that must have involved – among others – bomb handlers, maintenance personnel, munitions controllers, base security, squadron HQ, and people who could recode military grade software. We'd been cored from the inside out, not unlike the way termites work their way through a house. They leave it looking sturdy enough until you walk in one day, carrying a couple of cases of beer, and suddenly you're through the floorboards.

'Our problem is,' Petinski continued, 'given all the checks, procedures and security, what's happened is impossible.'

'Maybe believing it's impossible is what made it possible,' I said, thinking on the run.

'You care to explain that?'

I was afraid she'd say that. 'Well, it has to start with the loyalty tests. Those will definitely have right and wrong answers.' Actually, the more I thought about this, the more I thought I might have stumbled onto something.

'So?'

'You don't think candidates could be schooled to score high?'

'It's not just the tests. What about their family, next of kin, former employers? The background checks run deep.'

'When there are millions of dollars at stake, arrangements can't be made? Nothing's impossible, especially if the stakes are worth it.'

Petinski let the cool air continue to work on her face and neck. Eventually she said, 'If you're right and people have been schooled, it's possible that consistencies in test answers might flag potential conspirators . . . I'll pass it on.'

Did I just get a pat on the head?

Security at the main gate ignored us, checking only what came in. I turned onto East Craig Road and picked up the signs to the Las Vegas freeway.

'Oh, I forgot to mention we're on a red-eye at ten o'clock tonight,' Petinski said.

'Where are we going?' *By the calculations of my superiors, we've got nine days left.* Now that I had some idea of what was to be delivered and triggered, nine days didn't seem like a whole lot of time.

'Rio. Benicio von Weiss is under a watch order.'

'Who's doing the watching?'

'Local authorities, CIA and MI6.'

'The Brits? He steal a nuke from them, too?'

'No, they want him for passport violations.'

I snorted. 'The guy forget to collect a stamp?'

Petinski shrugged. 'Al Capone went down for tax evasion.'

'Hitting von Weiss with passport violations is like putting Jeffrey Dahmer away for unpaid parking fines. Here's a suggestion, why don't we just send in the Marines if we know where he is?'

'Brazil's not our country.'

'It's not?'

'O Magnifico is a cool customer. We'll get nothing—'

'O Magnifico?'

'That's what von Weiss's people call him.'

'Sounds like a circus trapeze artist.'

'As I was saying, Cooper, we'll get nothing from von Weiss. He's been in the weapons business a long time and he knows all the tricks. I want to concentrate on locating Randy. Find him and we'll get some solid clues about where the weapon is, and perhaps its intended use. Once we get a sniff of the W80 we can decide what to do with von Weiss.'

'We don't have a lot of time left. Why waste it hunting for someone who might be dead?'

'Randy's alive.'

'Despite what I said to Alabama, we don't know that – not for certain.'

'The profile on von Weiss tells us that if he killed someone he believed was a US government agent, he'd find a way to brag about it. In short, we think we'd know by now if Randy was dead.'

I wasn't so sure about Petinski's plan. Calling in the 82nd Airborne to secure the suspect so that we could ask him about the warhead with an M4's flash suppressor occupying one of his nostrils seemed the option more likely to yield positive results quickly.

I drove us back to the Strip and told Petinski about Shadow Bar. She wanted to pack and said she'd meet me there in forty minutes.

*

Petinski walked in twenty minutes late, by which time I was on my third Maker's Mark with rocks. It was early, barely seven. The evening crowd was still at least thirty minutes away. The dancing shadows, dressed in small tank tops and pleated ultra minis, were doing their best to mesmerize and by the second Maker's they were succeeding with me.

'Why am I not surprised?' said Petinski, appearing suddenly with a glass of Coke in her hand, looking around, checking the place out.

'I know another bar called the Green Room if you'd rather,' I told her.

'We don't have time.'

'Which reminds me, you're late.'

'I got a call from my boss.' She took the seat opposite while I crunched an ice cube. 'Stu Forrest was just an alias.'

'Forrest.' My brain was splashing around in a bath of bourbon. The name was familiar but I was having trouble recalling who he was.

'He did the fuel planning on Randy's flight. The guy who took off for Mexico just before we turned up at NAB . . .'

Oh, yeah.

'His real name was Ed Dyson – that's *Lieutenant* Ed Dyson. He was a Navy meteorologist with a masters in high-altitude wind modeling. He left the service a little over a year ago, discharged on medical grounds, and went straight to work with Morrow at NAB.'

'So he's a weatherman?' I smirked, picturing a chubby guy on daytime TV moving cardboard clouds around a map.

'Do you know anything about wind, Cooper?'

183

'I get plenty eating onions.'

'I'm serious.'

'It's no laughing matter, trust me.'

'Cooper . . .'

I sighed. 'Okay, you got me. Tell me what you think I should know.' Being serious, all I knew about wind was that it often blew onshore near the coast – something to do with the land heating up faster than the water. But I had a feeling my beachside experience was about as relevant to Petinski as my relationship with onions.

'It's important to know that when a physics package detonates, it generates clouds of lethal radioactive dust that get spread high and wide. Weather prediction – especially the movement of high-altitude winds – is probably the single most important planning aspect that goes into a nuclear strike.'

I put my drink down on the table. 'Why's it taken Defense Intelligence this long to ascertain the guy's identity?'

'Too many threats, too many budget cuts, too few assets. Don't tell me you don't know what I'm talking about.' Petinski had me there. 'Dyson also used a false social security card and passport,' she continued. 'And he was operating on the edges of our surveillance. If anyone was going to catch him out it would've been Randy, but perhaps he wasn't on the ground long enough to identify him.'

'Or maybe Randy got too close to Dyson, asked too many questions. Dyson contacted von Weiss, who was suspicious anyway, and Randy's next long-distance flight runs out of gas.'

That gave Petinski something to think about.

'And DCIS thinks Dyson flew south to link up with this Benicio von Weiss,' I said.

'That's the conclusion.'

Rio. I'd never been there, though a buddy of mine, after seeing the city's famous Carnival, said the place was like a twelve-mile erogenous zone. Maybe there was a silver lining to this nuclear cloud yet.

Fifteen

When we arrived at our hotel on the beach at Ipanema, Rio de Janeiro, I told the cab driver to keep driving. I liked the setting just fine, but the hotel was old and narrow, and according to a sign out front it had great dormitory-style accommodation.

'What are we doing?' Petinski asked, turning to look out the back window.

'Are you a backpacker?'

'No. Why?'

'Me neither.'

'Where are we going?'

'Don't know yet.' I leaned forward to have a word with the driver. 'You speak English, buddy?' I asked him. A grunt suggested he might. 'What's the most expensive hotel you got round here?'

'Copacabana Palace,' he said over his shoulder. 'You want to go there?'

I told him yes.

'It'll come out of your expenses, not mine,' Petinski warned as the driver hit the brakes, swerved and accelerated down a side street. I figured that if a nuclear bomb was set off somewhere, our hotel bill would be the least of anyone's concerns. And if we managed to prevent it, same

185

outcome. For once I was going first-class. 'If you're worried about it, we can share a room,' I told her.

'In your dreams.'

The Copacabana Palace on Copacabana Beach was all scallops, arches and French windows painted a pinkish shade of white. A plastic bride and groom perched on the roof wouldn't have been out of place. A Rolls-Royce was parked in the forecourt between a Lamborghini and a stretch Hummer. Petinski gazed up at the hotel out her window as the cab driver waited for a break in the traffic to turn into the forecourt.

'I can already see the zeros on the minibar prices,' I said. 'We should check in as an engaged couple.'

'And why's that?'

'Might give us options down the track – cover, and so forth.'

She gave me a look that said if I had an ulterior motive, I should get it out of my head.

I answered with a look that said, 'Who, me?'

The cab driver swung us into a gap that opened up in the oncoming traffic and planted us in the hotel's forecourt with a squeal of brakes. I paid the fare and two guys in their mid-twenties wearing crisp gray suits and flat, round pillbox hats arrived and held our doors open.

'You have baggage, sir?' asked the guy holding my door.

I could've mentioned my ex-wife but I said, 'In the trunk.'

Petinski and I got out. It was hot, different from the Vegas kind of heat. This was the wet, steamy variety, exhaled as if from nearby jungle. We followed our luggage to reception where we were met by chandeliers, vases painted into the recesses on the walls, smooth tiled floors and three South American glamour types working the counter.

'Good morning, sir,' said a tall dark-skinned woman with thick black hair, bright red lips and an exotic accent. 'Can I help you?'

'We're checking in.'

Petinski gave her a brief smile then melted into the background.

'Certainly. Name?'

'Cooper. Vincent Cooper.' I put my Visa card on the counter with a snap and her fingers went to work on a keyboard. Concern almost immediately began to trouble her unlined forehead. 'Um . . . did I mention that we don't have a reservation?' I confessed, confirming her fear.

'Oh, I'm not sure we have a room vacant, sir. We are fully booked.'

I noticed that on her finger was a gleaming engagement ring yet to be dulled by disappointment. The badge on her firm bosom told me her name was Gracia.

I dropped my voice. 'Look, Gracia, if you can help me out, I'd really appreciate it. I was hoping to ask my girlfriend here to marry me.' I gestured with an eye movement at Petinski, who was wandering around examining the wall art. 'But then her purse got snatched at the airport and our romantic getaway is turning into a nightmare. I need a little help to get the job done. Just a couple of nights. Really, whatever you've got . . .'

The frown intensified, but movement at the corner of her lips told me that I might possibly have mined some empathy. Her fingers worked the keyboard harder and she exchanged a few quick words with the woman beside her. After this discussion she returned to me, looking a little pained. 'I am sorry, we have only one room available, but the TV, it is not working . . .'

'Oh, that's okay.' I leaned across the counter and, with a vaguely conspiratorial smile, said, 'I was hoping we wouldn't be watching too much TV . . .'

Gracia returned the smile with one of her own, a cheeky curl on one side of her red lips. 'With taxes, the room is thirteen hundred dollars US per night. But perhaps I can give you a small discount because it has no TV. Is one thousand one hundred dollars okay?'

Eleven hundred bucks times two nights, maybe more. Arlen would pop his cork. 'Great,' I told her. 'We'll take it.' I filled in the forms and left an imprint of my Visa.

'*Boa sorte* – good luck,' Gracia said with a wink, handing me two plastic card keys.

Petinski and I followed a short hairy guy in a pillbox hat up to our room on the fifth floor, a generous space done up like an English cottage with printed curtains, framed paintings of birds and plants, polished wood and gold taps. It was the kind of place where the other half lived, the half with money. The guy gave us a quick tour, which concluded with a set of double doors opening onto a balcony overlooking the pool and restaurant in the courtyard. I tipped our guide and he left, closing the door quietly behind him.

'This looks expensive,' said Petinski, hands on hips.

'I got a discount.'

'Half price is still going to blow my budget.' Petinski gazed around the room. 'The bed's mine. Couch is yours.'

'Better than the doghouse.'

'Don't push your luck, Cooper. And what did you tell the woman on the front desk? Why was she smiling at me?'

'I told her that, as I was about to ask you to marry me, they should just leave a stack of clean sheets at our door.'

'Jesus, Cooper . . .'

'It's called thinking on your feet, Petinski. Let's move on. Speaking of which, what's our next move, workwise?'

'We've got a meeting.'

Shortly thereafter we were walking out through the hotel lobby. I glanced at the reception desk and my confidante there gave me a wave. I put my arm around Petinski's shoulder.

'What are you doing?' Petinski asked with a hiss.

'Playing the part. We've got an audience,' I told her.

'You *got* the room, Cooper. Don't think you're getting anything else.' Petinski shrugged off my arm the instant we walked through the door into the afternoon sunshine. After letting a number of cabs pass, she waved one down and gave the driver an address read off her iPhone. The driver took us through a long tunnel cut through solid rock, into another part of the city. Checking out the surroundings, I caught a glimpse of the famous statue of Christ up on one of the many hills overlooking the city. From this angle, the way his arms were out-stretched reminded me of Petinski's description of Josef Mengele with his arms out wide like an angel with its wings open, saying, 'Death to the left, life to the right . . .'

*

The shopfront said we were in a place specializing in tailor-made suits, an assertion confirmed inside by several well-dressed gents with a combined age of around a thousand years, slicked-back silver hair, pencil moustaches, and measuring tapes around their necks. But then one of them scanned a barcode off Petinski's iPhone, led us to a clothing rack in a back room and parted the half-made suits hanging on it, and a panel opened to reveal an elevator. We thanked the old guy and stepped in, and a few jolts later the doors opened on a trim black woman framed by an über-cool reception area of stainless steel, glass and chocolate wood, a large seal of the CIA on the frosted glass wall behind her. 'Mr Delaney is expecting you,' she said in an internationalized American accent I couldn't place. 'Please follow me.'

I was happy to oblige, a large part of the reason being her ass, a round and firm ass that moved beneath her loose black skirt like any second it was gonna break into a samba. We arrived at a plain woodgrain door with no name or title on it. Behind it was a small room with a simple black Formica table, bottles of water clustered in its center. A political map of the world hung on one wall, while the other three were bare.

'Take a seat, please,' said the woman. 'Mr Delaney will be with you in a minute.' She and her ass turned and left.

Pretty much exactly a minute later, Delaney strolled in – a guy of average height and weight, medium brown hair, small brown eyes, no distinguishing marks or features, wearing Levi's and a white shirt. He was so average even his own kids might have had trouble picking him out of a line-up.

'Jeb Delaney,' he said with a Jonny Hayseed drawl. 'Assistant Deputy Director.'

Hmm. The assistant to the assistant. We'd been sent straight to the middle. He shook our hands and sat at the head of the table.

'This place is a surprise,' said Petinski, small talking. 'Beneath a tailor's. Who'd have thought?'

'Yeah,' said Delaney, 'except that everyone in the Brazilian, Brit, Ruskie, Frog and Chink secret services have their shirts made by the boys topside, so I think the word's probably out about what's in the basement. Still, we're centrally located and it beats the crap outta workin' from the attaché's office in the embassy up in Brasilia.' He smiled. 'Rio's a bunch more fun than the capital in every way that counts.'

I had a sense that maybe ol' Jeb here wasn't talking entirely about the spy business. Petinski smiled back and flicked me a who-is-this-guy? glance. 'Thanks for taking the time to see us, sir,' she said.

'The pleasure's all mine,' Delaney replied. 'Fact is, ya'll been given the highest clearance I ever seen for non-Company folk, endorsed by Langley *and* DoD. Makes me inquisitive what this is all about, but, 'course, that ain't allowed.'

Petinski gave him another smile.

'Bottom line,' he continued, 'we've been ordered to provide you every assistance. You need anythin', just let me know. We have a line into the local PD as well as Brazil's security agency. And we drink with the folks over at MI6.' He took two cards from his shirt pocket and gave one to each of us, nothing on it except a cell number. 'When ya'll get a pickup, the codeword is "Landlock". Forget t' say it, ya'll get dial tone and the number'll be useless thereafter.'

'Got it,' said Petinski.

'Online coms can be routed to us through your agency in Washington.'

Something about Jeb's focused manner once the intros were done suggested the squeal-like-a-pig hillbilly shit he was going on with was an act. I hoped so. I wasn't a fan of the Company, but I had a feeling we were going to be relying on it pretty heavily here.

'Anythin' you need right off the bat?' he asked.

'We're interested in Benicio von Weiss,' said Petinski.

Jeb allowed himself a smirk that vanished almost as soon as it formed. 'Vee Dubyah, eh. Who ain't? We got more assets on that fella than flies on a corpse.'

'You've got a tail on him?'

'I hope so – yeah.'

'What's the Company's interest in him?'

'Whatever our Langley masters tell us to be interested in. But aside from that, Vee Dubyah's also rich, influential and bent like a mountain road. Actually, *I'm* interested in why *you're* interested in him. I'll be honest with you, I don't like it, but your clearance entitles y'all to a big chunk of our latest intel, assuming you want it.'

'We'll take whatever you can give us, sir,' said Petinski.

'You've just arrived, right? How ya'll gettin' around?'

'Cabs.'

'A tip: make sure those cabs are random. Don't pick one out of a rank.'

'Good advice, sir.'

Duh, I thought.

'I take it ya'll came here first. So what's next?'

'Get our bearings. Perhaps take a look at von Weiss's main registered address.'

Jeb looked at me. 'Ya'll don't say much, do you?'

'Looks like they make a nice suit upstairs,' I offered.

*

'What's with you, Cooper?' Petinski snapped as we watched the traffic zip by, waiting for a cab to appear. 'You were pretty damn rude back there.'

'I didn't say anything,' I replied.

'Exactly.'

'Look, Petinski, like it or not – and I don't – someone's decided I'm your trophy partner. As far as I can figure out I'm being paid to accompany you and look pretty.'

'Don't flatter yourself.'

'Do you know how many residences von Weiss has?' I asked, getting back on point.

'He has six safe houses in Brazil alone. Unofficially, as you know, he

191

also runs the gang that controls a major favela, which is a honeycomb of potential boltholes.'

'That would be the guacamole dip the severed hand was mailed from?'

Petinski sighed. 'Yes.'

'Do we know where von Weiss is now?'

'Twelve hours ago, before we got on the plane, he was down the coast from Rio at a place called Angra dos Reis, a seaside vacation town. He keeps his boat there. Delaney's going to update us when new information turns up.' She raised her hand and signaled to a cab.

'This guy just lets himself be tailed?'

'Look, Cooper, I know what you're thinking, but as I told you already, we've got no firm proof of his connection to the theft of the nuke. We've got nothing other than suspicion. Von Weiss has a reputation – he doesn't scare and he's got enough money to buy whomever he wants.'

'We've got nothing on him, but we're *sure* he's the guy?' I asked as the cab pulled over. I opened the rear passenger door for her.

'And I suppose you've never had a murder suspect with motive and opportunity who you're absolutely positive committed the crime, only you don't have any clues that'll stand up in court?'

For some reason I really didn't like it when Petinski was right.

Sixteen

We let the cab go and walked the last klick. Benicio von Weiss's three-story mansion was in a damp valley, buried in an overgrown jungle of fleshy palm fronds and tropical plants, set behind a wall fifteen feet high. The road snaked around in front of it and climbed the side of the valley, providing a view down into the place.

'Von Weiss got kids?' I asked Petinski.

'No. Why?'

'Big house for a single guy.'

'He's rich. And he has staff.'

Right, that other-half thing again. One wing of this place was longer than the street I lived on. I took a pair of compact binoculars from my pocket and trained them on the premises. It was set in a corner by itself, away from other dwellings, the nearest neighbor being fifty yards up the street. There were surveillance cameras on the wall with interlocking fields of view. Wire also ran around the top of the wall – electrified from the look of it. No doubt there were other sensors – motion, heat, Doberman and so forth. Von Weiss defended his privacy like Area Two defended its weapons.

Conveniently, the gate set in the wall slid open just then and a glossy black Mercedes M-class drove slowly out, accompanied by outriders on KTM dirt bikes. The Mercedes windows were heavily tinted. Nothing to see there. I moved the binoculars back to focus on the gap in the wall provided by the open gate and saw two guys in some kind of uniform: tan shirt and black pants, combat boots and black ball cap.

I ran the binoculars around the surrounding area. On the hill above the house was a jungle of trees, vines and fleshy plants that came to an abrupt end where a slum began, a trash heap of dwellings, hovels built on hovels, no rhyme or reason to their shape or location, no planning ordinances.

'That a favela?' I asked Petinski.

'It's the one controlled by von Weiss's people. Céu Cidade – Sky City.'

Céu Cidade, where the FedEx box sent to Alabama had been mailed from. 'I'd like to check it out.'

'We can't go there, Cooper, not without your friends in the 82nd Airborne. Rio's been cleaning up its favelas. At least trying to – getting ready for the Olympics and the World Cup – but there are still quite a few holdouts, Céu Cidade being one of them. It's a distribution hot spot for much of Rio's cocaine and weapons. Ask the wrong person the wrong question up there and you don't get out alive. Perversely, the place also has one of the lowest murder rates in the whole country.'

'Von Weiss runs a tight ship.'

'And Hitler built the autobahns, but only so he could move his armies around easily.'

'Okay, I get it – von Weiss is an evil prick. All the more reason to have a good snoop around. Randy could be up there somewhere.'

Petinski chewed the inside of her cheek. 'You're right . . . But how to get it done, that's the problem.'

'First things first. What's on the other side of that wall?' I motioned at the house.

'Breaking in will put von Weiss on his guard.'

'I'm sure he's already on it. We need to see what sort of guy we're dealing with. I'm going to give Jeb a call.'

'Why?'

'Because the Company has toys.'

'What are you going to do, Cooper?'

'Don't know, but that's never stopped me before.'

*

The driver had just finished making his delivery. We only had to tail him a short distance because he obligingly pulled into a side street off Copacabana Beach, walked a block and ducked into a strip joint offering happy hour – a beer and lap dance for twenty bucks. Great value. I made a mental note of the address.

Petinski and I doubled back to his truck, which was oily and smelled of baked engine grease. The vehicle was a virtual museum piece and therefore easy to steal. Best of all, behind the cabin was a bulk gasoline tank.

Petinski drove, taking direction from her iPhone. It was just after ten p.m. when we arrived in the vicinity of Castle von Weiss. We parked with a hiss of air brakes on the street's shoulder, in an area of deep shadow, the tires sloshing through mud. The first step or two in the plan was thought out. The rest was, well, loose.

'Get plenty of cover before you light 'er up,' I said.

'See you back here at ten-forty,' Petinski replied, adjusting the seat belt. 'Don't be late.'

Our wristwatches were already synchronized. I had exactly thirty-one minutes to do whatever I was going to do before my partner drove off in another stolen vehicle and left me behind. I climbed out and coughed through a cloud of gritty diesel smoke blowing down from the exhaust pipe behind the cabin's roof. Taking one of the small remote-detonated charges from the pouches on my chest webbing, I kneeled down and felt the magnet draw it onto the vehicle's fuel tank, mating with a solid click. I flicked the switch from 'standby' mode to 'armed' and waited for the red light to flicker green, informing me that the device was receiving a signal from the remote in the cabin with Petinski. The second charge I placed on the steel chassis beneath the big gasoline tank and went through the same routine, waiting for the green light.

The gears ground together and the truck moved off, shuddering with serious clutch trouble toward its date with the scrap heap. I jogged after it, keeping to the shadows, and watched the taillights disappear round a bend. A handful of seconds later, I caught up with those lights again when they flared briefly, a hundred yards down the road, Petinski having tapped the brake pedal. Then she jumped, at least that was the plan. The tail lights appeared to skip sideways a little, indicating that the vehicle had rammed something solid, as planned. Confirming this, the muffled sound of crumpling metal panels and breaking glass tinkling onto the ground came back to me on the night air. A couple of breaths later, a small bang ignited the vehicle's fuel tank and around forty gallons of diesel fuel burst into flame. A heartbeat later, a second explosion dwarfed the first as the truck's gasoline storage tank went off like a massive incendiary and a huge orange and yellow ball of burning fumes rolled up into the night like a smoke ring blown by hell itself. The sound arrived next, a deep clap that smacked into my chest like a two-by-four. Then the heat rushed past, impossibly hot against my face considering the distance from the source.

The wreckage of the truck was alight and burning ferociously. The silence imposed on the immediate vicinity by the shock of a big explosion was giving way to cries of surprise as folks came to their senses, or at least to watch the show.

Still keeping to the shadows, I ran hard toward the roaring orange flames. They licked at the base of a pall of black smoke that doused the light spilling down from the favela on the hill. Coming closer, I saw the gate in von Weiss's fifteen-foot-high wall open and several uniformed men run out. They formed a semicircle around the vehicle, probably trying to deduce whether some unfortunate soul might be cooking behind the steering wheel. Or maybe to see if someone was going to break out a pack of marshmallows to roast. Residents from the favela swarmed down the hill and were joined by their neighbors in the valley, rich mingling with poor.

I left the shadows and walked along the wall to the open gate as two guards rushed out, one carrying a bucket of water that he sloshed over himself, the other a fire extinguisher. The heat of the fire forced them back, along with the crowd, and the spectacle kept everyone entertained. I slipped inside the perimeter and flipped down the night vision goggles on my head.

Half the house was dark with no electric lights on. In the other half, it was a different story. Probably where the live-in security force bunked, I figured. Aside from money and privacy, I wondered what else this von Weiss character was so keen to keep to himself with all the security; perhaps a milk can that packed a kiloton punch, or a former Air Force pilot kept against his will. I headed for the darkened wing I believed to be unoccupied, taking a suppressed Glock borrowed from the Company out of the holster on my chest webbing. There was no point wasting time trying to finesse my way in, picking door locks that I figured were going to be top of the line. I had maybe five minutes to snoop around before the guards realized there was no one to rescue, lost interest in the truck and got back to the job of patrolling. I cocked the Glock's slide and fired three rounds into the door at the top hinge area, the solid hardwood splintering. The hinge at about waist height was next, followed by the one around eight inches above the marble stoop. A couple more shots sputtering from the suppressor into the wood around the lock did the trick and a slight push from my shoulder finished the job, the door giving way with a crack of seasoned timber.

I dropped the Glock's mag and exchanged it for a fresh one before inviting myself in. Out on the road, a helpful secondary explosion accompanied by several shouts and a cry from a woman reinvigorated the crowd's interest in the tanker while I stepped into a world that smelled of rosewood and furniture polish. The guards watching the security cameras in the other wings had better be distracted. If not, I'd know about it soon enough.

Opposite the front door was a wide stairway up to the second floor – bedrooms, I guessed. I took a random left-hand turn instead and moved across a spacious lounge room where the furnishings were old and heavy and from another era. From what I could make out, the oil paintings on the wall were mostly religious scenes illustrating various impressions of either heaven or hell. Others showed children walking alone or holding an adult's hand. There were busts, too – bronzes on marble plinths. The place felt less like a home and more like an art gallery dedicated to images that were a little on the creepy side. I kept working my way through the house – bathrooms, sitting rooms, a library and a reading room. I came to another locked door so I Glocked away its hinges. Inside was a study with a desk, a couch, a bookshelf, and a fish tank with a lamp pointed into it that flared brightly in the NVGs' lenses and made me look away. Completing the furniture ensemble was a glass wall cabinet displaying various military automatic weapons. Oh yeah, and two large red, white and black flags with swastikas crossed over a bronze bust of Adolf Hitler raised on a plinth.

Perhaps I shouldn't have been surprised at the display, given what I knew about von Weiss's lineage, but I was. At least my uneasiness about the decor was resolved. It paid homage to Germany of the 1930s – Hitler's Germany. A quick inspection of the books revealed them to be mostly German-, English- and Portuguese-language natural history reference books on snakes and reptiles – no surprises there. The light caught a familiar title, the words pressed into the spine and finished with gold leaf. There were two volumes. I souvenired volume one, stuffed it into my webbing and went back to scouting the room. On the wall opposite the flags was a panoramic hand-colored photograph of a Nazi rally, Hitler in jackboots facing a bank of microphones. He was addressing what could easily have been half a million men in uniform. Above and behind Hitler a huge eagle perched on top of a swastika like it was squatting on an egg.

The room was part study, part private shrine. There were other photographs on the walls of Nazi officers and officials. I recognized Himmler and Göring in separate pictures, in the company of another officer from the SS who didn't look so familiar. But I'd seen one of the buildings in the pictures many times over the years – railway tracks leading to an archway beneath an observation tower in a broad front of red-brown brick. I didn't have to read the caption to know this was the main gate to Auschwitz, the infamous Nazi extermination camp. Handwriting on the white mat around the photo confirmed it: 'Hauptsturmführer Mengele. Auschwitz II-Birkenau, Frühling, 1943.' In the photo, a line of around twenty sallow, skeletal male camp inmates dressed in black and gray striped pajamas stared at the ground. Two SS guards accompanied them, one of them a dog handler leashed to an animal with a sloping hyena-like spine. The caption fingered Mengele as the unknown officer in the other Kodak moments. In this one he was smiling at the prisoners, enjoying a moment of benevolence. Or maybe he was considering what he could do to them back in his surgery.

A shadow momentarily flickered in the small amount of light coming through the door. I had time to lift a hand to protect my head from the object swinging toward it. Something heavy gave my forearm a glancing blow and sent a bolt of pain shooting through the bone, and I backed away from the shadow, which was in fact a medium-sized guy with a flat, bearded face. He had a holster on his hip – empty. Maybe he was off duty when he saw the damage to the front door and came to investigate the reason for the excessive elbow grease applied to open it. He swung again before I could show him the Glock, but he misjudged the distance in the dark. Unless of course he was gunning for the fish tank, in which case he got plenty of wood on the ball. The glass shattered loudly, and then made even more noise when it all crashed onto the floorboards. I flinched, anticipating the rush of water, but there was none. The guard stood still, breathing hard, his eyes wide and suddenly frightened, looking at where the tank had been. He gave a scream, which strangled in his throat, dropped the brass candlestick dangling from his hand, and ran out the door. From the corner of the tunnel vision offered by the NVGs, I saw something long and black move across the floor, whippet fast, and disappear under a cabinet. Time to go before Rodriguez returned with more batters.

*

Two types of sirens approached, their interwoven wailing piercing the night. The fire brigade and the police, I figured. The crowd gathered around the burning truck had grown to about a hundred. Most of the ferocity had gone out of the flames though the bonfire was still generating plenty of heat. I stayed in the shadows as much as I could, keeping my back to the flames when I couldn't, and made my way up the road. Three police cruisers and two fire trucks blew past in a traveling thicket of flashing electric light. Petinski met me a couple of hundred yards farther on in a stolen Hyundai, hidden from the street beneath an overhanging tree, its headlights winking. I jogged over and hopped in through the open passenger-side door.

Petinski pulled onto the road and accelerated to the edge of wheel spin. 'What happened?' she asked when she saw me rubbing my forearm.

'I bumped into something.'

'You place the camera?'

'No, I only got as far as the ground floor.'

'Shit.'

'Things got a little hectic. I picked this up.' There was a book in my hand, an old book bound in lightly tanned leather, a black swastika in a circle of gold embossed on the front cover.

Petinski glanced sideways, read the title. 'Jesus – *Mein Kampf*, Hitler's anti-Semitic rant.'

I opened it up to the title page and saw an inscription handwritten with a fountain pen in neat, tightly controlled script. The writing looked old-fashioned. I flicked on the overhead light. Mengele's name was recognizable, but the rest was in German. My command of that language was limited to *schnitzel*, *bratwurst*, *bier* and *Oktoberfest* and all of those words were noticeably absent.

'You read German?' I asked. The signature began with a symbol in the shape of a lightning bolt, followed by an elaborate squiggle, just the kind of signature you'd expect from a Nazi.

Petinski did a double take at the book and immediately pulled over. 'You drive.'

I left the book on the seat, got out and walked around the front of the car. Unfastening the chest webbing, I tossed it onto the back seat.

'Might not be a good idea to check this car with valet parking at the hotel,' I suggested.

'We'll leave it at Ipanema. Local police will pick it up.'

It was getting toward eleven p.m., the traffic thinning out. Petinski stroked the book's cover lightly with her hand. 'This cover. It's human skin.'

'Human skin . . .'

'That's what I said. I've seen one before in a Holocaust museum. And the signature. It's Hitler's. The writing here says, "Dear SS-Hauptsturmführer Mengele, National Socialism and the citizens of Germany owe you a sincere debt of gratitude."' Petinski flicked through some more pages. 'Mengele returned from the Eastern Front in '42. This edition was printed in 1940. It was probably Mengele's personal copy, recovered sometime after he returned.' She flipped through more pages, fascinated.

'Mengele was on the Russian front?'

'In the Ukraine. The record says he was wounded pulling three men from a burning Panzer.'

'So the guy was a hero?'

'A *Nazi* hero.' She spat out the words. 'They awarded him the Iron Cross First Class. His wounds prevented him returning to the fighting so he was transferred to Auschwitz-Birkenau. He arrived there in '43. He made a name for himself performing experiments on people – children, and especially twins. Maybe that's the fine work the German citizens owed him a debt of gratitude for.' There was a tremor in her voice.

'What else is going on here, Petinski?'

'My grandmother lost her twin sister as well as her mother and three brothers in that death camp.'

I said nothing. Petinski might have been motivated by personal circumstances that went way beyond the facts of this case, but they weren't getting us any closer to finding Randy or the bomb. I hoped someone else out there was doing better than us because from my reckoning we had just rolled into nine days to go. Or perhaps eight days.

Or maybe six. Was the countdown specified on the note based on US Eastern Standard Time or US Western Standard Time or Northern Australian swampland time, or somewhere else entirely? Whatever, it was getting away from us fast.

I drove to the curb and stopped.

'What's the problem?' Petinski asked.

'We're running out of time. Can I have your cell?'

'Why?'

'To find us another way into that favela. I want to have a look at von Weiss's HQ up there. He must have one, right?'

She passed me her phone. 'Forget it, Cooper. We'd need a guide at the very least, someone from BOPE.'

'What's BOPE?'

'Batalhão de Operações Policiais Especiais. That's Portuguese for Special Police Operations Battalion – Rio's anti-terror squad. They've done a lot of the heavy lifting cleaning up the favelas.'

'Why trouble them? We'll know we're getting warm when we run into people with guns.'

'That's not practical.'

'Neither is calling in the local anti-terror boys.'

'Because . . . ?'

'Think about it. Who lives in a favela?' I asked.

'People who can't afford to live somewhere else.'

'What sort of work do they do? The low-paid service jobs. They sweep the streets, dig the drains. Probably they're the council workers, the nurses, the low-level government employees.'

'Where's this going?'

'What about police work? That's a low-paid service job too, isn't it? It is where I come from. Like you said, the favela clean-up wasn't all that successful. Maybe some of the folks asked to do the cleaning up have other interests, like being in on the action.'

'I'm sure they recruit those squads from out of town.'

'Do you know that, or are you speculating?'

'I'm assuming.'

'Anyway, what do we tell local law enforcement? That we're on their home soil looking for one of our missing agents and a nuke?'

'I get the picture,' she said.

Which was that if Uncle Sam wanted this shit kept under wraps, at least for the moment Petinski and I had no choice but to risk going it alone.

Seventeen

Céu Cidade – Sky City. As the name suggested, the favela held high ground. It sat on the saddle between two peaks with a valley on either side, the one where von Weiss had his home and the other given to warehouses. It was in this light industrial valley forty minutes later that Petinski and I crawled through mostly deserted streets, eventually parking among sprawling rundown buildings with shattered windows.

'Leave the car and it'll get stolen,' Petinski observed.

'Not if you stay with it,' I told her.

'Sorry – if *who* stays with it?'

'Who do you think?' I said.

Petinski sighed like she knew this was going to come up. 'Look, Cooper, I'm quite capable of taking care of myself. And if you get yourself into trouble, maybe I'll take care of you too.'

Sure. Petinski was well under a hundred pounds and, well, not to put too fine a point on it, a fair proportion of them kept her bra occupied. I turned toward her and was about to say, 'I don't think so,' when she took my hand and twisted my thumb in a way that felt like she'd dislocated it, providing a flash of intense pain that caused me to cry out. '*Okay!*' I snapped. My hand was released and the pain instantly evaporated. 'Jesus, Petinski . . . What the hell was that?'

'I gave gymnastics away after the Olympics and took up Jiujitsu and Taekwondo. I was US Women's Kumite Champion 2006 and 2010.'

I wiggled my thumb. 'So I'll stay with the car and *you* check out the damn favela.'

'No. Let's *both* do this,' she said, getting out of the vehicle. 'Forget about the car. We can steal something else later if we need to.'

You learn a lot about people when you travel with them.

We each drank some water from bottles we'd brought with us, stuffed the essentials into a small pack, and a few minutes later we entered Céu Cidade via a brightly lit section of road containing a Hamburger Bob's, a general store, a drinks and candy store, as well as shops selling furniture and welding services, a gas station, a motorcycle repair garage, a tire repair shop and a post office. I found a street number and confirmed that this was the post office on the FedEx package's consignment note. Petinski snapped off a photo with her phone for future reference, and then took a shot of some graffiti on an adjacent wall of three monkey heads side by side: one with no ears, one with no eyes and one with no mouth. The rules to live by in Sky City . . .

Above the retail area the streets darkened, became narrower, and the incline sharpened. The airless night was hot and thick with humidity and my t-shirt was already sticking to my back, my feet sweating in my Adidas. Starlight behind thin high cloud provided meager illumination. It was late and not too many folks were around for such a densely packed area – a few shirtless men in shorts doing late-night chores, the odd group of women sitting on stoops, the wet breeze funneling through open doors providing some relief from the heat. Dogs stood around, cats cantered between the darker shadows. Occasional motorcycles roared by, heading up or down. Almost no one paid us any heed.

Even up close the homes here seemed to be piled on top of each other. And they were constructed from whatever material could be slapped together quickly: brick, cinderblock, wood, corrugated steel, poured concrete, old auto panels, metal sheeting and some items I couldn't identify. Here and there light bulbs burned inside windows with no glass, electricity provided via a tangled spaghetti of black wiring over the streets and alleys. And in the air, hints of sewage, old grease, kerosene and samba music.

We climbed up through the human anthill, following winding paths, uneven stairwells and narrow lanes. At one point, three shirtless young men appeared suddenly from the shadows and followed their own pungent body odor down the narrow chute toward us. I tensed for trouble, but none materialized. We came out into a wider alleyway and saw the silhouette of a young guy ahead lounging against the wall, smoking, a Belgian FN FAL assault rifle in his other hand, muzzle pointed absently at his toes. A red ember glowed in front of his face and smoke drifted in our direction. I smelled weed. The guy was humming a tune, occasionally breaking into the lyrics, and stopping regularly to spit on the ground. Hmm. Stoned, bored and armed. In short, trouble. We detoured around him, backtracking ten yards or so to cut through a slit of a walkway between houses that leaned into each other and seemed to meet in the dank, airless darkness overhead, blocking out the stars.

We followed the walkway and exited soon after in a relatively open space, the intersection of a number of roads and paths. A view opened out to the east, toward Ipanema a couple of miles away, where the lights from another favela overlooking the beach glittered like gold dust tossed onto black velvet.

Farther behind us up the hill, above the intersection, a row of spotlights burned with a white-hot intensity unusual in these parts. It appeared to be coming from a collection of walled houses, some kind of compound. Two motorcycles roared up the hill toward us. I drew back into the shadows, my arm across Petinski's chest so that she got the message. The KTMs roared into view, passengers on the back armed with more assault rifles; they sped across the intersection and were cloaked by the shadows.

Schloss von Weiss was close. Keeping out of the open, we reconnoitered the intersection and found the cavern that had swallowed the motorcycles. The lane kinked back on itself, followed a tunnel between some houses and came out below those spotlights, which were blazing down from a high cinderblock wall built by folks who knew how to build.

We kept moving, scouting the wall. Twenty minutes later we had circumnavigated it and were back where we started. Down one end, back toward the location of the crooning doper with the FN, was a gate manned by four men. All were armed. One of them carried what appeared to be a light machine gun, a Belgian Minimi perhaps, or maybe the US version of the same, the M249. Whatever, it meant going through the front gate wasn't an option. Not tonight.

'What now?' Petinski whispered.

I looked around. Not much to play with. The compound wall was smooth. No way to climb it.

'What are you planning, Cooper? You can't storm it. There are only two of us, remember?' Petinski pulled a cigarette packet–sized box from her pocket, turned it on and held it up. 'A neutron detector,' she explained before I could ask her what she was doing.

'That's gonna pick up a bomb in a basement over the wall?'

'So they say. Uses a gallium arsenide wafer. Detects neutrons emitted from fissile materials. *Extremely* sensitive. If our bomb's in the area, it'll tell us.' She tucked the instrument into a vest pocket.

'Well, is it?' I asked her.

'Is it what?'

'In the area?'

'Doesn't appear to be,' she said.

I checked left and right. A house piled up in one spot near the wall had a roofline that extended beyond its neighbors'. I went up to it and found the front door – solid, and locked. I brought out *my* gadget – the Glock.

'You want to gain entry?' Petinski asked.

'That's what I had in mind.'

'Put the gun away,' she said, backing up half a dozen steps. She then bounded toward the brickwork beside me. At the last instant she leaped and hit the wall with her front foot and pushed up so that her hand found a ledge at least ten feet off the ground. In one fluid movement her other foot sprang off a crack and she was in midair, reaching for a pipe. I watched her swing herself completely around it and then push herself up, feet first. One leg hooked over a balcony and the next instant Petinski was over it and gone. The woman climbed like a monkey.

Moments later the front door opened. 'Coming in?' she asked politely.

I put my finger to my lips.

'Relax, the place is empty. Could be a shift worker lives here.'

Inside it smelled of boiled meat, cheap tobacco and urine. My least favorite Air Wick. Petinski led the way up a steep, narrow flight of concrete steps ending in a covered veranda, the one through which she'd gained entry. The top of the von Weiss compound wall was three feet above our heads, and about the same distance away. I looked down over the balcony and confirmed a drop of about twenty feet to the ground. Starlight caught on the jagged shards of broken glass set into the top edge of the compound wall's cinderblocks.

The home we were in was small and open to the elements on the side facing the wall. Plastic sheeting hung down from the ceiling, a makeshift screen against the rain. Behind the plastic and down one end was a stove with gas cylinder, a sink, a compact bar fridge covered in football decals, and a small table and chair. Down the other end, a narrow wire bed frame occupied the compact space with an old mattress on top. There was also a long plank of wood between cinderblocks on which stood various electrical appliances, magazines and football kitsch. A nearby floodlight on the compound wall lit the place like it was under arrest.

'Got any cash on you?' I asked Petinski.

'No, why?'

I took some *reals* from my pocket and left them on the fridge. Next, I grabbed the mattress. The smell of it reminded me of the A-Star as I hauled it out onto the veranda and set it down. 'Keep an eye on the guards at the front gate. Let me know when no one's looking.' I readied the Glock.

A few seconds passed. 'Now,' she whispered.

I squeezed the trigger, shot through the nearby floodlight's metal shroud and killed the light. No glass tinkled to the laneway below, which was the general idea. Passing the Glock to Petinski I hoisted the mattress to the veranda's wall, picked it up by its bottom end and half pushed it, half threw it at the top of the wall across the way. The mattress came to rest straddling the top edge, covering those glass shards. I went inside and came back out with the plank of wood. The damn thing weighed a ton – hardwood. I propped one end on the veranda wall and lowered the top end onto the mattress.

'Put a foot here.' I pointed at the end of the plank and Petinski secured it as I leaned on the makeshift bridge, testing its strength.

'Hurry,' she told me.

'I'm hurrying.'

'You call that hurrying. If it had been me up there we'd be in the bar ordering—'

'Something virginal with an umbrella in it,' I said. I shinnied to the top of the plank and popped my head over the wall. It was dark. Wrestling with the pack, I removed the NVGs and slipped them over my head. Then I got hold of the camera, a small remote video recorder attached to a sticky base. I popped my head over the wall again to ensure that the coast was clear. It was. There wasn't much open area on the other side of the wall, though more than was usual in this housing compress. Down the far end, behind the gate manned by the armed sentries, was a brightly lit courtyard. A black Mercedes SUV gleamed under those lights. Could it be the same vehicle that had driven out of von Weiss's compound earlier in the evening? Sure it was. What were the chances that identical black SUVs would be in both places? Limited.

This compound had been set up to operate like a fort. I already knew that a wall went all the way round it. Snipers in the rooms of the uppermost houses, plus a machine gun or two behind sandbagged emplacements up high, could keep an assaulting force with only small arms at bay for some time. Any attack would probably also have to deal with armed resistance sniping at it from the rear, from the homes farther down the hill. And no doubt there would be underground tunnels for escape if necessary.

I went back to concentrating on those armed guards at the gate. When I was sure the coast was clear, I threw the sticky camera at the wall of the house opposite. It stuck, finding a brick ledge above block. Lucky throw.

Eighteen

I opened my eyes. A light breeze rolled around in the folds of the translucent white curtain closing off the outside balcony. Beyond the curtain I could hear folks splashing about in a pool somewhere below.

The sun was already up and my Seiko was set to go off in a minute's time at six a.m. The pull-out sofa bed was as comfortable as any I'd ever slept on, or would have been but for the injury the swinging candlestick had done to my forearm. I turned my head and had a look at it. The skin was purple from elbow to wrist. I ran my fingers along the swelling, made a fist and rotated the arm left and right. Sore as hell, but nothing broken.

The Seiko buzzed.

The door to the bedroom was open. The bed was messed up but no one was in it. I got up, took a shower and mentally went through the leads we had to go on. We had so few that the review took no more than a handful of seconds, so I just stood under the water and tried not to think about the doomsday clock ticking down to midnight. Nine days, maybe less, and we were still going nowhere.

'That you in there, Cooper?' a voice called out. Petinski's.

'No, it's George Clooney,' I said. 'Cooper had to go out. You mind coming in and passing me a fresh bar of soap?'

'Breakfast is here and it's getting cold,' she said.

If I wasn't mistaken, we were sounding like an old married couple. And given that we weren't having sex, behaving like one too. If the woman down at reception got the hotel detective to check on our sheets, we'd be bounced out of here on false pretenses. Somehow I didn't think that line of reasoning would make Petinski any more accommodating. I toweled off and threw on the robe hanging from a gold-plated hook on the door.

Petinski's idea of breakfast wasn't mine. Where were the scrambled eggs, bacon and pancakes? All I could see on the tray was muesli and fresh fruit salad. Nothing here was gonna go cold, unless she was referring to my appetite.

'I'm having a swim first,' I said.

'After a shower?'

'Shower first, swim second. House rule.'

Petinski shrugged. 'Hurry, we have to get going.'

'Get going where?' I wondered. It was occurring to me that maybe I was being a little too managed. Spoon fed, even. I had no proper briefing, no resources, no intel beyond what Petinski chose to pass on.

'CIA has a lead on Randy's whereabouts. They've had a tip-off. They believe he could be in one of von Weiss's safe houses. You and I have been volunteered to help ABIN close the cordon. We have to roll out of here in an hour to make the rendezvous at eleven.' My partner was almost perky.

I picked up a handful of clothes, my wallet and the spare passkey. 'What's ABIN again?'

'Brazil's national intelligence agency – counter terror, et cetera.' I knew that . . . 'See you in twenty minutes,' she concluded.

'Okay,' I said, though I had other plans. My gut told me the safe house would be a waste of time. If nothing else, it seemed odd that the type of operation the Brazilians wanted us in on wasn't happening at dawn when most folks were dopey. This one was going down at brunch, a far more civilized time. My interest was in Céu Cidade, von Weiss's favela and Rio's mainline for drugs and guns patrolled by his private army.

The place was a rat's nest and we'd only scratched the surface. If I was von Weiss and had something to hide, that's where I'd hide it. 'Have you checked the camera? Are we receiving?'

'The Mercedes left twenty-seven minutes after we did, a tall man driving – not our subject. The resolution isn't great. Other than that, nothing of interest. Check the file after your swim. Just make it quick, will you?'

'Yes, boss,' I said as I walked out, a comment that earned me a good lip pursing.

The elevator was pulling into my floor so I decided to ride it instead of taking the stairs. The doors slid back. The box was pretty full, occupied by five large African males, all of whom were wearing sunglasses. I walked in, turned, and stood as the doors shut, the air reeking of sour animal, testosterone and Abercrombie & Fitch cologne. The way the men carried themselves – a kind of nervous aggression – was familiar. A sideways glance in the mirror confirmed that four of the men were bodyguards for piggy in the middle, a tall weasel-thin *hombre* with dusty matte-black skin wearing a cream-and-orange-striped knitted shirt and cream-colored pants, an ensemble that looked as natural on him as lipstick on a tarantula. Dime-sized diamonds were punched into the lobes of both ears. The four men at four points of the close protection box around him were heavy-set, bearded and needed a bath real bad.

The doors opened on the first floor and I offered to let the Africans out first. The bodyguards hesitated and looked me up and down. My own training told me that they were nervous about letting a stranger wander around behind them.

'Beautiful morning, isn't it?' I said complete with goofy smile.

I got four frowns in return, but they decided I was harmless and moved out. Their principal ignored me completely – no eye contact at all. Keeping the box formation the men turned right, heading for the pool, taking up as much room as possible so that other hotel guests had to walk in single file, hugging the wall to get past. I wondered who the veep was and what his story might be, because they moved like men used to ambush, almost as if they expected one to appear and cut them down at any moment. Housemaids, maybe, bursting out of the laundry and attacking them with boxes of Tide.

I gave a mental shrug. They were none of my business and I was none of theirs. I detoured to the pool shop and bought a pair of swim trunks because my undershorts, aside from being undershorts, had a hole in them. After changing, I strolled out onto the pool deck and saw that there was a casual restaurant facing the beach on one front and the pool on the other, where a breakfast crowd had gathered. The Africans had taken one of the larger tables out in the open, closer to the pool. A waiter was speaking with them, his notebook open. The bodyguards appeared to be more focused on the space they found themselves in than on ordering breakfast. I recognized the body language. They were getting their lines of fire worked out, noting the exits and so forth, in case of an emergency that had nothing to do with a burnt side order of sourdough toast. Again, I wondered who these guys were.

I grabbed a towel from the cabana boy and claimed a lounge chair, dumping my clothes and towel on it. Several guests were in the pool doing slow languid laps. That was about my speed, so I joined the queue flopping back and forth. After around ten minutes of this I came to a stop to catch my breath and blow the watery snot out of my nose.

Meanwhile, the situation at the restaurant had changed somewhat. To start with, there were a few more guests now and, at one large table in particular – the one occupied by the African party – the mood was rowdy. I did another lap underwater, coming up for breath at the shallow end, then pushed off the wall to do a lap in the silence at the bottom of the pool. I came up and hooked my elbows over the tiled ledge as a second party of Africans swaggered across the courtyard, heading for the tarantula and his pals, all of whom stood to welcome the new arrivals with various gangsta handshakes.

At the sight of all this, my heart rate soared and rang the bell at the top of the scale because *I recognized one of the new arrivals*. Jesus, last time I saw this guy in the flesh it was nighttime in a clearing on the top of a hill in the east Congo rainforest where he was touting the killing power of the claymore anti-personnel mine to a bunch of rapists and butchers. And shortly after, the thing almost blew my head off. Some faces you don't forget. Especially when you've taken the time to look at all available Interpol shots of that face in the hope that you'll meet it one day in a dark alley and you'll have a baseball bat in your hand.

The face's name: Charles White, arms dealer, killer and most recently the middleman who, according to Petinski, had somehow managed to get a W80 nuclear warhead out of continental USA and into the hands of this Nazi-loving von Weiss we were stalking. And now here he was, about to sit down to eggs Benedict. Only it was broad daylight, and where was my Louisville Slugger?

*

On closer inspection, I also recognized Falco, Charles White's older brother. And now that I thought about it, two more of the party – a couple of the bodyguards accompanying Charles White – also looked pretty familiar: muscle that had accompanied him in the DRC.

I glanced up at my balcony. The door was open, the curtain pulled aside, the room behind it a dark rectangle. I scanned the other balconies facing the pool: several other rooms also had their doors open and the curtains drawn back. Was ABIN up in one or more of those rooms, watching proceedings? Or maybe CIA? Or MI6? I scoped the restaurant. All I could see were waiters and guests behaving like waiters and guests. Where was the guy sitting on his own, reading the newspaper with the hole cut in the masthead? Or the nonchalant couple taking their newborn child for a walk in a stroller? If Charles and Falco were under observation, whoever was doing it knew their stuff.

I got out of the pool, walked to my lounge chair and toweled off. Bundling up my clothes, I wandered over to the hotel door without showing any apparent interest in the breakfast club. The casual act ended when I reached the hallway, where I broke into a sprint for the elevator. A couple of minutes later, I fell into my room on the fifth floor.

'Petinski!'

'Shhh, quiet,' she hissed from somewhere inside. I found her sitting cross-legged up on the TV cabinet with her camera, lining up the Africans through the open balcony doors. 'Charles and Falco White,' she told me without lowering the viewfinder.

Old news. 'Who's the guy with the close protection?' I asked.

'Don't know.'

I joined her in the shadows.

'We shouldn't be so surprised those two would turn up here,' she continued, her digital Canon peeling off rapid-fire shots. 'They've got money, the Palace is one of Rio's finest hotels, and this city's where they live.'

'I'm staying on these guys,' I said. 'ABIN can plug its own holes.'

'You don't like following orders, do you, Cooper?' Petinski said quietly.

'Orders I like just fine. It's stupidity I'm not down with.'

She climbed off the cabinet, removed the micro memory card from the camera and fiddled around with her iPad while I watched the tables down in the courtyard. A few minutes later she joined me at the cabinet as a woman entered the restaurant area, her back to Petinski and me. She wore a short bright-blue dress cut low at the back, and walked on low heels toward the focus of our attention. It was the kind of walk that makes men lick their lips – I licked mine.

'Look, the entertainment has arrived,' said Petinski.

When the woman was close enough, Charles White grabbed her, lifted her clean off her feet and sat her on his lap, side-saddle. She threw her head back and laughed, maybe a little too hard.

'Jesus,' I said under my breath.

'What's up?' Petinski asked.

'That woman down there. Her name's Sugar.'

'You know her?'

'She worked at Jubilee. She was involved with Randy and Alabama.'

It took Petinski a few moments to get around to asking the obvious question. 'Intimately?'

There was no way to soften it. 'Yeah, I believe so.'

'Both of them?'

'Unconfirmed on that score. And there have been other connections.'
Me, for example. I took out my cell and showed her the picture of Sugar
sitting with Ty Morrow in the Green Room several hours after he'd supposedly fled from creditors in his jet.

'Men are such fucking idiots,' she murmured.

Nineteen

The party was breaking up. The bodyguards stood first and formed a loose diamond around the table where their principals sat. Falco put his arm around the tarantula guy while Charles played the gentleman and saw to Sugar's chair, pulling it out for her. The four of them, surrounded by the muscle, strolled toward the lobby, laughing and chatting like they were off to a little league game.

'They're on the move,' I informed Petinski, who was hurriedly stuffing various items into a shoulder bag.

'Let's go.'

I was still wearing the robe, the swimming costume beneath it, and my feet squelched in a puddle of water on the carpet. I slipped the robe and dropped the trunks to the floor and suddenly realized that Petinski was staring at me. Man, I'd forgotten about her completely. 'Nothing you haven't seen before, right?' I said, toughing it out, turning to rummage through my clothes for clean undershorts.

'Excuse me?'

There was no way I was going to stand around blushing. 'Or maybe you haven't.' I stood up straight and square. 'Petinski, meet Little Coop. Little Coop, Petinski.'

Her eye line took an excursion. 'This is *totally* inappropriate behavior. There are rules, Cooper.'

'It's a he-said-she-said thing unless you have proof. You want me to vogue for your camera?'

Petinski glanced at her Canon as if considering it, then turned her back on me and walked to the door. 'Just hurry the fuck up, would you?' She snatched her bag, tucked it under an arm and stomped out.

I shrugged. It was easier to dress without an audience anyway and a minute later I caught up with her at the bottom of the fire stairs in the lobby.

'Evidence or not, Cooper, the bullshit you just pulled is in my report,' she snapped.

Down in reception, Gracia smiled at us as we crossed to the front entrance. I gave her a veiled thumbs-up and she returned it with excited silent clapping.

*

I waved down a cab while the stretch Hummer eased out of the hotel's forecourt, a Hyundai SUV following. A few moments later Petinski and I were heading through the tunnel separating Ipanema and Copacabana from the rest of Rio, tailing the Hyundai.

'What about ABIN and its cordon?' I asked, testing her.

Petinski's eyes were glued to the traffic in front. 'A bird in the hand, right?'

I realized I was sitting on a newspaper, and pulled it out. *O Dia*, read the masthead. *The Day*, I figured. An ad on the front page for women's underwear caught my eye. Then I clocked the main story of the morning, which included a photo of a burning vehicle outside a familiar home. There was an inset photo of von Weiss, and another of a snake with its black mouth open, fangs bared. I showed the paper to Petinski.

'Underwear, Cooper?'

'The house, Petinski . . .'

'Oh, sorry. It's just that I . . . I sometimes think you're, y'know, preoccupied.'

I passed her the paper. 'My mind is always totally focused on the job at hand.'

'Yes, it's just that I'm not sure what you think your job is,' Petinski countered as she examined the photos. 'That's a mean-looking snake.' She read the caption out loud, '*Preta de Mamba*,' then double-tapped an app on her iPhone, opening a translator.

We drove for several minutes, slicing through the traffic, catching several amber streetlights and running one red to keep the Hyundai in view.

'It's a black mamba,' Petinski announced. 'A venomous snake, it says here, found in central Africa. It's aggressive, and has been known to attack and even chase its victims. It's the world's fastest snake, apparently.'

I leaned forward and asked the cabbie, 'Can you read, translate and drive?'

He nodded so I passed the paper forward and tapped the story. Glancing at the front page he said, 'I have read this, *já*. A man who keep snakes at his house – he was robbed. The thief, he burn a truck to distract people and stole some valuable thing. This snake, it got loose and kill two people who work in the house. But now it has been caught. The man who owns the snake is rich and powerful. He offer reward for anyone who can give *policia informações* on the thief.'

I recalled the glass case being smashed, and seeing the thin black shadow whipping across the floorboards, too quick to identify before it vanished under a cabinet. A black mamba. A killer. Now I understood the cause of the fear I saw in the face of the guard who ran screaming from the room. He must have known what had slithered into the night.

The driver's eyes darted into the rear-view mirror several times, checking us out. We were paying him to follow someone, and now we were asking about a front-page crime. I didn't want him feeding anything to the police, concerned bystander–style.

'Journalists,' I told him, gesturing at Petinski and myself.

'Ah, *journalistas*,' he said. That seemed to do the trick and he went back to keeping track of the road ahead instead of his nosy passengers.

'Are you going to call someone?' I asked Petinski, opening the window to let in the traffic noise.

'I'm sorry?'

'You don't think you should inform whoever it is you really work for that we're tailing the criminals who stole the nuke?'

'I made a brief report when I uploaded photos taken at the pool. What do you expect should happen here, Cooper? You think we should just spirit them off to Gitmo? Think it through. We don't know where the weapon is and these people won't hand us a road map to its location.'

'Then we might as well sit on our hands, 'cause they ain't gonna lead us to it either.'

'No, but despite all the smiles and backslapping we've seen these people carry on with, they *have* to be feeling the pressure. A nuke is a long way from a case of M16s with erased serial numbers. Someone will cave, make a mistake, and when they do, we'll be there to exploit it.'

'Call in the 82nd like I suggested, Petinski, because if they don't crack and the weapon is used, the White brothers, von Weiss and everyone else connected with this will go to ground and we'll have nothing.'

'There's nowhere on earth they can hide where we can't find them.'

'Right, just like we knew where to lay our hands on bin Laden for all those years.'

Petinski refused to be diverted. 'I've been told to tail them and not lose sight of them. And that's what I'm going to do.'

'And what's my role in all this? To hold your purse?'

'If that's what it takes.'

'You want them to break, Petinski? Apply pressure.'

'You do *nothing* unless you clear it with me, Cooper.'

Over his shoulder, the driver informed us, 'Yes – to Pão de Açúcar. That is where they go.'

The road soon opened out into a circular area with a packed parking lot, far too many tourist buses for the available spaces clogging the place. Thick cables angled up from a terminal toward a vertical face of brown rock towering above the parking lot. I spotted Chas and Falco White trotting up the crowded stairs of the terminus with their unidentified friend and Sugar, the bodyguards in the loose diamond formation around them, a parting made for them through the sea of tourists by several uniformed police. There was a buzz in the throng, the kind brought on by the presence of celebrities. People held up their phones to get photos.

Our cab driver took us to the edge of the crush. Petinski paid the fare while I attempted to force a path through the mass, but it closed in solid behind the Whites and almost seemed to lift them up and deposit them at the doors of a cable car on the verge of departing. Eventually, when I reached the ticket office, I had to wait my turn behind a short, round, sweating tour guide with hair plugs who was having his book of ticket stubs checked by a meticulous young woman determined to find fault.

A buzzer sounded and a rotating orange warning light lit up in the platform area. The door closed on the cable car carrying our persons of interest. The car then slid slowly out of its bay and accelerated into a climb toward the rock face, a massive granite formation that seemed to burst out of the flat ground. Petinski caught up to me in time to miss the next cable car, and we only just managed to squeeze into the one after that.

Looking around, I figured either everyone in the confined space was CIA or MI6 or ABIN, or no one was. Cameras clicked and the atmosphere filled with *oohs* and *ahhs* as the rapidly increasing elevation provided views of several golden sand beaches lapped by blue water. And maybe in a few short days all that sand would be turned to glass as a minor sun burst from a milk can and bloomed over it.

The cable car docked on the crown of the hill and the load of tourists or secret agents, I wasn't sure which, followed the signs down to another terminal where a second car was to hoist us to the peak of Sugarloaf Mountain. Petinski and I had lost sight of White and the rest, but there was no place else to go other than up, so we joined the queue and waited for the second leg of the journey.

'I know we're not here for the view,' said Petinski, 'but that's a heck of a view.'

She was right; this was some panorama. The cream colors of Rio wrapped themselves around countless beaches and bays of blue-green water at the bases of what I could only describe as perky, surgically enhanced bumps poking up all over the place.

The cable car eventually docked on the top of Sugarloaf. Petinski and I threaded our way through the crowds milling about, and set off to locate the White brothers. The view was hard to ignore, but we did our best and concentrated on casing the small numbers of bars, fast-food joints and junk shops catering to the steady stream of tourists. But the White brothers and the rest of their party were nowhere to be seen.

'They have to be here somewhere,' muttered Petinski, hands on her hips, scoping out the vicinity.

Several tourists pointed at a Boeing passenger jet away in the middle distance as it banked and headed straight for Sugarloaf. It banked steeply again, just as I was getting nervous that it might land on top of us, and headed for a frighteningly short runway across the bay. The vultures wheeled on the air currents, moms and dads took photographs, and kids ate ice cream. I could have been on vacation. A helicopter suddenly shot around the side of the mountain and filled the air with the snarl of jet engines and rotor thump. Kids ran to the fence for a closer look as the chopper came to a hover abeam a heliport a little down the side of the mountain before the incline dropped vertically away. It was a large civilian job painted silver with thick blue and red stripes that ran from nose to tail rotor. I was familiar with the type, a French-made Eurocopter EC225, the civilian version of the military Super Puma. Aircraft like this ferried workers to oil rigs. It drifted toward the landing pad, wowing everyone who'd never fallen out of the sky in one of the fuckers, and sat in midair twenty feet or so over the pad before settling gradually onto its wheels with an eardrum-rupturing noise that cleared the sky of vultures.

I turned my back on the racket and was about to set off on another tour of the facilities to try to locate our suspects, when Petinski nudged me in the arm. Whadaya know . . . It was von Weiss stepping out of the aircraft behind a pair of bodyguards in expensive suits. He jogged slightly hunched over beyond the rotor downwash and shook hands like a visiting dignitary with the party that stepped into view: Falco and Charles White. So that's where they'd been lurking. Petinski took pictures, just one of many people doing so. A small crowd followed von Weiss out of the aircraft – no one I recognized. One of them was a girl in a short white dress, with shoulder-length golden hair and skin. She joined von Weiss's side and both were introduced to the tarantula in the cream and orange knit. I wondered how von Weiss – a neo-Nazi and probably also a believer in the master-race crap – felt about shaking hands with a black man. He seemed okay with it from this distance. Sugar was down there, too, I saw. Von Weiss didn't shake hands with her, I noticed, but she scored an air kiss from his girlfriend, the buttery blonde.

A four-man security team that had spilled from the Eurocopter, all of them fair-haired and well over six five, formed an Aryan diamond pattern around the party. The Whites' security team formed a looser, outer ring, and all of them moved slowly to the stairs that would bring them up to the main viewing area. I looked around for other helicopters. Good move on von Weiss's part. Arriving by chopper he could spot the tail; and indeed two other choppers were standing off a mile away in a stationary hover.

The turbines on the Eurocopter spooled up. It lifted thirty feet off the platform and pivoted slowly through ninety degrees. Petinski kept snapping away at it as it backed away from the heliport and then spiraled into the sky. One of the choppers holding station in midair started to move also.

'I think you got it,' I said to Petinski, who was still snapping. 'C'mon.'

The crowd's interest in the new arrivals evaporated once the aircraft had departed. Petinski and I drifted along, acting innocent, keeping the party in view. They moved to a bar, one of von Weiss's stormtroopers performing a quick site inspection before the principals ventured in. I noticed the bodyguard palming the bartender something, which resulted in two tourist couples being shown the exit. Von Weiss didn't care to share. Meanwhile a waiter organized a single large table from smaller ones for the group, and everyone sat. Drinks came next. Petinski anchored herself in some shade under a tree and took more photos. I wondered what they were talking about. It would've been good to have a microphone in there. The muscle lined up across the front of the bar facing the viewing area and suggested seeking other venues to the rare tourist game enough to approach and ask if the place was open for a drink.

'We just gonna sit here until they leave?' I asked Petinski.

'We've got the Whites and von Weiss in the one place. This is where the action is.'

From what I could see, the only action was sitting up there in the bar with von Weiss and the Whites in the form of Sugar and the sleek blonde. 'Meeting out in the open like this? Von Weiss is thumbing his nose at us. Showing us he can't be touched.'

'What do you want to do, Cooper, go up there and accuse von Weiss of stealing a WMD?'

She had a point. And she was right about me wanting to do *something*, but what? My mind was a blank.

'Look, we're not the only people on this, Cooper,' she again reassured me. 'But we're the only people on this *here*. We play it by the book and do what we can.' She motioned at her camera. 'Most importantly, we stay in the background and don't blow our cover. Fate has put us in the box seat. Let's just see what happens.'

I didn't like it, but I had no alternative.

Petinski removed the chip from her camera and thumbed in a fresh one. I glanced around. There wasn't much for me to do. 'You want a Coke or something?' I asked.

'Yeah, it's hot,' she said, glad to give her trophy partner a task.

'Back in a minute.' I brushed a wasp out of my face and went off in the direction of the vendor. Along the way I saw a sign pointing to the washrooms and decided to make a detour there first. I found them eventually on the side of the mountain, roughly below the bar occupied by von Weiss and company. According to a traffic cone, the women's was closed for cleaning but the men's was still open. A kid appeared in the doorway, struggling with his fly. His mother, loitering nearby, berated him for dawdling, their cable car on the verge of departure. I went around behind them into the dimly lit cinderblock structure. There wasn't a lot of ventilation inside, so I breathed through my mouth, leaned over the urinal and thought of running water. Halfway through the business, a man came and stood beside me, grunted, then exhaled loudly with relief. Neither of us acknowledged the other, both of us willing a veil of privacy around our personal space as we answered the call of nature.

Finished, and with a sense of being pleasantly unburdened, I zipped my fly, drew back from the urinal and washed my hands under a tap in a putrid basin. No towels in the wall dispenser. I shook the water off as the other guy arrived to take his turn at the basin. He came into the light: a heavy-set black man with meaty shoulders and traps so pumped up that he didn't appear to have a neck, except that his expensive pink-and-white-striped tie had to be looped around something. On his black cheeks the stubble was short, coarse, sharp as iron filings and uniformly arranged as if aligned by a magnet under his skin. A mid-length 'fro stood out on his head a couple of inches. He glanced sideways at me and our eyes met for less than a second – more than enough time for us to realize that we had met once before, and that I had to kill him before he killed me. He roared and charged at my midsection, buried the point of his shoulder into my solar plexus and drove me into the wall. My head slammed into the empty paper towel dispenser and I felt the box crumple with the impact. He then tossed me hard into the concrete-block wall and I dropped like an old suitcase with a broken handle. A kick to the ribs came next; the kick was his and the ribs were mine – I'd have preferred it the other way round. The air rushed out of my lungs and wouldn't come back. I couldn't breathe. He bent over me to smash his elbow into my face. I moved and he missed, which opened up the angle to his nutsack making it fair game for the toe of my boot. So I drove it up, burying it between his legs, using the last of my strength. The man cried out and slumped to the floor beside me, curled into a ball, groaning.

Air started to work its way back into my lungs. I managed to suck down a breath, then another. The man came unsteadily to his feet, standing over me. Maybe he had small nuts and my kick had missed the spot.

'Get up,' he panted.

I came to my feet slow, using the wall.

'Show me your hands.'

I showed them – empty.

His weren't, not entirely. A dull black Walther fitted with a suppressor the size of a pork sausage occupied his right.

He put the gun in his jacket pocket with some difficulty, the sausage making it tricky, and poked it at me. I didn't know this goon by name, but I never forget a face. And neither did he, it seemed. Around six months ago I'd laid eyes on him a couple of times in Cyangugu, a small town on the Rwandan side of the border with the Democratic Republic of Congo. US advisors were on the ground there training a force of former insurgents, preparing them for integration into the DRC's army. At the time, I was in-country on close protection duties, babysitting a pair of touring celebrities entertaining our advisors. This asshole was there riding shotgun for Charles White, who was selling stolen US-made weapons to all takers, including claymores like the one that almost gave me a haircut. I guessed he was aware that Chuck and I weren't on the best of terms.

'What now?' I asked him.

'We go for walk,' he replied with a heavy French accent.

'Then what?'

'You know what. Turn around.'

As I began to do as he asked, the metal hand-towel dispenser remodeled by my head pivoted off its bracket, dropped off the wall and fell with a ringing clatter onto the concrete floor. The suit with the gun flinched a little, blinked and half turned, taking the gun in his pocket offline. I had maybe half a second. I used it to grab his tasteful silk tie, and yanked it as hard as I could, pulling it toward me. His body was twisted slightly and the force came from an odd direction. He teetered on his front foot, off balance, which I compounded by pulling down one side of his jacket, pinning an arm. I aimed a right cross at his chin and shortened the blow an inch or two so that the point of my elbow crashed into his nose. His hands went to his face and he reeled back. I helped him on his way, grabbing a handful of 'fro and bouncing his head off the wall. There was a loud *clink* as his teeth came into contact with the water pipes running down to the basin, and a couple of them flew out of his mouth and dropped into it, rattling like glass marbles against the porcelain. The pipe also caught his forehead, dazing him, and he slumped to the ground, the Walther clattering out of his hand.

I looked around, panting, unsure what to do, my heart working over-time. I couldn't leave this ape in the toilet block, and I didn't want him raising any alarm bells with the White brothers and von Weiss. I had to get him out of here and dispose of him somewhere, somehow.

I picked up the Walther and stuffed it in the back of my pants, then frisked him. His wallet and three magazines of what looked to be armor-piercing rounds became mine. Obviously, this guy wasn't going to let a little body armor stand in the way of a kill.

'Hey, you in there . . .'

It came from outside. A woman's voice. It was a whisper, a hoarse whisper meant for me. It didn't sound like Petinski. I wondered if maybe it was police. If so, how'd they know to address me in English rather than Portuguese? Maybe it wasn't police . . .

A woman appeared at the entrance, blonde and attractive. I'd seen her before.

'I'm armed and dangerous, honey,' I said.

'That makes two of us.'

She showed it to me. Small, .22 caliber, gold plated, pearl handle.

Unsure about what to do, I propped the unconscious brute against the wall, leaned on him and checked the Walther in case I needed to use it in a hurry. 'What do you want?' I asked her, stalling, taking the Walther off safety.

'You're CIA, formerly OSI. Your name's Cooper. I saw a picture of you walking into the tailoring shop over the CIA station downtown.'

'And you're von Weiss's toy.'

'More accurately, I'm Emma Shilling, MI6. We've got three minutes, perhaps less, before someone comes looking for me. And in the meantime you're going to need help dealing with that.'

I figured she meant the sack of shit propped up like a drunk against the wall. 'Put your costume jewelry away and come in with your hands where I can see them.' MI6. I couldn't check that the woman was who she said she was, but I figured she'd've shot me if she wasn't.

Slipping the weapon into a gold mesh purse, she clickety-clacked into the lavatory block on strappy heels. 'What happened?'

'He splashed on my shoes.'

'You're fucking crazy. He's got friends just around the corner.'

'The guy jumped me. We'd met before – another time and place. My cover was blown in a heartbeat.'

'We have to get rid of him.'

'He's too big to flush. I tried.'

The MI6 agent – if that's what she was – wasn't exactly outfitted for body disposal. Her dress was a white pleated fabric only slightly heavier than air, and it floated as if in slow motion around her slim, fit body. The unconscious sack of shit had blood oozing down his chin. I took my jacket off and handed it to her. 'If you're gonna help, put this on.'

She took the jacket. 'Wash his face.'

She spoke with a clipped English voice, like any moment she was going to ask me if I liked fox hunting. It was an upper-class public-school accent. I've hung out with enough Brit SAS guys to recognize one when I heard it. Turning on the tap in the sink, I cupped some water onto his nose and mouth and rinsed off most of the blood. Two teeth had been trapped by the grate over the drain hole. I pocketed them. When I was done, the woman threw on my jacket, turned inside out and worn wrong way round like a smock, and hooked her arms under his.

'We're between cable cars,' she said. 'As soon as a fresh load of tourists arrives, a queue will form here, so we don't have long. There's a path down there, a kind of nature walk. Out the door, down some stairs and veer left.'

I shouldered most of the guy's weight and made for the door, his feet taking one step for every three of mine. The woman acted like a rudder, guiding him from behind. A middle-aged Asian male heading for the john cut across our path with his wife, a short, thickset woman wearing jeans and a tourist t-shirt with the statue of Christ on it, arms outstretched. Both stopped and gaped at us disapprovingly as if thinking surely it was a little early in the day to be falling down drunk.

'Something he ate. Too much iron,' I explained to them as we stumbled past.

The man hurried his wife out of our way and pointed her toward the lavatory block.

'Down there,' directed the nicely dressed British agent.

I half fell down the steps and dragged our now semi-conscious captive with me. He was a heavy fuck. I wasn't going to be able to haul him too much farther.

'Left,' said the woman.

The path cut a tunnel through heavy jungle. Beyond the leaves and scrub were glimpses of another part of Rio across the bay, rising whitely from more turquoise shoreline.

'How much farther?' I grunted.

'Thirty yards or so.'

The heavily concussed man staggering between us was regaining more control over his limbs with every step. He was going to snap out of it properly any moment and I wanted him down on the ground with a gun in his face when that moment arrived.

'To the right,' the woman said as a fork in the path appeared. We followed it to the right until the fence came to an end at a signpost warning of danger ahead.

'I need to ask him some questions,' I said.

'No, we have to get rid of him *now*. *I* need to get back to von Weiss, and you have to vacate the area as soon as possible, because this man is going to be missed and they'll come looking. We're stopping here.'

Gladly. I stopped, panting, sweating heavily. His legs might have been moving, but I was still more or less carrying him. I rolled the man off my shoulder, into some low shrubs, insects chirping unseen in the bushes around us.

The woman parted a branch, which revealed a sheer drop and an unobstructed view of the ocean and sky. Black vultures wheeled on the air currents rising around the rock. 'We do what the locals here do when they want to get rid of a body.'

'And that is . . . ?'

'Feed the birds.'

Kneeling down, she grabbed a handful of his coat and tried to roll him toward the edge. He rolled some, but not enough.

The man groaned, on the edge of consciousness. I lifted his arm, pushed him over onto his side and then shoved him with my boot toward the void. He rolled onto his front and then his side. Another shove and the incline took over, momentum gathering, and then he tumbled off into the sky, gone without further sound.

Twenty

The woman who'd identified herself as Emma Shilling had dropped my coat on the path. I recovered it and caught up with her power-walking back toward the lavatory block, checking her watch, agitated. 'I've been away ten minutes. That's too long.'

'The facility was closed – you had to wait.'

'The people I'm with are *very* tense. Paranoia levels are high.'

'They seem pretty relaxed.'

'Trust me, they're not.'

'Serves 'em right for using fake passports,' I said.

'You and I both know that's not what this is all about.'

'Really? What's it about?'

'Nice try. You're with the Company. Ask your people at Langley.'

'CIA? We've just met and already you're insulting me.'

'If you're not CIA, then what are you? You bloody Yanks have more bloody secret agencies than I've had sodding boyfriends.'

'I take it you get around.' She ignored that so I cut to the chase. Or a small part of it at least. 'Randy Sweetwater. The name ring any bells with you?'

We were close to the block and could observe it clearly through the trees. There were more people milling around – the cable car must've arrived. The cleaner's cone was now in front of the men's section, clos-ing it to the public, but a giant of a man nevertheless walked out of it and went straight into the women's without a moment's hesitation. I'd seen this guy earlier getting out of the chopper, directing the security: one of von Weiss's men.

'Shit,' the Brit muttered when she saw him and drew back into deeper cover.

'Who's Dolph Lundgren?'

She knew who I meant. 'His name is Julio Salvadore. He's a sociopath from Paraguay and he's von Weiss's right-hand man. He's come looking for me. This is not good.'

'Like I said, the facility was closed, and you went on a hunt to find another.'

She took a second to process the excuse before nodding, accepting it. Meanwhile, I wondered what the cleaners would make of the blood spat-ter. I hoped they got to it before Dolph did. Speaking of whom, he exited the women's toilet, a perplexed female tourist trailing in his wake, bin-oculars around her neck. She checked the signage on the wall, evidently wondering whether it was she who was in the right section, while the Paraguayan looked around the area, hands on hips. Yep, he was a big motherfucker: six five and maybe two hundred and fifty pounds.

The British agent opened her purse, took out a black Chanel tube and used it to paint her pink lips a shade pinker. 'How do I look?'

In fact, nothing like a woman who'd just helped wrangle a gorilla off a mountaintop. I picked a leaf out of her golden hair, which was dead straight and cut Cleopatra-style. Dark makeup accentuated pale blue eyes that shone like there was a light source somewhere behind them. Her skin was olive, smooth and free of lines or blemishes of any kind. I pegged her age at maybe twenty-five. She was a nice juicy goat staked out by MI6 to catch a lion. 'You'll pass,' I told her.

'Okay, here goes.' She turned to go down the path to work her way back to the bar from another direction.

I stopped her. 'Randy Sweetwater was a pilot. He worked for von Weiss. Firecracker coloring . . . good with women.'

The tiniest of lines formed between her eyebrows. 'American, right? Yes, I think I've met him. He was around a lot, but not lately. He was a friend of yours, wasn't he?' Shilling must have seen something in my face. 'Von Weiss has a sensitive nose for double agents. If he suspected him, even a hint, he'd have been disappeared.' She took a card from her purse and gave it to me.

I already knew that von Weiss believed someone in his inner circle was a double agent. Did he know there were at least two? 'What about you?'

'I didn't come into this without skills.'

'Neither did Randy.'

'This is how I pay the rent, okay? What do *you* do?'

I looked into her bright blue-gray eyes and was reminded of sunlight on stainless steel. She'd handled the disposal of a body as easily as most women order cocktails. Yeah, she had skills, but she was working in an environment where they could easily get overwhelmed. I glanced at the card. A logo – silver on blue. '"Olympe." What's that?'

'A restaurant. Von Weiss will be there tonight. You be there too, if you can promise me you won't kill anyone.'

'I can't be in the same room with White – he'll recognize me.'

'He won't be there. I'll try to find out what I can about your friend.' She started to move.

'Not so fast,' I said.

'I have to go *now*, okay?'

'The guy in the orange knit – who's he?'

'A business associate of von Weiss's. He's representing another interest – I don't know whose. An important customer. That's all I know. I've never seen him before today.'

'Find out who he is.'

'You're giving the orders now?' she asked.

'Find out who he is, *please*. And watch out for the girl on his knee.'

'Sugar?'

'Yeah. I think you're her type.'

*

233

I went back to the ledge to make doubly sure there was no evidence left behind. A little crushed foliage, but that was it. I leaned out over the ledge. The drop was sheer all the way to the bottom five hundred feet below. A steep incline of scree, clear of suspicious-looking lumps of clothing, rose to meet the rock face from a bed of dense, dark green jungle. It was as if the mountain had opened up and swallowed the body whole. Convenient. Not even the vultures seemed especially interested in anything other than working the updrafts. That would change when the body – wherever it was down there – began to decompose. In this wet heat, I gave it a few hours. My fingers found the teeth in my pocket. I took them out and tossed them at the wind.

A couple of kids were chasing each other along the path when I rejoined it. I took the steps three at a time, up to the populated section of the lookout where the concessions were clustered. And a few minutes later I rendezvoused with Petinski and her camera in the shade of her tree.

'Where've you been?' she asked.

'The head,' I replied.

She glanced at my empty hands. 'Weren't you getting me a Coke?'

I took the card from my pocket and handed it to her. 'I picked this up instead – an invitation to dinner. It's where von Weiss will be this evening.'

'What? How . . . ? Who gave it to you?'

'Emma Shilling.'

'Who?'

'The blonde number snuggling up to our chief suspect over there. She's MI6, so she says.' I motioned at the bar where Shilling had rejoined the table. The man named Salvadore came in a few seconds behind her, but from another entrance.

'Jesus, Cooper . . .' said Petinski as she snapped off some more frames of the changing situation at the bar.

I noted von Weiss leaning toward Shilling for an exchange of words. She smiled, adding a shrug, laughed vivaciously, put on a show. The man called Salvadore bent toward the boss's other ear, and then Charles

White got in on the act, beckoning one of his peeps over. The tarantula and Sugar sipped their drinks and observed. Moments later, White's two remaining bodyguards got up from the table and strolled off in the direction of the washrooms, presumably to hunt for their missing colleague.

They'd find no trace of him. The cleaning detail was an added stroke of luck. I couldn't have planned it better if I'd planned it.

'You want to tell me what you've done, Cooper?' Petinski asked, wary as hell.

'Applied pressure,' I said.

'Which means?' Something on my forehead caught her attention and led to a closer examination of my face. She gripped my chin with her fingers and turned my head from side to side. 'You've been in a fight.'

I opened my jacket and showed her the Walther's handgrip. Then I told her about the run-in with the Whites' bodyguard, that we recognized each other and, as a consequence, one of us had to die. I said I preferred it to be him. She said there was a hung jury on her preference. I told her about Shilling happening along at an opportune moment, and how she helped me dispose of the body. That didn't get me anywhere with the jury, so I defended my actions further with some backstory about the slaughter the newly dead guy and his boss were promoting in Africa. Jury, still hung. I got a lecture about professional conduct, and I was about to get it all over again when von Weiss's chopper roared around the back of the mountain and made further dressing-down impossible to hear. Giving her what little news I had about Randy Sweetwater would have to wait.

Charles White's bodyguards came back from their search empty-handed. Something had happened to their buddy – he'd just up and disappeared. And now they were leaving in a hurry. Pressure applied. Petinski caught the departure on her Canon.

The Sugarloaf Mountain lookout lost a lot of its appeal once our persons of interest had flown away, so Petinski and I caught the next cable car to the base station, and from there made a beeline for the Palace. Petinski wanted to check in with her superiors, whoever they were, and I wanted to have a shower and wash the bodyguard's killing off my skin. Petinski was sitting at a desk by the balcony when I came out of the bathroom wearing a towel.

'Why would reception send us champagne?' she asked, holding a half-bottle of Bollinger. She read from a card. '"From your friends at reception."'

'I think it had something to do with the thumbs-up I gave Gracia there this morning as we left. A little victory signal.'

'Thanks a whole bunch, Cooper.'

'Just maintaining our cover.'

Petinski shook her head.

'What have you got there?' I asked, seeing photos up on her iPad.

'Which of these men did you throw off the cliff?'

Three photographs taken at the bar earlier were lined up on screen.

'The guy on the right,' I said. His face was turned three-quarters to the camera lens. High cheekbones, broad nose and dark skin with black eyes beneath a heavy brow.

'I got us reservations at the restaurant. We were lucky – they had a cancellation.'

'So long as it wasn't von Weiss who canceled.'

'Good point. That reminds me, I had Langley check out Shilling. Her real name is Amanda Shaeffer. She's a captain in the Royal Marines. A commando – Green Berets, no less. These days she works for a counter-terror research group attached to the UK Ministry of Defence, which can mean anything, including MI6.'

Curiosity drew me back to the desk. On the iPad screen, shots of White's henchmen were replaced by a publicity photo of a woman crawling through a muddy trench with a light machine gun in her hands. Amanda Shaeffer. I barely recognized the woman I'd met earlier. The accompanying assessment sheet said she'd graduated from the Royal Marines Commando Training Centre at Lympstone, Devon, on her first attempt – a rarity.

'Britain doesn't let women fight on the frontlines,' said Petinski. 'I guess the Ministry of Defence found a way to tap into her talents.'

'I asked her about Randy,' I said.

Petinski looked up. 'And?'

'She's seen him around, but not for a while.'

'How long's "a while"?'

'She didn't say, and there was no time to elaborate.'

My partner scowled, well aware that pulling a disappearing act around von Weiss could mean the worst.

'We'll find him,' I said, only because I couldn't say much else.

She sat back in her chair, let her arms hang loose by her side and closed her eyes for a few long seconds. 'I appreciate the encouragement, Vin,' she said when she opened them. 'But Randy knew the risks. It's important to me that you know my concern for him isn't about our personal relationship. That ended before this mission began. I don't even have the right to resent Alabama. She was just next in line. If it wasn't her it would've been someone else. I'm concerned because Randy was my partner, professionally speaking.'

'Vin?' I said, a little stunned. 'Have we broken through something here, Kim?'

'Is that all you took out of what I just said?'

'Of course not.'

'You're not making this easy, y'know.' She fingered the card from the restaurant. 'You're good at what you do, Cooper. It's random and it's not my way, but I have to admit it's effective. You made contact with MI6 and now we're going to be able to stay on von Weiss and maybe gain some intel on him in real time. I've been pretty uptight. I'm sorry that we haven't worked more as a team.'

'Is this an apology for being an abrupt, blunt, aloof, snooty, humorless, uncommunicative ice maiden?'

'What?'

'Apology accepted.'

'Don't you ever take anything seriously?' she asked.

'Who's joking?'

Petinski blinked at me.

'One thing, though. You mind if I stick with Petinski? Calling you Kim just feels like some other person.'

She stood up.

'Where are you going?' I asked.

'To take a bath. That okay?'

'You get an answer from Washington on this unknown guy with von Weiss?'

'No,' she snapped impatiently. 'He's not in our database. They're checking with our friends and allies. There's nothing we can do for the moment. So, if you don't mind . . .'

'Go right ahead. Hey, I might review the photos you took today. Where do I find 'em?'

'There's a folder on the desktop.' Petinski disappeared into the bathroom and I heard the water run.

I went to her collection of Mac products, selected the laptop, opened the folder and set up the six hundred and thirty-seven photos in it to run as a slideshow. At two seconds a slide, that would be a little over twenty minutes viewing time. I poured two Glenfiddich minis into a short glass with rocks, sat back and watched. I skipped the chopper landing and went straight for the party settling into the bar. First up: Sugar. She really was as hot as I remembered her and I felt a certain tingle, the memory of our time in the Bally's pool coming back. Her smooth coffee-colored skin, that cute button nose and a pair of full lips that could suck the shell off a boiled egg. In the photo I was looking at, the tarantula was beside her, leaning back, one arm hooked over the back of his chair. He was smirking, his other hand unseen under the table. Knowing Sugar, and from the smile on her lips, I could guess at what it was up to. 'Lucky bastard,' I murmured.

A procession of photos of Falco and Charles White came next, a continuous series of them dealing with the waiter, placing orders. Seeing photos of Charles White sitting happily instead of lying face down on the ground with the back of his head blown out was hard to take. Their dead bodyguard featured in several shots. Knowing the guy's immediate future chased away the bad feelings and replaced them with a happy glow.

Individual shots of von Weiss and then Shilling followed. I paused the show on a photo that captured them together. Von Weiss's attention was directed at someone opposite, out of view, probably the tarantula, while Shilling's was focused on von Weiss. On her lips was a Mona Lisa smile. I wondered what she was thinking.

I examined von Weiss. His face was peeled and implanted to the point of absurdity – like an extreme makeover gone horribly wrong. He was one of Brazil's richest men, an arms dealer, a suspected killer, the illegitimate child of an infamous Nazi war criminal, a world authority on snakes, and – given that he'd somehow managed to get his hands on one of our nukes and intended to use it – also something of an evil genius. A complex character. I wondered what type indicators would sit at the bottom of *his* emails.

Back to Shilling/Shaeffer. If I had known nothing about her, her presence at the table wouldn't have been surprising. Von Weiss might've looked a little freakish, but he had money, and money, generally speaking, seemed to help beautiful women overlook plenty. Shilling fit the part of the rich guy's trophy perfectly: perfect golden hair, perfect golden skin, eyes that hinted at infinity, perfect body. They seemed the perfect couple. Only, as Shilling herself had said, it didn't take much for von Weiss to disappear people who weren't who they said they were. Given what I knew about the real Emma Shilling, I could see a few bumps ahead in their relationship. I hoped she knew when to run.

I sipped at my single malt and watched one of White's bodyguards get directions to the head, followed not too long after by Shilling, who excused herself, stood up from the table and also took directions from one of the bar staff, right around the time I was being stomped on.

The slideshow continued while I chose an ice cube and rolled it around in my mouth. Von Weiss summoned Salvadore, who took the same exit Shilling did, presumably because she wasn't back from the powder room quick enough for his liking. More photos of the Whites, the tarantula, von Weiss, Sugar and the bodyguards. Eventually Shilling reappeared, followed by Salvadore.

With the chopper's arrival, the party vacated the bar and headed for the heliport in a hurry. Petinski had snapped off shots of the arriving chopper, and then swung her camera back to von Weiss's party, and then back to the chopper. There were close-ups of the aircraft's registration and other markings. It pivoted and approached the heliport with the cockpit front-on to the camera. Close-ups on the aircrew followed. It was when she brought the lens to bear on the pilot that I nearly choked on the ice cube. I went through several photos to make doubly sure, and then enlarged the clearest of them. Jesus, there was no doubt. I knew this pilot. His name was LeDuc. He was the little French fuck who'd double-crossed me and a bunch of others back in the Congo. He'd flown us into a trap on a UN chopper and then sprung it. People died because of this asshole's perfidy. LeDuc was AWOL from the Armée de l'Air, the French Air Force, and had made Interpol's Most Wanted list. He was near the top of mine. I owed this cocksucker a strike with a rusty machete to the side of the neck, and seeing his Frog face suddenly back in my world I renewed the vow to collect.

That LeDuc was part of von Weiss's troop made sense. The weapons the Whites were trading in central Africa came from the Brazilian arms dealer. And in the Congo, LeDuc was teamed up with Charles White. LeDuc, White, von Weiss – they were all in it together. The blood pounded in my temples. I downed the rest of the single malt, put the laptop back on the desk, stood up, turned to go to the fridge and ran straight into Petinski – hard. She rebounded off me. I grabbed her hand so that she didn't end up sprawled on the carpet, and her towel almost fell away. In a panic, she snatched it and held it against her breasts. We were close. I could smell her peppermint breath and her moisturizer. I grinned and said, 'Oops,' as I released her hand.

Our lips were only inches apart. Did I read something in her eyes – a weakening of her resolve, perhaps? I closed the gap between us an inch or so, reading her signals, feeling the electricity.

'Don't even fucking think about it, Cooper,' she whispered.

Twenty-one

The cab pulled up outside Olympe forty minutes ahead of our booking. We were early because the layout of the place had to be known to us before von Weiss arrived. The restaurant was in a small stand-alone wedge-shaped building in the Rio 'burbs, situated at the end of a narrow one-way street. We expected to be the first patrons to arrive, but inside the door I was surprised to see the maître d' accompanied by a gorilla in an expensive suit, with a jaw like reinforced concrete and wearing an earpiece. I recognized him from the excursion to Sugarloaf. If nothing else, the forward planning told me the people handling the security for von Weiss were pros.

'I must examine you,' he informed us once the maître d' was satisfied we had a reservation.

'I've had my yearly check-up,' I told him. He frowned like he didn't understand, so I made it easier for him. 'I don't think so, mac.'

'We are sorry, sir,' said the maître d', wincing, seemingly pained by my reluctance to submit, 'but tonight there is security. We have a VIP coming to Olympe. If you will not satisfy this request, then we must postpone your reservation for another night.'

'Go with it,' Petinski advised me.

241

The inspection rankled, but I put my arms out from my sides anyway and allowed myself to be patted down. He found nothing.

'Your wife now,' he said.

'Fiancée,' I said.

Petinski took half a step forward.

The man bent down to run his hands up the inside of her calves. 'Careful, pal,' I said, 'if you value your thumbs.' He hesitated, probably wondering what the hell I meant, but took his paws elsewhere anyway. There wasn't much to check. Petinski was all breasts and legs in a flimsy almost see-through babydoll number that hung barely to mid-thigh. After buying it in a hurry from a dress shop at the Palace, she'd told me it wasn't her style. I told her it should be.

The security guy finished the job by feeling the hollow of her back, and withdrew against the wall with a grunt and a flick of his hand to send us on our way.

The maître d', a middle-aged guy with a big nose and a tub of product in his hair, directed us to our table.

'Who's your VIP?' I asked him.

He shrugged. 'Sorry, sir, I cannot say.'

I let it go. I knew who was coming to dinner anyway. The dining area was split into two sections, a room with a couple of larger tables in the center and, off to one side, a long red-paneled seat that ran the length of the wall faced by smaller tables. We were being led to the wall, which meant that either Petinski or I was going to have to sit with our back to the room. I drew the short straw – back to the room.

The maître d' flipped out the napkin, put it on Petinski's lap and said, 'Please, my apology for this.' He meant the security check rather than the seating or the napkin. 'Can I get you a drink? It is a courtesy of the house.'

Petinski chose something from the menu, some local extravaganza with pineapple pieces and cherries that looked and sounded like a Carnival float. I ordered my usual, a fine selection of single malts in plain view at the bar.

'You said you didn't drink,' I commented.

'You're not the best influence, Cooper.'

I looked her up and down. 'It's what I do, but you're resisting.'

'Are you referring to the moment back at the hotel?'

'Maybe. Have you given it some thought?'

'Haven't you learned that getting involved with your partner is not such a great idea? I have.'

'Who wants involvement? I was thinking more along the lines of a shallow meaningless roll in the hay. And you haven't answered the question.'

'Despite what you might think, I'm not an *ice maiden*, Cooper.' There was the suggestion of a smile in her eyes. 'Of course I thought about it and I decided against it. Now, can we get back to work, please?'

We spent a few minutes in comfortable silence, looking around, taking in the surroundings. The maître d' returned with our drinks on a tray. He set Petinski's on the table in front of her, then mine in front of me. Petinski picked hers up and took the straw between her lips and went back to keeping an eye on the front of house.

An excessive number of waiters stood around, hinting at the size of the tab Uncle Sam would be picking up for Petinski and me. This was no cheap eatery. The bar was not actually a bar but a bench where drinks were prepared. Behind it through a slatted blind was a kitchen half the size of the seating area, staffed by chefs in white aprons and tall white hats.

I excused myself, got up and went to the bathroom. The facilities for men and women were side by side, located behind a screen at the rear of the restaurant. The men's was the size of a closet, with only enough room for two. A small window on the back wall was locked partially open, and barred. The layout of the women's probably wouldn't be any different. I wasn't sure what Shilling had planned, but separating her from von Weiss without raising suspicion, even for a few seconds, was going to be a problem. At least without a little help. I took out my cell and put in a call.

As I returned to our table more diners arrived to experience the unusual greeting at the front door. No one seemed to mind it all that much, which was surprising. Perhaps getting frisked was a regular feature of the fine dining experience in Rio. I understood the reason for the security. In this place, if a gunman with a grudge came through the front door there'd be nowhere to go for von Weiss but straight to hell. I liked to think that White's missing bodyguard might have had something to do with all the precaution, but then, maybe not. If *I* was von Weiss's security, I'd have vetoed this venue. The conclusion I came to at the end of all this consideration was that von Weiss was quietly confident, at least in his hometown.

The joint began to fill fast. I checked my watch: seven twenty-five. Von Weiss was late. And then the door opened and Dolph Lundgren walked in, ducking slightly to avoid bumping his head. Yeah, he was a *big* motherfucker. He had a few words for his colleague getting personal with the dinner patrons, and then went back out. He came in again a handful of seconds later, another goon following, then von Weiss walked in with Shilling and both were fawned over by the maître d' and the chef, who raced out from the kitchen. Two more bodyguards brought up the rear, immediately breaking off and going on an inspection of the restaurant, double-checking the facilities, entrances and exits.

'Turn around, Cooper. It's impolite to stare,' I heard Petinski say.

'Just fitting in with the general trend,' I said, noting that pretty much everyone in the restaurant, men and women, had also forgotten their manners.

In my case the reason for the etiquette slip was Shilling, who was peeling herself out of a tight-fitting coat to reveal a long filmy canary-yellow dress with no back and barely a front that glimmered in the low light. Her hair did likewise while her skin glowed with a touch of the sun.

'She's beautiful,' said Petinski, stating the obvious.

'Scrubs up okay.' I again compared the woman handing her coat to the maître d' to the one hauling a Minimi light machine gun through the mud. 'What's von Weiss doing?'

'Being shown to their table.'

Behind me, I could hear the maître d' chatting away, being super friendly, laughing. The mental picture I had of the restaurant told me that von Weiss and Shilling had been allocated the single table in the area behind ours, rather than seating against the wall. The bodyguards, with the exception of Dolph, had taken up stations at strategic points in the restaurant: by the front door, outside the restrooms, outside the kitchen. I glanced over my shoulder quickly and saw that Dolph was standing close to his boss, but not too close.

I was right about where von Weiss and Shilling were seated. Petinski had a clear view of both of them over my shoulder. 'This is not good for any meeting with Shilling. They've got the place bottled up,' she murmured.

'Let's see what develops,' I said.

'What are you up to?'

'Let's eat,' I said, motioning at a waiter.

'We're not here for the food.'

'I'm hungry.'

I sensed movement behind me, followed by the scent of expensive perfume. Then I saw Shilling walking to the facilities, every male head in the joint following her progress. The lummox guarding the restroom stood aside to let her past.

Petinski cleared her throat and glanced briefly down at her lap. Something was up. 'What just happened?' I asked her.

'Von Weiss looked at me,' she replied, leaning forward, using my bulk as cover. 'It was a certain kind of look. I need a shower.'

'It was just a look.'

'Trust me, there was a lot packed into it.'

*

The atmosphere in the restaurant settled down into a kind of normalcy, despite the heavy security and the fact that the staff took every opportunity to grovel over their extra-special guests. Meanwhile, however, I managed to even the score with Petinski over her breakfast effort and ordered a plate of barbecued meats to share. Genuine conversation between us was almost non-existent, though Petinski put on a good show, giggling occasionally, leaning forward to touch my hand, doing the things couples in love do when it's dinner for two at a swanky restaurant.

Shilling got up again to go to the bathroom. This time I followed her a minute later. Maybe there was something about this restaurant I hadn't considered, a way we could communicate that I hadn't spotted. The security guard's eyes bored unblinkingly into mine as I approached, issuing a kind of primal challenge.

'Evening,' I said with a smile as I tried to edge by. 'Need to do number two.' I got no sense that he understood anything other than my desire to visit the john. He stopped me, blocking the way, just to show me who was in control, I figured.

I put my hand in my pocket and brought out some loose change. 'Hey, you keep a nice bathroom, buddy,' I told him and pressed a few coins into his giant paw. 'Nice clean towels. I like a clean towel.'

As I sidled past him, I saw the guy look at the money in his hand like it was something picked up off the pavement, drop it on the floor and wipe his hand on his trousers.

I did what I had to do in there, which was basically to inspect the space again. Nothing. Shilling was on the other side of the wall. I tapped on the brickwork but received zip in reply so I washed my hands, dried them with the air blower and went back to my table.

The doorman growled at me as I thanked him again.

'Darling,' said Petinski, 'you're back. See what that nice rich man over there has just sent us?' A bottle of Krug sat in a silver bucket on a tripod beside her elbow. A waiter placed two frosted flutes of cut crystal on the table and pulled the bottle from the ice. I glanced over my shoulder and gave von Weiss a friendly nod, which he returned. Out the corner of an eye I saw Shilling angle her way back to her seat, silencing the conversations at the tables she passed. 'And look what else he sent me,' Petinski continued, motioning at a silver tray in front of her that I hadn't noticed. On it was a small black plastic envelope with gold trim. A *condom*! Fucking cheeky bastard.

Petinski smiled a fake smile at me and said, 'Measured response, Cooper.'

I picked up the rubber, pushed my chair back and went to have a few indignant fiancé-type words with the man who'd just tried to pick up my bride-to-be. By the time I got there, two goons were already standing behind their boss, one of them being Dolph, ready for whatever I might choose to do in retaliation.

'What the hell's the meaning of this?' I said to von Weiss, slamming the raincoat onto the table in front of him.

'Your girlfriend is very beautiful, Mr . . .'

'She's my *fiancée*, pal. You're lucky I don't bust you in the nose.'

'Oh, you are American. Where are you staying?' he said, looking up at me pleasantly, a long way from being threatened, full of accommodation. 'You must allow me to—'

One of his security doofuses, the guy monitoring the front door, walked in a hurry across the room and interrupted us to have a word in his boss's ear.

And suddenly the front door of the restaurant burst open and four helmeted men in black overalls and body armor tagged with the word *Polisi* stormed in. Consternation filled the room, along with the blue and red flashing lights from law-enforcement vehicles outside the windows. One of the police made an announcement in Portuguese, which drew a muffled scream from a woman somewhere in the room, and everyone was instantly on their feet, rushing for the door.

I grabbed the maître d' by the arm as he ran past. 'What's going on?'

'Please, there is a bomb threat. We are being evacuated.' His eyes were wide with fear. I released him and he made a break for the door, pushing in front of restaurant patrons.

Petinski arrived beside me, dabbing the corners of her mouth with a napkin. 'Great. Just when we were making progress . . .'

A worried police officer with an MP5 submachine gun attached to the ammo rack across his chest approached us. '*Senhor, senhora. Desta forma, por favor. Pressa, pressa . . .*' he said and ushered us toward the exit.

Once at the door, we got some notion of the pandemonium outside. It wasn't just the restaurant that was being evacuated, but the entire street outside the Olympe along with the one beside it, two blocks at least. Many of the buildings in the area were apartments, which meant a large number of occupants – frightened people of varying ages being moved along. Here and there, folks were having their IDs checked by police with powerful flashlights and German shepherds. Dark blue police vans were everywhere, along with bomb squads and bomb detection dogs. Fifty yards from the restaurant, a beat-up white Toyota van had been taped off and surrounded at a distance by police. I gathered that's where the device was.

Dogs barked, lights flashed, infants bawled and people shouted at each other. I was about to say something to Petinski when I realized that she was no longer beside me, the generalized panic having separated us.

'Cooper, come with me, please.'

It was a police officer, suddenly materialized in my face. He had to say it again before the fact that he knew my name registered on my brain. I looked at him. Black helmet, black armor with the word *Polisi* on it, side arm strapped to his thigh. He looked familiar.

'Hey, Cooper, wake up there, boy. Jeb Delaney, here to do some good.'

Recognition. 'Hey, Delaney.'

'This way,' he said.

Four armored Polisi formed a box around us and we hustled across the street to a double-parked white Ford Explorer with darkened windows.

'Let's go,' Delaney said, pulling open the door.

Inside I caught a hint of gold dress. Emma Shilling. The door slammed shut behind me and the Explorer hauled ass, a blue light flashing up behind the windshield, the siren chirping on and off, people scattering in its headlight beams like schools of frightened fish.

'This bomb scare your idea?' Shilling asked me.

'No,' I said.

Delaney looked over his shoulder from the front passenger seat and grinned. 'Well, actually, Cooper, it was, kinda . . . You called and said you needed some action, and that's what y'all got.'

'Jesus, Cooper,' Shilling huffed, 'you're determined to get me bloody well killed, aren't you?'

'Relax. Your boyfriend will be convinced,' said Delaney. 'This is genuine, at least as far as the police are concerned.'

'You didn't need to do this,' she insisted.

'How were you gonna pull off a meeting at that restaurant?' I asked.

'Subtlety.'

'Subtlety . . .'

'You wanted the name of the man von Weiss has been entertaining, right?'

'Among other things.'

'Look in your right-hand pants pocket.'

I leaned back to get my hand inside and felt around in there – loose change, some gum, a lint ball and a card. Everything in there I already knew about except the card. I took it out as the Explorer bucked viciously over a curb and accelerated into the general Rio traffic, the sirens and lights by now killed off. There was handwriting on the card. I glanced at Shilling.

'I slipped it in there when you stormed up to defend your fiancée's honor,' she said. 'Subtlety.'

I angled the card at the streetlights strobing through the window. 'Gamal Abdul-Jabbar. Who's he?'

Shilling had her own question. 'Where are we going?'

'A safe house,' said Delaney.

The British agent scanned the streetscape through her window. 'How far away is it? Not in another bloody country, I hope.'

'It's a couple of minutes from here,' Delaney reassured her.

'What about von Weiss?' she asked. 'He doesn't like it when people go missing, unless he's the person who ordered it.'

'Don't worry about lover boy. We figure you've got forty minutes breathing space.'

'Forty minutes? No. He'll call me.'

'I don't think so. We killed cell reception in the area. Don't want our terrorist setting off his car bomb remotely now, do we.' He winked at us.

The Explorer veered off the main road and reduced speed as it climbed up a hillside. Several wild corners later, we came to a stop.

'We're here,' Delaney announced.

'Good, I think I'm about to be sick,' said Shilling.

Out the window was a narrow gray terrace in an old rundown neighborhood. Delaney dangled a Smurf hanging from a key at us. 'Who wants it?'

'Twenty minutes and not a minute more, okay?' said Shilling, snatching the little blue guy. 'Then you take me back.'

Delaney agreed, 'Okay, twenty minutes. The alarm code is CIA-have-a-nice-day.'

Shilling rolled her eyes and we both got out.

Inside, the safe house appeared to be someone's home. Football trophies were arranged in a glass case, photos of kids playing the game shared the walls with cheap artwork from the tourist market. On the floor, old green carpet complete with stains. In the kitchen, an ancient fridge painted up like the Brazilian flag contained some cheeses, various bottles of spices and condiments, plates of leftovers and so forth.

'So what do I call you?' I said. 'Shilling or Shaeffer?'

'Shilling. Let's keep it in character.'

'You want a drink if I can find anything?'

'Love one. There's sure to be a bottle of *cachaça* somewhere.'

'What's that?'

'National drink of Brazil. If there's a choice, I'll have scotch.'

The woman had taste. 'You get the glasses,' I said. 'I'll have rocks.' I found the liquor in a cupboard. 'What's *cachaça* distilled from?' I held a bottle of the stuff with a graphic of a squid on it.

'Sugarcane.'

'Not calamari?'

'No.'

I was intrigued, but I put it back anyway and found a liter of Cutty Sark moored in the back of the cupboard. Shilling had glasses with ice on the benchtop. I took the card she'd slipped into my pocket and flicked it over, repeating my earlier question. 'Gamal Abdul-Jabbar – who is he?'

'A Somali pirate. He was involved in that cock-up back in '11 with the Italian cruise ship. The one where three of the crew were shot. We think he might've been one of the shooters. Before that he was a hit-man for Al-Shabab, killing opposition elements in Mogadishu. Not particularly skilled, just your average psychopath. He's twenty-two, illiterate and already has five million US in a Swiss account. He's learned that crime pays.'

On my cell, I pulled up a photo that Petinski had sent me of the tarantula guy taken poolside and showed it to her.

'Yep – that's him. We going to have that drink or we going to let it age in the bottle a little longer?'

I grinned and poured. 'What's he doing with von Weiss?'

'Don't know. Not exactly. He's not a direct customer, not a buyer. London suspects he's acting on someone's behalf. He's a middleman, or a lieutenant perhaps. More than likely he's representing a big fish back home in Mogadishu, one of the city's war lords. Several of them are von Weiss's regular customers. What's your interest in him?'

The only question that mattered was whether he had anything to do with a missing W80, but I couldn't go there. 'Is it possible Gamal might be striking out on his own?'

Shilling picked up her drink. I followed her out of the kitchen into the front room where she turned on a lamp and switched off the main ceiling light. I noticed she wasn't wearing underwear.

'London doesn't think so,' she said. 'But you don't know until you know, right?' She clinked my glass with hers. 'Cheers, Vin Cooper, number twelve on the World's Sexiest People list.'

'You googled me.'

'Of course.'

'No biggie. Homer Simpson was number eleven.'

She sipped her drink. 'I also read about your escapades in the Congo with those celebrities. What were they like?'

'Like you'd expect they'd be.' I went back to the business at hand and scrolled through the photos on my cell till I found the one I was looking for.

'Yes, that's Randy,' she said when I showed it to her. 'Nice photo. Who's the woman?'

'His girlfriend.'

'She's pretty.'

'At the moment, she's pretty worried.' The photo was a headshot of the both of them, laughing, the Vegas skyline at sunset in the background. 'You manage to get anything more on Randy's whereabouts?'

'No, not in the few hours since this morning's escapades. I can't exactly go round asking direct questions, you know. I pick things up in conversation, or not at all. I'm just an ornament with ears.'

And now that she mentioned it, those ears of hers had ornaments: a three-carat stone on a fine platinum chain swung from each lobe, the light refracting through the facets, breaking into rainbows.

'Get those on a captain's salary?' I asked.

Shilling knew what I was referring to and her fingers came up and fiddled with one of them self-consciously. 'They were gifts. And even though I've bloody well earned them I don't get to keep them. As for Randy, I'm sorry – especially for his significant other.' She rested up against the edge of a table. 'I wish I knew more.'

The fact that he just seemed to have disappeared was making me think of the vultures up on Sugarloaf.

Shilling sipped her drink. 'He tortures people, you know. There was a man not so long ago – von Weiss had his hands smashed, all of his fingers and knuckles. Then he beached him on an island off the coast here called Queimada Grande. The place is full of venomous snakes. Von Weiss laughed his head off watching the poor sod die.'

'You were there?'

'On the boat.'

Snakes. Queimada Grande. The FedEx package sent to Alabama. 'His name was Fruit Fly,' I said.

She was surprised. 'You know about that?'

'There's something big going down in, we think, around eight days time,' I said.

'But you can't tell me what it is?'

I shook my head. 'No, but we think it involves this guy.' I brought up a photo of Lieutenant Ed Dyson, alias Stu Forrest, the weather guy who stole a plane from Nevada Aircraft Brokers and flew it south at pretty much the moment Petinski and I turned up there to ask questions.

'Yeah, I've met him before. Several times. He stayed with us just yesterday, and then he left.'

'Headed where?'

'I walked in on a conversation between him and von Weiss. I heard Dar mentioned.'

'Where?'

'Dar es Salaam.'

'Africa?'

'D'uh.' Shilling smiled, glints in the flecks in her eyes matching the ones in her diamonds. 'Anyway, as you say, there is a kind of countdown going on in the von Weiss world. I don't know what it's about – you do, obviously – but O Magnifico's up to his neck in it. I've been told to pack. We're leaving tomorrow or the next day. Meanwhile, everyone's jumpy as hell. And pulling that vanishing act on White's bodyguard today didn't help.'

'You travel with von Weiss a lot.'

'Yes.'

'Does he usually tell you where you're going?'

'Yes.'

'But this time he's being vague about it.'

'I don't think the vagueness is directed at me. Even though I've heard it mentioned, I just don't think we're going to Dar es Salaam. Berlin is more his speed, sometimes Rome. Just lately he's taken a shine to Moscow.' She examined my face. 'You think because he hasn't told me where we're going I'm under suspicion?'

'Would you jump ship if you thought you were?'

'In a heartbeat. Von Weiss takes great pleasure watching people die.'

I wasn't convinced she'd be going anywhere in a hurry. Shilling was a conscientious employee and maybe too eager to please for her own good.

'Hey, I know what I'm doing, okay.' She poured another splash of

Cutty for herself and a regular sousing for me. 'Anyway, along with the usual suspects, I've heard Dubrovnik mentioned, along with Cape Town, Tel Aviv, Malta. Von Weiss knows there are other moles in his organization, aside from the ones he's unearthed. Not being specific about our destination is just him being careful. Loose lips and all that.' She took a big mouthful of whisky and passed it from one bulging cheek to the other like she was rinsing her mouth.

I showed her another photo. 'How about this man?'

'Sure. That's Laurent Duval, von Weiss's personal pilot.'

'His real name is André LeDuc, formerly of the French Air Force. He's a deserter. He's also wanted by Interpol and the Générale de la Sécurité Extérieure for illegal weapons trading, murder, conspiracy to murder, and extortion.'

She smiled. 'Yeah, but can he fly?'

The jury was out on that one. 'The one time I flew with him he crashed the plane, so maybe not.'

Shilling snorted. 'Jesus, this just keeps getting better.'

'How about this guy?' I asked, pulling up another mug shot.

'Yeah. He came to dinner on von Weiss's boat over a month ago. Can't remember his name.'

'Ty Morrow.'

'What's his claim to fame?'

'Attempted murder, conspiracy to murder, conspiracy to import drugs, illegal weapons smuggling.'

'Well, you wouldn't expect von Weiss's pals to be missionaries. Do you *really* know what's going on? What von Weiss is up to? Or is this just a CIA fishing expedition?'

'I'm not CIA,' I told her.

'Jesus, Cooper, of course you bloody well are. Maybe you just don't know it. Your partner, Kim Petinski – I've seen her before. In London a year back at some US Embassy bash. Before I came here. We weren't introduced, but she was pointed out to me as a Company girl.'

Petinski, CIA . . . Of course I knew that. I just hadn't been prepared to accept it.

'So, you know of course that von Weiss is a snake expert, and now you know he enjoys making people suffer. Oh – and he's a big fan of the Nazis, which is connected in his mind, I'm sure, to his bastard father, Josef Mengele.'

'We know,' I said.

Realization dawned on her. 'Hey, it was *you* who broke into his home, wasn't it?'

'I didn't break anything. The door was open.'

'You took his *Mein Kampf* signed by Hitler. You know that's his most treasured possession? O Magnifico was mad as hell when he realized it was gone. There's half a million dollars on your head because of that.'

'That's a lot of money. I might turn myself in.'

'Well, it's not on *your* head, exactly,' she said. 'Von Weiss doesn't know who stole it, but the word is out. The man who tries to sell that diary will end up like Mr Fruit Fly.' Shilling finished her drink and put the glass down on the table beside her. She was getting edgy, conscious of the time.

'What can you tell me about von Weiss? What kind of man is he?'

'Well, for one thing, he hates the United States. And perhaps hate isn't a strong enough word for it. He's in a constant rant about what he calls "the American evil".'

'What's his problem?'

'He's convinced that if we hadn't entered the war, Hitler – his big hero – would've won.'

'Maybe he's right,' I said. 'And maybe someone should remind him it was Adolf's fault for declaring war on us.'

'I'm sure he knows that.'

'How does he feel about you guys – the Brits? You won that war too, didn't you?' I grinned at her.

'We're okay. We're Anglo-Saxons, almost as pure as the Aryan master race, don't you know. The Nazis saw us as brothers in the great fight.'

'The great fight . . . ?'

'The one against the Jews. The fact that the States is such a supporter of Israel is where his tirades usually end up.'

255

Was von Weiss's hatred of the US the driving force to steal a nuke and use it against us?

'He rubs his hands together with joy at the problems you're having in the Middle East – with Iran, with Afghanistan and Pakistan. He believes Islam will one day triumph. All they need is a standard to rally behind. Or a leader perhaps.'

I drank my drink. Von Weiss – when all was said and done he was just another nutcase with a grudge.

'What else can I tell you about O Magnifico,' she said, joining me in a sip. 'Well, fortunately for me, he's not the kind of man who likes to fuck.'

'Then what kind is he?' I replied, doing my best to keep my tone nice and even while wiping my nose with the back of my hand, catching the trickle of Cutty I'd just snorted back through it. Shilling was cool, the way a gin and tonic in a long tall glass with ice and a slice of lemon is cool. I had to admit thoughts about the nature of her relationship with von Weiss had crossed my mind.

'He's the kind who prefers to watch. He likes to dress women in uniform – a Nazi SS uniform, preferably – and watch them masturbate with whatever comes to hand. He's got a python. He likes to watch me do it with that.' She picked up the bottle. 'Y'know, I probably shouldn't drink scotch. It's my own personal sodium pentothal . . .'

Twenty-two

I swallowed hard. Just then, a key fumbled in the front door lock.

Jeb Delaney strode in. 'That's twenty minutes. Time's up, y'all. Let's go.'

'Give me a minute,' said Shilling. She put her glass down and went to find the bathroom.

I was still thinking about her little bedroom admission.

'In the confusion, we made sure Vee Dubyah and a couple of his flunkies got caught up with the anti-terror cops,' Delaney reported. 'We separated him from one of his bodyguards so it wouldn't look too suspicious. Ms Shilling couldn't be the only one of his people to get cut from the herd. Just got word they had to let Vee Dubyah go a couple of minutes ago. The guy was screaming for his attornies.'

The British agent walked back into the main room off the kitchen, her hair and makeup fine-tuned.

'You hear that?' I asked her.

'Yes.'

'We'd best get you back soonest, ma'am,' Delaney told her.

'Please,' she said.

'What about Petinski?' I asked.

'Yeah, they stalled her too,' Delaney said. 'Got caught up in a group of about a hundred people with Vee Dubyah and co. ID checks and so forth. The local boys put on a good show. Looked completely legit.'

'How do you want to handle the return?' I asked Shilling.

'Get me to a place where I can catch a cab,' she said, walking to the door. 'I'll take it from there.'

'How do I contact you?' In fact, what I wanted was to stop her returning to von Weiss's snake pit, but there was no way I could make that happen. And I had a suspicion Shilling wouldn't allow it even if I could. She was doing what she was trained to do, the total professional.

'You don't, Cooper. *I* do the contacting. If something happens and I need to get hold of you, I'll find a way.'

*

'Why didn't you tell me that's what you were doing?' Petinski asked when I walked back into our room at the Palace.

'Me? I didn't *do* anything,' I told her. 'I didn't tell you about the bomb scare because I didn't know there was going to be one. I called Delaney up from the bathroom at the restaurant and asked if he could cause a diversion, something that would give us some time with Shilling, on account of we couldn't get near her. The bomb scare was what he came up with.'

'I turned around when we got outside and you were gone.'

'Same,' I said.

'What did you get out of her?'

I took the card from my pocket and handed it to her. 'The guy we saw poolside this morning with the Whites, the man von Weiss has been entertaining. His name is Gamal Abdul-Jabbar. He's a Somali pirate, as well as being a hit-man. He likes to shoot Italians.'

'I know,' she said and turned her iPad around to face me. Abdul-Jabbar's mug shot and rap sheet were up on screen. A CIA logo was in the bottom right-hand corner. 'He's working for this man.' She pressed a key on her laptop and another rap sheet came up.

The face on screen was the color of an oil spill, black and shiny, with a cheekbone that had been broken at some stage of his life and poorly reset. Slap this guy on the back and one of his yellow eyes might pop out.

'His name is Mohammed Ali-Bakr al Mohammed,' she continued. 'A former Al-Shabab, an Islamist who's decided he prefers money and power to achieving martyrdom. He's set his sights on being Somalia's number-one war lord, and he's a real charmer. There's an unverified story that he took human heads after a battle against a rival gang and used them in a bowling tournament with his lieutenants. Over the last few years, he's had several piracy operations thwarted by American warships. Word has it he's vowed revenge on us.'

'I'm trembling,' I said.

'She tell you anything about Randy?'

'No, nothing further. But she has placed Ed Dyson with von Weiss,' I said. 'Ty Morrow, too. Shilling positively identified both of them. That's a breakthrough.'

She nodded. 'Yes.'

The way she said it suggested a problem. 'What?'

Petinski took a deep breath and let it out. 'Langley doesn't think von Weiss is the man we should be chasing.'

I blinked, mock-stunned. 'That's Langley, as in the CIA?'

'Yes, Cooper, I'm a Company employee. I'm sure you've figured that out by now.'

She had *that* right. 'So why the subterfuge?'

'Thank your supervisor.'

'Arlen?'

'He said you wouldn't be so keen to work with the Company. It was his idea to keep up the NTSB cover and then switch to some other federal agency. The DCIS just seemed to work best.'

'And the sudden burst of honesty is because . . . ?'

'Because we're done here, washed up. As I just told you, Langley's shifted focus.'

'That is bullshit, Petinski. We—'

She held up her hand to stop me going any further. 'You know there are other teams on this case. Stronger leads have been chased up, other suspects. Top of the list is some one star and a colonel, both of whom were formerly at Bragg and are now in the DoD. Imagine that, seems Mr Big and his pal were right under everyone's noses.'

'What about that lecture I got from you about having a murder suspect that you're sure has done the crime, blah blah?'

She shook her head.

'And what about Ed Dyson – weatherman, nuclear fallout expert – hanging out with O Magnifico? We've got that *confirmed* now.'

'Forget it, Cooper. The people who pay my salary have changed their minds. I'm off the case.'

'Then what are we chasing here in Rio if it's not a nuke?' I asked.

'What you started out with in the first place, probably – weapons stolen from US bases and sold to the highest bidder. That's von Weiss's operation. It's just not the Company's priority right now – understandably.'

'I'm sure you'd agree that Langley has gotten it wrong before once or twice.'

Petinski was unmoved.

'What about the severed hand with Randy's ring and the damn ransom note? What about that whole "trigger" shit you were so fired up about? What about the deadline?' My voice was raised.

She saw mine and raised her own. 'Jesus, Cooper, *none* of it has taken us *anywhere*! We've got no leads – nothing except a few air miles. And the deadline . . . No one's buying it anymore.'

'What about Randy, Petinski? You turning your back on him too?'

Petinski jumped up, fists clenched. '*Fuck* you, Cooper! *Jesus!*'

I took some breaths, got my heart rate under control and waited for Petinski's anger to come off the boil. 'So what now?' I asked as she turned her back on me and walked a circuit of the room. 'Put your feet up?'

'You want me to tell you again what I think *you* can go do, Cooper? I head home and get rebriefed. More than likely I'll get reassigned.' I caught a glimpse of her face as she snatched open the door to the bathroom. Plump tears were rolling down her cheeks. She went in and slammed the door behind her. A few seconds later, I heard the shower running.

So that was that. Case unsatisfactorily closed. Nothing more to do than pour a couple of Glenfiddich minis into a tumbler with ice and bitch about my employer. I got up, went to the minibar. As it looked like this was my last night in the Palace, I figured I might as well drink like a king. With a glass in hand, I sat at Petinski's command station set up on the desk and fiddled, pulling up the footage feeding through from the camera in the favela. It was still doing its job, unlike Petinski and me, its motion sensor kicking it into life whenever something moved within view. I watched twenty-four hours of footage compressed into minutes: a dozen or so changing of the guards at the front gate and the arrival and departure of a number of motorcycles, the time code jumping forward with each cut. Nothing exciting. I switched the view to real time. It was now after one a.m. and the activity had dropped to zero. For something to do, I changed the program's preferences so that the computer chimed when the camera began rolling. The bell went off almost immediately and a small box on the computer screen opened to show two bikes leaving through the main entrance, a pillion passenger on one of them waving a machete around his head. Then the box on the screen closed and the security system went back to sleep. Maybe I should do the same. I yawned, and took a gulp of single malt.

The water in the shower had stopped running for a while, though I'd only been vaguely conscious of that. The bathroom door opened and Petinski came out in a hotel toweling bathrobe, her hair up and her face covered in some kind of shiny goop. She turned her back on me and put pajamas on under the robe before tossing it onto a chair.

'I'm going to bed,' she announced as she climbed between the sheets. 'You're still on the couch.' She reached over and turned out her bedside lamp.

Damn, if Petinski wasn't starting to remind me of my ex-wife . . .

*

'Cooper, wake up for Christ's sake . . . !'

I came awake to Petinski shaking my shoulder like she'd tried doing it gentle but gentle hadn't worked.

'Okay already,' I snarled. I had a Glenfiddich hangover, which is to say a quality hangover aged in the cask for twelve years. My body was locked solid in the seating position facing the various blinking and winking standby lights of the electronics gear assembled on the desk in front of me. I pulled myself out of the cramp, stretched out, leaned forward then back, the odd bone cracking.

'Have some water.' Petinski handed me a bottle of chilled Evian from the now almost empty mini fridge. 'Why didn't you go to bed?'

'I forgot,' I said, drinking the Evian, enjoying the feeling of ten or so chilled US dollars sliding down my throat.

Petinski checked the minibar drawer. Empty. 'Jesus, Cooper . . .'

I was too hung over to care.

'Here,' she said, putting a couple of Advils into my hand. I threw them back, which wasn't the best idea, my head pounding with the movement.

'Did you wake me for a reason?' I asked her, my voice croaky.

'Yes,' she said. 'Get dressed.'

I looked down and realized I was in my undershorts. I also noticed at this point that Petinski's pajama bottoms had been replaced by pants. Her boots were on. She leaned across me and tapped the keyboard, and the screen brightened with a frozen frame from the security camera. 'This woke me. Look,' she said, motioning at the screen.

She tapped the space bar and the recording from the security camera played, the time code beginning at 03:37:42. What followed sobered me up good and proper. The black Mercedes SUV, the one I'd seen coming and going from von Weiss–owned territory, arrived inside Céu Cidade's main gate. All four doors opened and those Aryan bodyguards spilled out. Two of them went to the rear of the vehicle, opened the tailgate and hauled out a person whose head was covered with a hood: a woman. Her hands were tied behind her back and she wore a t-shirt and brief underpants.

The extra-big one – Dolph – put her over his shoulder in a fireman's lift and carried her out of view. The hood slipped a little and blonde hair fell out. The screen froze on the last frame. Thirty-one seconds of footage.

'That was Shilling,' I said unnecessarily, aware of the cold sweat on my back.

'I've called Delaney. He's going to meet us at the Céu Cidade post office.'

'Is he bringing a tank?'

'No, a unit of BOPE, the local anti-terror people.'

'Those guys? You're filling me with confidence.' I got up and found my pants, crumpled on the floor. 'Maybe we should just get Salvadore's number from von Weiss and let him know we're coming.'

'Can you please hurry?' she asked.

'Can you slave the camera feed to your iPad?'

'Of course.'

'Then set it up and bring it along. Some real-time intelligence might be helpful.'

We were in a cab five minutes later, speeding across town in a tropical downpour, water filling the gutters, water vapor steaming up the windows. The Advils had done the trick, clearing my head, and twenty minutes later we pulled up in the warehouse area below the favela and let the cab go. It was a five-minute jog to the rendezvous, fog drifting slowly across the slick roads.

'Where you been?' Delaney asked when we arrived.

'Sleeping,' I said.

'You carrying?'

I showed him the Walther.

'Where'd you get that?' he asked, but then thought better of it. 'Actually, I don't want to know. Kim?'

'No.'

'Here,' he said, passing her a Glock 23 and three mags.

She said thanks, checked the weapon over, pocketed the mags, then secured the pistol in the back of her belt.

Delaney went back into a dirty old white Hyundai. 'Here, put these on,' he said, and producing two urban black armor vests and Kevlar helmets from the back seat.

A black truck lumbered around the corner and came to a stop behind us with a squeal of brakes.

'I see you passed on my suggestion about the tank,' I said to Petinski. She looked at me and adjusted her armor.

The tank was actually more like a security vehicle, only with a top-mounted machine-gun turret. A door opened and a squat, bull-necked man climbed out of the front passenger seat and jumped onto the road.

'*Hola*,' Delaney said, raising his hand, and went to meet him. A rapid-fire conversation in Portuguese followed between the two men as they walked slowly back toward us. 'This is Sergeant Adauto Robredo of the Batalhão de Operações Policiais Especiais,' Delaney announced when they were close enough.

Petinski and I introduced ourselves, shook hands. Robredo's was warm, hard and a glossy gunmetal black. His arms and neck appeared to be made from the same material. A short, coarse beard covered his face and followed the contours of his cheeks and neck. His coveralls were black, the only color being the emblem on his shoulder, a white skull impaled on a dagger with two crossed flintlock pistols behind it.

'The sarge's English ain't so good,' Delaney explained, 'so he asked me to tell you not to worry that he and his men haven't been in this favela before.'

'I'll try not to,' I said, and gestured at the turret on the truck. 'It looks like they're expecting trouble, or is this standard practice?'

Delaney translated and got a grin and a burst of Portuguese from Robredo. Delaney said, 'Adauto says it won't be needed, and he says he's got enough men to handle any situation that might arise.'

'How many men?'

'Ten, includin' himself and the driver.'

Meanwhile, Petinski, fiddling with her pack, had extracted her iPad. She fired it up, presented the screen to the sergeant and said to Delaney, 'Inform the sergeant we have a camera in the favela. It'll allow us to check out what's going on in there when we get closer.'

From his smile, Robredo was either enthusiastic about this, or her – I couldn't tell.

Petinski seemed pleased that he was pleased.

I would be pleased to inform him that there was a chance she could do the splits. Maybe later.

'Please, for you to get in truck now,' Robredo said haltingly.

Yeah, pretty much everyone seemed pleased.

Delaney locked his vehicle with the remote and we followed the sergeant to the rear of the truck. As he opened the door, a wave of body odor and gun oil rolled out over us. Inside, men in helmets and body armor with FN FAL 7.62mm assault rifles between their knees were pressed together like black-clad sardines. The sergeant barked an order and room was made for us somehow.

Petinski stepped up first, followed by me, then Delaney.

'*Agent* Petinski, now, is it?' I asked her behind. It chose not to reply.

Petinski got to her seat, shaking everyone's hand along the way. The door closed and red light flooded the darkness, illuminating all manner of equipment on the walls of the truck, from axes to climbing gear. The truck shuddered as it got underway, the smell of diesel exhaust leaking into the cabin. We accelerated up the hill, everyone swaying from side to side, then lurched around a corner. The incline got steeper and the corners sharper, but that didn't seem to slow the truck at all. Either Robredo and his driver were in a hurry, or they didn't care to be a slow-moving target.

I heard Petinski's iPad chime. Its screen came to life and the men beside her turned their faces away quickly to preserve their night vision. After a few seconds, she glanced at me then back to the screen, a scowl on her face. Something wasn't pleasing her.

'What's up?' I asked.

'The camera.' She handed over the device. 'Press rewind.'

I touched the arrow and the white noise in the frame became the picture of a lanky man in loose clothing pointing a handgun at the camera from the street below, holstering the gun in the front of his pants, then walking backward out of view, into blackness. I ran it forward and watched the lanky guy in loose clothing walk out of the blackness, take a gun out of the front of his pants and point it at the camera. An instant later, white noise.

'They got the camera,' she observed.

Fuck. Who finds a tiny camera nestled into a darkened corner at four thirty-five in the morning, for fuck's sake? I let Delaney know that we'd lost the camera.

'Don't worry about it,' he reassured me. 'These guys know what they're doin'.'

I needed reassuring.

Petinski stuffed the tablet into her pack as the truck came to a stop and the handbrake ratcheted on. External speakers squawked, and Robredo's voice boomed into the night.

The truck's back door burst open and Petinski, Delaney and I were almost pushed out by the eagerness of the men to get their boots on the ground.

'What's he saying?' Petinski asked Delaney as the PA gave the night a good shake.

The CIA deputy yelled over feedback, 'He's sayin' that if anyone makes any trouble, his men will bring hell into their beds.'

Seemed like the perfect segue into a joke about my ex-wife, but there wasn't time. Meanwhile, the men had formed up in a line in front of the truck. Petinski, Delaney and I stayed behind them, mist that was more like steam drifting around us. About fifty yards farther up the hill, the floodlights on the compound's wall illuminated the night. Due to a narrowing of the street, the truck could get no closer, at least not without bulldozing through someone's front steps. It was a still, windless night. Nothing moved, other than the mist. Maybe Robredo's threat worked. Speaking of the man, he got out of the truck and joined us. Delaney had a quick word with him then informed us, 'I told him about the camera. He said it didn't matter.'

I wouldn't have expected him to say anything different and I should have felt the same way; so why didn't I?

Robredo barked a command and the unit advanced up the street in a line abreast, Delaney, Petinski and I bringing up the rear. But then a sudden boom split the night and the man in front of me fell backward, splashing me with warm wet fluid. I looked down on his face and saw that there wasn't much of it left, explaining the warm wetness, the remains of his steaming skull reminding me of a large half-eaten Easter egg full of strawberry ice-cream. I turned to look for Petinski and a round cracked like a dry stick as it zipped past my ear, the boom from the rifle that fired it following an instant later.

Jesus! I ducked. Robredo's men had split up and run for cover. I was alone with the body spread-eagled on the road. I grabbed the man's rifle in one hand and his collar in the other and dragged him back behind the truck as Robredo's men began returning fire. I patted down the dead man and located four mags for the FN in his ammo rack along with a Ka-Bar knife. I stuffed all of these into various pockets and relieved him of his rifle. Then the body at my feet began to shake, the heels of his boots tapping a random beat against the ground.

I ran back up the street, hugging the shadows. Accurate single shots . . . there was a sniper up ahead somewhere. There were plenty of towers up inside that fortress, perfect hides for a shooter. The dead man had been right in front of me. If he'd moved a couple of inches to the left or right, it would be me doing a tap dance on the pavement. And if I hadn't turned my head to look for Petinski . . .

Robredo had taken a knee behind a rough retaining wall and was shouting into his cell phone. His men were on the move, teams of two leapfrogging each other, closing the distance to the compound, using whatever cover presented, shooting as they went.

'Cooper! Here!' Petinski. I scuttled up to her position and found Delaney beside her, Glock drawn, eyes wide.

'Thanks,' I told her.

'What for?'

'Being here.'

Muzzle flashes sparkled just inside the compound's main entrance. Full automatic fire from a belt-fed light machine gun. Red fluorescent pencils of light lanced through the night and skipped off the road beside us, and shouting filled the blackness along with gunfire. Lights, weak incandescent lights, went on here and there as the people of Céu Cidade woke up to the gun battle. Ahead, the searchlights on the compound wall snapped off. The world went dark but for the little multicolored floaters that hung in front of my eyes. I couldn't see for shit. Shots rang out from somewhere in our rear. We were being cut off, the situation deteriorating fast.

Robredo's men began retreating, not firing, unsure where the attacks were coming from. Two of the men were wounded, being helped along by their buddies. The sergeant joined us and spoke rapidly with Delaney.

'Another two units are on the way,' said Delaney, passing along Robredo's news. 'And there's a chopper inbound.'

I hoped it had a minigun. Failing that, sharp shooters in the doors. I tapped Petinski on the shoulder. 'Follow me. Stay close.'

'Shouldn't we wait for the reinforcements?' she asked.

'No.'

Petinski hesitated, but then changed her mind. 'You're impulsive, you know that, Cooper?'

I made a dash for the truck, giving Petinski no choice but to follow. Impulsiveness had nothing to do with it. I just didn't want to arrive too late to find another person I knew – Shilling – killed.

The truck wasn't far, and we made it in a handful of seconds. I jerked open the back door, Robredo's men swearing and shouting around us, pissed at being pushed back, and helped myself to a coil of rope, a pair of flashlights and a tomahawk. I ditched the rifle, threw the coil over my shoulder, handed Petinski one of the flashlights and we went off to find the alley reconnoitered the previous night.

We broke into a run. This time, Petinski was half a yard ahead. I pulled the NVGs from my rucksack and juggled them with the tomahawk as the path zigzagged up the hill. We soon came out of it into the open intersection, the golden lights of the favela I'd seen away in the distance the night before now glowing a dirty yellow behind a veil of fog rising up the valley.

'What're you going to do?' Petinski asked, adjusting her NVGs before fitting the straps over her head. 'Wait a minute . . . you don't know, but that never stopped you before, right?'

'We're going over the wall, hence the rope.' I gave it a pat while I considered the details.

'And the tomahawk?' she asked.

'Scalps,' I replied.

The passage at the base of the compound wall was as dark as a drain. I slipped the NVGs' double lenses over my head and the world became the familiar Kermit green. I scoped out the intersection and found what I'd hoped to find – a nest of densely tangled electrical wiring feeding into a large drum: a substation. A cluster of those wires disappeared over the compound wall. I pulled the Walther and shot three rounds into the drum. A section of the internal compound went dark. That should do it. Now that the lights were off, I didn't want them being turned back on.

'This way,' I said, and jogged down the lane, stopping twenty yards or so from the dwelling Petinski vaulted into on our last visit.

'Again?' she asked and took off the NVGs before I could answer. She handed them to me. 'Can't climb with these on.'

Sucking in a few deep breaths, one foot forward, she bobbed back and forth, judging distances and heights, getting her balance sorted out. And then she was running at the wall and I saw a blur as she scaled it. I jogged to the front door and waited. Something inside came crashing down. Then a heavy thump. I put my ear to the door. Nothing. I tried the handle. Locked. Petinski was taking her time. I heard a bang, not a gunshot.

The lock gave on the fourth swing of the tomahawk. I kicked the door in and raced up the stairs into some kind of storeroom. Three males were slumped on the floor, broken shelving and various cans and other items around them. A fourth man had Petinski in a headlock, her feet off the ground. They'd been making so much noise that they hadn't heard me. Petinski was in a chokehold and was starting to go into convulsions. I swung the axe backhand at her assailant's neck and the blade bit deep into his spinal column and stuck there. He collapsed to the right, his legs falling away like a wall with its foundations sapped. He didn't cry out. He wouldn't need an MRI to tell him he was now

269

a quadriplegic. Still, somehow the guy's left hand went for a weapon tucked into his belt. I had no choice and put the toe of my boot into the tomahawk's head, pushing the blade all the way through into his esophagus. The guy stopped going for his gun.

Petinski propped herself up on one elbow beside him and hacked a few dry, choking coughs. 'Thanks,' she croaked. 'I got three of them. Fourth one jumped me. Didn't see him.'

Ambush. They knew we were coming and baked us a cake.

'What's that smell?' I said, but I knew exactly what it was – the unmistakable funk of corpse.

'Out there,' she said, motioning at the veranda.

I went to have a look and the smell got worse as I went out into the open. Lying on his back, a black male, one-eighty pounds, maybe five ten. The eyes were empty, death having repossessed everything. His throat had been cut and a curve of blood spatter arced across the plastic sheeting that hung from the guttering. Blood pooled under the body's neck and shoulders. I could hear a few flies buzzing around the corpse. Petinski walked out of the storeroom, rubbing her throat with both hands. I lifted the arm a little and the whole body moved: rigor had set in. I wanted to know when he'd been murdered. A corpse loses roughly two degrees Celsius every hour. A thermometer up the bunghole would've been the correct method to check the core temperature, but as I had no thermometer, I placed two fingers in the crease of the armpit. Though it was still vaguely warm in there, his sweat was cold.

'How long's he been dead?' asked Petinski.

'A few hours.'

'Perhaps the folks over the wall thought he helped us plant the camera.'

Or maybe he played loud music once too often. We had no time to mourn the guy. And offering an apology for perhaps getting him killed wasn't going to help him at all. I stood up, pushed the plastic sheet aside, grabbed the mattress and repeated the procedure from the night before. Once the plank was in place, I secured one end of the rope around the pipes under the sink, and threw the coil up and over the mattress.

'Me first,' Petinski demanded, climbing up onto the plank. She refitted her NVGs, took the rope in one hand, and sprang up to the mattress. Then she turned to face me, the rope around her back and shoulders, and was gone in an instant.

I didn't get it done quite so elegantly but the result was the same, and a minute later I dropped beside her at the base of the wall inside the compound. No alarm was raised. No shout. In fact there was no movement anywhere that I could see. The shooting had stopped. Outside, sirens were *whoop-whooping* but here inside the wall all was quiet except for a humming sound. It was a large generator. Emergency power. I went over and had a look at it. The lights throughout the compound were now all off, and while the place seemed deserted, power was still being used somewhere. I levered open the control panel with the Ka-Bar, hit the kill switch and the motor died instantly.

Scanning the area I saw a window about fifteen feet up, some kind of retaining wall beside it. I pointed it out and we ran at a crouch toward it. 'Me first this time.' I said as we paused to catch our breath.

Petinski nodded and rested her hand on my arm, so I rested a hand on her sports bra.

'What are you doing?' she asked.

'Cashing in my brownie points for saving you back there. They dissolve unless you use them quickly.'

'You want to keep that hand?'

I removed it and told her to wait until I gave the all clear. Shinnying up the wall, I then scooted along a top edge that stepped up several times. The window was open, a leap of three feet or so to reach it. I jumped out, my fingers finding the ledge, and pulled myself up with a grunt, re-bruising my forearm. A last effort and I was inside, panting. Petinski was inside too, sitting on a chair at a small table, waiting.

'I found a door and used the stairs,' she said with a shrug.

'Thanks for telling me.'

Another shrug. 'The place feels like a morgue. There's no one around.'

Proving her wrong, a gun battle erupted somewhere close, a large volume of automatic fire.

'Call Delaney,' I said, squeezing past her into a stairwell. 'Get him in here. I'm gonna see if I can locate the shooter's hide.'

Around fifteen minutes later, after getting lost in this deserted rat's nest several times, I stumbled on a circular staircase to a room with a trapdoor in its low ceiling. Using a chair I opened the door, lifted myself up and found a 7.62mm sniper rifle with a night scope set up on a table, its bipod and wood stock resting on sandbags. Half a dozen casings were on the floor. The window had a view down the hill, which was swarming with fifty or so BOPE troops, the gunfire now sporadic, a chopper roaring in a hover overhead while its spotlight quivered over the compound's entrance.

'Cooper,' Petinski yelled out from somewhere below. 'You up there?' Her head came up through the hole in the floor. 'Been looking for you. Come down. There's something you need to see.'

Twenty-three

Petinski led the way through a series of rooms and narrow passageways, ever downward into the bowels of the place, passing BOPE personnel who were either directing the occasional sullen cuff-locked male or carrying large numbers of captured weapons. The von Weiss compound was in fact a warren of twenty or more individual homes interconnected by doorways cut through adjoining walls and trapdoors in the ceilings and floors.

Eventually Petinski led me to a large storeroom full of packaged and tinned food, sacks of grains, sugar, flour and so forth. Preparations for a siege, perhaps? One end wall appeared to be hinged at the floor and ceiling and was pushed out of alignment, revealing that it was, in effect, a secret door. Delaney and Robredo and a couple of his men loitered outside it, waiting for us.

'How'd you find this?' I asked Delaney.

'There's a control room. What's inside this room was up on one of the screens. They just kept searching till they found it.'

'Why? What's inside?'

'Take a look,' said Delaney, patting his stomach with his hand as if he had a bad case of indigestion.

On the other side of the door was a large well-lit space, a cross between an operating theater and a forensics lab. The floor was tiled, a stainless-steel grate set in its center. A stainless-steel table stood over the grate. Along the three walls were benches with equipment, much of which I couldn't identify other than to guess that it was medical. Placed on benches were glass cases lit from above with heat lamps, and large jars containing reptiles, animals and various unidentifiable gizzards suspended in formaldehyde. A flat-screen TV on one wall showed a dozen small windows that recycled surveillance camera views. But all this was incidental because beside the stainless-steel table was a large mass covered by a sheet of black plastic. Small rivers of red ooze ran like capillaries to the grate in the floor from whatever was under the plastic.

I had a bad feeling about what it might be, but I didn't have too much time to ponder as one of Robredo's men pulled the sheet away. Yeah, as I thought, a body. But not Shilling's, and that was a relief. The sight of what had been done to it still made me catch my breath, though, because sitting strapped into a chair was a man, naked, and the state of him was just plain disturbing. His limbs, hands, fingers, feet and toes were swollen to ridiculous proportions. What I was looking at could have been a grotesque balloon animal. There were splits in the skin on his arms and legs where the swelling appeared to have exceeded the skin's elasticity. His tongue was black and bloated, and had forced its way out of his mouth, spreading the jaw so wide apart that it appeared to have been dislocated from his skull. His eyes were hidden beneath puffy pillows of flesh. His neck had inflated to at least twice its normal size, a small pressure-split through a tattoo of a skull inked below his ear. A thin steel wire tied to the back of the chair cut deep into the skin around where his Adam's apple would be, and blood had run from the wound. Quite possibly, as he'd puffed up like the Michelin Man the unfortunate bastard had garroted himself.

'Who is he?' I asked.

Delaney produced a driver's license taken from a black leather wallet – the victim's. 'Accordin' to this, Gustavo Santos. He was one of von Weiss's security team.'

Delaney passed me the license. The photo bore almost no resemblance to the male duct-taped into the chair, except that a little of the skull tat-too was visible, an identifying mark that was as good as anything.

'Why do you think von Weiss would do this to one of his body-guards?' I asked. 'He must have had a reason.'

Delaney shuffled. 'Um . . . Santos was the guy we separated from von Weiss during the bomb scare.'

I digested that. Shit, not good news. We already knew von Weiss was paranoid and believed his inner circle had been infiltrated. If Santos had been killed, then what about Shilling? She'd been isolated, too. 'We saw von Weiss's men bring Shilling to the compound earlier,' I reminded him. 'We've got it on tape. That's what brought us here in the first place. So where is she? Why've we found this guy and not Shilling?'

'Because they staged it,' said Petinski. 'They put on a show. They let us see them bring her here. They lured us into a trap, hoping to kill you and me. And when they were sure we were on our way, they disabled the camera.'

If that was true then Shilling's cover was definitely blown. She was in mortal danger. The discovery also explained the shots fired at my head from the sniper rifle, the ambush in the house where the guy had his throat cut. Perhaps I'd been seen planting the camera. The facts sure pointed in that direction. Maybe, like Petinski said, we'd been played. And now Shilling was going to pay the price – or had already paid it – and if she paid it like the unfortunate individual we'd found here? Jesus . . .

I gestured at the body. 'What would cause that kind of swelling?'

'Anaphylactic shock,' said Delaney.

'You mean like nuts?' I asked.

'No, like snakebite. Robredo says he's seen this kind of reaction before.'

'Snakes,' Petinski said. 'The personal von Weiss touch.'

Was it my imagination or was I starting to hear thunder every time I heard this guy's name? 'I want to see that control room.'

Robredo, Delaney, Petinski and I arrived there five minutes later, a small, windowless air-conditioned shoebox stuffed with computers, phones and screens. Several personnel were already occupying chairs behind the equipment.

'Everyone here BOPE personnel?' I asked Delaney.

'No, sir,' said a woman with a broad Kentucky hills accent sitting in the chair in front of me, raising her hand.

'Tyra's on the cultural attaché's staff,' Delaney explained. 'Tyra Marr – Vin Cooper and Kim Petinski,' he said, introducing us. Delaney refrained from mentioning her sponsoring agency openly, although 'cultural attaché staff' was code for CIA.

'Hi, y'all,' the woman chirped.

'Can you drive this boat, Tyra?' I asked her.

'Sure, no problem.'

'You mind skipping through the security cameras one at a time?'

'All hundred and seventy-three of them?'

A hundred and seventy-three? 'We'll make ourselves comfortable,' I said.

'You want to view the cameras out in the favela too?'

'He's got the whole place wired?'

'Your suspect sure is a nervous bunny.'

Tyra shared a few words in Portuguese with her colleagues, and a black and white image of the familiar front entrance of the compound came up on the main screen. A view of the compound in its entirety appeared on a smaller secondary screen, a red wedge showing the camera's direction and range, together with various digital readouts nailing the specifics.

'The resolution is full HD and output can be provided in all the usual spectra. How do you want it served up?'

'Infrared. How big are the cameras?' I hadn't seen a single one in the entire joint.

'The lens is the diameter of a pinhead.'

That explained that.

'How long do they keep recordings filed?' Petinski asked.

'How far back you wanna go, honey? They got terabytes of memory.'

The camera Petinski and I wanted turned out to be number

fifty-seven. Tyra took the recording back to the previous evening, at about the time I was poised on top of the wall, surfing a mattress, and there I was in glorious thermal black and white. Petinski's guess was right. The assholes had known about our attempt at surveillance from the beginning. Which meant that when von Weiss sent Petinski the French champagne with a side order of prophylactic, he was just toying with us. I felt like a putz – outwitted, outplayed and outsmarted. But it was Shilling who was going to get voted off the island.

'What about the cameras down in von Weiss's playroom?' I asked.

Tyra pushed some buttons and moved a joystick. 'If you're hoping to get him on camera committing murder, babe, it ain't gonna happen, I'm afraid. That history's been wiped.'

Okay, so having the guy smiling for the birdie while his victim blew up like a football bladder was too much to hope for. I tried another angle. 'Let's see if we can get that Mercedes SUV arriving with Shilling.'

'Nope, no good, neither,' said Tyra, after isolating the relevant cameras and checking the recordings. 'Wiped.'

Only straws were left. I took one. 'Then let's see if we can pick up the SUV coming into the favela. There are only two entrances, right?'

'Let's take a look,' said Tyra as her team went to work. 'No, wiped also,' she said eventually.

'They've been thorough,' Petinski observed quietly.

'What about checking the car's departure?' I asked. Petinski shook her head like it was a lost cause. I wasn't ready to give up. 'The Benz isn't here now, so it must have left. We're going to dot the t's before we call it quits.'

Using as a starting point the time at which the recordings had been wiped at the compound, Tyra stayed on the camera with a view taking in the post office down in the valley. She then took a stab at the approximate time the Mercedes would have arrived at that point. Nothing moved on screen at all until a couple of dogs moseyed across the road. She rewound the view at five times the speed for the equivalent of ten minutes. Nothing. Then she did the same going forward. She was shaking her head and about to stop the show when headlights grew out of the shadows.

'Hey, there it is.' Petinski pointed at the screen as the SUV glided around the bend.

'It took the car thirty-five minutes to leave the compound and arrive at that point,' said Tyra. 'Seems a little long.'

'They stopped somewhere along the way,' Petinski concluded.

Was it possible that von Weiss's men had gotten lazy or maybe run out of time to erase *all* trace of the vehicle's passage through the favela? 'Check the cameras along the route. See if you can find where it stopped.'

The vehicle's departure from the compound had been wiped, along with its journey most of the way to the post office. It took an hour, but Tyra and her team eventually found a camera picking up the car as it crawled out of a narrow lane.

'Good hunch, Cooper,' said Petinski. 'You were right – they took a detour.'

'Find the turnoff,' I said.

Within minutes, Delaney, Petinski and I were racing in a convoy of BOPE SUVs down the main road, swerving around a stream of ambulances heading back up the hill. Overhead, the BOPE chopper worked the area we were headed to with its searchlight, looking for movement.

'Cooper, I've been thinking,' said Petinski quietly beside me. 'Von Weiss has been one step ahead of us all the way. This could be another setup. Perhaps he *wants* us to search this area.'

I looked at her.

She shrugged. 'It's possible . . .'

Yeah, it was possible. I passed it along to Delaney. 'Jeb, tell your friend Robredo to be careful. Could be another trap.'

*

Roadblocks were set up in the area and Robredo's men began searching house to house. Petinski, Delaney and I were kept out of it, this being BOPE turf. After twenty anxious minutes, the sky to the east beginning to lighten, a BOPE officer appeared from behind a building and ran toward us. 'Please, this way,' the man said with a heavy accent when he reached us, out of breath, sweat soaking his forehead. We followed him at a jog along an alleyway that doubled back on itself and climbed through the chaotic stacked housing, and eventually arrived at a doorway guarded by Robredo and his men, their weapons at the ready.

'What makes them think this is the place?' Petinski murmured.

Delaney spoke briefly with Robredo, who answered him in a hurried whisper before snapping an order at one of his men. The officer responded, producing two large hand grenades of an unfamiliar type from his webbing.

'They found these explosive devices rigged with tripwires at the access points to this house,' Delaney said. 'For our safety, the sergeant wants us to back it up a little.'

A pair of officers escorted us around the end of a wall and almost immediately a brace of flash bangs detonated, the ear-splitting racket amplified by the brick and cinderblock cavern. As the echoes subsided, screams and shouts from the people living in the vicinity increased in intensity and rained down on us from above. An empty beer bottle came down and smashed on the paving. A stream of urine followed along with a bucket of shit.

Robredo appeared from around the corner, breathing hard, his face haggard, and ignored the neighborhood anger. He motioned at us to follow him as he spoke to Delaney.

'What did he say?' Petinski asked.

'He says this is the place,' the CIA deputy confirmed as we walked toward a heavy red door. 'There's a body inside. It's not good.'

I prepared myself. I had a feeling this was going to be worse than Mr Soufflé with his anaphylactic shock. The home we walked into was surprisingly modern and spacious inside with expensive light fittings, warm white marble slabs on the floor and classical bronze sculptures of naked women lining the walls. But I couldn't take my eyes off the woman lying on a white mink rug in the center of the room, and my testicles felt light and vulnerable as I walked around her. It was Shilling. The familiar golden hair. She was on her side, naked. Splotches of blood stained the white mink rug and spattered her shoulders. Her olive skin was flawless, but for a triangle of paler skin across her buttocks where an ultra-brief bikini had prevented tanning. Shilling could have been asleep, except for a couple of obvious signs to the contrary, the lesser of the two being that she plainly wasn't breathing. But that was far less striking than the other reason: her eyes, which were open and staring. I remembered them as being a steely blue and yet now they were a bright sulfurous yellow in color. Both oozed a trickle of blood and fluid from punctures. They stared out of her skull at nothing, grotesque. Petinski's hand went to her throat as she turned away in horror. 'Mengele. That's what he did in Auschwitz,' she said. 'His experiments. He killed people trying to change the color of their eyes.'

I took a step toward the body, but a terse word from Robredo made me hesitate. Something moved in the shadows thrown by Shilling's legs and torso. It was a large brown snake the thickness of my arm and at least as long as the woman's body. The thing moved again, this time bringing its head up and over Shilling's legs and along her side. Its forked tongue flicked from its mouth every few seconds, tasting the air as it brought a coil across her ribs and breast. The damn thing was challenging us.

A rapid exchange ensued between Delaney, Robredo and one of his men. 'It's a bushmaster, Cooper,' the CIA deputy said. 'It's deadly. Very aggressive.'

I found myself wondering if it had killed the British agent before von Weiss applied his handiwork. Robredo's man, who seemed to know what he was doing, took out his knife and slashed at the snake, lopping its head off. He then kicked it scudding across the floor. The serpent's headless body immediately slid into tight coils before falling off Shilling's body and writhing beside it.

'He told her it was a python,' I said.

'How do you know that?' Petinski asked.

'She told me some things.'

I made a pact with myself at that moment that I was going to kill von Weiss, and I was going to do it mean.

Petinski was down on her haunches, examining Shilling's eyes. 'Doing this – pulling shit like this out of his father's handbook. It's a challenge of sorts. He has to know we've dug into his past.'

Robredo spoke into his shoulder mike and a couple more BOPE officers came in, stared at the naked woman on the floor and then began searching the room. Another man walked in with a blanket and threw it over the body. The cop in me thought about the crime scene being compromised, but after what we'd seen, all of us were beyond that now. Shilling was a casualty of war.

'You'd have t' say von Weiss is out of the favela business permanently,' Delaney remarked. 'After this shit, the asshole's burned his bridges. There ain't a man in a BOPE uniform that wouldn't shoot the fucker on sight.'

'You had a tail on von Weiss, right?' I said. 'So let's pull him in.'

Delaney glanced at the ground and looked anywhere other than at Petinski and me. 'We . . . er . . . we took the tail off him yesterday.'

'Why?'

'Washington told us he was no longer a person of interest.'

I stared at him.

'The Rio desk's not big. We got resources issues, other priorities . . .' He chose not to finish this mealy-mouthed bullshit. Maybe he heard what he sounded like.

'What about a couple of von Weiss's low-life associates, Falco and Charles White?' I asked. 'You know them?'

'Yep – arms dealers, former US citizens, and now residents of Brazil. We don't have a watch on them neither, but we know where they live.'

'Where's that?'

'In a ritzy apartment block beside the Copa Palace – your hotel. They both keep penthouse suites there.'

'You're shitting me,' I said, although it did explain why I'd seen them breakfasting at the hotel. For all I knew, the brothers had egg-white omelettes poolside at the hotel every other day. All this time I could have just strolled next door, taken a ride in a lift, knocked on Charles White's door and evened our account with a little lead deposited between his ears. 'Meet us there in an hour. Bring a fuckin' sledgehammer.'

*

It was early but already hot, the sky a misty blue, the beach across the road filling fast. The folks on the sand were mostly too preoccupied oiling themselves up to notice a BOPE van with roof-mounted gun turret squeal to a stop in the forecourt of the Excelsior, the apartment block overlooking the pool at the Copa Palace.

The rear doors flew open and Robredo's troops almost threw themselves out, itching to get to the men in the two rooftop apartments who, they'd been briefed, were involved in the killing and wounding of their comrades at the Sky City gun battle a short while ago. They ran at the double to the main glass doors and burst straight through them. The concierge attempting to block the way with a raised hand was brushed aside. The men charged up the fire stairs while Delaney, Petinski and I took the elevator, accompanied by two detectives from the local PD who were armed with a warrant to make the search legal. We arrived on the top floor in time to see a length of railway track with handles take the door clean off its hinges at apartment number two. The door to apartment number three got the same treatment. Flash bangs were thrown in to make a statement. After the splintering crash and the aftershocks of breaking glass ceased, men surged into both apartments, shouting, weapons shouldered, ready for violent retribution.

Unfortunately, no one was home.

The apartments were on the spare side of comfortable: white leather couches, African art, zebra-skin rugs, designer touches, lots of dark wood and plenty of glass, most of which now crunched underfoot.

'There are wall safes,' said Delaney as the railway-track battering ram was called up. 'PD says their warrant's good for us to take a look inside.'

The first one, in Falco White's apartment, withstood two blows. Inside, fuck-all of significance – some share certificates, rental agreements and so forth. The boys had their technique down pat on the second safe and stove the door in with one hit. The detectives took over and removed a handful of documents, most of which appeared to be on various bank letterheads. Large envelopes containing cash of different currencies were also removed along with three passports. One of them, a Brazilian passport, was Charles's. The other two had his photo, but the names and nationalities were different.

'Passport violations,' I muttered. Emma Shilling would've rubbed her hands together.

Wearing gloves, Petinski leafed through one of the passports. 'Everyone involved in this is going to be traveling on false documents.'

Robredo handed an elaborate leather box to Delaney along with a fancy printed envelope. 'This was found on the dresser in the bedroom,' Delaney said, lifting the envelope flap and extracting a card with childlike printing on it. He read aloud: '"A small tocan of my apreeshea-shon." It's signed Gamal. Who's Gamal? From the spelling, an English major, obviously.'

I was surprised he had to ask, but then I remembered he had no need-to-know.

'Gamal Abdul-Jabbar,' replied Petinski.

'A spider from Somalia,' I added, 'fond of knitted shirts. He's here on business. What's in the box?'

Delaney opened it and whistled. 'A Patek Philippe.' The box held a man's wristwatch.

'I take it that's a good one.'

'If expensive is good, then this baby's around forty-five-thousand-dollars worth of good.'

Gamal had bought the watch for White to show 'apreesheashon' for the entertainment provided – Sugar. And I was sure she'd earned every cent.

'You're going to have to coordinate a sweep of all the known residences kept by von Weiss,' I said. 'Will your station chief cooperate?'

'She'll be fine with it.'

'What about city hall?'

'After what happened up at Céu Cidade? *Não problema, senhor.*'

'Another avenue that might be worth checking: von Weiss has a pilot by the name of André LeDuc, alias Laurent Duval. You can check him out further with Interpol and the Générale de la Sécurité Extérieure. Might be worth seeing if the asshole's recently lodged any flight plans.'

'Sounds like you know him.'

'Only well enough to want to kill him,' I said.

Twenty-four

Aside from a brief catnap, we'd been up the best part of twenty-four hours. I yawned wide and long and leaned against the wall while I waited for Petinski to locate the key.

'I'm going to bed for an hour,' she said as she unlocked the door to our suite. 'What are you going to do?'

'I can join you for a few minutes if you like,' I said.

'I'll be in a coma within a few seconds.'

'That's okay. *I'll* still have fun.'

'On the couch, Cooper.'

*

I came awake, ripped from sleep, eyelids fluttering open. The room was quiet, the sun a little higher, the air a little warmer than it was when I fell onto the couch. I lay still and listened to the sounds coming through the open balcony doors – friendly sounds of the pool filter gurgling, kids splashing, the beat of a bird's wings in the enclosed courtyard, the toot of a distant horn out on the street. Sleep had been an exhausted shutdown, like the kind that follows combat. I shouldn't be awake, and yet I was. Nightmarish images began to drift across my mind from the night before: the cored cranium of a dead BOPE officer; the man on

285

the balcony with his throat cut, stiff with rigor mortis; the heel of my boot kicking the axe blade through a man's spinal cord; the puffed-up security guy who reminded me of the Michelin Man; and, of course, Shilling . . . These were images I'd be trying real hard to forget, but there was resistance. They were demanding some daylight hang time before slipping into my sleep to fester among my dreams.

I felt a weight across my shins move slowly. I wondered what it was, and then it moved fast. My brain was about to ask what the fuck when, suddenly, a black mouth appeared inches from my face, lunging, a dark cavern of death with curved white hypodermics on either side. I lifted the sheet to protect my face, pushed up and back and those fangs went straight through the fabric, a clear drop of oily fluid splashing onto the webbing between my fingers. A powerful sinuous cable writhed, making a sound that was half hiss, half gag. I stumbled out of bed with the sheet, a long length of uncaptured snake waving around between my legs, and ran across the room toward the bathroom.

'What are you doing?' Petinski asked, sitting up in bed, angry about the rude awakening.

'The laundry,' I shouted, wrestling the bedclothes into the bathroom. Opening the glass shower door, I threw the bundle into the recess and slammed the door shut. Within seconds the snake had disentangled itself. The body was long and yellowish green and it lifted its head up and out of the sheet, circling the glass cubicle, rising ever higher, hunting for a way out.

'Jesus,' said Petinski, her hair a fright, a mixture of exhaustion and fear on her face. 'Is that a black mamba?'

What else? What I wanted to know was how many black mambas there were in this city. I doubted they were at plague proportions, regularly turning up in five-star hotel rooms. This had to be the same reptile that lived in a glass case in von Weiss's study, the snake that had made a run for it and subsequently attacked and killed two people. We'd been paid a visit, another attempt to conclude unfinished business, namely the deaths of Petinski and me.

With each circuit of the glass cubicle, the thing was learning, pushing off the corners. I remembered Petinski's commentary about these fuckers. They were fast, aggressive and lethal. They'd been known to get into village huts in Africa and kill everyone just because their disposition was mean. I went back into the bedroom and searched for a broom. No luck. What was I thinking? They had staff for that here. I went to one of the closets, pulled Petinski's clothes off the rack and ripped out the length of pole.

'Cooper. Get in here . . .' Concern rippled through Petinski's voice. I went back into the bathroom. The snake had used the hot and cold taps for leverage along with the showerhead coming out of the wall above them, and its head was now waving around the top edge of the glass. Shit, the fucking thing had to be well over twelve fucking feet long! I whacked its small head with the pole and it slipped back into the recess, its body sliding off the taps, forked tongue lashing the air in front of those fangs. It fell and banged against the opposite glass wall and immediately began its climb all over again, only this time more aggressive, more determined. More fucked up.

'Call room service,' I said.

'And tell them what?'

'I dunno – get 'em to send up a snake charmer.'

'Just tell me where you put the Walther.'

I gave the reptile another whack on its scone. 'Is it hot in here?' I asked.

'Not especially,' she said. 'The Walther. Where is it?'

If it wasn't hot, then why was I was sweating like old dynamite? Jesus . . . The room spun a hundred and eighty degrees and suddenly I was sitting on the floor, my left hand feeling as though it had been dipped in lava. I held it up, expecting to see burns. A red stain had spread across the back of it, a yellow sweating blister forming in the webbing between my first and second fingers. Also, my arm had blown up and it reminded me of a thick uncooked sausage. I thought of the Michelin Man – the guy we'd discovered in von Weiss's playroom. Had I been bitten? My heart was beating weirdly fast. I fell sideways, unable to keep myself upright.

'Cooper . . .' I heard from somewhere far away.

My mouth and eyes were open; couldn't move my tongue. Arms heavy. Vomit gushed out from between my teeth. Then the diarrhea started.

Breathing hard, I could blink only with difficulty. I felt myself being dragged backward out of the bathroom, the door slammed shut. I tried to move, but couldn't. Everything too heavy. Breathing in short breaths. I was moving on a gurney, in an ambulance, wheeled under hard, white lights. Catheter, fluids, hypodermics. Shilling, yellow eyes . . .

*

As far as I was concerned I was awake for the whole ordeal, but apparently I was out cold for three hours or so. And when I say cold, I'm talking ice bath, a full hour immersed like a big lime in an even bigger caipirinha.

I remember asking Shilling what was going on, the MI6 agent sitting on the end of the bath in her shimmering yellow dress, which her eyes now matched.

'You should be dead, y'know,' she said. 'They've given you two shots of epinephrine, three bags of saline and two shots of black mamba anti-venom.'

I wondered why Shilling was now talking with an American accent. Either seconds or hours passed before I opened my eyes again and Shilling was gone. In her place was Petinski. 'Am I dreaming you?' I asked her.

'No.'

'Where's Shilling?'

'You don't know?'

'She's dead,' I said.

'You had me worried. Not so long ago you thought I was her.'

'Was it you who told me they gave me two shots of epinephrin?'

'You remember that.'

I nodded. 'Did I get bitten?'

'No, black mamba venom's unbelievably potent. You got some of it on your hand where you had a cut. The doctors believe you're hyper-allergic to it. They thought you were going to have a heart attack.'

'But I didn't.'

'No, you didn't.'

'It was lucky for you they had anti-venom on hand. And they only had it because of the trouble the snake caused here a couple of days ago.'

'What happened to it?'

'The snake?'

I nodded.

'I dragged you out and shut the door on it. Then I called Delaney. He called the Rio Zoo. The ambulance took you away, and a couple of herpetologists arrived not long after and captured the snake.'

I took a deep breath and did a sense check and felt remarkably okay, almost refreshed. I flexed my hand, a catheter taped to my wrist.

'The book's gone,' Petinski said.

'What book?'

'*Mein Kampf*. Whoever put the snake in our room took it.'

'Lucky I read the last page so I know how it turns out.'

Petinski looked at me blankly. Right. I gave a mental sigh. The skin on my palm felt tight, itchy. 'So now what?' I asked her.

'They're keeping you overnight for observation.'

'I'm fine.'

'You're not.'

'And von Weiss?'

'Disappeared.'

'So we've got nothing?'

'Maybe, maybe not. Delaney put out some feelers on your old friend, André LeDuc. Nothing came back. But then some bright spark on the Buenos Aires desk searched the flight records of all aircraft owned by known von Weiss corporations, noted the various aircraft your friend had been flying lately, and ran a search on all the tail numbers. Flight plans for two aircraft owned by von Weiss companies had been sub-mitted within the last twelve hours. One was a smallish twin-engine Baron on a flight from Asunción, Paraguay, back here to Rio. The other, a Gulfstream, was flying Buenos Aires–Jo'burg–Dar es Salaam. Your friend LeDuc is checked out on the type.'

Dar. Someone else had mentioned the place recently. But who? And why?

'What's the matter?' Petinski asked.

'Do you know anyone who lives in Dar?'

'No.'

'Does Delaney?'

'How should I know?'

'Dar es Salaam has come up in conversation recently. I'm just trying to pin it down. You haven't mentioned the place before?'

'No.'

I closed my eyes and tried to will the connection into my head. But the harder I tried the more the vague sense that Dar was significant began to fade. I gave up. Maybe I just got it wrong. Maybe I wasn't all here yet, my body still fighting off the effects of the snake venom.

'Try not to stress about it. You've been through an ordeal.' She gave me a there-there look.

'You make it sound like I'm an old guy with dementia who can't remember where he put his diaper.'

'Fine. Whatever.'

'That's more like it.' I noticed she was wearing makeup – lipstick, eye shadow and so forth. 'What's with the war paint?' I made a gesture over my face and the tube hooked up to my wrist rattled against the bed frame. 'You going somewhere?'

'Home.' She glanced at her watch. 'On a plane in four hours.'

'What about the case?'

'What case?'

'Didn't von Weiss just make another attempt on our lives? Doesn't that make you want to even the score?'

'I work in intelligence. I don't even scores.'

'How do you know von Weiss isn't hunkered down in some other Rio hideout?'

She shook her head. 'Forget it, Cooper. He's gone.'

'Who put the snake in our room? Who stole the book we stole?'

'It wasn't von Weiss. We've got surveillance footage of an unidentified man in a jacket and ball cap stealing a room-service passkey, taking the elevator to our floor, opening the door to our room, throwing in a paper bag and leaving. The snake was in the bag.'

'And the book?'

'Also gone. There've been simultaneous raids on all von Weiss's known addresses throughout Brazil since you've been in here. They found nothing except dazed employees who believe he's left the country. BOPE, CIA, you name it, everyone agrees he's gone.'

'What about his boat? What was his boat called?'

'*Medusa*. It's fallen through the cracks too.'

'It's a big boat. Must be a hell of a crack.'

'Brazil has a million uninhabited rivers and tributaries to hide it in.'

I let it go. Charles and Falco White and that asshole LeDuc had also slipped through the net, not that the pathetic attempt at surveillance could be called a net. Gamal Abdul-Jabbar had left town. Shilling had been killed. And whatever was going down appeared to have moved to a new address.

This was pissing me off. I jerked the saline line out of the catheter. Then I pulled out the catheter and pressed down on the hole the needle left behind to minimize the bleeding.

'Hey! What are you doing?' Petinski demanded, appalled.

'Going to Dar es Salaam.'

'That's ridiculous.' She looked about the room a little panicked, clearly wondering what to do, who to call.

My clothes were in a neat, washed pile on the visitor's chair. 'Where's the rest of my things?' I lowered my feet to the floor.

'At the Palace. For Christ's sake, get back into bed, Cooper.' Petinski stepped toward the door, I figured to rat me out to the nurses' station.

'No, gotta go.'

'Jesus . . .'

'Am I under arrest?'

'Don't be ridiculous.'

I sat on the edge of the bed and felt lightheaded. The real test would come when I stood up. A nurse walked into the room, shrieked a little when she saw me out of bed and ran off – I assumed to get help, or a hypodermic with a sedative, or both. The lightheadedness passed and I took the steps to my clothes without further difficulty. I picked up the pile and took it back to the bed. Petinski turned away when I dropped the nightgown.

'Don't think you'll be able to hold yourself back, huh?' I said. 'If you like we could just pop into the bathroom together, take a shower and say goodbye properly.'

'Are you finished?'

My pants were on. 'Yes.'

'I can't stop you?'

'What do you think?'

She sighed deeply. 'Okay, well, I've enjoyed working with you. It's been an education, I'll say that much.'

I felt myself getting stronger with all the activity. I threw on socks, pushed my feet into boots and tied the laces. Outside, wind lashed the trees and lightning flashed, the thunder following a split second after. 'What's up with the weather?' I remembered it being sunny.

'Nothing serious. Afternoon thunderstorm. It'll pass.'

A flash of lightning grounded somewhere out in the parking lot just beyond the window, the almost instantaneous thunderclap vibrating the pane. And then it hit me. 'Dar. Hey, I remember now. Ed Dyson – the nuclear weather forecaster guy. He flew to Dar es Salaam a couple of days ago.'

'How do you know that?'

'Shilling told me. I didn't think much of it at the time. But now von Weiss's G5 is headed there too. In the land of no coincidences, that's significant.'

'Not to me it's not. I can't do anything about being reassigned. And if I were you, Cooper, I'd contact my supervisor immediately.'

'If you were me you'd ignore that advice, because I am me and that's what I'm doing.' I stood up and, like a drunk, almost fell back as the nurse and a doctor rushed in, ready for action. Holding up my hand to stop them I said, 'I'm fine, and I'm going.'

'No, no. You stay!' insisted the doctor.

'That's what I told him too,' said Petinski.

There was a prickly, tingling sensation along my arm and hand. I scratched it. Whatever was below the dressing on my left hand, between my fingers, felt like a small volcano about to spit something molten.

'See? There is poison still in your blood. If you move around too much, you will again swell up,' said the doctor, picking his way clumsily through the English language.

'I'm going,' I repeated.

'Okay, then you wait a minute, please,' the doctor instructed before dashing out the door.

'Did you check us both out of the Palace?' I asked Petinski.

'No, you still have a room.'

The doctor reappeared with a sling, a small white plastic container and a tube of cream. I wondered what he was going to try to do with them. He shook the container and it rattled. '*Antihistaminico*. You take two, three time every day. You start now.' He said something to the nurse, who poured a glass of water and handed it to me. 'Cream is *antihistaminico*. Put on three time a day.'

'Can I drink booze on that?' I asked. The doctor seemed puzzled so I made the universal sign of lifting an invisible glass to my lips.

'No. Alcohol will taste bad.'

I took the advice with a few grains of salt. Maybe the guy just had it in for the sauce. 'And the dressing?' I held up my hand.

'Change tonight and in morning. If finger turn black, or it makes . . . er, *podridão* . . . er . . . rotting smell, then you come back.'

That sounded bad. I told him he had a deal, bundled up the remaining personal effects under my good arm, the one with the yellow and black bruise. The doctor looked at me all concerned as he passed me the sling.

By the time Petinski and I made it to the exit the worst of the storm had passed. We pushed through the doors, went to the cabstand and

Petinski picked the third car in the line-up. I held the door open for her, thunder booming in the distance.

'No, Vin, you take it. I'll get the one behind,' she said. 'I'm going to the airport.'

'Can't change your mind?'

'I can't just do whatever I like. God knows how *you* get away with it.'

I never called in, was how.

She held out her hand to shake.

'We should catch up for a drink one day,' I said, taking her hand. It was small and cool. 'After the bomb goes off lunchtime this Wednesday, right?'

The smile well and truly gone, she said, 'Good luck.'

'You too.' I got into the taxi, told the driver the Copacabana Palace and turned to watch Petinski climb into a cab as we pulled away.

Twenty-five

The rooms at the Palace had been thoroughly cleaned, but that didn't stop me checking under the bed like a nervous six year old. Satisfied that there weren't any more surprises laying low, I opened my laptop for the first time in a while and checked my email. I ignored the in-box clogged with the usual cc'ed crap, and sent a note to Arlen letting him know that I was okay, in case he was wondering, and to provide him with some details of my travel plans. I also added that I was enjoying my vacation hugely, thereby muddying the waters if someone believed I should be someplace else, earning my pay. I sent it off and received an answer almost immediately – an automated out-of-office reply. The guy must've taken more vacation time and headed back to St Barts and Marnie. I could hardly blame him. A call to Delaney was next on the list.

'Hey,' he said, recognizing my voice. 'Why you callin' me? Y'all s'posed to be takin' it easy, lookin' at all the pretty nurses.'

'I'm cured. It's a miracle. Listen, can you do me a favor?'

'So you're not callin' from the hospital?'

'No.'

'Aren't they keepin' you overnight?'

'I want to thank you for all your help,' I said.

'No problem. I'm sorry things got so fucked up.'

'Yeah.'

'Sounds like you're leavin'.'

'Tomorrow. Petinski has already left.'

'I know. She called me.'

'Do me a favor?'

'Sure, what do you need?'

'Whatever you've got that's recent on Dar es Salaam – pirate activity and so forth. Plus anything you can give me on Gamal Abdul-Jabbar and his current employer, Mohammed Ali-Bakr al Mohammed. Use my secured email address.'

'No problems.'

'What resources has the Company got on the ground in Dar?'

'They have a nice building, but the people there are not chilled like me. Unless it's official, take my advice and stay off their radar. Make waves for them and they're likely to pull y'all in and you'll wake up somewhere out of the way, like Auckland, New Zealand.'

'I'll keep it in mind. And thanks for everything.'

'Come back next year for Carnival.'

I said I would, along with a bunch of other things that added up to goodbye, and ended the call. Next, I fixed a Glenfiddich with rocks, took a sip and managed to stop myself throwing up, but only after a couple of dry retches. I cursed the doctor for putting a temporary hold on my hobby and called the concierge desk. I needed a travel agent and I figured a hotel like this would have a preferred supplier with proven reliability. An hour and a half spent patiently mucking around with airline schedules and the agent had me booked on the six a.m. to São Paulo with connections through to the only lead I had – Dar es Salaam. The trip would take thirty-six hours, and that was assuming all those connections lined up as planned. I didn't think much of my chances but I didn't see that I had another choice. The nuke was still out there somewhere and the clock was still ticking, but there were other agents on that. As far as I knew no other resources were looking for Randy Sweetwater, and he was still out there somewhere too. Emma Shilling was also on my mind. Who was going to avenge her?

I called room service next, ordered a club sandwich, latched the front door as well as the doors onto the balcony, and took a bath, avoiding the shower. When I was done I threw on the robe and fiddled with the TV in an attempt to get it working. I gave up, opened up the minibar again and considered giving the Glenfiddich another try. The doorbell rang and I walked over and checked the peephole. Outside in the hall was Gracia from the front desk, the tall, striking woman with the big brown eyes and thick black hair who'd found my fiancée-to-be Petinski and me a room with a busted TV. Accompanying her was a guy pushing a trolley.

I opened the door. 'Room service, *senhor*,' the room-service guy said as he wheeled in the cart, setting a silver-domed tray down on the coffee table. I checked under the dome, confirmed club sandwich, signed the docket, tipped him and off he went.

'*Senhor* Cooper,' Gracia said when he'd gone, concern on her features. She nodded at my hand. 'You are okay now?'

'The doc says I only got forty years left.'

The concern remained on her face. She cleared her throat. 'Please, I wanted to come and say in person, on behalf of the Copacabana Palace, how unhappy we feel about what has happened.'

'That's okay, Gracia, it was just one of those things,' I said with an offhand wave, as if finding a black mamba on the bed was like discovering a hair in my soup.

'The bill for your stay here has been – how do you say? – canceled.'

That was a surprise. 'Canceled?'

'There is no charge, *Senhor* Cooper.' She handed me the invoice with the balance showing zero *reals*.

'Thank you. That's very generous,' I said. And now I wasn't going to have to explain a bill to Air Force finance that ran to quite a few thousand bucks. I should've ordered lobster.

'Also, I am sad that your woman and you, you are not ...' She muttered something to herself in Portuguese in frustration. 'I do not know the word. *Casar . . .*' She took a ring off her finger and put it back on.

'She told you the engagement was off?' I said. That was so Petinski – clearing the decks.

'*Sim.*' Gracia nodded. 'She told me you are not get married. I am feel apologize for you.'

'You feel sorry for me?'

'No, no, I feel *sad* for you. My English is okay, but could be better. I speak some of many languages, but none so well as Portuguese.'

'I don't suppose you know any useful Swahili?' I asked her on the off chance.

'What is Swahili?'

'It's what they speak in Dar es Salaam.'

'Oh, you are leaving us?'

'Tomorrow – early.'

She gave me another brief smile and took a step toward the door. 'Well, I must go. It has been a big day for you, I think. You rest.'

Gracia had soft brown eyes with long lashes, and as I'd already noted she was tall at maybe five eleven. Tall enough to be a topless tall. An open blouse revealed a hint of a purple and pink lace pushup bra. Looked to me like maybe Carnival was already going on under there.

'Hey, here's a thought,' I said, spider-to-the-fly-like. 'Why don't you have a drink with me before I leave?'

She shook her head. 'No, I must go.'

'You'd be doing me a favor. As you said, it's been a big day: I've been attacked by a killer snake, spent most of the day in an ice bath, and my fiancée has walked out on me.'

Gracia hesitated.

I spun out a little more web. 'Never mind. Look, I understand: you're on duty and I don't want to get you into trouble. Thanks so much for everything.' I held out my good hand to shake.

'Why did your fiancée leave?' Gracia asked, taking my hand.

'I really don't know.' I looked at the floor and shook my head, the image of pathetic jilted blubber. 'She just . . . left.'

'I am sorry.'

'Me, too.'

Gracia glanced at the clock on the DVD player, the fly not even real-izing that it was caught. 'I am not on duty now. Perhaps one drink. You have *cachaça?*'

'I think so,' I said, making a move in the direction of the minibar.

'Please, I will do it. You must eat your dinner. You want *cachaça* also?'

'Sure, I love the stuff,' I said with every intention of leaving the drink untouched. I took the dome off my sandwich, removed the toothpicks and took a bite. It tasted good.

'Did you love her?' Gracia asked, setting a glass tinkling with ice down on the table.

'Yeah,' I said. I knew this lie was going to get difficult if I didn't change the subject. I looked for her engagement ring. From memory it was a freshly cut diamond set in white gold, or maybe platinum, but it wasn't on her finger. Hmm, this was tricky. Ignore it, or mention it? 'Your ring,' I said, rolling the dice. 'You're not wearing it.'

Gracia pushed the ice down into her glass with a long pink mani-cured fingernail. 'My engagement. It is also . . .' She made a gesture with her hand like whatever was in it had gone *poof*, into the air, and she couldn't care less about it.

'What happened?'

'My girlfriend. She went on his Facebook. She told me there were photos.' Gracia took a long drink, her throat moving, the ice making music in the glass. She rolled the glass between her palms. 'I looked too. The woman he was with . . . it was my mother step.'

'He was doing your stepmother?'

She nodded. '*Sim.*'

*

Gracia sat upright, threw her head back and held her thick hair off her neck. Then she rested her hands on my ribs and blew air upward across her face to cool down. My turn next. She blew on my chest, her lips forming a perfect O. I reached up and ran the tips of my fingers along the top of a breast, the gentle curve reaching toward a dark nipple, the sheen of perspiration on her skin. Damn, this woman had control.

'Where'd you learn to move like that?' I asked her.

'Samba,' she said, lifting her ass off my hips and rolling it in a circular motion a couple of times while keeping me inside her, demonstrating the motion. Little Coop was still hypersensitive and his jangled nerves made me catch my breath.

She stopped moving and went all serious. 'Why don't you stay another day, maybe two?'

'I'd like to, but I can't.'

Gracia got off me, kneeled on the bed and held her breasts like she was lifting fruit, presenting them to me, an offering. 'You like these?' she asked.

'Sure.'

'You have them again if you stay.'

'That would usually be an unbeatable offer, but I have to go back to work.'

'What is your work?'

'I chase bad guys.'

'Then you are a good guy?' She shook her head. 'No, I think you are a bad guy too. Especially with women.'

The comment made me think of Shilling. The memory of how we found her – what von Weiss had done to her – made me shudder.

'So now you are cold?' she asked, running her hand along the goose-flesh on my good arm. 'This, I can fix.'

Reaching down, Gracia pulled up the sheet from the bottom of the bed and it billowed over us like a parachute canopy. As it settled, descending slowly, full of her scent and perfume, she wriggled down and I felt the warm wetness of her mouth close around me.

Twenty-six

I arrived in Dar es Salaam a little after three p.m. two and a half days later, a delay in Rio plus the various flights and long layovers, especially in Jo'burg, chewing through more than the expected thirty-six hours. In fact, if I'd still been listening to the ticking clock mentioned in the ransom note that arrived with the amputated hand, there'd be only around four and a half days left on it before *kaboom* time, and maybe a lot less depending on which time-zone calculations Randy had used.

The arrivals hall at Julius Nyerere International Airport was new, but the AC was down and it was hot, airless, bustling and smelled of dust and sweaty armpit. I joined the impatient queue for a visa and paid the required hundred and fifty bucks to get it. Out in the hall I chose a hotel called the Southern Sun off an ad on the back of a luggage trolley, then walked through a gauntlet of people who were keen to sell me their local knowledge, like where to find a cabstand. This turned out to be the front entrance, where a motley collection of vehicles were lined up. The drivers sitting in them flashed their lights to attract attention. I strolled over.

'Taxi?' asked a driver, leaning across the front seat of an old Renault. He was at the head of the queue, but I pulled the rusting rear door open and got in anyway.

The driver was a tall thin man of black and Indian descent, aged in his mid-twenties. He wore sandals, loose black cotton pants and an off-white shirt. Thick, round-rimmed glasses magnified his dark eyes. There wasn't a lot of room in the vehicle, front or back, and his legs were up around his armpits, reminding me of all the time I'd just spent in economy. Music blared from the radio, a kind of African hip-hop I wasn't familiar with. 'You know the Southern Sun?' I asked him.

He pulled into the departing traffic on the wrong side of the road, until I realized that's the side they drive on here, like they do in Britain and Australia.

'The Southern Sun. Yes, yes, that will be fifty dollar.'

'Turn your meter on.'

'No meter. No meter in Dar es Salaam. Taxi from airport to city is fifty dollar. Special fare.'

Specially steep. The city was barely eight klicks from the airport.

'How long you staying? You need a car? You must hire me, ha ha. You are Westerner. If you don't take taxi, other taxi will follow you until you take one.'

Interesting sales pitch. He laughed as he talked, either the nervous type or he found the fact that I seemed prepared to even consider paying his price hugely amusing.

'Five hours is one hundred fifty US dollars,' he continued and again followed it with a laugh. 'This very good price.'

'Sounds like highway robbery to me,' I said even though compared to the run to my hotel it seemed reasonable enough.

'Okay. I make it one hundred. We have a deal, ha ha?'

'I'm here for the sights.' In fact, I wasn't exactly sure what I expected to see in Dar es Salaam, let alone where to start looking for it. Gamal Abdul-Jabbar caught a plane here. A von Weiss G5 possibly piloted by LeDuc had lodged a flight plan to this city. And Shilling had said that Dar had been spoken about by von Weiss. Was there something of specific interest here? Or was it just a stop-off to somewhere else – Somalia, perhaps, to meet up with pirate boss Mohammed Ali-Bakr al Mohammed?

'You want to see the sights?' he asked. 'Then you need a guide also. I am driver *and* guide, two people in one. For two people you must pay one hundred fifty dollar. Ha ha ha. Plus fare from airport to hotel is two hundred dollar. Okay? Deal? What you like to see? We have many wonderful things in Dar. Beautiful beaches, beautiful churches. If you like, I take you to—'

'I'll make it an even five hundred bucks if you get me a boat – something small, quiet and fast.' Both Abdul-Jabbar and Ali-Bakr al Mohammed were pirates. Pirates were interested in ships, and Dar es Salaam, according to the information emailed to me by Delaney, was the last stop for seaborne cargo bound for Mogadishu, Somalia's friendly capital seven hundred or so miles up the African coast.

He mulled over my offer for a few seconds. 'Taxi with driver and guide and boat for five hundred dollar. Yes, I can do.'

'Included in the deal is a handgun and spare rounds of ammo. I'm not fussy – Glock, Tokarev, Makarov – whatever you can get.'

'Ha ha ha ha ha ha ha.' The driver's eyes darted from the road to the rear-view mirror to the road to the mirror. Fair to say I had the guy's full attention.

'What's your name?' I asked him. Those eyes of his continued to dart. 'Your name,' I repeated. 'You got one?'

'Fakim,' he said. 'It is Fakim.'

After that, the conversation pretty much dried up, so I did a little of that sightseeing out the window to get some idea of the lay of the land. We were moving through a light industrial slum, the kind that gloms onto most airport access roads. On the left, the buildings were built low and cheap and mostly of the warehouse type; on the right, homes and shops. Every home had a shop out front, and every shop a home behind or on top of it. There seemed to be kids roaming around all over the place. Listless dogs were everywhere, the air hot and steamy. And as the road was unsealed, it was dusty, too – the exposed earth rusty orange in color. So far, Dar reminded me of Kigali, which reminded me of the Congo, a place I was keen to forget.

Things became more strictly residential once we turned off the main road, the homes gray and slapped together and tightly packed like they were bundled for recycling. Ahead, a car had driven nose-first into a pothole the size of a bomb crater and steam gushed from under its hood, the dazed driver wandering around with a hand to his bloody forehead.

'How far is the Southern Sun from the port?' I asked.

'Not far. Two, three kilometer.'

After passing the oil refinery and the railway sidings, I caught a glimpse of the docks. Ships of various sizes were tied up to a long pier running the length of the near shoreline: a container ship, a vehicle transporter, a grain ship and a couple of tankers. More merchant vessels were moored out in the middle of the harbor. Several beat-up fishing boats chugged back and forth. They didn't seem particularly seaworthy, though seaworthiness was something I didn't know much about. For all I knew they fished as far up as the Gulf of Aden and out to the east toward the Seychelles and Maldives. Small outrigger-style canoes also drifted along, limp triangular sails attempting to catch the exhausted breeze.

Fakim hooked into a turn away from the water, taking us toward the ritzy end of town where, it seemed, the folks could afford some greenery. Not long after, he pulled into the forecourt of the Southern Sun and stopped at the front stairs. A guy in hotel uniform approached the car but I waved him away.

'So what do you say, Fakim?' I said, flattening a ball of notes extracted from my pocket. Two hundred dollars was all the US cash I had on me. 'Two hundred now, another two hundred when you pick me up later and take me to the boat, and the balance when I get the gun.' I held the greenbacks toward him. He stared at the wad, wanting it but reluctant, seeing the strings attached. 'I know what you're thinking – that you could always just take this two hundred and drive away, but there's more where this comes from, so much more.'

'Money for gun – extra.'

'How much extra?'

'Not much.'

We were getting beyond my cash reserves and my preparedness to haggle. 'Okay – my final offer: four hundred for you, a hundred for the boat and a hundred for the gun. Six hundred in total. If you can get the gun and boat for less, you make more profit. If the boat and the gun are no good, you get nothing. Take it or leave it.'

Fakim glanced out the window at the surroundings, considering the deal. 'Okay,' he said finally, taking the two hundred and putting it in his top pocket. 'I do this and you still owe me four hundred.'

'And you still owe me a boat and a handgun with spare ammo.'

'Yes, okay. We go to Magogoni Street.'

'What's Magogoni Street?'

'Where boat lives. It's near. I will come back at four o'clock. That is good time, ha ha?'

Suited me. 'See you then,' I said. The risk was that laughing boy here would keep on driving, but I had a feeling he'd be back. Money didn't look like it was all that easy to come by in this town. Tourists were walking wallets, even the seemingly violent ones like me.

'What is your name, sir?' he asked.

'Vin.'

'Yes, Mr Vin. Ha ha.'

Right.

Though I hadn't booked, I got a room at the Sun easy enough, the occupancy low if the empty reception area was anything to go by. The four-star hotel was furnished in a great-white-hunter-swaps-elephant-gun-for-Nikon kind of way, with pictures of the big game found in Tanzania replacing the stuffed trophies that would've graced the walls of a place like this not so long ago.

On the way to my room, I stopped at an ATM to get some cash, and then called into the business center. I fired up a Hewlett-Packard, opened Google Earth, and five minutes later had a bird's-eye view of the Dar es Salaam harbor which, from a couple of thousand feet up, reminded me of a pancreas, or maybe a stomach. On the day the satellite passed overhead, the ships attached to the buoys out in the harbor channel were a couple of what appeared to be naval frigates. A little digging around on the CIA site confirmed that the US Navy visited Dar on a regular basis, particularly since the formation of Task Force 151, the multination naval effort to stamp out piracy in the region. Maybe what I was looking at here were US Navy vessels. I dug around a little more. The carrier *Enterprise* and the cruiser *Leyte Gulf* had recently joined the task force. Serious firepower.

Settling into the room, I unpacked my toothbrush, took a shower and sent my dirty clothes to the laundry. Call me strange but I prefer to shoot people in clean undershorts. Next I took a short nap to nip the jet lag in the bud, and woke at three fifty-five p.m., the phone on the bedside table ringing. Answering it, I was told by the concierge that my driver was in the foyer.

*

'Hey, Fakim,' I said as I walked up behind him. 'You came back.'

'Yes. Ha ha ha. Please,' he said and led the way to the Renault parked in the forecourt.

'How'd you make out with those items we talked about?' I asked.

'Yes, Magogoni Street. We go see man now.'

After a slow mile and a half crawling through narrow backstreets that reeked increasingly of burned trash and excrement, we exited suburbia at a place where a dozen fishing boats with broken keels were pulled up on a white-sand beach. Men were working on the boats, nets and other gear. Fakim rolled down his window and talked briefly to one mahogany-colored old guy hobbling beside the road on a crutch fashioned from driftwood, dressed in raggedy knee-length pants and a faded pink Pepsi-Cola t-shirt. He had one leg, one eye, three teeth and a voice that sounded like it was being passed through a cheese grater. All the guy needed was a parrot. He pointed toward the beach and drew a map in the air while he talked in, I guessed, Swahili. Fakim drove on a little way and parked near a yard of rusting cars and other relics.

'Please, you follow, Mr Vin,' Fakim said getting out.

We went down to the boats lined up on the beach, the sand a minefield of human turds and gobs of soiled newspaper. Plastic bags, bottles and paper rolled in the gentle wavelets flopping onto the shore, the air thick with top notes of shit, diesel, fish and rotting wood. Fakim stopped to speak with an old Arab sitting smoking a fat hand-rolled cigarette in the shade of one of the boats, who pointed at another man sitting farther down the beach.

'That man there, he owns boat,' Fakim explained.

The boat owner stood up as we approached: lean, black and short, a cigarette stitched to his lower lip, and ancient threadbare shorts and undershirt hanging off his body. He'd been sharpening a long curved blade on a whetstone. He waved the blade around, exchanged some kind of local greeting with Fakim, and the two men went into an intense negotiation. The breeze shifted and essence of unwashed body hit my nose and made my eyes water. When the dialogue ended, the guy beamed a cigarette-stained grin and Fakim laughed his nervous laugh.

'He agrees to the price,' Fakim announced. 'One hundred US dollars. You pay now.'

'What am I paying for, exactly?'

'You can use boat for twenty-four hours. If you break the boat, you must get him new one. Also, he will kill my parents if we do not return it. Ha ha.'

As Fakim was saying this, the boat owner went over to a patched canvas tarpaulin and pulled it back on a beaten-up single-hulled boat with a gleaming new fifty-horsepower Honda outboard motor hanging off the back.

'You like the boat, Mr Vin?' Fakim asked.

'Perfect.'

'You want to use now?'

There was still maybe an hour till the sun snuffed itself out in the smoke haze hanging around above the horizon. 'Sure, why not,' I said, and sealed the deal with a hundred in tattered notes, which I passed to the owner. He grinned broadly and said something that was either 'Thank you' or 'Sucker, this baby's not even mine'. I figured a receipt was out of the question.

He then went back to the boat, ratcheted up the hull with a car jack, placed two wheels under the rear of the boat, pulled the jack, lifted the bow and hauled the ensemble to the water's edge. Jumping in, he pumped fuel from the tank and started the motor with the press of a button. He then motioned me over and introduced me to the systems, all controlled from a small command station toward the front of the boat. A Mercedes-Benz three-pointed star was glued into the steering wheel boss.

Fakim stepped awkwardly into the back of the boat and fell onto the bench seat.

'What are you doing?' I asked him.

'I am coming.'

I'd figured that much without his assistance. 'Yeah, but why?'

'My parents would wish it.'

Obviously, trust was yet to blossom between us.

'What about the gun?' I inquired.

'Later for gun.'

The old guy gave us a push off and I opened the throttle. The bow came up steeply as the prop bit and then settled down, the four-stroke motor barely murmuring. I steered us out into the center of the pancreas and turned inland. The ships moored out in the channel were a good place to start looking. I wasn't sure what I was looking for exactly, but I was certain I'd recognize it when I saw it. The first of the ships in the queue was a red and black oil tanker. No one was visible walking about on deck that I could see, though there were high-powered lights already lit up along the hull and superstructure. They were aimed down toward the waterline. I took us around the ship's stern and read the name, *Morning Star*, registered in Panama. No sign of life back here either.

Next in line, three hundred yards behind, was a compact container ship. It was painted off-white, rust breaking through the skin like a spreading cancer. I steered toward it, carving a white trench in the warm green harbor waters. Its name was *Sun Trader*, registered out of Liberia. Like the *Morning Star*, *Sun Trader* also seemed deserted, though lights were on in some of the small windows puncturing its superstructure. A third ship completed the queue, some kind of general bulk carrier. It was low in the water, suggesting its holds were full. A man was standing on the bow, smoking a cigarette. Fakim waved at him. No acknowledgment. I motored down the side of the ship painted dark blue and got a look at the stern – *African Spirit*, Liberia. It was an old-style bulk carrier, the type you didn't see so much pulling into Western ports these days, a couple of cranes on it, presumably between the holds. Nothing more to see here; I steered toward the pier where there were other ships to inspect, the vehicle carrier from South Korea and so forth.

After checking them out, all seemed to be more or less ghost ships with virtually zero human activity on board. What was there to do on a modern ship when it was sitting on a mooring anyway? The harbor tour continued. I took us farther inland where the water turned black and individual rainbow slicks of oil merged into one continuous blanket that reflected the dying light. Over the city, the twilight sky was filling with the smoke of a hundred thousand cooking fires, all fuelled by trash if the smell was anything to go by.

I'd been wrong and there was nothing of any interest to see out on the water after all. Spinning the Mercedes wheel, we scribed a tight one-eighty and headed back to the beach. By now the sun was below the horizon. With daylight largely gone, the lights on the ships had some authority, burning bright to discourage the approach of unwelcome guests. It was the same out in the channel, where the ships were lit up like exercise yards. There was one exception to this, the *African Spirit* at the back of the line, which was no more than a vague gray shadow.

Keeping a hundred yards or so from the line of moored ships as we headed back, I glanced idly up at the darkened *African Spirit* as we motored by. And that's when I caught sight of the thing I knew would be significant when I saw it. A surge of adrenalin punched my heart rate into triple figures. I turned away to avoid attracting suspicion and looked ahead to the steel cliff that was the next ship in the row rising out of the black water. What I'd seen up on the deck of the *African Spirit* was a guy with an assault rifle dangling carelessly in his hand, a light-enhancing device propped up on his forehead. Everyday garden-variety pirates would probably have assault weapons, but I doubted they'd be equipped with NVGs. No, the guys guarding this ship were *special*. All of which meant one thing – I was gonna need that handgun.

A few minutes later I drove the runabout up onto the sand. Fakim fetched the wheels and helped me beach it high and dry. We threw the tarp over it and I ducked back under to retrieve the ignition key. There were another twenty-three hours of ownership with my name on them and, given the security bond Fakim had put up, it was only fair not to make the thing too easy to steal. The boat owner materialized out of the night and I put the key in his gnarled hand.

'Tomorrow, tomorrow,' he said when I told him thanks.

'What if I need it sooner?' I asked.

Fakim exchanged a few words with the guy and said, 'You come back any time. He will be here. He guards the boat.'

'Now let's go get a gun,' I told Fakim as we walked up the beach.

'No. Later for gun.'

'So you keep saying.'

'First we must eat.'

Food. Did I have time for that? The guard I saw on the *African Spirit* with the NVGs didn't look particularly alert, but there'd be others. It'd be pointless and dangerous trying to get aboard before fatigue set in among the watch. I had a few hours to kill. And, now that Fakim mentioned it, I was hungry for the first time since my brush with snake venom, though the smells I was coming to associate with Dar weren't exactly making me salivate for the local cuisine.

We passed by two men barbecuing the small carcass of some unidentified hairy animal over a smoking fire set in a cut-down fifty-five-gallon drum.

'I don't suppose you got Burger King in town?' I asked.

'Ha ha ha,' he replied.

'What makes you think I'm joking?' I said.

Fakim drove through narrow backstreets for a while, the unsealed roads choked with people and street animals, and eventually pulled into an open square, folks milling around, some moving to the beat of blaring music, hawkers selling food out of portable stalls. I settled for Fakim's recommendation – chicken à la newspaper. At least, I think it was chicken. I unwrapped the newsprint. The sinewy carcass was covered in hot spices and peppers, served with some boiled stringy vegetable matter, and was a little hard to positively identify. I was thinking squirrel. Somehow Fakim managed to get his hands on a couple of chilled Cokes.

The chicken tasted like something else that tasted like chicken. Like squirrel maybe. I left most of the greenery and the Coke was, well, Coke. We were done by nine forty-five and went back to his car.

'Okay, now the gun,' I told him as we got in.

'Yes, Mr Vin, the time is good for gun,' he replied.

I wasn't sure what he meant by that – maybe it was just his English – but I let it go. We drove for another twenty minutes or so, into another part of town more decrepit than the last, if that were possible. Fakim eventually pulled over in a street that was part residential, part warehouse. No kids running about here, and there were no hawker stalls, no music, no dogs, and only a trickle of light from a window here and there. Fakim turned to me and said, 'Gun is down there.' He pointed to a nearby narrow pathway completely engulfed in shadow.

'Down there,' I said.

'Yes.'

'Now, money please?'

'What?'

'You have paid two hundred dollar of the four hundred dollar for car, for driver, for guide. You now pay two hundred dollar you owe me for boat, and also a hundred dollar for gun.'

'So what do I get for this hundred dollars?'

'I show you where gun is.'

'And it's up to me to go and get it?'

'Yes, yes.'

The guy had an interesting business model. 'So the gun is down that darkened alley somewhere, and you want me to give you the money for it now.'

'Yes, the gun is down there. You pay me. All three hundred dollar, please.'

This deal didn't add up in all the ways that counted, but mostly because he wanted the balance of the cash now in case I didn't make it back outta there alive.

'Ha ha ha.'

'I'll give you a hundred dollars now and another two hundred when I return with the gun.'

He looked at me hard, no doubt weighing the odds of my return.

I told him my problem. 'Once I pay you, what's to stop you driving off the second I get out of the car?'

'Oh no, no, no, Mr Vin!' he said.

Yeah, right. 'A hundred now, two hundred later. That's the only deal on the table.'

He exchanged his look of injustice for a frown of surly defeat. 'Okay . . . deal.'

There was a length of broom handle on the floorboards beside him. 'I'm gonna borrow your nightstick.' I motioned at it. 'It's in the fine print.'

'You pay me first, please.'

On the whole, it was an interesting lesson in economics Dar-style. I counted out the hundred dollars, swatted them into his open hand and he passed me the broom handle.

Fakim wasn't to know that I was cleaned out, cash-wise. I'd have to figure something out on that later. I left the car and walked across the road to the alley, the stick in my left hand held behind my leg. I stood at the entrance to the black hole that was the alleyway, off to one side so as not to be silhouetted, and waited a minute or two for my eyes to adjust to the darkness. The air stank of old ammonia – dog, cat and human piss. What the hell was I walking into? The faintest glimmer of mustard-colored light beckoned from down the far end of the black hole. I moved toward it, breathing hard, broken masonry and glass underfoot, along with plastic bags, plastic bottles and bottle tops, paper and stinking, sucking mud. The alley went through a kink and then another kink and broadened into a small square, an open sewer running through the middle of it. Ahead, against the far wall, three males and a female. Two of the males were chatting, smoking, leaning against a beat-up Toyota van with its parking lights on. The female had her skirt hitched up around her waist. She was presenting her huge dimply rear end to guy number three, a runt behind her whose sweat pants were around his skinny knees. He was jigging back and forth like a ferret in heat as he screwed her. The woman was grappling with a column of masonry to keep her balance while she looked back over her shoulder, smiling and murmuring encouragement.

'Excuse me,' I said to the two smokers, finger raised, lost tourist–style. 'Can you fellas point me in the direction of the nearest automatic teller machine?'

The men stared at me open-mouthed the way a prospector might regard a gold nugget that had just fallen out of the sky and landed at his feet.

'Hey!' one of them shouted at me after a protracted second or two, once they realized this gold nugget was no apparition. He reached into the front of his pants, pulled out a massive nickel-plated pistol that still managed to flash in the dimness, and skipped across the square toward me with his buddy a few steps behind, the weapon pointing in my general direction like an artillery piece. I was actually relieved to see this move on their part because it meant that the moment of maximum danger had passed. If I were them, I'd have dropped me first and asked questions later.

When the guy in front came within range, I swatted the weapon aside with the hidden broomstick, then followed through with an elbow to the side of his face, and finished off the ensemble move with the broomhandle, a smack down low that took his legs out from under him. One, two, three. He went down on his back with a thud, the mud settling under him with a farting sound. His buddy put the brakes on

313

and pulled a knife, so I bent down and picked up the gun, which made him back up, spin around and run for the nearest exit. The hooker was also running, having reorganized her clothing. She vaulted the open sewer with the grace of a hippo and disappeared into a doorway. Ferret guy was following his buddy, trying to run with his pants still around his knees.

I regarded the man at my feet. He was in his early twenties, maybe a hundred and thirty underfed pounds that were a mixture of black and Arab. His clothes, if they weren't Chinese rip-offs, were expensive – Everlast-branded sweat pants, Lonsdale t-shirt, Adidas high-tops. His mouth was opening and closing like a beached fish. He was winded, finding it difficult to fill his lungs. I crouched beside him, patted him down and found a wallet – empty – a switchblade, a handful of candies wrapped in plastic, seven hand-cut dum-dum bullets and a snub-nosed .38 revolver with a half dozen layers of duct tape wound around its handle. I checked the cylinder. No empty chambers. Up for inspection next, the nickel-plated job. It looked new. It was a heavy hitter, a .44 Magnum Desert Eagle. A useful weapon as long as you didn't have to hold it extended for any length of time, a real hand cannon. Removing the magazine revealed two rounds with a third in the chamber. I sniffed the barrel. It had been fired fairly recently. Being shot by a .44 slug was just a little worse than hitting the sidewalk after stepping off a twenty-story building. I relieved the guy of the handguns and ammo and left him with his other possessions.

'Two guns for price of one. I should ask for double,' said Fakim, shaking his head when I climbed into the passenger seat and showed him the weapons. 'So, where you go now? Back to hotel?'

'No,' I said. 'Take me to the most expensive brothel in town.'

Twenty-seven

The frown on Fakim's face was Sunday school–teacher stern. 'A brothel. This is illegal in Tanzania, Mr Vin. You want to make with woman, we go to Uwanja wa Fisi. It is famous.'

'Never heard of it.'

'It is also called Hyena Square.'

'Still never heard of it.'

'You buy woman there for five hundred shillings.'

I did the calculation. 'That's thirty cents American.'

'You can bargain with them, make love for three hundred shillings.'

On the basis that you get what you pay for, what could you expect for thirty cents or less? In Dar es Salaam, I didn't want to think about it. 'Let me put it another way,' I said. 'If you had *a lot* of money in this town, and you wanted to meet a *nice* bad girl, where would you go?'

Fakim thought about that as we moved off and said, 'Yes, I know good place.'

Twenty minutes later, and in a better part of town, we cruised slowly past a joint called the Q-Bar Restaurant and Nightclub, a bar open to the street where white guys mingled with black women, drank beer, played pool and, from the look of the comings and goings, took aforementioned black women back to their hotel rooms, wherever that happened to be.

'This the best place to get laid?' I asked.

'Yes, Mr Vin, best place.'

'Okay, well, go down the road a ways, do a U-turn and come back. Park where I tell you.'

Fakim nodded, massaged the gas pedal and we drifted on past the bar. I couldn't see anyone I recognized as we cruised by, but did I really expect to? I reminded myself this was a long shot. I was going to have to get lucky – a different kind of lucky to the lucky going on at the Q-Bar.

A short while later we were coming back down the street. Several parking spots were available. 'There,' I said, pointing to a gap thirty yards up the road from the bar and on the opposite side. Fakim squeezed us into the spot. There was no street lighting to speak of around us, so the bar punched out of the gloom. Bon Jovi was on the playlist, a pair of African women moving to the beat in long slinky sheaths accentuating their slender height.

After ten minutes of doing nothing but sit, Fakim asked, 'What is happening?'

'Not a lot so far,' I said as I watched an old white guy with a paunch, gray hair and a bald spot lead a young African woman wearing a midriff-baring top to an old Toyota Tarago van.

'When will there be something?'

The Tarago edged into the street and drove off.

'Fakim, you watch television, you know what a stakeout is?'

'Yes.'

'Well, that's what this is – a stakeout.' That seemed to satisfy him for the moment. I killed ten minutes or so re-examining the confiscated firearms, glancing back at the Q-Bar every now and then. The .38 was an ancient weapon with its numbers crudely removed, a classic throw-down. You killed someone with a piece like this and left it at the scene – untraceable. The barrel was filthy and the grimy duct tape around the handle was sweating glue, leaving little balls of tacky black sludge in the palm of my hand. I wondered how many deaths it had been responsible for. I cleaned the metal with a scrap of rag scrounged from the backseat area, pushing it through the barrel with a pen from a holder on the dash. The gun could do with some oil, but I had none. Obviously the previous owner had never seen what happened when a dirty weapon blew up in your hand.

The Desert Eagle was a different story to the .38, though the barrel had flecks of powder caught in the rifling. Its action was, however, dirt-free and well oiled. After wiping it down with a fresh strip of rag, I ran the strip through the .38 to transfer a little lubrication, and then reloaded its cylinder with the dum-dum rounds. These nasty little fucks had a grooved cross cut in the tip so that the slugs expanded and broke up on impact with human flesh, the pieces tearing and gouging their way through.

During the clean-up, a couple of vehicles came while others went, the to and fro movement at the Q-Bar featuring some of the hottest women I'd ever seen, African or otherwise. Other than that, there was nothing of particular interest going on.

Three hours later, it became apparent which of the women were doing more of the coming and going than the others. Fakim had long since fallen asleep, snoring against his window.

'Fakim.'

Nothing.

'Fakim,' I repeated.

He woke with a loud fart. 'Yes? Yes?'

'There another entrance to this bar?'

'Yes, Mr Vin, there are others,' he said.

'Great,' I muttered. It was now just after two a.m. The whole exercise had been a goddamn waste of time, the futility of it magnifying my exhaustion. The fault was mine. I'd failed to ask the question, fuck it all. I yawned. 'Let's go.'

'Where now?' he asked, turning the key in the ignition, the motor hiccuping into life.

I was thinking my bed back at the Southern Sun. I'd chosen this place to stake out in the belief that the pirates out on the *African Spirit*, being in the employment of von Weiss, would have more money than the average john and therefore would choose to come to the best little whorehouse in Dar when they were ashore – assuming any of them were ashore tonight. Maybe this assumption was flawed from the beginning. Maybe Hyena Square for a thirty-cent doink was more their speed. 'Head to the docks,' I said. 'Wake me when we get there.'

I burrowed into the seat and thought about closing my eyes. But at that moment I saw two white guys leave the bar with three women, one of whom was well over six and a half feet tall. Sleep could wait.

'Hey, will you look at that,' I said, sitting up.

'Yes, she is very tall. I think she is Maasai. They are warrior tribe – grow very tall, taller than her.'

She'd be a shoe-in for a job at Donn Arden's Jubilee Showgirls.

The party got into a minibus with a Holiday Inn logo on the driver's door.

'Follow them,' I said.

'Oh, Mr Vin, you like tall women? You do not need to follow *her*. I know another place where—'

'Just don't lose them,' I said, cutting him off. It wasn't the Maasai woman I had an interest in but the two white guys with her. I'd met one of them before a couple of times back in Vegas. It was Ty Morrow, owner of Nevada Aircraft Brokers, suppliers of aircraft to drug cartels, arms traders and Benicio von Weiss. Running into Morrow all the way down here? Well, that was completely unexpected. And I'd have been more than happy to have had that opportunity on its own, but a big fat bonus came with him. It was his wing buddy. This guy I'd never been introduced to, though I now knew him well enough through his service record and recognized him from his photo: former lieutenant Ed Dyson, US Navy, discharged due to some obscure (and, for all I knew, bogus) medical disorder. Petinski's weather professor. As I watched, Dyson closed the door behind the Maasai woman as she pulled in her long legs, then ran around the back of the minibus and climbed in the other side. Whadaya know, a gentleman. Emma Shilling had told me she'd overheard Dar es Salaam being mentioned in a conversation

Dyson had with von Weiss. And now here he was in living, breathing, horny person. Motherfucking jackpot. If these guys were here, then surely O Magnifico himself wasn't far away. Maybe Morrow and Dyson would lead us right to him.

'Wait till they pull out,' I told Fakim.

Whoever was driving the minibus took their time getting their shit together, enough time for the vehicle parked in front of it to depart and provide the minibus with an easy exit. The minibus driver took it and accelerated hard, taillights disappearing in a rolling ball of dust up the road.

I barked, 'Move it!'

'Yes, yes, Mr Vin.' Fakim jack-knifed into the traffic. A horn blared and a headlight crashed into our overhanging fender with a dull crunch of metal and plastic.

'Oh, oh . . .' Fakim wailed.

'Wonderful,' I muttered. Fakim slumped his head against the steering wheel, his fists against his temples.

The vehicle that had hit us backed up a few feet and its front doors flew open. Seconds later a flashlight came on and swept over Fakim and me.

'Is that you, Cooper?'

Petinski!

'Jesus,' she snapped. 'What the hell are you doing here?'

'Get out of the car,' said a man accompanying her in a voice I didn't recognize.

Several patrons from the Q-Bar were wandering over to watch the show. Fakim opened his door with difficulty, eventually pushing it out with his feet. I got out and leaned on the roof. 'Why don't you watch where you're going, Petinski?' I asked her. 'Or was it your buddy here driving?'

'You know this clown?' inquired the guy with the flashlight.

'Be nice, Ken,' she told him.

Ken was neatly dressed and slightly built with a good hairline. He looked like a Ken. He shone the beam full in my face.

'You wanna put that away, Ken?' I told him, and then to Petinski I said, 'Do I call you Barbie now?'

She snatched the Maglite from her partner's hand, turned it off and tossed it into their car. 'You were following Morrow and Dyson?' she asked, short of patience.

'About to,' I said. 'Until you and Ricky Bobby here arrived.'

The guy glanced at the ground and then over at the Q-Bar as if maybe we were talking about someone else.

'We've been sitting twenty yards up the road for the last six hours,' Petinski said.

I watched Fakim examine the damage to his vehicle. 'Is it drivable?' I asked him.

He tugged at the fender but couldn't manage to pull it away from the tire. 'No, but it's not so bad.'

The Renault was a patchwork of different-colored panels anyway, evidence of numerous past accidents. Life was hard for a car in Dar. 'Don't worry about it,' I told him. 'The Company will pay to get it fixed.' I turned to Ken. 'Won't it, Ken?'

'Who is this joker?' Ken asked.

'Don't push it, Cooper,' said Petinski. 'Can we get back to the business at hand? How long you been following Morrow and Dyson?'

'I was going to ask you the same thing. Weren't you being reassigned?'

'This *is* my reassignment.'

'Which is?'

'None of your business.'

I looked at her flatly.

She sighed. 'Okay . . . Chasing the weapons obtained illegally in the United States from military bases.'

It annoyed me to hear that. That was the case *I* wanted. Fakim had finished checking over his car and he wasn't happy either. 'Give him your card,' I said to Ken before Fakim could arc up at me.

'But it wasn't my fault,' Ken whined.

'There's an independent witness who says otherwise,' I said.

'And who's that?'

'You're looking at him.'

Ken stared at me a moment or two and wisely decided I was serious. He reached for his wallet and removed his card. It read: *Lieutenant Ken Bushell, US Navy, Assistant to the US Military Attaché, Kenya. US Embassy, Mombasa*. A weight of fancy non-standard gold embossing on the lettering told me Bushell had had them printed up himself. These Navy types . . .

'Nice card,' I told him. 'When'll you be back in the office?'

'I don't know. Next Monday or Tuesday. Who knows.'

'Petinski, can you loan me three hundred bucks?'

She hesitated.

'C'mon, you know I'm good for it.'

She put her hand in her pocket, removed a money clip and pulled most of the bills off it.

'Two-fifty's all I got.'

'Thanks,' I said. 'I owe you.'

'You do.'

I handed Ken's card to Fakim along with one of my own. I also gave him the two hundred and fifty dollars and told him it was the balance of what I owed him, plus fifty bucks for a cab. 'Contact Mr Bushell here. If you can't get through, give my office a call.'

'Yes, yes, Mr Vin. I will. Ha ha. If you want to use boat, your friend at Magogoni Street will be waiting. But please to bring back, okay?'

'Relax,' I said.

He passed me a card, a photo on it of his Renault with him standing beside the vehicle, his hand raised, and the words *Fakim's Luxury Taxi*. 'For next time you come to Dar,' he said.

'Thanks for your help, Fakim,' I said, shaking his hand.

'*Asante sana* – thank you, Mr Vin, ha ha.'

'You going somewhere?' Ken asked.

'Yeah, with you and Petinski.' I gave Fakim a final wave and then climbed in the back of their light-green Ford before Ken could get his tongue around an objection. 'The Holiday Inn, right?' I said. 'Let's go.'

Petinski shrugged and got in. Ken didn't have much choice. He turned and opened the driver's door.

'So you're from the Mombasa station,' I said to Ken, leaning forward between them. 'A little out of area, aren't you?'

Petinski answered for him. 'I told you we've got problems in Dar. The station chief has been relieved for taking bribes. Langley thought it best to use out-of-towners.'

'What about von Weiss?' I asked as we moved off. 'Where's he?'

'Couldn't tell you. We're after your two pals Charles and Falco White.'

'They're here?'

'At the Holiday Inn with Morrow and Dyson.'

'And this has nothing at all to do with the other things you and I were investigating?'

'No.'

Ken eyeballed Petinski beside him, whispered something to her.

'Relax, Cooper's one of us,' I heard her say.

'Hey, I resent that,' I said.

'You always got a smart mouth, Agent Cooper?' Ken asked.

'Only when there's good material to work with.'

'Anything turn up on Randy?' Petinski said over her shoulder.

'No, nothing.'

'In a way that's something, I guess.' She meant that as a body hadn't turned up there was still a chance he was alive.

'How'd you track down Morrow and Dyson?' I asked her.

'Morrow piloted von Weiss's G5 from Buenos Aires to Dar. Laurent Duval was his co-pilot. Ken here had the airport staked out and picked up the tail when they landed.'

I was more familiar with 'Duval' by his real name. 'André LeDuc,' I said, this time unable to suppress the grin. 'He's here too?'

'I thought that would make you happy,' she said.

'Delirious. So what's going down?'

'We think Charles and Falco have been negotiating deals with Somali pirates. We're here to get the proof.'

'A deal to do what?' I asked.

'Weapons shipments.'

Her use of the word 'shipments' made me think of the *African Spirit*. 'What about Morrow, LeDuc and Dyson? What are they doing here?'

'We're not sure. Hence the tail.'

'But everyone's still convinced it has absolutely nothing to do with what we know to be missing.'

'What's missing?' Ken asked.

'Tell him,' I said. 'We need to talk and time's running out.'

'You tell him.'

'A nuke, Ken, one of ours.'

'*Shit?!*'

'Yeah, lots of it.'

Petinski shook her head, not happy that I'd spilled the beans. 'There have been arrests.'

'What arrests?' Being at thirty thousand feet in economy the last couple of days, I hadn't heard dick.

'OSI swooped the day before yesterday and detained a number of people: four NCOs who worked in Munitions Control at Area Two, along with six armorers and three weapons handlers. All but two of them had moved on from the 896th MUNS to other posts.'

'There goes Colonel Challis's perfect record,' I said.

'The colonel shot himself.'

He shot himself? 'Was he under suspicion?'

'No. He left a note.'

'Why'd he do it?'

'Shame, basically. Also, you remember the one-star general and the colonel I told you about, the two officers who were under suspicion? The FBI took them into custody. They were spirited away to a safe house somewhere in Maryland.'

'What did they get out of them?'

'A couple of corpses.'

'*What?*'

'Both were murdered. One was electrocuted in the bath, the other shot. Whoever did it then torched the house and burned it to the ground.'

That didn't seem possible for a whole bunch of reasons. 'What about surveillance cameras? They give up anything?'

'Temporarily disabled.'

'What the fuck is going on?' I wondered aloud.

'Good question,' Ken echoed.

'Stay out of this,' Petinski warned him. 'Loose ends, Cooper . . . Three NCOs who served with the 99th Security Forces at Area Two have died recently in various car and motorcycle accidents.'

'And no one's talked?'

Petinski shook her head. 'No one's saying a word. There's a nuclear weapon involved. There aren't going to be any deals cut.'

'Anyone we know been taken into custody?'

'Staff Sergeant Sailor. You remember him?'

I nodded. Sailor – the black guy the size of a plains buffalo who'd accompanied Petinski and me on the orientation tour.

'More arrests are expected,' she said.

'How'd they figure who had their hands in the cookie jar?'

'You remember your idea – the one about the psych tests where people learned the answers?'

I prepared myself for a pat on the back. 'Yeah?'

'Well, the people who *really* know about those things laughed at the suggestion.'

I shrugged. It was a long shot anyway.

'But they reviewed *all* the background security checks. Irregularities were picked up. Turns out around half a dozen people who had clearance and access weren't who they purported to be. They're all now in custody and high on the suspect list. The whole system's going under review. Again.'

Traffic was banking up. Ken doll swerved to avoid a pothole and then hit the brakes, the air full of brown dust choking the headlight beams. 'What now?' he muttered.

Folks in the vehicles stopped in front were leaving their cars. Some were running away, appearing and then vanishing in the murk. Petinski, Ken and I got out and went ahead, pushing through people fleeing past us.

At the head of the traffic jam was the minibus with the Holiday Inn logo on the door. It was sitting on its rims, the tires shot out. The doors were full of bullet holes, all the windows smashed. Thin ribbons of smoke rose from several places. Blood spatter ran down the paintwork from the rear passenger windowsill. From ten feet or so, a mass of hair and blood was all I could see inside the car. Dust rose around the van, illuminated by headlight beams. Steam swirled from a puddle of fluid gathering on the ground between the front wheels. The attack had only concluded moments ago. I surveyed the area quickly but couldn't see the shooters. Petinski, Ken and I jogged to the van. The Desert Eagle rubbed the skin in the small of my back. The throw-down was inside my sock, bumping up and down painfully against my ankle, the glue on the handgrip tugging at the hairs on my leg. I was tempted to pull one of the weapons, but decided to leave them where they were until absolutely necessary. The last thing I needed, in the vicinity of the shot-up minibus, was witnesses who said they saw a firearm in my hands.

I checked the vehicle's interior and confirmed that everyone in there was deceased. Six bodies, several of which smoked with all the hot lead buried inside them. I recognized Morrow and the Maasai woman. Morrow's fly was undone and her head was in his lap. A tight bloody ball of US dollars was scrunched in her hand. In the seat in front were Dyson and the two other women. His head was back against the head-rest, half his neck torn out. The women had holes drilled in their cheeks and foreheads and chests. I reached in through the driver's window and turned off the ignition to reduce the risk of fire.

'This can't have been random,' Petinski concluded as she looked in on the carnage.

Duh, I thought.

'Anyone speak English?' Ken shouted into the night. 'Anyone see what happened here . . . ? Anyone?'

'Hey, you want taxi?' a man called out to us, seeing the opportunity to maybe pick up a little business. I waved him away.

And then three men burst through the dust and the traffic at a run, yelling and pointing down the road behind them. They were excited about something. As they flew past I broke into a run, heading in the direction they'd just come from.

A hundred yards farther on, round a corner, a square opened out. In the middle of it I could see that a pothole the size of a bomb crater had swallowed a pickup. The vehicle's rear axle and diff were clearly visible poking up over the edge of the crater. Traffic had already built up around the accident, a multitude of headlight beams diffused by the raised dust washing the scene in dirty yellow light. Two men were lying sprawled on the road, moving slow. Rifles – assault weapons, FN FALs – were scattered around them. Several other men were staggering around in circles, recovering from the pickup's nosedive. One of them wandered up drunkenly to a Toyota van at the head of a line of stalled traffic, pulled the door open and hoisted the driver out onto the road. He then pointed his weapon at the man and shouted some kind of warning at him before going back for his pals, who were now all getting up on their hands and knees.

Petinski and Ken appeared beside me. 'Were they the shooters?' Ken asked.

'Don't see anyone else running around with assault weapons, do you?' I said.

'What do you want to do about it?' Ken inquired, ready for action, reaching around for the Smith & Wesson holstered in the small of his back.

Maybe I'd misjudged him.

Twenty-eight

'Easy, tiger,' I said. 'Not a good place for that.' Ken took my advice and left his weapon where it was. It wouldn't have been smart to engage these men in a firefight in the middle of this crowded square – too much potential collateral damage wandering around. And unless Ken had a bazooka nestled back there between his butt cheeks, we were seriously outgunned by these guys, as well as being outnumbered.

'You were right from the beginning,' I said in an aside to Petinski.

'Right about what?'

'It's von Weiss. And what's going on now only reconfirms it.'

'Why's that?'

'Von Weiss managed to get his hands on the W80 and he's about to use it, just like Randy said in his note . . .' I looked at the timer on my watch, '. . . within the next seventy-two hours. The one star and the colonel – the FBI's prime suspects? They were decoys. I wouldn't be surprised if they had nothing to do with this mess at all. But now it's time for von Weiss to clean house. He's whacking everyone connected to the scheme and now, obviously, it's Morrow's and Dyson's turn. I don't like LeDuc's or the White brothers' chances of making it to sunrise.' And in regards to those guys, if I was right, I was genuinely disappointed that

327

it wasn't going to be me pulling the trigger on them. But then a hard reality suddenly dawned on me: we were going to have to try to keep them alive. 'Shit,' I muttered.

'Eh?' Petinski was only half listening, watching the last of the attackers peel himself up off the road. He was nursing a badly broken forearm as he lurched toward the Toyota.

'We're gonna have to protect LeDuc, Charles and Falco White. If we don't manage to keep someone connected to von Weiss breathing, he could walk away clean.'

'He's not the one, Cooper. Langley knows what it's doing.'

'Since when?'

The stolen Toyota van started to roll, the driver keeping his hand on the horn to clear a path. A police siren was still a long ways off, the world moving in slow motion. As the van crawled along, its rightful owner approached the driver's window, his hands out in a beseeching gesture. The carjacker responded with his rifle, poking its muzzle in the guy's face till he backed away.

'I'm not getting into this fantasy with you now, Cooper.'

'Listen – Emma Shilling told me von Weiss is hot for revenge against America.'

'Why?'

'For bitch-slapping the Nazis in the war, and for driving his old man, Mengele, into exile. And now, with Ali-Bakr al Mohammed and Gamal Abdul-Jabbar, he's found people to help him do the deed.'

'Cooper—'

'This is von Weiss's moment, Petinski. It's the one he's been working toward for a long time.'

'Where is this going?'

'I think our W80 is sitting on a ship out there in the harbor. Von Weiss has given the bomb to those two pirates to use against us.'

Petinski gave me her weary look. 'And how're they going to do that, exactly?'

'Do I have to do *all* the work here, Petinski?'

'*Hello* . . .' Ken said impatiently breaking us apart. 'We need to get back to our rental before it's stolen.' He turned to me. 'You coming?'

'No,' I said.

'Then what are you going to do?'

'I don't know.'

'But that's never stopped him before,' said Petinski, sporting a look of triumph. 'Right, Cooper?' She turned and followed Ken back to the rental.

*

That shitty fudged ESTJ manner of hers aside, I knew I'd put some doubt in Petinski's mind about the situation confronting us – just as her refusal to accept my theory put some doubt in mine that I was completely right. Nevertheless, I was struggling to find another that fit the facts – or the facts as I knew them, anyway.

I watched as the Toyota van carrying the gunmen slipped through a hole in the traffic, the van's owner shouting and shaking his fists at its receding taillights as the dust and the night slowly engulfed them. It was a gutsy performance. I felt sorry for the guy. Maybe the car was all he had in the world.

An antique Nissan Pathfinder 4x4 pulled up beside me, the driver leaning across and winding down the window. 'Hey, you want taxi?'

'Sure,' I said.

He'd read my mind, only unfortunately for him he hadn't also peeked inside my wallet along the way because maybe then he'd have kept driving. The door was rusted on its hinges but I managed to open it and then pull it almost all the way closed. The driver reached across, grabbed a piece of thin cable dangling from the door, yanked it shut with practiced technique and hooked the cable around a bolt welded to the remains of the dashboard. 'Where you want to go?'

I pointed down the road the gunmen had taken. 'I have to catch up with my friends. They're driving a Toyota van.'

'Fifty US dollar, okay?'

'Ten,' I said, just to generate a little respect.

'Okay, twenty-five is good price. No problem. We will catch your friend,' he said, laying into the horn to clear the way as the Nissan shuddered into movement.

I wondered how we'd managed to settle on twenty-five dollars but went with it.

'Where are they going?' the driver asked.

'I don't know. Just driving, having a look around.'

'Can you see this van ahead?' he asked, peering forward, leaning against the steering wheel. 'Toyota van is popular.'

I caught a glimpse of one several cars ahead caught in the headlights of the vehicles stopped at an intersection. Maybe that was it. But then, down a side street, I saw taillights of another van that could have been the gunmen's. Passing us on the other side of the road, heading back the way we'd just come, was yet one more Toyota van. Hmm, yeah – popular. 'Just keep going straight ahead,' I told the driver.

I counted four more Toyota vans within the next ten seconds.

'Where's Wally?' I said.

'What?' the driver asked.

'Forget it.' Maybe this was a lost cause. I considered another plan. 'The port. Where is it from here?'

'We are going the wrong way. It is in the other direction.'

That came as a surprise. I believed the gunmen to be pirates, so naturally I'd assumed they'd head straight for the docks where they'd take a boat out to the *African Spirit*. Perhaps the van had pulled a one-eighty. This was looking hopeless, but I decided to give it another couple of minutes.

'Please to put window up, sir,' the driver said.

I wasn't keen to, the temperature being somewhere in the low nineties, the humidity nudging a hundred percent. The .38 had gummed itself to my ankle and a free-flowing river of sweat had formed between my shirt and the seat back. But then I took a look at what we were driving through and saw why he wanted it closed. The homes hereabouts were shanties. Listless, glassy-eyed young males hung around smoking pot or openly dealing drugs while slack-jawed, barely clothed women sat on the earth with crying babies, which they ignored completely.

Kids barely able to walk just stood like they didn't know what to do or where to go. This was truly the end of the road. I glanced down a side street leading into the heart of the damned and saw the van crawling along.

'There,' I said, pointing it out.

'No, not going down there. Your friends are lost, gonna be in a lot of trouble.'

'I'll pay you another ten dollars on top of your fee. I can't just leave 'em here.'

'Okay,' he said reassessing the dangers.

Obviously, ten bucks was worth more than ten bucks in this part of the world.

'We are near Uwanja wa Fisi,' the driver said.

That sounded familiar. 'Hyena Square?'

'Yes. Everyone knows Hyena Square. Your friends have come for women.'

'Maybe,' I said as he turned into the muddy lane. As long as the guy kept on the tail, he could believe what he liked. Meanwhile, the van didn't come to a stop but kept inching along seventy yards ahead.

'Don't get too close,' I told the driver, not thinking.

'You do not want to join them?' he said, eyes darting to me, uncertain.

'Actually, no. I've decided to surprise them. Let's just see where they go.'

The streets became gradually wider, the mud and the ruts deeper, the smell of human excrement more powerful. We entered a square where the buildings were a little less temporary. The van pulled up outside a windowless cinderblock bunker that could have been a toilet facility, only they didn't have those in Dar, at least not where you could crap right on the street. Two men loitered outside the bunker, smoking, and the smell of pot and shit hung heavily in the night air. Six men got slowly out of the van, carrying rifles. The guy with the broken forearm held it to his chest.

Two men appeared from nowhere. They ran past the Nissan drunk-enly, weaving about, one chasing the other with a broken bottle. The one giving chase got close and threw it, but then lost his balance, fell and did a faceplant into an open sewer.

I glanced at the cab driver. He was nervous as hell, head swinging around, scoping out the scenery. 'What we doing here, sir?'

'I'll give you another fifty dollars to relax,' I said.

The look I got told me he was finally realizing that my story about catching up with friends stank as bad as the general area. I pulled the .38 out of my sock, the tacky handle giving my ankle a light wax job, and put it in my lap. Next I removed the Desert Eagle, confirmed that a round was chambered and that it was on safety before tucking it behind the belt in the front of my pants. It might only have three rounds in the bank, but iron like that made the right kind of statement. I checked over the .38, was reassured by those dum-dums and gave the cylinder a spin. The driver's eyes were wide, staring at the ugly little killing machine in my hand.

'Take a deep breath,' I told him.

'What are you going to do?'

'Nothing for the moment. Just gonna wait and see what develops.' I said that to reassure myself as much as him, because now I was even more outgunned and outnumbered than I'd been with Ken and Barbie back at the bullet-riddled Holiday Inn minibus.

Fifteen minutes later the cab driver and I were still sitting in his Pathfinder, nothing going on at the bunker down the road. It was just past four a.m. I felt like I'd been up for forty-eight hours. Something that sounded like it wanted to be set free growled in my stomach and lack of sleep was making my eyeballs feel as dry as glass marbles rolled in sand. If not for those little adrenal glands pumping away deep inside, I'd be trying to dream something pleasant, like Petinski feeling frisky in an Olympics leotard.

A door suddenly burst open. Men surged out of the toilet block – I counted twenty. Some of them had faces that were pale in the darkness, which meant they weren't African. Interesting. From this distance and in this light, making a call on their nationality wasn't possible. They dispersed and piled into the carjacked van and three other vehicles.

Pretty much everyone seemed to be carrying an assault rifle and a bag of some description. The convoy moved off quickly, the vehicles low on their springs, tires churning through mud and shit.

I unhooked the door and kicked it open before I realized what I was doing. Apparently I was going to check out that bunker whether I wanted to or not. To the driver, I said, 'How much do I owe you?'

'Eighty-five dollar.' The concern on his face told me he was not confident about collecting.

'I'll make it an even hundred.' I made the offer to counter his desire to split as soon as he hooked the door shut. 'Just don't leave this spot.'

'One hundred twenty-five,' he said.

'One hundred ten.' That just came out.

'Okay, but we must go soon. This is very bad place.'

That last observation was like saying water is wet because, aside from the gunmen and the glass-wielding sewer divers, I'd stepped calf deep into the foulest smelling mud in the history of foul-smelling mud. As I lifted my feet it sucked, clawed and gurgled at my boots like it was trying to dissolve them. I picked my way across the roadway to the side shared with the toilet bunker and moved toward it slow and stealthy. Before I got there I could see that the armed guards that had been seated out front earlier were gone. The place looked and felt deserted. Both sides of the block supported mean little shanties built from stuff most folks threw out. If at all possible, I didn't want to disturb the people who lived in them, or damage these homes in any way.

My sweating palm kneaded the .38 gummy bear. The door was clearly a wafer-thin sheet of veneer, and gaps all round leaked a yellow glow from within. I could also hear the local R&B playing somewhere inside. Pressing my ear against the door, I heard the music a little louder and clearer, but no other sound that suggested habitation. Twenty guys with bags and guns had piled out; I hoped that was everyone. My heart rate was up. There was only one way in. I thumbed back the .38's hammer, pulled out the Desert Eagle, cocked it and thumbed off the safety.

I put my bodyweight behind a front kick that blasted the door clean off its hinges, and moved in quickly, stepping over it. The hall was low and narrow and stank like the place had been washed down with urine, bong water and charcoal. A room off to the right. No door. A dark rectangle. I went in, staying low. Empty. Rubbish littered the floor – food packaging, plastic bottles. Kicking the trash aside I found two bottles of water, unopened, seals still intact, but nothing else of note. From the smell and the state of the blackened floors, cooking fires had been lit in this room. No windows, or other doors, though there was plenty of ventilation with the roof raised several inches above the walls. No people, either – clear. I turned and went out, keeping low. Another room like the last was off to the right of the passageway. Nothing but trash and old bedding in there also. I backed out. Not much hallway left, a heavily padlocked door sealing the end. One last doorway remained; dim light came from within. That's where the music was coming from. A flash bang would've been a handy thing to throw in there before my body filled the doorway.

I counted to three, moved to the other side of the opening, stopped. No reaction from within. I put the .38 around the corner, followed by my head, briefly. In, out. A table, an automobile battery on it, wires leading to a car headlight bulb burning dully. Nothing had moved. I put my head around a second time, saw the battery on the table again. A tub was bolted to the wall along with a workbench. Two mattresses were on the floor. A man lay on one of them, overnight bag on the floor beside him. I went in. He was plainly dead, staring open-eyed at nothing on the soot-stained ceiling. A neat bullet wound like a squashed raspberry colored the center of his forehead. His forearm was broken, a red and white bone end breaking the skin like the bow of a sinking ship. I was pretty sure he was the man injured in the car crash. I figured his buddies had fixed it so that it wouldn't bother him anymore, or slow them down. Not much of a healthcare plan.

I checked his pockets and found a few US dollars and two Somali thousand-shilling notes in the bottom of a thigh pocket, which was probably as much in the way of identification as I could hope for. Next I opened the bag. It stank of sweat, tobacco, grass and something my nose couldn't identify. I dug around. Two empty AK-47 mags; standard terrorist ski mask, black; a cheap plastic spray or rain jacket with hood; a pair of pants, dirty; a ratty blue t-shirt with holes; a red scarf. The source of the unusual smell lay in the bottom, a bundle of damp leaves bound tightly together inside a banana leaf. I pulled out the bundle and took a sniff. Christ, this smelled foul, like old meat soused in vinegar. I'd seen pictures of the stuff before in DEA handouts, but never come across it. *Khat*, drug of choice in Somalia, Yemen and Kenya. From what I remembered reading, the stuff produced an effect similar to speed when chewed or brewed up like tea. I threw it back in the bag and pulled the zip shut. The spray jacket told me the dead guy spent time at sea, the ski mask and AK mags said bandit, the Somali shillings and the *khat* suggested his nationality. In short: Somali pirate. His vessel had to be the *African Spirit*. Maybe the NVG-wearing bandits I'd seen aboard had captured it along with the men bivouacking in the bunker. I wondered why the port authorities hadn't challenged the vessel. Maybe they'd just been bribed to look the other way.

Moving on, the music I'd heard had come from an antiquated cassette/compact disc/radio player. It was on the floor, covered in trash. The battery levels on the player's face hovered in the red. The floors in the other rooms were thin concrete slabs but here the floor was wood. I noticed an empty foil fruit-juice container sticking up between the boards and brushed it aside with my foot but it refused to budge. It appeared to be jammed in the seat of a trapdoor. Further investigation revealed a knot in a rope recessed into one of the boards and a hole in the floor beside the trapdoor. I pulled on the rope and a section of floor came with it. I lifted it completely out, revealing a dark square of nothingness beneath. The rungs of a ladder disappeared into the jet-black void.

I holstered the Desert Eagle in the small of my back, and shifted the .38 to my left hand. A hand free, I carried the battery to the hole in the floor, set it down and dangled the globe into the basement. The bulb flickered off and on several times until it stopped swinging, the connections dodgy.

Lowering my head into the hole, I saw . . . Jesus Christ, it was a man hanging by his wrists from a chain bolted to the ceiling. I gagged. The air smelled putrid in there – of blood, shit and death. I had no choice but to climb down into that stinking hellhole to get a better look. The man, a white man, was stripped to his undershorts and covered in dirt and human feces, festering machete cuts, burns, bruises and welts. The animals had been shitting on this guy through the hole in the floor above. He had to be dead, but then I saw a bubble of mucus grow out of his nostril and pop. The guy was alive. I checked the chains to see if I could get him down quick. They were covered in thickly clotted blood. And then I saw why. The manacles attached to those chains were secured with bolts that went clean through the poor bastard's wrists.

'Can you hear me?' I said. 'I'm gonna get you down.'

I spun around, looking for something that might help get the job done. There were more auto batteries here – three of them wired together. Other wires were attached to the terminals with alligator clips. The ends were wrapped in sponges, one of which dangled over a bucket of filthy black water.

The man hanging by his wrists started to whisper, a dry exhausted rasp. His lips and tongue were cracked and I couldn't make out exactly what he was saying. This guy needed water bad. I climbed back up the ladder to get the two full bottles I'd noticed upstairs, returned and poured some water into his mouth. Most of it he coughed straight back up. His lips were moving. He was saying something. I went up close.

'I toe there noth . . .' he whispered.

'You told them nothing?' I said, taking a guess.

He nodded.

'Attaboy,' I said, wondering what information the guy had that the fucks holding him wanted.

'I toe there nothi, nothi . . .'

'What's your name?' I asked him. I kicked a pile of trash to one side and saw a hammer and an old wrench, probably what had been used to bolt the guy in.

'I toe there noth . . .'

'Who are you? What's your name?'

He swallowed, coughed up a blood clot that ran down his chin and made his Adam's apple jerk up and down. 'Weewarah. Ran Weewarah. Ran Weewarah . . .'

Randy Sweetwater. My heart backfired. 'Fuck! Randy! That's you?'

Tears streamed from his eyes. 'Waity, waity, waity?'

'Waity?' I asked him.

'Waity,' he said, over and over.

Waity? And then it hit me. 'You mean W80? The nuke?'

Apparently it did because with the burden of this knowledge passed along, Randy slumped to his knees, unconscious, pulling the chains taut and jerking his arms violently in their sockets.

*

Being out cold did Randy a favor. It wasn't easy getting the manacles off those bolts with a slippery, rusty wrench. It wasn't easy getting him up through the hole in the floor. And it wasn't easy carrying him to the waiting cab across the river of mud and shit. Most difficult of all was convincing the cab driver to let me put the bleeding feces-covered agent on his rear seat.

The promise of another ten bucks overcame the problem. But where to take him? There was a hospital up the road from the Southern Sun offering a nice view over the water. But Sweetwater was in a bad way and a nice view wasn't going to be enough. Some of the deep machete cuts on his legs and back had gone septic. He was also badly dehydrated and who knew what the fuck else. I'd given him more sips of water from those scavenged bottles, but he hadn't been able to keep much of it down. His captors believed he was as good as dead, which was probably why they'd left him breathing. Maybe they just wanted to make his death as ugly as possible – torture the guy a few hours more before he died alone, from blood loss and septicemia.

'We take him to hospital?' the driver wanted to know.

'How far is the US Embassy from here?'

'Twenty minute.'

'Go there. Hurry.'

The driver stepped on it while I sat in the back with Randy to stop him sliding onto the floor. I wanted to ask him where that nuke was, who had it, what they intended to use it for, and when they intended to use it. None of which was possible, the guy being unconscious. So instead I kept brushing the persistent flies off him and counted the machete strikes on his legs and back. I counted more than a hundred before giving up. Some of the cuts were over a quarter of an inch deep. His wrists were a mess. I'd chosen to leave the bolts where they were in case I severed vital blood vessels pulling them out. God knows how the arteries hadn't been destroyed when they were hammered through.

'How much farther?' I shouted forward.

'Ten minute, a little more perhaps.'

Randy stirred briefly, distracting me, then returned to his previous limp state. Alabama had been right about him being alive, and with odds I believed were overwhelmingly against it. I wanted the opportunity to ring her to give her the news, but someone from the embassy would eventually have the pleasure of doing that, though maybe they shouldn't be too hasty about placing the call. I'd seen enough battleground casualties to know that while some people recovered from devastating wounds, others died from injuries that seemed little more than a scratch. Just because Randy had made it this far didn't mean his prospects were good. As far as I could tell he had no broken bones or major punctures in his chest cavity or back, which was reassuring, but he'd lost a lot of blood from those cuts and some of them wept yellow and green pus. I took his pulse. His heart rate was completely off the scale, windmilling like a fan in a storm. The guy could blow a gasket any moment.

'How long now?' I shouted.

'Ten minute! Ten minute!'

You said that last time, pal. A pre-dawn tropical downpour was now drenching the scenery out the window. We were well out of the bad end of town, this area resembling the one around my hotel, with plenty of gardens and so forth, though nothing appeared particularly familiar in the darkness.

The cab ride was giving me time to consider whether taking Randy to the embassy was such a smart move, given what Petinski said about the situation there with the station chief taking bribes. I had no idea who he'd been taking bribes from, or if the bribery related to this case. For all I knew it was von Weiss or one of the White brothers doing the paying off. And were there others besides the chief still dug in at the embassy, selling their country out the back door? Or was the cancer entirely cut out with his removal? Too many questions with no answers. All I knew was that the medical aid at the embassy would be first world.

Besides, indecision was a luxury I couldn't afford. I had to get back to Petinski and Ken, convince them to drop their stakeout and form a boarding party. And, of course, I could give Petinski the news about her former partner. Speak of the devil, he groaned.

I leaned in close. 'Randy? Randy . . .'

'Eye dee,' he whispered. 'Eye dee.'

'What? Eye what? Idea?' I asked him. He was drifting in and out.

'Eyee dee, eyee dee,' he repeated before his mouth went slack and he slipped back into unconsciousness.

'Sir, we are here!' the driver said. 'US Embassy.'

There was now a wall beside the road. I couldn't see the end of it. It was high, too, and blast resistant, featuring anti-truck bollards disguised as potted trees placed at regular intervals a distance out from the base. With a wall this long, the compound behind it had to be *massive*. That massiveness felt reassuring. And so was the sight of the Stars and Stripes hanging from a towering flagpole behind the wall, transfixed in the crossfire of floodlight beams.

A roadway opened up on our right, leading to a parking lot. The driver turned into it. A gatehouse lay ahead. The lights were out. Heavy steel anti-collision gates prevented access to the compound beyond.

'Wait here,' I told the driver as I got out and ran to the gate. Shit, no buzzer to press, but there'd be cameras on this entrance and, in this part of the world, someone somewhere would be watching monitors. I ran back to the cab.

'You got a pen or pencil?'

He shook his head. 'No, sir.'

'A cell phone? Let me make a call? You can add it to the bill.'

He handed it over reluctantly, an ancient Nokia with a cracked screen and the battery held in place with a bit of old electrical tape. There was a notice on the wall with an emergency number to call. I dialed the number. Nothing. I examined the phone's screen. Signal strength one bar out of five. I tried it again with the same result.

'Sometime it work. Sometime not.' The driver shrugged.

Shit. I gave him back his phone, went to the gutter, found a piece of rock and used it to scrawl on the asphalt. The rain instantly washed it away. Double shit. Four twenty-five a.m.: time was getting away from me. I went back to the cab and opened the rear door wide.

'Sorry, buddy,' I said as I put my arms under Randy and lifted him out. Last time I saw him he was maybe a hundred and ninety pounds, but not anymore. On top of everything else, his captors had starved the poor bastard. The good news was that he was easy to carry when the ground underfoot wasn't a river of poo. Taking extra care of his wrists, I set him down on the asphalt in a puddle of light in front of a surveillance camera, then ran back to the cab, grabbed the dead Somali's overnight bag and stripped the cover off the back seat.

'Hey!' the driver snapped.

He didn't know what to say when I pulled the headrest out of the front seat. 'The bill – add another twenty,' I told him and rushed back to Randy. The rain was still coming down hard. The guy wasn't moving, but he was breathing. I repositioned him on his side, put the headrest under his ear and spread the seat cover over him. I took the clothes from the bag, laid them on the cover and then put the rain jacket over the top. That'd have to do. Randy wouldn't be lying there long. But to make sure of that, I took the .38 from my sock and fired it into the air once, twice, sharp cracks ringing around the wall and bouncing off the gatehouse.

'What are you doing? You will make them angry!' the driver wailed as I jumped in the back seat. He wrenched the wheel to one side and stood on the gas pedal.

'I couldn't find the doorbell,' I said, as we snaked out of the lot. Whoever was watching those security screens would see a body placed outside the gate by a guy firing a gun. An alarm would be raised and folks would rush out to see if the body was alive or dead. That was my plan, at any rate. I just had to hope that Randy would regain consciousness long enough to tell someone who he was and what was going down, because I'd run out of options for the moment on that score. 'Okay. You know the Holiday Inn? That's where we're going.'

'No! I want money! You pay *now*!'

I was tempted to remind him that I was the only one in the car with a gun, but chose the next best option and lied in the most soothing voice I could muster. 'The Holiday Inn is where all my cash is. I've got nothing on me.'

'*What?!*' he squealed like someone was squeezing his nuts. 'Two hundred dollar you owe me!'

Did I? I'd lost count. That seemed a lot.

'You have no money?'

'Yeah, I've got money, but like I said, it's at the Inn. And if you don't get me there pronto, I'll take ten off.'

The driver swore at me in Swahili, downshifted and hauled ass.

'How long till we get there?' I asked. 'Lemme guess, ten minutes?'

'Yes, ten minute,' the driver snapped, giving me the evil eye in his rear-view mirror.

In fact it was eight.

Up ahead on the left, just before the hotel, was a vehicle with its hazard lights flashing and its alarm honking. Parked in front of it was Ken's light-green Ford. On the other side of the street was a prefab concrete block of around ten stories lit up like a bad party in a variety of colors the hotel probably described as 'fun'. The Holiday Inn 'H' was displayed in a concrete frame just off the sidewalk and the forecourt was clearly visible. Petinski and Ken had chosen a good vantage point from which to keep the place under surveillance.

'Here is good,' I told the driver, leaning forward and pointing past him at the space behind the Honda Acura with its lights flashing.

He pulled over. 'I'll be right back.' He gave me a look like he expected me to run.

I strolled past the Honda with its taillights flaring orange in time with its horn. No one was paying any attention to it – just another car alarm set off by a passing truck or something. I looked ahead to the Ford and worked on something irritatingly clever to say to Petinski and Ken. It was then that I saw small glass crystals scattered on the roadway beneath the driver's door. On the asphalt beside the Ford were the black skid marks of a vehicle that had come to a panic stop. Through the Ford's rear window, I could see Ken slumped sideways toward the passenger seat.

Adrenalin glands over my heart mainlined a bucket of juice into my left ventricle. I covered the remaining distance in a jump. There was blood on the passenger-side window as well as the windshield. I reached in, checked Ken for a pulse but couldn't find one. The attack must have only just happened, though: even the sweat on his forehead was still warm. So where was Petinski? The passenger door was slightly ajar. I checked the rear seat and saw a canvas bag – hers. Was this a random attack, or was it planned? I knew what my gut told me, but I had to be sure. I opened the bag. A separate zip-up Chanel makeup bag, deodorant, a change of underwear, a t-shirt, a Lakers ball cap, a small packet of mixed berry juice with a straw attached, and two Weight Watchers energy bars. I took the food and drink, shoved it in my pockets and put the bag back on the seat. Patting Ken down, I found his BlackBerry. His 9mm Glock was in its holster, wallet in his rear right-hand pants pocket. Opening the wallet revealed a thick wedge of US dollars and receipts. The fact that he still had a wallet with money in it, as well as his weapon and phone, said that this was no opportunistic smash and grab. Petinski's open door and her bag still on the rear seat indicated abduction. But who'd done the snatch? Petinski and Ken had been staking out the White brothers. Had Falco and Charles shown up? Or was it the Somali pirates from the bunker? I took most of the cash, leaving some in the wallet before replacing it in Ken's pocket. I also left the Glock where I found it. Petinski's most recent partner had been whacked. I didn't want the local cops drawing an easier conclusion – like theft – from the crime scene. I punched a few buttons on his BlackBerry. The screen asked for a password. I punched in four zeros on the off-chance – no joy. Fuck. The thing was useless to me.

A couple of guys from the hotel had walked down the driveway and were looking across the road toward the car with the sounding horn still going bananas.

'Hey, you!' one of them called out to me – a Brit, from the accent. 'What are you doing?'

I dropped the BlackBerry onto the floor and walked back to the cab, keeping a nice easy smile on my face.

'Two hundred dollars, right?' I asked the driver, taking the front passenger seat.

'Yes, two hundred.'

He was unaware of what had happened in the green Ford, and that suited me fine – the guy was spooked enough already. I counted out two hundred and twenty from the wad and handed it to him. 'You know Magogoni Street?'

'Yes, I know this,' he said, now beaming.

'That's where I'm going. Hurry.'

The two guys from the hotel were getting gamer, about to cross the road.

'It is near, only five minute,' he said, still grinning, counting the money and noting the tip.

Five minutes, now. Amazing what a few bucks will do.

Twenty-nine

Where had they taken Petinski, and for what purpose? Were the fucks gonna hammer bolts through her wrists too? I was concerned about her, but I had another, more pressing job to get done. As much as I didn't like it, putting her life first would compromise it big time. I had no choice but to put her out of my mind.

Randy's timetable was screwing with my head. Wednesday the fifth was still three days away, but what had the timing been based on? 'Twenty days', the note had said. Were they all twenty-four-hour days, or was Day Twenty a twelve-hour day? It would have been far more convenient, to say nothing of more accurate, if the note had said it would be delivered at three p.m. on Wednesday the fifth, Pacific Daylight Time. For all I knew, the physics package was already beginning to smoke. Whatever, there wasn't a lot of time left in which to warn Uncle Sam about how, where and when. I just had to get on with it and hope I wasn't too late. Sticking with my original timetable, I still had roughly seventy-two hours left, give or take, to do something – whatever that happened to be.

The way I figured it, Ed Dyson had been murdered because an expert weatherman's services were no longer required. He'd ceased to be essential to whatever the plan was because, quite simply, the

W80 was on the brink of detonation and the weather was locked in. Morrow's murder was probably just an opportunity that presented itself, a handy second bird killed with the same stone that took out Dyson. I stifled a yawn, shook my head to clear it, and tried to focus on what I had to do next.

Out my window I saw my hotel, the Southern Sun, its neon glowing in the night sky. My bed was in there somewhere. More than almost anything else, I wanted to crawl into it. It was four thirty-seven a.m. and within around an hour, the sky would begin to lighten and the day would heat up. Frankly, I wasn't ready for it. Jet lag on top of no real shuteye for far too long, plus the effects of successive adrenalin hits ebbing and flowing through my system had taken its toll. Thinking straight was a problem.

Pulling out the energy bars taken from Petinski's bag, I tore the wrappers off both and stuffed them into my mouth. They were chocolate coated and caramel flavored and tasted sickly sweet, but they were Weight Watchers so at least they wouldn't go straight to my hips. I drank the juice to get rid of the taste of the bars. Then I needed something to get rid of the taste of the juice, which wasn't really juice, and the aspartame hit fizzled after a few seconds.

I rubbed my face and slapped my cheeks. I was dragging along the bottom, the world moving in slow motion. I yawned – unstifled this time – my mouth wide, lips stretched tight against my teeth. The cab took a sharp corner and the pirate's overnight bag on the back seat rolled and thumped heavily against the door. I pulled it into the front with me, set it on my lap and the foul smell of those leaves leached from its pores. *Khat*. The pirate pick-me-up . . . *produced an effect similar to speed when chewed or brewed up like tea.* I pulled the zip back and the meaty vinegary sour sweaty stench floated out of it like an evil cloud.

'You have *khat?*' the driver asked, the smell obviously familiar to him.

I took the bundle out of the bag. It reeked of pickled decay.

'This is good,' he continued, attracted rather than repelled by the stink. 'I have this for when I drive day and night. This is your *khat?*'

If I said yes I was sure he was going to ask if we could be pals. 'A friend's,' I replied.

'You have had before?'

'No.'

'You chew some. You look tired.' His concern was touching.

'How much do you take?'

'Three leaf, no more. Chew good. Not to swallow.'

Was not swallowing this stuff the equivalent of not inhaling? I could promise him that there'd be no swallowing because the smell was so vile I figured they wouldn't stay swallowed for long if I did. I pulled three leaves with their long stems from the bundle. I had a big day ahead. In fact, the day ahead filled me with dread, especially if I was right about what was on board the *African Spirit*. And meanwhile, as I said, keeping my thoughts corralled was proving a real challenge. The damn things kept wandering off.

The decision was made. I put the leaves in my mouth and started to chew. The taste was bitter – opposite to the super-sweet chocolate bars and berry-flavored water I'd just had. I chewed, lowered the window and spat.

'No, no! You waste it. You swallow this,' he explained, waving his fingers generally around his mouth, 'not the leaves.'

I assumed he meant I had to swallow the saliva. Nasty. I hit the button to close the window, then stuffed a few more leaves in my mouth.

'You have *khat* for me also?' he asked.

I looked at him.

'I give you discount . . .'

Discount? Wasn't I in credit here? 'Does it affect your driving?' I asked.

'Yes. Make driving easy. Car drive itself.'

Hmm . . . maybe I should have asked that question before I started chewing. I was hoping for a wakeup call from this stuff, not Lucy in the Sky with Diamonds. I noticed that my heart rate was up. I'd also started sweating and breathing harder, a tingling sensation running through my butt and legs like a low-voltage current. The exhaustion was lifting.

'How long does the effect last?' I asked him.

'Sometime two hour. You like *khat*?'

'How far now to Magogoni Street?' I asked.

'We are here.'

Yeah, it was dark but the road was still familiar, and so were the smells being fanned through the vents.

'There's someone I need to speak with here, and I'll need you to translate for me.'

'I will do this for ten dollar.'

'You'll do it because I've already paid you a fortune.'

I chose that moment to pull the .38, flick the cylinder to one side and replace the two empty chambers with spare rounds from my pocket.

The driver regarded me with horror. 'I will do it,' he said, getting the message. 'We are friends now, yes?'

'Drug buddies.' I returned the gun to my sock.

'Yes.'

I gave him three leaves from the bundle and tucked the rest inside my shirt. I then fished around in the bag until my fingers found the ski mask and scarf. 'Park here,' I told him, motioning at the wrecking yard.

He pulled carefully off the packed dirt into the sand. I tucked the ski mask inside my shirt, tied the scarf around my neck, grabbed the bag and got out.

'Good *khat*,' the driver told me, now standing on the other side of the vehicle, rolling his eyeballs.

I spat the quid onto the road. Whether it was good quality or not, all I knew was that I now felt great, like if I shut my eyes and thought about it hard enough, rockets would sprout from my heels and to hell with the boat I'd come here to collect. 'This way,' I told him, and walked toward the beach, resisting the desire to break into a canter.

There was no moon and my own hands were no more than dim shapeless forms. I led the way between a couple of beached hulks, the driver still with me, and cut along parallel to the waterline until I found the tarp covering the boat I'd rented. My heart was thumping away like jungle drums. Grabbing a handful of tarp, I flung it back. But then I stopped, every muscle frozen, because a long curved blade was being held under my throat, my whiskers scraping against the honed steel and making it hum. Stale tobacco, sweat and fish stench filled my nostrils. A familiar combination. It was the toothless old man who'd rented me the boat. He pulled the knife harder against my throat when I tried to speak. But then just as suddenly the steel was removed. He made some exclamation of rec- ognition and slapped me on the arm with the flat of the blade, pals again.

'He say, he was n-not sure it was you,' the driver stammered. 'He was about to kill you, then me.'

The sound coming from the old man suggested a giggle.

'What changed his mind?'

'He say you smell bad. He remember it.'

Right. 'Let him know I'm here for the boat.'

The driver started talking and the two of them went back and forth like I wasn't here.

'Hello . . .' I said after a good minute of this.

'I tell him you have had *khat* – first time for you,' said the driver. 'He said he hopes you are okay.'

'What about the boat?' I said, ignoring the subplot.

'He want to know why you want it now. It is dark, there is nothing to see. Do you want to fish?'

'Tell him I need to get aboard the *African Spirit*, one of the ships out in the channel. Let him know I have to get on it without anyone seeing me.' In this part of the world, I figured telling him the truth about what I wanted would be like jumping in a New York cab and saying, 'Follow that car.'

Another conversation in Swahili blossomed between the two men.

'He say he cannot do this,' the driver said finally.

'Why not?'

'He say he cannot do it with the boat you have paid for.'

I sensed a loophole. 'But he can get me on the ship some other way?'

'Yes, this is correct. He say for this you can pay him in *khat*.'

'But I paid him in advance already,' I said.

'You pay for this boat,' the driver replied, slapping the single hull dinghy under the tarp. 'Not for *this* boat.' He pointed at the faint outline of a desiccated outrigger hauled up on the sand nearby.

I was starting to feel like a fleeced American, outfoxed by the wily locals.

'He say he want six leaf for this boat.'

I sighed, pulled the wad from my shirt, counted out the right amount, then handed an extra leaf to the driver. 'A tip,' I said, 'for handling the negotiation.'

'It was a hard negotiation.' His hand stayed out. I sighed again and folded out two more leaves. 'Thank you,' he said.

The old guy walked a little up the beach to a jumble of packing crates and began unstacking them. A few moments later he returned with a small portable outboard motor in one hand and a makeshift ladder in the other. He mumbled something to the driver and walked over to the outrigger.

'You must help get the boat to the water,' the driver told me.

The way I was feeling I could toss it into the drink with one hand tucked behind my back. I went over, lifted a hull and dragged it to the water's edge, then trotted back for the bag.

'So how is this going to happen?' I asked. 'How's he going to get me aboard the *African Spirit*?'

The two locals went into a huddle.

'You are lucky,' the driver told me when they broke for air. 'Achmed say the sides of your ship are low to the water and, as you can see, he has brought a ladder.'

The low-tech solution was dubious but I didn't have a lot of choice. I checked my watch. Sunrise wasn't far off. It was now or never.

'Achmed say there are many boats like his out fishing this morning and this will help.'

Out on the water the only boats visible to me belonged to the lights out in the channel, hard white points of light on the cargo vessels. The *African Spirit*, though, was still running dark.

'If you do not need me, I will go now,' said the driver. 'Good luck with your mission.'

'. . . that you won't tell anyone about,' I said.

'Of course not,' he replied, a hand on his heart.

Sure.

He and Achmed said goodbye with a handshake.

'Hey,' I told him, raising a hand. 'Thanks for your help.' I'd put the guy through plenty. He'd complained but he hadn't buckled.

'Yes. Thank you also, sir. Now I will not have to work for a long time.' He waved and walked away, disappearing in the darkness.

The old guy's papery voice piped up. From his hand movements, I worked out that he wanted me to drag the boat into the water and then jump on. I took the .38 out of my sock and stuffed it in the front of my pants. The old guy gave me an encouraging gummy smile and braced himself at the back of the outrigger. He pushed, I pulled, and the worn old craft released its grip on the shore and moved into the warm wavelets phosphorescing green and blue as they rolled through the trash onto the sand. We jumped in at the same time, the old guy grabbed a paddle and stroked a few times before throwing it in the bottom of the boat and firing up the outboard.

Within moments we were scooting across the harbor in the general direction of the channel. Achmed was right about the fishing, and there were hundreds of outriggers like the one beneath me out on the water, netting and fishing with lines. He circled the row of cargo ships to scout the best approach, pointing out the positions of men he could see on the *African Spirit*'s deck. I couldn't see a thing. He brought the outrigger toward the ship from an angle close to its stern. Other outriggers were fishing in close to it.

I slipped the ski mask over my head and dropped it down so that it covered my neck. The scarf I retied around my head so that some of the fabric flopped down over part of my face. As a disguise, it was only slightly better than wearing a clown suit with big floppy shoes and a flower that squirted water. I was at least twice as broad as any of the pirates I'd seen and wouldn't pass for one of them for more than a split second. So basically, this was going to go well, or I'd be fish food. No middle ground.

Achmed cut the motor and the outrigger drifted between several identical boats. A low-frequency hum was immediately audible coming from the *African Spirit*. Its diesels were turning. The ship's hull rose out of the water to a height of around ten feet. I didn't see how getting me aboard was going to be done. The old guy was fiddling with the ladder, pulling it out from the bottom of the boat. Then he laid it down so that it formed a walkway out to the smaller outboard hull. He motioned at me to come quick. I scampered back to where he was and saw what he was pointing at. There were small rungs and indentations in the side of the ship that began at around the height of my shoulder. No time to dawdle, I ran across the ladder to the small outboard hull and then leaped up when I got to the side of the ship. The fingers of my right hand found the rung and I dangled there for a second or two, wondering what would have happened if I'd missed it. Glancing down, I saw the boat had been replaced by black water, Achmed allowing his craft to drift back among the other fishing boats nearby.

My body pressing against the steel of the *African Spirit's* hull, I could feel its mechanical heart beating within, a pulse that felt almost alive. I twisted around and hauled myself up, getting my hand within reach of the next rung. This was my damaged hand, the one still swollen from the snake venom, and it ached painfully when it took my weight. But my boot found the lowest of the footholds pretty much right away and up I went.

My eyes were now fully adjusted to the dark. Looking toward the east, there was still no hint of the sun's arrival, but it wouldn't be long in coming. Raising my head slowly above the edge of the gunnel, I could see two of the pirates on watch, smoking and talking. They wore black urban assault body armor, FN FAL assault rifles slung over their shoulders like the guy I'd seen the night before; they also had NVGs, though one had his set pushed up on his head while the other's dangled uselessly around his neck. The smell in the night air told me they were smoking weed. Off they strolled to the opposite side of the deck, having a nice chat and a joint. Their training mightn't have been worth a pinch of shit, but their weapons loadout was top shelf. Two words popped into my head: von Weiss.

I waited another minute, listening, observing. Close by, sitting on top of the hatch cover over the hold closest to the ship's superstructure and taking up a lot of room, was something beneath a canvas tarp. Hearing and seeing nothing else noteworthy, I hopped over onto the deck and went to investigate what it might be. Ducking under the bottom edge of the canvas, I crawled in. It was dark in there even though the sky was now hinting at the coming dawn. Though I couldn't see a thing, my fingertips reported the smooth hull of a boat. Working along to its stern, I found three large outboards hanging off the back.

A deep rumble that thrummed up through the steel plate beneath my feet combined with a slight loss of balance to inform my senses that we were moving.

Shit.

Thirty

The tender's fuel tanks were enormous, and further augmented by a collapsible 270-gallon bladder. So not only did this baby undoubtedly have some go, it also had range. The light improved as I continued to investigate, locating a cooler stocked with – among other things – thirty bottles of chilled mineral water. Lucky for me because, with the sun climbing above the horizon, there was already enough heat under this tarp to bake a chicken. Those other things, by the way, included a dozen bottles of Krug champagne, several kilos of smoked salmon, cured hams and salamis, a selection of cheeses and four large tubs of Ben & Jerry's Chocolate Fudge Brownie ice cream – a cut above the usual survival rations, in my experience.

I found no IDs on the runabout, but I did find a locker beneath the floor. Inside it were two pairs of shooter's gloves, size large; two FN FAL assault rifles and half a dozen extra mags to go with them; two pairs of NVGs; half a dozen M26 frag hand grenades; two black urban assault body armor vests with webbing; and, most surprisingly, a drum-fed Atchisson AA-12 fully automatic assault shotgun with spare drum. I'd seen this weapon demonstrated but never used one. From memory, it could pump out three hundred rounds per minute and packed a kick like Chuck Norris with a hangover. Food, horsepower, guns and gas:

was this some kind of escape pod, or a means for the *African Spirit* to project a little power? It was certainly capable of both.

Small holes and tears in the tarp provided ventilation and gave me a view across the deck Within an hour of sunrise, we were well out to sea. I'd counted eight Somalis so far, a couple heavily armed, the rest not. All were thin, underfed specimens in cast-off clothing. Two fair-skinned men in their forties hurried by wearing neatly pressed green coveralls. These guys looked vaguely Middle Eastern in origin. Iranian, maybe. In all, an interesting cast of characters. I wondered how many of these fuckers were among the deadbeats who'd given Randy the treatment back in Dar.

And then two guys came by who got me all excited because, for one thing, they wore flat caps at a jaunty angle, had solitaire diamonds in their earlobes and looked like gangstas from a Snoop Dogg video. And, for another, I recognized them from Rio and from my brief time in the Congo. They were members of Falco and Charles White's close protection squad, colleagues of the guy Shilling and I had rolled off Sugarloaf Mountain. Even more exciting than that was seeing the bodies they were guarding: Gamal Abdul-Jabbar, alias the tarantula, and Mohammed Ali-Bakr al Mohammed, the Somali pirate kingpin.

The state-of-the-art military technology, the high-powered luxury tender, the presence of the Whites' security team, the pirate boss and his eight-legged assistant . . . I'd landed square in the middle of von Weiss's plan as it was being put into effect. Only, what exactly was the plan? As I considered this, Ali-Bakr al Mohammed stopped to urinate over the side of the boat. If he'd been alone, I could have dropped a major fly in von Weiss's ointment by giving the guy a little push, dropping him in the drink.

There had to be others on board who hadn't conveniently wandered past my hide. How many, I couldn't be sure. And what about those Iranians? Were they, in fact, Iranians? If they were, what were they here for? They seemed out of place. Did they have something to do with the W80? And was the bomb actually on board the ship? I believed it was, and presumably so did Randy. Was it tucked away in one of the holds?

At some point, I'd have to leave the safety of my hide and search the ship. That gizmo Petinski had shown me – the arsenic wafer or whatever it was called – that would've come in handy. It could've told me for sure if the bomb was here somewhere. And that got me to thinking: if it was on board, then what was I gonna do about it all on my lonesome? I finished off another bottle of chilled Evian water, sweated, and put an eye up to one of the holes. The way *khat* scrambled my thoughts was starting to get on my nerves . . . Gallium arsenide wafer – that's what it was called.

From the position of the sun, we were heading roughly north. Time, nine a.m. I was stuck here slowly cooking till the night came down in around ten hours time. And in maybe three days time the hands on Randy's nuclear clock would be chiming midnight; after which the world would be a very different place, with the knowledge that our nuclear stockpile was fair game for criminals. I urinated into the now-empty water bottle, peeped through the holes in the tarp, and hoped the effects of the damn *khat* would just hurry up and wear the fuck off so that I could get some damn sleep.

A horn sounded over the decks and all the armed men immediately ran for cover inside the main superstructure, leaving the unarmed Somalis, who continued doing whatever they were doing, which was mostly smoking, spitting and picking their noses. I released the ammo drum on the AA to get a feel for the weapon's action, and because the crap in my system just wouldn't let me sit still, then snapped it back into place. A few seconds later, I heard the sound of jet engines. I got a visual on them through a tear in the tarp – a flight of two Navy F/A-18 Super Hornets, flaps lowered, going slow, cruising parallel to our course. They ran past us, heading in the opposite direction, around three hundred feet off the drink. There was a lot of ocean out here. Without doubt, they'd come specifically to check us out. A couple of the Somalis gave the fighter-bombers a friendly wave as they roared on by. There was no second pass, which suggested that the *African Spirit* had checked out just fine. The horn sounded a second time across the decks, two short blasts, and the armed men came back out.

The presence of the Navy Super Hornets told me there had to be a carrier within the vicinity – probably within two hundred miles of our position. It had to be the big E – *Enterprise* – the carrier that had recently joined the multinational anti-pirate Task Force 151 operation.

I yawned and closed my eyes. I needed to shut down for a few hours. I rested my head against the side of the tender, put my feet in the chiller, lay a couple of packs of smoked salmon over my head and snuggled up to a cold leg of ham. Sleep. Please just let me sleep.

*

My wish was granted, but I was only aware of it when I woke with a start and saw that the hands on my watch had advanced nine and a half hours as if by magic. Jesus, that was a big chunk of time. Now when I looked out of the tarp the orange sun was touching the horizon behind a gauze of heat haze.

I found a small paring knife and cut a chunk off the now body-temperature ham, ate some sloppy Ben & Jerry's and drank a half-gallon of warm water. The chiller had stopped working, the batteries now well and truly exhausted. But unlike them, I felt okay. The *khat* was sweated out of my system along with the last vestiges of snake venom. And the food in this joint really was first class.

I killed the half hour till twilight tidying up the boat and surveying the activity on deck. Some unfamiliar faces wandered by, Somalis and more of those maybe-Iranians. A few wore ski masks, hiding their faces. I figured there had to be at least twenty men on board, possibly as many as twenty-five, many of whom were heavily armed. The Atchisson AA and I couldn't take them all. But maybe there was a smarter approach. First priority, I had to scout the ship to see if the W80 was aboard. And, with a bit of luck, perhaps there were just enough folks of different shapes, sizes and nationalities for me to pass at least a casual inspection, as long as I dressed right.

The body armor went on first, webbing over that, and I filled the ammo rack on my chest with the spare FN mags and velcroed in a couple of M26s. I tied the red scarf around my neck and pulled on the ski mask.

Over that I fitted the NVGs, turned them on and tested them, taking in the view through one of the larger tears in the tarp. The gadget worked fine, the evening sky a bright green above a green-black sea. In the front of my webbing, below the FN mags, was a velcro pouch that fitted the Desert Eagle perfectly. The .38 and its sweating handgrip went back in my sock. The remaining spare rounds – five – were still in my pocket. Finally, I slipped on a pair of the shooter's gloves. As for the AA, I hadn't seen anyone else packing one, which meant I had to leave it behind for now; carrying it around would instantly mark me out as someone different. So I placed it on the deck beneath a flap of the tarp, along with the spare drum loaded with twenty rounds of twelve-gauge double-aught. If I needed it in a hurry later, it'd be easy to pick up on the run.

By the time I'd done all this and familiarized my hands with the positions of everything stored around my body, it was well and truly night. There were stars, but the haze cut their brilliance. I had no idea what the moon was doing, there being too much smoke hanging over Dar to know whether it was up or down. With any luck it wouldn't appear. A small amount of light from the boat's superstructure fell onto the darkened deck, almost unnoticeable with the naked eye but amplified by the NVGs. The deck up this end of the ship, close to the superstructure, was clear of activity for the moment so I ducked under the tarp and came up in the cool night air. I shivered when it hit my skin, downright cold compared to my sweatbox hide.

I assumed the easy stroll of the armed guards I'd seen and ambled nice and slow toward the bow. A man approached me from the other side of the deck, one of the Iranians. I tensed. I hadn't known he was out here. Had he seen me pop out from under the tarp? My finger twitched against the trigger guard of the Desert Eagle and I took the selector off safety. He started babbling at me. And in Farsi. That was a language I recognized the sound of. They spoke it in Afghanistan. It was also the national language of Iran. Interesting. Maybe I was right about where these guys were from after all.

There wasn't a lot of illumination up this end of the deck. To anyone not wearing light-enhancing hardware, I'd be little more than a dark mass on two legs. The guy produced a cigarette, holding it in front of my NVG lenses, letting me know what he wanted – a light. I waved him away and kept walking, but he stood his ground, deriding me for being uncomradely. So I turned and patted down my pockets, making like I was going to accommodate him, and pulled something from a pocket. That quietened him down. I stood between him and the wind as if to shield the flame. We were close to the gunnel. He never saw the hit, a short, sharp rip to his midsection. I held him up by his shirtfront and he gawked at me with horror and confusion while he attempted to suck in some air. I scanned the deck, confirming that we were still alone. We were. 'Sorry, pal,' I whispered, pushing him back. He took two small steps, overbalanced, and slipped over the side without any kind of sound at all, into the wash boiling off the bow. One down. I pocketed the lighter, which was in fact one of the dum-dums for the .38.

I stepped up onto the steel plate doors that sealed the forward hold to investigate a sliver of light from below, escaping up through a crack. Why would a cargo hold need to be lit? Next stop, the bow. When I got there I stopped to have another look around to get my bearings and let the wind dry the sweat out of my clothes a little. The horizon, what I could see of it unobscured by cranes and superstructure, was completely empty. A door opened in the superstructure and light flared bright green and then died as the door closed behind an armed guard. I turned and walked back toward him. My intention was to shoot him if he made any fast moves, but the guy ignored me completely when I passed him – not even a nod.

I kept walking toward the superstructure, alongside the boat beneath the tarp. I flipped up the NVG lenses and then opened the door, yellow light flooding out along with oil fumes. I stepped inside and closed the hatch. The immediate area was empty, the steel walls painted cream above and red below, the floor painted green and all of it covered by a layer of grime. There were narrow ladders up and down, and passageways heading back toward the rear of the boat and along the front of the superstructure. Somewhere deep within, the heart of the ship whined louder, the pulse of it here more certain than it was out on the deck in the wind. A sign on the wall had a man slipping on a jagged red arrow pointing downward. Captions in both English and Arabic advised that care should be taken on the ladders. I took the advice and got a firm grip of the railing.

When I was halfway down, two Somalis arrived at the bottom and waited for me to complete the descent. Somewhere nearby, music was playing – Arabic or maybe Iranian. Arriving at the base of the steps, I ignored the Africans and got the same treatment in return.

An Iranian and a couple of armed Africans were moving around, coming from somewhere and going someplace. This looked to be the accommodation deck. I went on a recon stroll along a dimly lit passageway, the dead air heavy with human funk, pot and tobacco smoke. A door was open here and there, revealing tiny steel cells with small beds and no personal effects. An Iranian squeezed past carrying a spool of electrical wire in each hand and a pack on his back. I decided to follow him.

He took me on a tour down four decks, then through a series of passageways and bulkheads, working forward away from the engine noise. Down here the walls, floors and ceilings were spotted with corrosion cancers and glistened as if they were sweating. A bulkhead hatch opened ahead and three Africans ducked through into a blaze of white light. I followed the guy with the wire spools through the hatch. Once inside the hold, what I saw caused me to gasp. The people I took to be Iranian were climbing over the cargo, at least thirty fifty-five-gallon drums painted gray and ordered in neat rows. The word GASOLINE was stenciled in black on most of the drums. The Iranians were working hard at fitting electrical relays, detonators and Primacord to the drums. If I didn't know better, they were rigging the boat for a massive explosion.

Stepping down onto the deck, I made my way to one side where enough room had been left beside the drums to provide a walkway. Ahead, I could see that a large section of the bulkheads between the holds had been roughly cut out, effectively creating one very large hold. In the center and forward holds were more lights, more drums, more Iranians, more Primacord. And in the forward hold, raised up on a bench with a rig, were two people in suits marked NBC – Nuclear Biological Chemical – working on something that looked a hell of a lot like a bulk milk can. My mouth was open. Our W80. *Our fucking nuke!* The damn thing *was* here. I took a few idle steps, concentrating on stopping my knees from shaking. I felt like sitting, and hard. Sweat bloomed on my forehead, the smell of gasoline in the hold suddenly suffocating. It was tempting to rip the ski mask off, though I wasn't sure what purpose that would serve other than to get me instantly killed. I left it on and tried to make my brain think of something a bit more constructive. It stammered that it didn't have enough information to make a call on my next move, so my legs took my brain forward into the second hold to see if that would help any. I moved slow and hoped I appeared nonchalant. There were more gasoline drums here, ordered just like they were in the first hold. Same again in the forward hold. Every second drum was rigged to blow, the ones in between sporting some kind of pump.

A head count told me I'd misjudged the number of people aboard by a significant margin. Including the folks I'd seen already, there had to be close to fifty personnel. Minus one, I reminded myself. I noted four men scattered around the scene, armed and dressed pretty much just like I was, even down to the ski mask. I kept moving and thought about how I might contact the US Navy steaming in the same patch of ocean. And then someone stumbled into me; more accurately, it was me who did the stumbling. Served me right for not watching where I was going – I couldn't take my eyes off the bomb and the people working on it.

'Hey!' the guy snapped. 'Watch where yo goin', moth' fuck.'

My eyes went wide with surprise. Of all people, I'd knocked over Charles White. He picked himself up off the deck. I took a step back and held up a hand in apology.

'Take yo' ass someplace else,' he shouted angrily. 'No need for yo here, useless fuck.'

I gave him a nod and backed away, but not before I saw his brother Falco behind him, hands on his hips, ignoring his brother and me while he surveyed the goings-on around the nuke with Gamal Abdul-Jabbar and Ali-Bakr al Mohammed. The Somali pirate with the wrecked eye socket turned to have words with a small group of Iranians perched over a pair of laptop computers. I doubted it was internet porn on those screens. This had to be the command center for the floating bomb. Those laptops probably controlled how and when the thing would blow. Four of Charles White's bodyguards were lingering in the vicinity, paying no particular heed to security other than providing their presence. They were heavily armed with M4s and anti-personnel M26 frag grenades bulging from their webbing. They were also well trained. Taking them out would be a long way from easy.

The White brothers, a couple of Somali pirate kingpins, a nuke and a ship full of gasoline. A picture was forming and it wasn't pretty. I didn't want to risk further eye contact with Charles White, or Gamal for that matter, so I crossed to the other side of the ship behind the ragged remains of the bulkhead. I walked slow, attempting to seem like just another guard on patrol. The different route changed the angle on the Iranians working over the W80. From where I was now, there appeared to be a separate device attached to the side of the bomb. It was under three feet in length, a very long shoebox fashioned from aluminum. I wondered what it could be. And why *Iranians?* If Ali-Bakr al Mohammed and the Whites needed outlaw nuke experts, why not North Koreans or Pakistanis? Iranians weren't nuclear bomb experts as far as I knew, despite their blatant nuclear weapons program. And the bomb itself was next to useless as a nuclear device. Without codes, *all* the experts said that it couldn't be detonated.

I looked back down toward the stern, over the tops of countless barrels of gas and detcord and relays and blinking red LEDs. The platoon of technicians working on them mostly appeared to have finished the job, only a few remaining on improvised catwalks over the barrels, checking connections and switches. What the hell was the plan? I thought about Sweetwater. Did he know what it was? He was onto the nuke early. He'd tried to warn the authorities without blowing his cover, sending his academy ring to Alabama along with the amputated hand of a known associate of von Weiss. And now a random series of incidents had brought me here, solo. The Lone Ranger with no Tonto.

Sweetwater – I hoped he'd made it. I didn't even want to think about what might have happened to Petinski . . .

Eye dee, eye dee . . .

I pictured the guy lying on his side in the rain outside the US Embassy compound back in Dar. Had he managed to pull himself up and out of his pain long enough to tell me what was going down here?

Eye dee, eye dee . . . Eye dee, eye dee . . .

And just like that, I had an epiphany. It hit me like a bucket of ice water. I suddenly knew what that odd shoebox attached to the side of the bomb was, why the Iranians were here, what von Weiss had planned, and why Ali-Bakr al Mohammed and his buddy were central to it.

Now I had no choice but to seize the ship.

Thirty-one

What Randy had been saying was eye-*ee*-dee. He'd tried to tell me that the W80 was to be used as an IED – an improvised explosive device. The *African Spirit* would be detonated in close proximity to von Weiss and Ali-Bakr al Mohammed's mutual enemy, the forces of the United States. But it wasn't just any IED; this one would be a hugely destructive dirty bomb scattering the W80's deadly plutonium core into the wind. That's what the box on the side of the bomb was all about, and why the Iranians were doing the rigging. *It was a shaped charge*, no doubt a variation of the type perfected by Iran for use against coalition forces in Iraq. Its job was to smash the W80's physics package a split second before the fuel load detonated and lifted the shattered plutonium core into the sky downwind of the target. Von Weiss and his Somali war lord would be hoping to nail one of the ultimate symbols of American power – the USS *Enterprise*. An attack like that would take the Big E offline for a very long time.

Making my way back to the hatch I came in by, I noted that a lot of folks were standing around, waiting. A clanging alarm bell sounded and the waiting turned into hurried evacuation. A line immediately formed at the exit hatch I was intending to use, so I cracked the one on the opposite side of the bulkhead closer to my position. The hatch opened out onto a small space with a ladder, which I raced up as technicians and Somalis came through the bulkhead behind me.

I was among the first to arrive on the open deck, so I moved quickly toward the tender and felt around under the tarp where I'd left the Atchisson and the spare drum. I got my hands on one of them just as a group of Iranians filed through the hatch. I racked a shell into the chamber, safety on. Then I jumped down from the raised hatch and headed for the bow.

Blinding white light flooded the decks. Several Somalis raced to the tarp covering the tender and began folding it back. Charles and Falco White arrived on deck with Abdul-Jabbar, Ali-Bakr al Mohammed, the bodyguards and a bunch of Iranians, all of whom were wearing lifejackets. The crane arms swung into place over the tender. The deck swarmed with armed men, the Somali guards shouting instructions at everyone else.

Hooks from the crane were attached to eyelets on the tender's gunnels. The White brothers climbed in with the Somali war lord and his number two, and all the Iranians. With everyone seated, the crane hoisted the tender off the deck and swung it over the side of the ship. The Africans swarmed to the side, yelling at the crane operator and flapping their arms to lower the load or to raise it. A sudden upbeat mood among them suggested that the operation was a success, and shortly after the tender appeared on a divergent course to the mothership, powering away into the night.

The Somalis waved their boss goodbye. I gave him the bird. Time to move while everyone was distracted. I made a beeline for the superstructure. The floodlights over the deck were doused and people bumped into each other, their night vision shot to shit. Flipping down the NVG lenses I ran to the hatch in the superstructure and lifted them up again before going through into the light. I ran up several ladders till I could get no higher, then sprinted toward the back of the superstructure. A final ladder brought me onto a small area open to the elements off to one side of the bridge. Jesus – there was an MSTAR set up in the space, a man-portable target surveillance and acquisition radar. Von Weiss had helped these people get the job done with some pretty neat toys. I had wondered about the alarm sounded over the deck thirty seconds or more before those two Super Hornets cruised past overhead. The MSTAR would've picked up the aircraft when they cleared the horizon. Cables ran from the hardware onto the bridge, through a hole roughly cut at the bottom of the access door. Those cables would be connected to a display module providing the folks on the bridge with their hands on the steering wheel all kinds of information on potential threats in the air and on the sea. A canvas tarpaulin lay in folds at the equipment stand's feet. No doubt it was simply thrown over the gear to prevent the ensemble being spotted by overflying aircraft. *Innocent* cargo ships didn't sport this kind of military-grade intelligence-gathering gear. I glanced at the horizon. Nothing but an empty expanse of ocean. Above the bridge, the standard radar tower with a rotating transmitter providing the bridge with weather and ship-to-sea information about nearby vessels and hazards.

So, in regard to the bomb, I believed I knew the where and the what, but *how* were these assholes going to pull it off exactly? There was a lot of ocean out there. I took a peek through the window onto the bridge. It was dark in there, the only illumination provided by dim red lights and small red or green LEDs on various panels. Three Somalis occupied the space: one with his hands on his hips, standing beside a small metal steering wheel with wooden spokes that I figured was probably the helm; one leaning over a map on a bench; a third just staring out the window at the sea beyond the bow. The guy at the bench gave me a half-hearted glance and then returned to what he was doing, checking over a map. From his point of view, through the small glass panel in the door, he'd caught sight of a heavily armed guy wearing a ski mask – nothing to worry about, plenty of those around.

A siren started wailing over the deck. The alarm sent everyone down there scurrying for the walkways beside the gunnels. Then the hatches over the cargo holds began to slide back, opening up the holds to the night air with a sound that was part rumble and part squeaking grind. Also, I could see renewed activity around the ship's lifeboats. They were being readied for departure and a rabble of Somalis had formed around each one.

The door onto the bridge opened. I was suddenly face to face with a Somali. He asked me something, damned if I knew what. He repeated the question a second time at twice the volume. The third time was almost a shout. The guy was getting agitated. I wasn't giving him the right responses, or indeed any response. His buddy came out from behind him, an FN in his hands, and they stood shoulder to shoulder at the doorway to the bridge. Both of them jabbered loudly at me; things were getting out of hand, and then the guy with the FN began turning the barrel of the weapon toward me, so I shot him. The impact of the double-aught in his chest sent him sailing backward through the half-open door. I kept the pressure on the trigger finger. The din of two more shots crashed off the hard steel around me and the second guy slumped to the deck, the Atchisson having blown his heart clean through his back and flattened it like road kill against the steel wall behind him.

This wasn't how I wanted things to go, at least not in a timing sense. I went through the door onto the bridge, stepped over the deceased just inside and slid on the pool of blood spreading from his vented chest. *Bang.* A gunshot. Close range. The sound caused me to jump. The slug went through a glass pane behind me. The third guy – I'd forgotten about him. He'd come out of the charthouse, a small room off the wheelhouse, and his rifle was shaking in his hands. He was pulling the trigger repeatedly and nothing was happening. Maybe he had a jam. Maybe he only had one round in the mag. Maybe this was my lucky day. It sure wasn't his: I shot from the hip and a big red hole surrounded by ragged cotton and strips of flesh appeared in his thigh, just below his nuts. A gush of warm blood from his shredded femoral artery hosed me down before I got off another round, better aimed than the first, that removed his jaw on its way through his spinal column.

Blood had soaked through the ski mask so I tore it off and threw it on the floor. All the men down on the deck were staring up at the bridge, in the direction of the gunshots, with 'what the fuck?' looks on their faces. Great. I double-checked the drum, and then put a reassured hand on the mag packing twenty rounds still tucked into my webbing.

There wasn't much time till the bridge was stormed, maybe a minute to scout around and hopefully find an escape hatch. A quick hunt told me there wasn't one. But I did find a small cabin with a cot, a fire extinguisher, a basin and a handy stainless-steel head – just what I needed for the nervous dump coming on. I heard shouting outside, getting closer. My date with the shitter would have to wait. Aside from the small cabin and charthouse off the bridge, there was also a radar room. The display monitor hooked up to the MSTAR out on the wing showed nothing airborne in the vicinity and, according to the ship's own radar, the sea surface was also clear. On the wall were pictures of the USS *Enterprise*, the USS *Leyte Gulf* and half a dozen other ships of the French, British, Australian and Indian navies. It was an identification wall showing targets. I considered putting a shell or two into the electronics in the room but then immediately thought better of it. Maybe there was a trigger for this floating dirty IED somewhere among all the flashing LEDs. Just as easily, there could be a way to defuse it, perhaps the *only* way to defuse it.

I took the stainless-steel chairs from the chartroom and repurposed them to jam shut the access doors onto each of the open-air wings. Next I removed the .38 and the Desert Eagle from the webbing and laid them on the floor in the cabin. Checking the dead guys for weapons and ammo I found three FNs with two full mags between them. I readied one of the rifles with a spare mag and placed it on the floor beneath the helm, then put myself flat on the floor in the cabin beside the handguns and took a bead on the nearest wing door.

A command was yelled into the bridge. Being in Somali, or whatever language they speak in Somalia, I couldn't understand it but I figured it was probably something like, 'Whoever the fuck you are, come out with your hands up.'

I answered with silence.

Their response to my response was a volley of shots that removed the glass panel I was aiming at. And then the flash diffuser on the end of an FN barrel appeared cautiously over the bottom edge of the opening and half a magazine was emptied into the bridge. The rounds smacked, pinged and whirred off the steel walls, floor and ceiling, some smashing out the forward-facing windshields. I kept my head buried under my arms till the noise stopped, then glanced up and saw several misshapen, full-metal-jacketed rounds spinning on the steel floor just in front of my face, bleeding off the last of their energy.

The barrel came through the hole in the door again, a face behind it this time. A round from the Atchisson made it disappear in a puff of red mist. I turned to the side, pulled one of the frag grenades off my webbing, gripped the spoon handle tight against the body of the weapon and removed the pin. This was risky. If I missed the hole in the door and it rebounded back into the bridge, it could get messy. For me. I decided against the lob, scrambled to the door instead, released the spoon, counted off three seconds then popped it through the hole. I heard screams and yells and a mad scramble and then a loud metallic crash as I dived for the floor in the radar room.

Moments later, I got up, ran to the door now pockmarked with dents, ripped the chair away and ran out onto the wing. Four bloody, smoking men lay slumped in a pile on the floor. Maybe half a dozen others were running down the alleyway toward the stern. I fired the Atchisson in their direction on full auto for a second and a half, dropping three of them. I ran back inside the steel walls of my stationary tank just as an axe smashed out the window of the door onto the wing opposite and a frag grenade sailed in. It hit the floor, bounced once and rolled into the corner. I dived into the cabin again and made it with barely a moment to spare. There was an unbelievably loud explosion just around the steel corner. It rang in my head and jangled as the pressure wave blew through the nasal and sinus cavities in my face. I yelled at the top of my voice with my mouth wide open to try to clear my ears.

The door the grenade came through was being battered by something. The top hinge bent and then broke. The center hinge was going the same way. And then the door burst inward and half a dozen men stormed in behind it shouting and screaming some kind of war cry.

I opened up the Atchisson and five rounds per second of twelve-gauge double-aught hacked into them at point-blank range, silencing them, but not before they managed to get off three or four wild shots of their own in my direction.

The drum mag emptied, I considered dropping the weapon and picking up the FN, but the shrapnel from the grenade had rendered it useless. Instead I replaced the drum on the Atchisson as two men made another attempt at storming the bridge, but they slipped on the blood on the floor like I had and both went down, smacking their heads on the steel. For dessert, they each chewed a couple of mouthfuls of double-aught.

My foot was wet. I looked down and saw that my leg was leaking blood, a pool of it forming on the floor around my boot. One of the FN rounds that had ricocheted had caught me in the calf muscle. Movement at the door. Through the empty panel I saw a man running toward me, bottle in hand, poised for the throw, a flaming rag hanging from its neck. A burst from the Atchisson cut that idea short and he crumpled to the deck. The bottle shattered and he was instantly engulfed in flames. Suddenly, the world around me was also in flames, my clothes catching fire. A Molotov cocktail had been tossed in through the door behind me. They'd attacked from both sides simultaneously.

My hands were alight, and so was the Atchisson. I put it on the floor and kicked it into a corner of the bridge. Shit, shit, shit. Flame ran up my arms. Back in the cabin, on the wall, wasn't there a fire extinguisher? I took a step and fell. My leg wasn't working. I got up, took a few half steps and dived for the red bottle on the wall. Ripping it off the bracket, I turned it on myself, releasing a torrent of foam that gushed from the nozzle, covering me and everything else in the vicinity. The trigger jammed open, quickly filling the small cabin with expanding foam. The flames were snuffed out, but the skin on my arms and neck throbbed like it was still on fire. And my lower leg was starting to feel as if someone was twisting my torn flesh with pliers.

The extinguisher stopped gushing just as a grenade rolled across the floor of the bridge. It stopped rolling. I dived under the foam as the thing went off and sent shrapnel pinging and clattering into the walls and ceiling around me. Two men raced in behind the detonation, screaming and yelling and firing indiscriminately. I felt around on the floor till I found what I was looking for. I came up on one knee, a big blob of foam armed with the Desert Eagle. The two men gaped wide-eyed at the massive hand cannon pointed at them. Single shots accompanied by a gout of flame jumped from the weapon's muzzle and large caliber rounds hit like runaway streetcars, slamming them into the steel and glass wall at their backs. I'd seen what death looked like enough times not to bother checking pulses.

Blood from my wounded leg was turning the foam on the floor red and pink. I stood up, popped my head around the corner to get a look at the doors at opposite ends of the bridge and see what was coming next. There were scorched bodies and blood and little pools of fire still burning here and there, and the air was filling with foul-smelling black soot. I couldn't see anyone moving but there had to be Somalis still alive on the ship. It wouldn't be long before they regrouped and had another go at dislodging me. They'd have to – I was in control of where their dirty bomb was going.

I unwound the scarf that was still around my neck and used it as a tourniquet, tying it just below the knee. I couldn't see what was going on back there on my calf, though the blood wasn't spurting out, so a main artery hadn't been hit. The tourniquet seemed to cut the blood loss some. Didn't do much for the pain, though. Putting some weight on my foot I tried to lift my heel . . . Jesus. I braced my hand against the wall to steady myself and waited for the rush of pain to subside a little. Walking would be tough; running was out.

I went over and collected the Atchisson from the floor, keeping an eye on both doors. The shotgun had stopped burning, but I could feel the heat of the handgrip through the foam-soaked shooter's gloves. I checked the drum. Five shells, all scorched pretty bad. Could I trust them? No, maybe not. I dropped the weapon on the floor.

I limped out into the wing closest to the sleeping cabin to see if anyone was moving down on the deck. Flipping down the NVG lenses

I got an eyeful of foam so I wiped it away and readjusted the lenses. Nothing appeared to be moving in Kermit world. But then a loud bang sounded, followed by a rattle, and I turned just in time to see a lifeboat slide down its rails and disappear from view over the side. Rats leaving the ship. I hoped that was all of them. I hoped they wouldn't call for reinforcements. I hoped someone would wake me from this nightmare soon.

One round remained in the Desert Eagle. I recovered the .38 from the floor. Wet and foamy, the handgrip had swollen to twice its previous width. The piece of crap would be impossible to aim and I trusted it less than the Atchisson, so I tossed it back into the suds on the floor. Next stop, the radar room. In here, little appeared to be damaged, the focus of the attack having been my position in the cabin. The feed from the MSTAR had been rendered useless, however, the hardware out on the wings reduced to junk by grenade shrapnel, gunfire and stray shotgun pellets. But the ship's radar was functioning just fine, and the screen showed that the *African Spirit* was on a course tracking the coastline. It showed that we were about twenty-five miles out to sea in international waters, south of the Kenya/Somalia border.

The room was full of radio and satellite comms gear. There were also two Toshiba laptops connected to a black sealed unit, a single small green LED on top indicating that it was on. I opened the laptops. Both appeared to be running diagnostics on either themselves or the sealed unit, except for a window on one of the screens with a countdown timer that read two hours thirty-five minutes, followed by seconds and also hundredths of a second, which suggested something different, as did the words at the top of the window that read *Run time*. From my rough calculation, Randy's timetable had the bomb going off in around forty-eight hours. His clock and the one I was looking at didn't tally. Maybe von Weiss had brought the operation forward, or Sweetwater had miscalculated. Maybe the watch he wore to replace the one he'd given the guy who'd ended up fish food in northern Australia was running a little slow. Whatever, it appeared that we were getting close to showtime.

I pressed the on/off button on the laptop's keyboard, just in case disarming the thing was that easy. Another window appeared with the word *Warning!* flashing within it, and below that: *Power loss will cause instant detonation.* The cold feeling that comes with a need to sit on the head again flushed through my system. The situation was clear. Around two and a half hours till this bomb went off – or sooner if I tried to mess with it.

Chatter came through a small radio speaker. The radio! *Duh.* Perhaps I could send out a warning for shipping to keep clear. I snatched the microphone off its mount, depressed the *send* button on the side and said, 'Mayday, Mayday, Mayday. This is *African Spirit, African Spirit,* around twenty-three nautical miles abeam northern Kenya. Anyone receiving? Over.'

Nothing.

I checked the frequency – it was fine – then repeated the call three times and got three nothings. Perhaps they didn't say 'Mayday' when ships were in trouble, or perhaps there was something else more fundamental amiss. I played with the *send* switch on the microphone. Depressing it didn't cut in on any external messages or make any sound through the speakers – not even a click. It felt dead. Unauthorized radio transmissions were probably considered no-nos by the computers and their little black unit.

I went to the helm on the bridge, the wood-spoked steel wheel. The ship was making sixteen knots on a heading of thirty-four degrees – a lot of knots for an old tub. Assuming a constant speed since leaving Dar, the *African Spirit* would've covered a distance of a little over three hundred and thirty nautical miles. A light on the small control panel indicated that the autopilot was on. Would the computers allow me to take the ship off autopilot? I flicked the switch and the light went off. Yes, they would. So manual course corrections were permissible. Okay, now I had control of the ship. Only, where was I going to take this bucket of poison? I figured the *Enterprise* had to be somewhere to seaward, so heading east wasn't on the dance card. I switched the autopilot back on and the light on the panel lit up. I had to find an answer down in the hold, some way to defuse the situation before I did anything else. I hobbled on over to the wing on the other side of the bridge, closest to the cabin. The carnage out there was as horrific as anything I'd ever seen, but I didn't dwell on it. The cards I'd been dealt had given me no choice but to go ballistic. The salt-laced wind out on the wing was fresh and strong, blowing hard from the west southwest – roughly from the direction of land. I pumped a few lungfuls in and out to clear my head, then turned down the passageway where three large lumps dotted the floor, Somalis gunned down by the Atchisson. I hobbled down and confirmed all three were dead, and relieved one of his FN. Checking the mag, I found just one round, with another in the chamber. Between the three corpses I recovered a measly eight rounds altogether.

My leg was giving me some issues. The wound was still oozing blood, though the rate had slowed. I loosened the tourniquet for a few seconds, then tightened it again. Making my way back down through the superstructure, the going wasn't so bad. I took the ladders in two steps, gripping the rails with my hands and sliding like I'd seen sailors do. Coming back up wouldn't be so easy.

I reached the hold without incident. Opening the bulkhead revealed a sea of blinking green LEDs in the darkness. The engine hummed loudly through the hull, a trace of gasoline fumes competing with the smell of bunker oil. I headed for the walkway down the side and dragged my leg toward the bow. The W80 was still where I'd last seen it, mounted on the rig with that elongated box welded to its side. I stopped by the table where I'd seen the Iranians hunched over laptops. Those computers had gone. Cables linked the weapon and the explosives attached to the fuel drums to a stack of black boxes with LEDs – relays, probably, to those Toshibas in the radar room. I resisted the temptation to empty a few rounds into those black boxes, the risk of detonating the weapon if I messed with the system still fresh in my mind. Pulling the plug's not an option, Cooper, I told myself – unless you're happy to have your atoms scrambled.

I yanked the detcord from two of the barrels, but it was solidly attached and didn't come away easy. There were a lot of barrels. Too many.

I went over to the raised platform and climbed the stepladder up to the weapon. The rig was specially made from heavy-gauge steel covered in congealed foam, which I figured was probably fire-resistant. The bomb itself was mounted in some kind of gimbal secured to the rig with titanium bolts. It occurred to me that being close to the weapon wasn't smart either. The men I'd seen working up here had been wearing NBC suits; for all I knew the breached W80 was spewing neutrons that were quietly broiling bits of my body I was fond of – my testicles, for example. The thought stopped me mid-climb. Really, there was nothing I was going to be able to do up there unless I found a big red emergency stop button on the side of the weapon. Unlikely.

I stepped back down onto the deck, feeling defeated. The program was running and I could do one-fifth of fuck-all to stop it. And then it started to rain. I glanced up at the sky – it was cloudless, oddly full of rain and bright NVG-enhanced starlight. The rain burned my skin, because it wasn't water coming down but a fine mist of gasoline. The mist was spraying from nozzles attached to plastic pipes running up the side of the hull. Some of them also spanned the openings overhead. Tracing one of those pipes, I found it led to an electric pump attached to a cluster of drums. Investigating a little farther, I found a lot of these pumps. Jesus, the hold was filling with an explosive mixture of atomized gasoline. The damn countdown had started.

Thirty-two

I got out of there as quick as I could, but by the time I reached the hatch separating the hold from the superstructure I was soaked through with gasoline, choking on it, spitting it out. The stuff was burning my eyes, nose and throat, stinging the burns on my arms and neck. I dragged myself up the ladders and tried to think about what I could do. The best I could come up with was to change course, bring the ship around one-eighty degrees. Maybe the answer lay in the opposite heading to the one programmed into the autopilot.

On the way to the bridge, I stopped by a dead Somali wearing a scarf. I took it off him and used it to wipe the gas off my face, hair and forearms. A satellite phone was lying in pieces in the pool of blood beside him. Shit, I could've used that phone.

Standing up, I checked the surroundings. It was then that I noticed an oil fire burning in a fifty-five-gallon drum down on the stern, sending up a column of smoke that probably trailed behind the ship for miles. Why hadn't I noticed it before? Probably the fact that it had been night had something to do with it. But now the sky had lightened out to the east. Within half an hour, it'd be full daylight. Looked like another perfect tropical day on the way – blue sky, fresh winds, mushroom cloud.

When I arrived back at the wing, another surprise greeted me: a voice. The wind made it impossible to hear exactly what was being said, but someone was on the bridge. I drew the Desert Eagle, released the safety and then stole a quick glance around the edge of the door. Nothing. The wheelhouse area was empty, just as I'd left it. But someone was talking. And he was in the radio room, sending a radio transmission. I stepped into the bridge, out of the wind, got down low, crept forward and heard an African-accented voice say, '. . . we are sinking by the stern following echo romeo fire. Require urgent assistance. Crew taking to the boats.'

There was a pause of around five seconds. I tensed, got ready to move, then the message repeated, 'This is MV *African Spirit*, one forty-nine zero three south, forty-one fifty-two eleven east. SOS. We are sinking by the stern following echo romeo fire. Require urgent assistance. Crew taking to the boats.'

Second time around sounded identical to the first transmission – no difference at all in the wording, the inflection or the tone. I edged along the wall and peeked around the corner. The radar room was empty. The message was a pre-recorded duck call. So this was how they were gonna pull it off. The oil fire off the stern was part of it, probably detonated by an ignition device remotely activated by the Toshiba twins. And when the assistance hurrying to the rescue was nice and close, where Ed Dyson predicted the best results – downwind – this big dirty bomb would detonate.

Now that I knew *how* von Weiss and the White brothers intended to pull off their attack on US naval assets, I could also come up with a plan for a counterattack. I grabbed the latest weather information off the radar display. The wind was out of the southwest at eighteen knots. If the *African Spirit* was roughly in position now to cause the most potential damage, then what were probably the targets – *Enterprise*, *Leyte Gulf* and possibly other ships assigned to Task Force 151 – were currently lying just over the horizon to the northeast. So it followed that the best course of action was to take this tub to a place where there was a chance the winds were blowing onshore. In short, the only option I had was to drive this tub onto the beach. From memory, there wasn't much in the way of habitation in this part of the world – no coastal towns or villages. I wasn't a hundred percent sure about that, though, so it was a gamble, but the only other option I could see was to find a life ring and jump.

I made the decision quickly – holstered the Desert Eagle in my belt, hopped to the control panel, flicked the switch disengaging the auto-pilot and spun the remaining spoke in the wheel counterclockwise. The ship immediately responded, leaning to the right as it carved a wide arc to the left, the spherical compass mounted overhead on the ceiling bobbing and rotating in its bath, coming onto a roughly west-northwest heading.

'Step back from the helm!' demanded a voice suddenly from out of nowhere.

The unexpected intrusion made me jump. Je-*sus*! I turned and saw Charles White. The fucker had come back and brought a small posse with him. *The damn satellite phone* – a call must have been made. He stepped through the scorched and battered door armed with an FN, and one of his bodyguards and a Somali squeezed through behind him.

'An' I thought von Weiss was jerkin' me off, man,' said White. 'I remember yo' ass from the Congo. It was *you*, wasn't it? An' you wuz down in the hold, snoopin' around. It's Cooper, right, asshole?'

My hand was still on the wheel spoke, the ship still coming around to its new heading. 'Where's the rest of your party?' I asked.

He smirked. 'One o' me's more than enough to take care o' the likes o' you, man.' He raised the business end of the FN and pointed it at my face. 'Now step the fuck back from the wheel, motherfucker,' he repeated.

I did as I was told and took a step back. A small step.

'Who do you work for? The Brits? CIA?'

'Alabama Thornton.'

'What . . . ? Who the fuck's that?'

'She's a topless tall.'

'What?'

'A showgirl from Vegas.'

'Don't shit me, asshole. You CIA, man. Have to be.'

'Insults will get you nowhere. What about Kim Petinski? You killed her, too?'

'What do you think, dipshit?'

'You're not getting off this boat is what I think.'

He replied with a smile, shared with his bodyguard. 'Tough talk for a fuck who's walkin' dead.' He sniffed the air. 'What's that you wearin', man? Eau de Fuckin' Exxon?' He laughed and took a cigarette from behind the ear of the Somali standing beside him and put it in his mouth. He snapped his fingers and the Somali passed him a gold Zippo.

'Blowing this ship up with the nuke. What's in it for you and your brother?' I asked him.

'Bin Laden gets a replacement.' He sneered. 'Mohammed Ali-Bakr al Mohammed, most audacious war lord who ever lived. And he'll be in our pocket.'

'Don't bet on him living long,' I said. 'A hundred nukes gets you respect, one nuke just gets you assassinated.'

'Let's talk about killin'. You whacked one o' mine up on Sugarloaf. Was you, right?' He flicked back the Zippo's lid and rolled the lighter along his thigh. Sparks and a flame jumped onto its wick. He brought the flame to the bent hand-rolled smoke between his lips, talking around it. 'I figure you the one who pushed him off the mountain.'

I gave a shrug that partly said I had no idea what he was talking about and partly said fuck yeah.

'In case yo' wonderin', yo' English bitch gave that up before we snuffed her, while von Weiss watched me givin' it to her in the ass.' He tossed the lighter at me. It hit my leg, just above the knee. My world slowed. The flame found the gasoline soaked into my pants. It jumped and danced and expanded with excitement. It engulfed my leg, and then jumped to my other leg. It caught my webbing next and, within seconds, I was a torch. Heat exploded around me. Through the orange flames I saw Charles White laughing. My immolation was a joke and he was sharing it with his bodyguards and the Somalis. I shook my arm, tried to shake the flame off it, but it was glued to me. I took a step backward, then another, turned around and around, the heat unbearable. And then I ran, until I found myself in the cabin where I dived onto the floor, into the foam. The flames were snuffed out in an instant, choked by the chemicals. I rose up from the floor, covered in the stuff, and I was not happy. White was standing in front of me in the doorway. The smile died on his lips when I pulled the trigger on the Desert Eagle. A shot of yellow flame spewed from the barrel. An instant later, the .44 slug ripped the arm and shoulder clean out of his body. The force of the impact spun him around and I glimpsed his exposed heart beating in the raw hole where his arm and shoulder used to be.

The Somali was first to react. He raised the Atchisson AA-12 I'd discarded to his shoulder and pulled the trigger. The shotgun barked and the Somali screamed as his hand blew off at the wrist. Half his face was also airborne as he fell to the floor, shrieking. The bodyguard and the remaining Somalis were going for their guns as I raised the .38 and started pulling the trigger again and again. The soggy, foamy weapon jumped around in my hand, but at the distance of a few feet not even this piece of shit could miss. It wasn't a pretty handful of seconds, dum-dum rounds being about as anti-personnel as small-arms ammo gets.

Sometime during all the gunfire, the Somali with the missing hand and face stopped screaming. I hobbled over to the mess on the floor that was Charles White. He lay sprawled and bloody against the forward bulkhead. His eyelids fluttered open and his eyeballs rotated upward, attempting to focus on me. Okay, so I admit that killing him felt good, like a reward for effort. And the fact that he knew it was me who killed him – well, that just made the good feeling complete. The vacuum his death would create in von Weiss's world would be filled pretty much instantly by some other piece of filth, but just at that moment I couldn't care less. It was personal for me with Charles White. His eyelids and eyeballs went slack as his chest contracted and his dying breath wheezed from his slack mouth. I put a bullet in his ear to make doubly sure of it. And, yeah, if my calf had been up to it I'd have busted a move.

Next stop, the helm – what was left of it. There might be others returned to the ship making their way to the bridge. Outside, the sun was now over the horizon, the air noticeably warmer. My Seiko told me that we were well inside the last hour of Toshiba time. I checked the radar display and turned the spoke half a rotation to ensure I was taking the fastest route to the beach, ten miles ahead – around forty minutes away. It also told me there was a vessel in pursuit of the *African Spirit* and it was closing fast.

Jets screamed by, barely clearing the bridge. US Navy Super Hornets. They'd come from the south and were gone from view in seconds. The ship giving chase, the jets – shit, maybe that pre-recorded SOS was working. The aircraft passed by low overhead again, coming from behind the stern this time, and the shriek made the fluid in the overhead compass dance. I watched them scribe a tight turn off the bow, washing off speed. They continued the turn and I followed them through it until I lost them somewhere behind the ship, the view obscured by the superstructure. Seconds later they appeared again on a parallel course to the ship, their gear and flaps lowered, rocking their wings from side to side. Okay, so the Navy was aware of the engine fire and had answered the SOS. Most likely they or the ship in my six o'clock, or the *Enterprise*, or *Leyte Gulf* or any number of other Task Force 151 vessels out there were trying to contact me, but with the *African Spirit*'s comms rigged the way they were, it wasn't being received and I couldn't make any reciprocating calls even if I heard them.

The US Navy flew another circuit. When they came around again, I went out onto the wing, stopping to pull a ski mask and a rifle off one of the corpses. I put on the mask and waved the rifle over my head. I did that so the pilots would get a different picture to the one they'd been briefed on. They'd come to buzz a ship that had broadcast an SOS, and instead they'd find one occupied by pirates. I wasn't sure how that would shake things up, but I was hoping for caution on the part of the Task Force. The aircraft finished their pass, went to afterburner and vanished so fast it was like matter transfer had been involved in their disappearance.

I stood on the bridge, watched the approaching coast and tried not to faint. I don't know how long I stood there, listening to my breathing, my thoughts flicking between the violence of the night just past, of what had happened to Sweetwater and what might be happening to Petinski if she was still alive.

I don't know what snapped me out of it, but when I did, the radar screen said the shoreline was less than ten nautical miles off the bow. It also showed that the vessel giving chase to the *African Spirit* had halved the distance and was now five nautical miles behind. It had to be doing thirty knots to our fourteen. It had to be military. I limped to the stern to see if I could get a visual. The column of black smoke off the stern stretched for miles, climbing high into a sky that was a clear bright blue. A fleck of gray sat on the horizon. It was too far away to get a fix on the type of ship. I swept the line separating sea from sky and saw four black specks above it, off to the northeast, closing the distance fast. Helicopters – Seahawks from the *Enterprise* or *Leyte Gulf*. They'd be overhead in three to five minutes and their crews would be con-fused about what was going on aboard the *Spirit*. A comment I'd made to White came to mind, the one about a hundred nukes getting you respect and so forth. Did I really think I was getting off this tub alive?

Heading back to the bridge, I stopped out on the other wing. A line of thick white clouds had settled over the shore and the color of the ocean was changing from deep blue to blue green as the seabed rose to the continental shelf. Checking my Seiko, the ship-bomb was programmed to blow in seventeen minutes. If I was still on board, I'd be aware of the detonation for perhaps a spilt second before the concussion and heat wave sent my ashes to hell. The *Spirit* would ground itself on a shoal or run up onto the beach at roughly the same time. The prevailing wind still seemed to be coming from the southwest. Maybe this little plan of mine was futile. Meanwhile, I'd seen no sign of anyone else on board. There were no more surprise guests. The ship was mine. I had no idea how to reset the autopilot, but the *Spirit* was pretty much going where it was pointed. But just to make sure, I took the singed scarf from around my neck and wrapped it around the remaining steering wheel spoke and tied it off so that it was jammed in position. The exposed skin on my arms and neck was throbbing. Blisters were forming. My calf was aching. There wasn't much left to do, but some *khat* would sure be handy to help me get it done.

Flat snarls heralded the arrival of several Sea Kings. I hopped out onto the wing. Two of them were a quarter of a mile away on a parallel course to the *Spirit*. I didn't stay out on the wing too long. There might be SEALs on those choppers, and I might be considered a legitimate target. The nearest chopper was flashing a light at the bridge. I figured it was probably Morse, but as I didn't know any Morse other than dot-dot-dot dash-dash-dash dot-dot-dot, the code for SOS, I had no idea what was being communicated.

The water was now light green and I could clearly make out a line of white where the surf was breaking onto the sand a mile ahead of the bow. Time to move. It was maybe less than three minutes till this tub blew its dirty secret into the sky. I could already visualize the headlines. Heads would roll. Mine would be toast.

I headed for the back end of the boat a last time. My leg was well and truly seized. The ricochet or bullet fragment or whatever it was that had performed a little impromptu surgery on my calf muscle had cut through a nerve, or was lodged against it, sawing through it with every step. I pushed myself along the wall, using it as a support, trying to keep my weight off that leg. I wasn't looking forward to negotiating the three ladders down to the open deck, but I took them as fast as I could and tried to ignore the screams ripped from my own throat when I stepped onto each of the metal decks. I opened the hatch out onto a burst of sunlight. Down at sea level, the ship seemed to be going faster, overtaking the swell lines. The water was a pale green now, the sandy bottom clearly visible. The naval vessel was close, turned side-on about half a klick away, its commander probably nervous about running aground. The ship appeared small – it was some kind of destroyer or frigate and not one of ours, but the Seahawk hovering over its stern probably was.

I peeled off the body armor and dropped it onto the deck, along with the .38 rounds in my pocket and the NVGs flipped up on my head. I climbed up onto the gunnel with difficulty. The turbulence coming off the propellers boiled with puffs of sand. I didn't think too hard about jumping, in case thinking about it changed my mind, and stepped off into midair. Half a second later, I hit the wash.

Coming to the surface no problems at all, I watched the *Spirit* charge full steam toward the beach less than a klick ahead, a surf beach. I could see the backs of the waves crashing onto the sand. Beyond, the yellow sand was a thin line of low khaki-colored scrub. I couldn't see any vehicles or smoke indicating habitation. Nothing to indicate wind direction either. Small fish nibbled at my calf, drawn by the blood, followed by something a little larger that hit my leg and started tugging at it, its teeth caught in the tourniquet.

I lifted my eyes and saw the ship suddenly pitch sideways and roll a little. It had struck the bottom. And then the sides of it bulged and three geysers of bright orange flame, one from each of the holds, shot several hundred yards into the sky. A split second later the entire vessel was engulfed in a vast expanding ball of gasoline that rushed toward me along with the shock wave. I ducked below the surface as the concussion pulse punched through the water. It punched the air out of my lungs and threw me around like a cork in a bath. Dazed and disoriented I bounced off the sand bottom, the world above the color of flame as the pall of ignited fuel spread over the air and sea. My lungs were raw and hot, close to bursting. Secondary detonations pulsed through the water pummeling me like body blows from a heavyweight. I needed air, but I was trapped below. I had to breathe or die. Nowhere to go. The oxygen-starved world was turning gray. I began to slide toward the bottom. Or the top, I wasn't sure which. I opened my mouth, lungs and chest convulsing. Water rushed in. I choked. My lungs were bursting, seared, the taste of copper and gasoline in them. 'This is it,' a quiet voice said somewhere inside, a moment of peace. 'You're gonna die. It's not so bad. Just accept it. Breathe . . .'

Thirty-three

I felt something clamp against my jaw, tentacles wrapping around my arms. My eyes and mouth opened and bubbles filled my blurred vision as a rubber mouthpiece was jammed almost down my throat, and the second stage cleared. Sucking hard, I breathed in, out, in, out . . . Sweet Jesus, motherfucking air! I breathed again and felt the relief that came with it surge through me. The tentacles turned out to be arms and the clamp a man's hand. A mask slipped over my face and I cleared it like I'd been trained. I saw that there were six men in the water around me. The trident insignia I saw on someone's neoprene shoulder told me they were US Navy SEALs.

I reached into my shirt, but my hand was pulled short. One of the SEALs showed me the pneumatic spear gun in his hand. I held my hands up in surrender and one of the SEALs reached into my shirt and pulled out what I was about to show them – my dog tags. He took a closer look, gave the other divers the 'okay' sign and patted me on the shoulder. He then pointed in a direction away from the burning *African Spirit* and made a bunch of signals that asked me if I could swim on my own, or needed assistance. I pointed at my calf, informing him that swimming was unlikely, then untied the laces and kicked the boots off my feet.

*

The ship was an Indian guided-missile destroyer – a new, sleek one. A party in NBC suits armed with M16s met me coming aboard and accompanied me back to where a temporary enclosed shower had been set up to one side of the helipad. A Geiger counter was passed over me, and then I was directed to get in the shower. Once inside I was doused in some kind of foaming solution for a few minutes, which tore into the burns on my arms, neck and face, and then the Geiger counter came out for another pass. I saw a few nods between the guys in the suits, which said either, 'Yeah, he's clean,' or 'Yeah, he's fried.' I figured it was the former when I was handed a towel and a pair of khaki coveralls and folks started zipping themselves out of the NBC suits. I noticed that the M16s had also disappeared. While I was moved into another tent, I caught a glimpse of the *Leyte Gulf* steaming down from the north. I also took in the scene over on the beach. The air was full of Seahawks, a pair of the aircraft landing equipment and US Marines on the beach. Above, I could see a flight of four Super Hornets in a two-plus-two formation flying combat air patrol at around five thousand feet. Meanwhile, the object of all this attention, the *African Spirit*, was on its side, surf pounding into its cracked hull. The tub was well and truly alight, burning ferociously, a thick pall of black smoke drifting *toward the beach*!

'Yes!' I said to myself under my breath.

'Please . . .' said an Indian medical officer, gesturing at a gurney. 'If you would be so kind. Do you need assistance?'

I shook my head, climbed on, and was then ferried inside the ship to a nearby medical examination room where he and an orderly gave me a quick once-over. Without saying a word, they applied some cream on those burns of mine, put me on a table and x-rayed my leg. A local anesthetic in my calf came next before a twisted bullet fragment was pulled from the wound.

'Good as new, sir,' the doctor said when he was done stitching and bandaging me up.

The orderly began to push me along on the gurney, but I stopped him and asked to walk. He shrugged and helped me off and I followed him at a hobble back outside onto the helicopter landing deck, where another party was waiting impatiently. This one included a US Navy master chief and a unit of Marines. They came toward me, led by an Indian officer wearing a turban.

'Good morning,' the Indian said with an accent more British than any Brit I'd ever heard.

'Good morning, sir,' I replied, resisting the temptation to add, 'Splendid weather we're having.'

'Welcome aboard the *Mysore*,' he continued. 'I am Captain Raf Sanghera, commander of this ship. You gave us quite a chase.'

'Yes, sir.'

'Well, I am not sure how long you will be with us, but you are welcome for the duration.'

'Thank you, sir.'

I wondered if he was going to mention the burning, smoking hulk rolling languidly on the foreshore, but no. Instead he shook my hand and then stood aside for the US Navy master chief petty officer, whose nametag said Beale.

'Special Agent Cooper, United States Air Force OSI,' he said, identifying me formally.

'Master Chief.'

'Made quite a mess for us to clean up, haven't you?'

I glanced over again at the *Spirit*. The sea around the vessel was also alight. No doubt there'd also be an oil spill.

'The whole world is going to want you debriefed pronto, Mr Cooper.'

I figured that.

He walked a little away from the Indians and motioned for me to follow. 'So the package. It *is* in that wreck, right?'

'Yes.'

'Well then, something's not right.'

'Like what?'

'Like we're not picking up much in the way of bee-queues. Almost nothing beyond the usual background radiation. Not even downwind. Doesn't make sense.'

'Bee-queues, Chief?'

'Becquerels – a unit of radiation measurement.'

'The weapon's in there. I saw it – touched it.'

'Well, we're gonna have to wait a little for things to cool off before we try to recover whatever it was you saw and touched,' he said dubiously.

I was distracted by the sound of an approaching Seahawk. It was intending to land.

'That's for you,' Beale shouted over the growing engine noise. Indian sailors went to work, packing away the temporary shower and other gear and herding everyone off the landing deck into an observation bay.

*

From an altitude of a couple of thousand feet, the *Enterprise* could have been a solid ingot of gray steel, except that it happened to be floating. As we drew closer, I watched two Super Hornets catapulted off one end of the ship as an early-warning aircraft was trapped aboard the other end.

We came in over the side of the ship, a pair of yellow shirts wanding us down onto the main angled deck close to the safety nets off the lip of the runway. Once the wheels had settled, a white shirt ran across from the opposite side of the deck and approached the Seahawk's open side.

His eyes searched around inside the cabin area. 'Agent Cooper?' I raised my hand. He handed me a canvas helmet with built-in ear protectors to put on. 'Come with me, please, sir.'

Hopping down onto my good leg, I limped after him to the ship's island where two armed Marines met me, their blond hair cut like matching shoe brushes. They tag-teamed with the white shirt. 'This way, sir,' the one with the stripes of a gunnery sergeant said over the noise of a taxiing jet.

I followed them along a narrow steel passageway, down a narrow ladder and along another narrow passageway, eventually stopping at a room guarded by two more armed Marines. This appeared to be a no-smiling zone. The Marines showed me into the room, a big steel box dominated by a large U-shaped table covered in laptop computers and cabling, attended by at least a dozen people I didn't know, and one that I did. There was a lot of talking that stopped sharply when I ducked through the bulkhead, the way it does when the people you walk in on are talking about you. Maybe it was my imagination.

'Vin!' said Arlen. He stood and came over. 'We were just talking about you.'

Right. 'Hey,' I said, happy to see the guy, happy to be seeing *anything* given my last twenty-four hours.

His eyes swept my face, neck and arms. 'Jesus, I was told you'd picked up a few burns . . .'

'Looks worse than it feels.'

'I sure hope so, buddy, 'cause you look like crap.'

A small cheer followed by a sudden burst of relief swept through the room. Two Air Force majors high-fived.

'What's up?' I asked Arlen as a short, balding Navy commander came over.

'Mr Cooper,' he said, grabbing my hand and almost shaking it loose. 'You've done a great job . . . a *great* job. We've just heard from the recovery team. They have the weapon, and it's intact.'

'It didn't go off?' I asked, surprised.

'Nope.'

'That's wonderful news, sir,' said Arlen.

The Commander was grinning like someone who'd won first prize in a beauty pageant, and motioned us into an adjoining cabin. 'This is going to give Washington complete deniability over the incident,' he continued. 'It never happened. There was no nuclear clean-up team, no compensation, no damage for the diplomats to repair.'

Maybe the bomb was a dud. In which case the last three weeks, including the murder of Emma Shilling, the kidnap and possible murder of Kim Petinski, and the abduction and torture of Randy Sweetwater – all of it had been for nothing.

'Do you know why it didn't detonate, Sir?' I asked.

'Possibly just bad sequencing,' the Commander replied. 'When you ran the ship aground, Mr Cooper, perhaps the fuel load on the ship ignited before it was supposed to. We're still waiting on all the specific details, but it appears the heat of the gasoline fire burned off the explosives in the shaped charge attached to the weapon. Our people at the recovery site have said that the bomb's plutonium core is a little scorched, but that's it. Let me say it again – good job, Mr Cooper.'

I thought he said I'd done a 'great' job. By tomorrow it would be an okay job, and in a week's time no doubt I'd be getting hauled over the coals for not doing a good enough job.

He smiled, shook my hand all over again and left, as did the other folks assembled in the room beyond.

'Was that your plan?' Arlen asked once we were on our own. 'To get that floating bomb to fire out of sequence?'

'What do you think?'

He shook his head and snorted. 'I think you're the luckiest bastard alive.'

Speaking of luck, 'How's Randy?' I asked.

'He's going to make it through okay. That was a neat trick you pulled in front of the security cameras at the embassy gates, by the way. They got to him quickly because of it. CIA traced the registration plate on the cab, interviewed the driver, and we pieced together your movements from there.'

'Did Randy regain consciousness?'

'Apparently – told us enough about the *African Spirit* and Ali-Bakr's plans for it.'

That was a better outcome than I'd expected. I wouldn't have been surprised to hear that Sweetwater had passed away. 'What about you? I thought you were in St Barts.'

'They made me number two assisting the general charged with cleaning up this mess. I was in Qatar interviewing personnel formerly stationed at Area Two when I heard you were in Dar. So I hitched a ride on a C-2 from the *Enterprise* doing a mail run.'

'What about Kim Petinski? Any news?'

He shook his head. 'Nothing. She's vanished. And so has von Weiss. He could be anywhere.'

'He'll turn up in Brazil,' I said.

'Why Brazil?'

'Because he's got the place wired – support systems, local knowledge and so forth. There's no better place to hide than South America. Ask any Nazi. You've spoken to Jeb Delaney, right?'

Arlen nodded.

'What does he know about the W80?'

'Nothing, I hope.'

'What does he think about von Weiss's whereabouts?'

'Same as you.'

'Are we gonna kick his Nazi ass?' I asked.

'The profilers believe he's more likely to be in Eastern Europe, closer to the memory of his father.'

'That doesn't answer my question.' Arlen was looking uncomfortable. 'What aren't you telling me?'

'We can't connect von Weiss to the theft of the W80,' he said.

'No one's talking?'

'Actually, they're now singing like birds, but von Weiss was smart. The operation was compartmentalized from beginning to end. We've got theories and assertions, but there's no evidence, other than Randy's accounts.'

One eyewitness wasn't enough to build a case on. 'There are no wire taps, phone records, photographs linking him to the bomb?'

'Nope, nothing concrete. Charles White might be able to give us something – when and *if* we find him . . .'

'Charles White is dead. I killed the son of a bitch.' Arlen didn't say anything. 'He didn't give me a lot of choice,' I continued.

'Would it have mattered if he did?'

My turn to add nothing. So instead I said, 'Charles's brother, Falco, was also on the *Spirit*. He jumped ship several hours before sunrise. He's still out there somewhere.'

'It'd be good to have him, of course, but Charles was point man.'

'There's also Ali-Bakr al Mohammed and his exec, the tarantula.'

'The *what*?'

'A Somali pirate.' I thought about filling Arlen in on the reason for the bomb's detonation in this nowhere land off the coast of Somalia, but I figured Randy had already spilled those beans.

'Having them under lock and key would be helpful,' said Arlen. 'They cracked our tightest security. We want every little piece about how they pulled it off.'

'Except that it sounds to me like we're getting ready to let von Weiss walk.'

'There are other charges.'

'Let me guess – outstanding parking tickets?'

'He'll never come to trial over the W80. You can't jail someone for something that never happened. They're kinda mutually exclusive, don't you think?'

'I'm going back to Rio,' I said.

'You've done enough. Let von Weiss go.'

'This has nothing to do with von Weiss. I'm going back for Petinski.'

'She disappeared in Dar. What makes you think she's in South America?'

I pictured the condom on the tray. 'Von Weiss took a liking to her. If we find him, I'm betting we'll find her.'

'So it *is* about von Weiss. Jesus, Vin.'

'This is about finding Petinski alive,' I insisted. 'I've lost one partner; I'm not keen on making a habit of it.'

Arlen's lips were set in a seam. I knew what he was thinking, could see it on his face. He believed it was already too late. Petinski was already gone – used in some sick experiment, her body disposed of in such a way that her final terrifying moments would never be known. If he was right about that, and I happened to find von Weiss, *I* wouldn't be letting him walk.

'You're not an executioner, Vin.'

I looked at him and sucked something from between my teeth.

'Excuse me, gentlemen.' It was the gunnery sergeant who'd accompanied me to the room earlier, standing in the doorway.

'What's up, Gunny?' Arlen replied.

'Sir, Commander Beale asked if you would both please join him on the flight deck.'

We followed the Marine and came out of the island into warm sunshine, into the teeth of a steady forty-knot wind. Two Seahawks were coming in to land, angling in over the whitecaps. Commander Beale and several officers were standing by with a large unit of armed Marines. The choppers touched down and the Marines marched across the deck to meet them.

'Thought you might like to see this,' Beale shouted at us over the wind and the rotor noise as he approached.

The doors of the choppers opened, disgorging a cargo of more armed Marines accompanying a group of around twenty males – the Somalis and Iranians off the *African Spirit* – their wrists cuff-locked in front of them. Last out of the lead chopper were the familiar faces of Abdul-Jabbar, Ali-Bakr al Mohammed and Falco White with his bodyguards.

'The *Leyte Gulf* picked them up,' the commander explained. 'They were out in the middle of nowhere, squawking on the radio for assistance. Their boat was foundering.'

Three members of the Marine unit that had taken the motley crew into custody stopped to have a quiet word with Beale. The Somalis, the Iranians and White all hung their heads, utterly beaten.

'Beale finished talking with the Marine.

'Where'd they find 'em?' Arlen asked him.

'On a launch. Strangest thing. Their engines were dead, fouled by Ben & Jerry's ice cream. They found a whole tub of the stuff sloshing around in the auxiliary fuel tank.'

Thirty-four

I had an official debriefing session with Arlen and Beale, followed by one with Naval Criminal Investigation Service and then another with CIA. When it was all done, I told Arlen I was heading back to South America on the next available. He wasn't happy about it, but he swung it anyway, organizing a C-2 to take me to Mombasa, the nearest international airport. From there I hopped international flights back to Rio.

Connections were better flying west to east and only twenty-one hours later I met Jeb Delaney as the sun came up at airport arrivals, Galeão International.

'You look like a chilli dog left on the griddle too long,' he said when he saw me.

'I tan weird.' I debriefed him on what I was permitted to say, which wasn't much, before asking the question uppermost on my mind. 'What you got on von Weiss?'

'To be honest with you, Vin – nothin'. And Adauto Robredo has even less, though he's been crackin' heads all over the place tryin' to get us some leads. But he does have a theory.'

'He agrees with us that von Weiss is in-country?'

'He does.'

'The profilers back home think he's holed up somewhere in Euro Disney.'

Delaney grinned.

'Did I tell you when von Weiss met Petinski, he gave her a condom?' I said.

'A condom . . .'

'Maybe he was out of flowers.'

'That's fucked up. You think he kidnapped her?' Delaney wondered.

'I hope so.'

'Not a pleasant thought.'

'It's a better one than outright murder.'

'What's to say she's not dead? He kidnaps her, does whatever he's gonna do, *then* kills her.'

'That's what my boss thinks. And meanwhile, we've got nothing on von Weiss.'

'Same problem here,' said Delaney. 'The authorities couldn't prove he was behind the shit that went down in Céu Cidade. He's a crafty SOB.'

'What about the black Mercedes SUV? I saw von Weiss's number two – whatshisname, Dolph Lundgren, the big blond guy – driving it.'

'Salvadore?'

'Yeah, him.'

'The vehicle was found dumped in the sea. It was registered to a little ol' lady in the 'burbs with no connection to anything. Forensics got nothin' from it.'

'And nothing from the surveillance hard drives at the favela?'

'We've got some frames of Salvadore escortin' a woman from the vehicle at the main entrance to von Weiss's citadel. We thought it was Shilling. Turns out it was a dancer from a nightclub, a decoy. The whole fuckin' thing was a setup played out for your camera. Authorities got nada.'

I gave my face a vigorous rub.

'I know how you feel,' Delaney said. 'So do Robredo and his men. He's gonna meet us at your hotel to work through what we do next.'

'Where am I staying?'

'This time around, a few rungs down from the Palace. Our station doesn't have much of a slush fund.'

'Yeah, sure.'

A short drive later, we pulled up at a bargain hotel off Copacabana Beach, two doors down from the strip joint I'd seen on my last visit that offered a beer and lap dance for twenty bucks. I was too late – the offer had expired. I signed in at the hotel, dumped my overnight bag in a small room that had the stale sweaty protein smell of a porn theater about it, and met Delaney back down on the street. The mid-morning crowds were heading to and from the beach in a steady stream, the Havaianas flip-flops on their feet making scuffing sounds on the sand-sprinkled sidewalks. The CIA agent was on his cell, looking around. He spotted what he was hunting for, stepped out on the street and waved at a blue Hyundai SUV idling along.

'Robredo,' Delaney told me when I arrived beside him.

The sergeant pulled up, a man in a BOPE uniform in the passenger seat beside him – a pale rope-thin guy sporting a pencil moustache. He looked like a carney, the type that rode the dodgem cars and carried a switchblade in his shoe.

We got in and Robredo turned and said hello, along with a bunch of other things in Portuguese I didn't understand. He introduced the carnie beside him as Officer Pedro. More handshakes. Delaney and the two Brazilians then went into another lengthy discussion before Robredo sped off carelessly down the street, weaving through the flip-flop traffic.

'What was all that about?' I asked Delaney.

'Pedro here has a number of strings to his bow. He's a BOPE tactician as well as being a profiler.'

'A shrink.'

'Be nice. Anyway, Pedro and his colleagues think von Weiss is gonna know we're strugglin' to come at him with the law because, one, he's planned it that way and, two, we're sure he would've had the word confirmed from the street that we're spinnin' our wheels.'

'If he knows that, what's he hiding for?' I asked.

'Because he's afraid.'

'Of what?'

'In this part of the world, the rules of the game can get bent out of shape to favor the authorities. There's that, and he's worried that if he shows his face someplace like Berlin . . .'

'His ass will get redacted and he'll find himself waking up on the Gitmo express.'

'Yeah.'

'So now what?'

'BOPE has its own unofficial intelligence network of snitches. And because no one has seen von Weiss or any of his people on the street, they've come to the conclusion that he's not *on* the street.'

'Then where is he?' I asked.

'On the water.'

I remembered discussing this very possibility with Petinski the last time von Weiss vanished, right after the encounter with the black mamba in my hotel suite had put me in hospital. *Brazil has a million uninhabited rivers and tributaries to hide it in.* Petinski hadn't thought much of this suggestion at the time; I wasn't sure I thought much of it now, but it seemed somehow vaguely ironic that it was the only straw we had left.

The Hyundai turned onto a pontoon bridge, the end of which disappeared into the haze a mile or two away across the water. 'Where are we going?' I asked.

'The naval station over on Niterói. Pedro was a lieutenant in the Brazilian Navy before he joined BOPE. He has contacts.'

Ten minutes later, we pulled up at a guard station. Robredo showed his ID to a man in an unfamiliar uniform, and the officer, Pedro, leaned across to have a word. The guard stuck his head in through the driver's window for a look-see and Delaney and I both gave him a nod. The boom came up and we were waved through. Pedro gave directions left, right and then straight ahead. We eventually stopped outside a long whitewashed building that had the look of a dormitory about it, within sight of the bay. A Brazilian Navy officer jogged over, chatted to Pedro, made a vaguely welcoming hand gesture at the rest of us, and then led us to a small airless briefing room where the temperature was sitting on a hundred degrees with no intention of moving. The walls were covered in maps – some old, some new – as well as photos of various Brazilian Navy ships. A digital projector hung from the ceiling. There were three tables, two computer workstations on all but one of the tables where maps were opened out.

Pedro, Robredo, Delaney and the new guy, whose nametag told me I should call him Marchèse, went into a huddle while I went to the wall and got a hint of the enormity of the task ahead. There was well over a thousand miles of coastline to look at, puckered by the delta of the Amazon River.

'We've got a patrol boat for two days,' said Delaney.

'Great. Who's got the beers?' I asked.

'What do you mean?'

'Might as well get something out of it.' I gestured at the map detailing the coastline south of Rio. 'He could be *anywhere*.'

'Von Weiss has villas at several spots south of Rio and São Paulo. Angra dos Reis, for example. There are plenty of deserted inlets and bays all along this area. He could disappear quite easily around here and still feel close to home.'

I didn't have a better idea and Angra dos Reis sounded familiar. Shilling had mentioned the place.

*

The *Grajaú* wasn't a big ship – a little over forty meters long, a crew of around thirty, a Bofors 40mm cannon up front and a 20mm cannon facing aft behind the superstructure. A brass plate in the wheelhouse said she'd been commissioned in '93, none of which interested Delaney in the slightest as he was violently seasick from the moment we left the dock. We motored down the coastline, stopping occasionally to investigate any large expensive vessels that looked like they might be on the lam.

The town of Angra dos Reis was located in a bay surrounded by soaring granite peaks covered in green jungle, and was a picturesque playground for the rich. I joined the crew scanning the shore with powerful binoculars, most of which appeared to be focused on finding topless babes sunning themselves on the beaches or boat decks. I was thus diverted once or twice myself. Okay, maybe three times.

Von Weiss's villa was located a mile south of town in a private bay, its own golden sand beach and a private impenetrable backyard jungle. The rigid-hulled inflatable boat was launched and Robredo, Delaney, Pedro and I went with an armed party of sailors to have a closer look at it. The villa itself was an ultra-modern concrete box floating on a single stressed concrete beam in the center. The place was locked up tight. It presented like no one had been there for some time, the utilities all turned off at their mains. The inspection was a complete waste of time. We piled back into the RHIB and motored out to the mothership, and kept heading south to waste even more of it. I found myself wishing Pedro was ex–Air Force with contacts in a helicopter squadron. A Super Puma could investigate in an hour what the *Grajaú* could cover in a day.

We called it quits at nightfall, the *Grajaú*'s commander taking the boat out to sea for more general duties. I stayed up for a while, out on the deck, and spent the time going over in my mind conversations I'd had with Emma Shilling and Petinski, one dead and the other almost certainly dead. I wanted the opportunity to give their deaths some meaning. I wanted von Weiss. I wanted to find him and I wanted to spend some time watching him crap his pants while he faced his own mortality. But I probably had more chance of winning the New Jersey lottery, a lottery I never entered.

The ship's first sergeant found Delaney and me bunks in a closet the size of an overgrown footlocker, where there wasn't enough room for me to lie on my side. Sleep didn't come easy, due partly to the cramped quarters, partly to Delaney, who was in the bunk above heaving loudly into a bucket, and partly to the burns on my arms, legs and neck throbbing in time with the ship's diesels.

The search of the coastline resumed at first light. Delaney didn't look so great, but everything in his stomach had long since been expelled so at least the hurling had stopped.

'You look like they just pulled you from a trash compactor,' I told him when he joined me on the rolling deck.

'I wish I felt that good,' he said, the rancid meat-like green tinge nevertheless gone from his face.

The sun blazed up over the cloudless horizon like it was expecting a fanfare. We rolled slowly through the swell and resumed the search, scanning the line of jungle meeting the water, interest increasing with the occasional sighting of a luxury cruiser, which inevitably came to nothing.

It was a quarter to ten, the heat from the morning sun almost crushing, when I took a break and went down to the mess to rustle up a paper cup of ice water. On the way back I stopped in what was probably the officers' wardroom to have a look at a framed map on the wall of the coastline around São Paulo and see if I could place the ship in relation to it. The name on a speck of rock more or less adjacent to São Paulo caught my attention. I went back outside and found Delaney. Everyone up on deck seemed pretty happy, and then I saw why. We'd pulled around a headland and a big pleasure boat was moored in the protective nook of a little bay. Three oiled-up women – two black, one white – were lying naked on the deck just behind the bow. They were young, maybe twenty-three. A couple of the seamen were waving at them. One of the black women stood up and waved back, her shining breasts wobbling back and forth.

'Queimada Grande. Ring a bell with you at all?' I asked Delaney.

'What?' said Delaney, distracted, a big smile on his face. The black woman turned around and showed us her ass. It was a nice ass. Nice legs, too. The sailors whooped. An officer made an appearance and snapped at the crew, and the feeling that we were on a pleasure cruise evaporated.

'Queimada Grande,' I repeated. 'Have you heard of it?'

'Yeah. It's an island crawlin' with poisonous snakes. What of it?'

Jeb Delaney hadn't seen the autopsy report on the hand sent to Alabama, which mentioned the venom detected in its veins. He didn't know about Fruit Fly, alias Diogo Jaguaribe, and how he'd died; he hadn't been briefed about Randy Sweetwater's ring on the amputated hand's finger; or where and how Roy Rogers's horse fit into the picture.

'Do you know where the island is?' I asked.

'Off the coast of São Paulo, I think.'

'It's close. We have to go there.'

'It's off limits. No one goes there.'

I looked at Delaney and watched the tumblers line up in slow motion.

'Oh, shit,' he said.

*

It took three hours of motoring along at the *Grajaú*'s maximum speed, the bow peeling white curls out of the blue water, to bring us within a few miles of the island. The captain took his ship over the horizon so that the only indication of land was a line of thin cloud. It was explained to Robredo and Pedro, who passed it on to Delaney, who passed it on to me, that if there was a vessel moored at Queimada Grande, it would most likely have dropped anchor on the western side of the island, sheltered from the Atlantic groundswell. That meant there was a good chance we could sneak up on it, the landmass obscuring the *Grajaú* from radar.

The island was a weathered haunch of rock in the middle of nowhere, covered mostly in grass and jungle. A tiny white light-house was visible at one end of the island's spine. Waves pounded the rocky shore and flocks of birds wheeled around it. The horizon was utterly empty in every direction, and certainly no boats were vis-ible. The *Grajaú*'s commander changed course, cut the throttle, and an announcement came over the ship's speakers. An armed party of sailors ran up on deck.

Robredo and Pedro handed out lifejackets and helmets. Robredo then looked around and, when the coast was clear, palmed Delaney and me a Glock each. I checked the mag and the chamber before holstering it beneath the lifejacket.

A few minutes later, we climbed down into the RHIB and sped for the southernmost tip of the island. As we rounded it, the water smoothed to glass and the driver pushed the throttle to the stops.

Coming around another rock spur revealed a quiet inlet, a sleek white hyper-luxury vessel over a hundred feet in length moored in the center of it. The name on the back of the boat, written with intertwined snakes, was *Medusa*. Von Weiss's boat. *Hoo-ah!*

A man on its bow looked up and around, the serenity broken by the sound of our outboards. He saw us an instant later, froze for a second, then ran toward the ship's wheel. The navy boys knew what they were doing and ran the RHIB up to the ship's stern, cut the motor then reversed it hard, which stopped it on a dime. With perfect timing, a seaman leaped onto a low ramp used to launch the tender and intercepted the guy, stopping him with a gun in his face before he could reach the wheelhouse and warn anyone.

I jumped across, following two seamen, and extracted the Glock. The man from the bow was one of those tall, blond, well-built Aryan Chippendale stereotypes. I recognized him from the night at Olympe, and from the meeting on Sugarloaf.

'Do you and the boys also do bachelorette nights?' I asked him as the seaman cuff-locked his hands. He looked at me strangely, but nothing I hadn't seen plenty of times before.

I followed the boarding party, becoming one of them as they swept through the boat. We'd managed to achieve complete surprise. Mostly the crew of the *Medusa* was going about its lawful business. They were hired by a crook, which didn't mean they were themselves crooked. However, to avoid confusion, everyone was shown a pair of cuff-locks and confined under guard at the stern of the boat.

I followed two seamen into one of the bedrooms and found the guy I called Dolph Lundgren standing naked in the middle of the room with his eyes closed. A black woman was kneeling in front of him. The shock of our arrival, which she caught in the reflection of a mirror along one entire wall, caused her to gag. She threw up violently into his crotch. Dolph yelped and was about to slap her until one of the sailors jammed a gun in his ribs. The woman raced for the bed, pulled the red satin sheet off it and wrapped it around herself.

'Hey, Sugar,' I said. 'Nice to see you again.'

She wiped her mouth with the back of her hand and eyeballed me, scared but indignant. If I'd been within slapping range, I believed she would have tried.

Dolph, alias Julio Salvadore, sat on the bed, pointing at the mess between his legs, complaining bitterly. He got laughs from the seamen, plus a set of cuff-locks.

'Von Weiss. Where is he?' I asked Sugar. She was too preoccupied with her own situation to want to help, so I left her and Dolph with the men from the *Grajaú* and went back out into the main passageway. It came to an end at a set of double doors. Three seamen already had it covered, and were about to breach and clear the room behind the doors. They tried the knob. Locked. I whistled at them, low and breathy and more of a hiss – not loud, just enough to catch their attention. I signaled them to give me a little room. When they were clear I ran and hit the doors in the center, all my weight behind a front kick. Something went crack and the doors flew open.

It was a big room, the shape of it following the bow of the ship. Von Weiss sat in a chair. He was naked but for a pair of jackboots on his feet and a black Nazi SS peaked cap on his head. In his left hand was a WWII-era Luger P08 pistol. In his other was his erect member. The scene reminded me of Shilling's confession, if that's what it had been. Beside von Weiss was a king-size bed covered with a swastika, the bed itself flanked by crossed flags of the Third Reich. And behind the bed, watching on, was a large portrait of a scowling Adolf Hitler. Various high-powered rifles and handguns were racked up in a glass case on the wall. Von Weiss was pointing the classic pistol at a woman I barely recognized, standing in the center of the room.

'O Magnifico,' I said.

He swung the Luger toward me.

I pulled the trigger. The Glock fired and von Weiss dropped his antique with fright. The slug missed his head by an inch, a round hole of sunshine now punched in the curved wall behind him. I meant to hit him. Maybe I was fatigued.

'Move and the next hole goes in your eye,' I said. 'You have a thing about eyes, right? Or was that your old man's thing?'

'Vin,' Petinski whispered, the thick makeup on her face streaked with tears and lined with terror. She was wearing an SS cap identical to the one on von Weiss's head. He'd dressed her in the black blouse of an SS officer, decorated with an iron cross, the buttons open down the front revealing her breasts. From the waist down, Petinski was naked. Her outstretched arm was shaking. A large golden-colored snake was wrapped around it, forked tongue darting from its lance-shaped head.

'How much money do you want?' I heard von Weiss ask.

I took aim and blew the snake's head off.

'No!' he shouted.

*

I gave the signal to the seaman. He pulled the lever, reversing the RHIB's engine, and the boat backed away from the shore.

'Thanks, Cooper,' was all Petinski said.

'No problem.' I put my arm around her shoulders and gave them a squeeze.

Von Weiss was standing on the rocks in his birthday suit and a peaked Nazi cap yelling at us, shielding his head from the angry birds diving on him. He was yelling that we should come back and get him. Or maybe to get him a pair of pants – I wasn't entirely sure which. He looked ridiculous and scared. I'm no shrink but I thought the image would help give Petinski back some of her strength.

'We can't leave him there like that,' Delaney said.

'You mean semi-naked?' I asked.

'No, you know what I mean. Hell of a lot of poisonous snakes on that island. He won't survive.'

Petinski flicked the hair out of her eyes.

Von Weiss had terrified and humiliated her. He'd also murdered Shilling, tortured Sweetwater, tried to kill me with a black mamba, and stolen a W80 that he'd hoped would ignite a fresh wave of global terrorism. A dangerous fuck of the first order. Maybe if he was allowed to walk he'd learn from his mistakes and next time we wouldn't get off so easy.

'No, he probably won't,' I said.

Petinski smiled and squeezed my arm, popping a blister beneath her fingertips.

Epilogue

I took the steps two at a time up to Alabama and Randy's home and tapped on the door.

'It's open,' Randy shouted from somewhere inside.

'Shouldn't you ask who it is before you invite them in?' I heard Alabama ask in a low voice.

'It's Vin, if that makes a difference,' I called out from the stoop to help them make a more informed decision.

'Hey, man,' Randy called back. 'Come on in, for Christ's sake.'

I eased the door farther ajar in time to see Alabama walk into the room. She looked good in a white tank top and old faded jeans cut into shorts, her hair up and off her neck in the Vegas heat, a broad smile on her lips. She opened the door fully and kissed me on the cheek. 'You made it.'

'Just for the day. Gotta head back to DC tonight,' I said.

'Randy will be pleased to see you.'

Speaking of the devil, he pushed himself into the room. He was in a wheelchair, so I'd have to say I'd seen him look better. Of course, he was in far worse shape the last time I saw him, lying half dead, curled on the road beneath a security camera outside the embassy in Dar. But that was three weeks ago and a lot can happen in three weeks.

'It's not permanent,' Randy said when he saw the look on my face. 'Picked up a touch of encephalitis. It's in my spine.'

Fluffy the cat jumped up into his lap and began to immediately purr. Randy scratched behind its ears and then shooed it off.

'He gets headaches,' said Alabama. The way she said it, I gathered they were bad.

'Getting better every day, babe. You wanna beer, Vin?'

'Thanks,' I said, and Alabama went off to the kitchen.

'So,' Randy said under his breath when Alabama was out of the room. 'That was a hell of a ride. I heard you got badly burned.' He was checking out the dressings that still remained on my arm and neck.

'Mostly first degree.'

'*Mostly?*'

'Nothing serious,' I said, and I wasn't playing the tough guy. True, I'd picked up a few second-degree burns, but only two third-degree burns that had required skin grafts. It could have been far worse. And compared to Randy's wounds, mine were insignificant.

Alabama reappeared with Heinekens and handed them out.

'Cheers,' said Randy, clinking bottles.

'I'm going to leave you guys to it,' Alabama said, 'go pick us up some lunch. You feel like anything in particular, honey?'

'Let's have seafood,' Randy suggested.

'Just what I feel like,' Alabama agreed. She lifted her chin at me. 'Vin?'

'I eat anything,' I said. 'And often do.'

They kissed and Alabama gave me another smile as she brushed past and picked up a shoulder bag from a chair beside the front door. 'Won't be long.'

'That'll give us forty minutes, give or take,' said Randy when the door closed. 'We can talk.'

I took a seat on the couch.

'The doctors say there's a chance I might not walk again. But the doctors don't know shit. I'll be shooting hoops in a week or two.'

I believed him. Randy was a fighter. A lesser man would have died in that cellar.

''Bama doesn't know,' he said, before upending the Heineken, his academy ring, back on his own finger now, tinkling against the glass.

I didn't believe that for a second. Alabama would know more about Randy's condition than Randy, because she'd make it her business to find out. That was the kind of woman she was.

'I see you got your ring back,' I said.

'Yeah.' He examined it. 'Still waiting on the Breitling. I have to say that was the dumbest shit I ever pulled – the whole severed-hand business.'

'Why's that?'

'Once I knew what was going down in von Weiss's camp, I could've walked. I *should've* walked. You know, come in from the cold.'

'If you'd done that, von Weiss would have changed his plans, brought the timing forward. You couldn't have risked it.'

'Maybe. Maybe not. Anyway, I got cocky. I thought I could pay some lowlifes to do what I told them, take care of the details and keep it to themselves. But they went straight to von Weiss, got another payment, and dropped me in the hole. Fucking literally. One minute I was on the team, working in with Gamal Abdul-Jabbar and his Somalis; the next those fucking animals were slicing me up, shitting all over me, cutting me, frying my ass, trying to get me to talk.' He was getting agitated, the memories returning, playing in his head.

'Don't be so hard on yourself. The ring, the snake venom, the finger-prints, the note – it was all there. Once we figured it out, the clues were like a roadmap.'

'Too clever for my own good.' Randy gazed at his lap, a moment of reflection, then looked up. 'And I got Anton killed. He was just a kid.'

'Anton?'

'The pilot who flew the King Air. I heard how he died in Australia.' Randy looked at his hand, scratched one of his palms. 'The note. I wanted Alabama to contact Anna, I didn't know that Anna had, you know . . .'

Died. I nodded.

'And I didn't know you and she were an item, either. The Kevin Bacon factor – amazing. Lucky for me you stepped in.'

Lucky he had a partner like Alabama. 'Hey, Petinski told me to give you her best.'

He grinned and checked around conspiratorially. 'And her best is pretty damn good, am I right?'

The grin was infectious. 'I wouldn't know.'

'Sure you wouldn't.' He rubbed his quads and the grin faded. 'I heard von Weiss took her. I also heard about what happened to Shilling. He's a sick fuck.'

'It's in his genes.'

'I've been reading the papers. Maybe it would have been better if you'd left von Weiss on that island.'

I'd have done just that if a Brazilian Navy Puma hadn't turned up and taken him away. 'Yeah, maybe,' I said.

We both took the opportunity to drink.

'I didn't know Shilling was on our side,' he said quietly.

'She didn't know about you, either. Tell me, did you cross paths with von Weiss's pilot – a Frog by the name of LeDuc? He also went by the name Laurent Duval. Short, dark and treacherous.'

Randy thought about it for a few seconds before shaking his head. 'No. Though I'd probably recognize him if I saw him.'

The slippery little fuck had wriggled through the net *again*. His capture was now up to Interpol; indeed, he'd climbed to the top of their hit list.

'So what's going to happen to von Weiss?' Randy asked.

'He's facing a raft of charges. Most of them are thanks to the work you did undercover – illegal arms trading, drugs importation, deprivation of liberty. He'll go away for a long time, along with his people.'

'Don't bet on it. I note you haven't mentioned the W80 thing.'

'What W80 thing?'

'Right. The fucker . . .' Randy shook his head. 'Well, you ran him down. Can you tell me about that?'

I gave him the ins and outs of everything I knew. Some of it he wasn't supposed to know, but I figured Randy had earned the right to hear about it. When Alabama came back we had soft shell crab and fresh fat

Pacific shrimp for lunch, cold Heinekens, and the day went by too fast. When it was done, Randy and I said goodbye and promised to catch up soon, then Alabama gave me a ride out to McCarran. We were maybe fifty yards down the road when, out of nowhere, she said, 'The doctors told me there's only a ten percent chance Randy'll walk again. At first they wouldn't tell me because I'm not next of kin. Can you believe that? I forced it out of them.'

As I knew she would. Having someone like Alabama in his corner – Randy was a lucky guy.

*

I glanced out at the seating in the auditorium from around the side of the wall. I was surprised to see that it was mostly filled. There were half a dozen other servicemen and women aside from me who were also receiving decorations. The Secretary of the Air Force had turned up, as had most of the staff from OSI here at Andrews. There was even a smattering of celebrities in the crowd: the rapper Twenny Fo' and Leila, his R&B fiancée, folks I'd come to know quite well after some close calls we shared in the Democratic Republic of Congo not so long ago. Ayesha, Leila's heavily pregnant personal assistant, blew me a kiss, as did Marnie Masters, sitting with Arlen. He didn't want to be left out and blew a kiss also.

A female second lieutenant stepped up to a lectern and asked everyone to stand as the colors were brought out – the Stars and Stripes, as well as the Air Force flag – and placed in the center of the stage by the color guard. Then the official party was called onto the stage: the SecAF, the base commander, the photographer, various colonels and, finally, Brigadier General James Wynngate – everyone in their dress blues.

The lectern was vacated so that Wynngate could say a few words. Unlikely, I thought. My CO was a lot of things but a man of few words wasn't one of them.

'Ladies and gentlemen,' he began, after clearing his throat and pulling a sheaf of paper from his inside blouse pocket. Five minutes later he surprised me and finished. He also surprised me by saying a bunch of nice things about me. Maybe that's why the speech was short by his standards, there being not so many nice things he could find to say about me, aside from the fact that my type indicators said I was an ESFJ and he believed that I was an exemplary example for others with similar indicators to follow.

Right.

The lieutenant took control of the lectern again, and said, 'Attention to orders.' Everyone on stage came to attention, and the audience stood. The lieutenant continued, 'In accordance with special order number 1835, the Secretary of the Air Force hereby awards the Silver Star for gallantry in action against an opposing armed force to . . . Major Vincent Cooper, United States Air Force.'

That was my cue. I walked out onto center stage in military fashion, stopped two paces from Wynngate, then did a crisp left face toward the audience.

The narrator went on to read the citation, which was based on the action in Kabul, Afghanistan, less than six months ago, where I'd volunteered for close protection work. I'd been leading the team, chauffeuring around a crooked Afghan politician wanted by the Taliban. We'd walked straight into an impromptu ambush, or maybe it was planned – that had never been properly determined. A suicide bomber took out the politician, and then my team was caught in a killing zone that grew in intensity. I happened to be in a good position to deal with some of the opposing force, and then returned to my people and helped get them out without further injury.

Luck should also have received a decoration because there was a lot of that involved.

'His unit secured inside the remaining functioning transport, Major Cooper stayed behind to provide covering fire, which enabled his personnel to withdraw from the engagement without further casualties. Major Cooper returned to the base by other means,' the lieutenant concluded.

The other means was a pushbike. The details of the engagement brought it all vividly back to mind. The dust, the bullets, the noise, the deafness and the dead US Army Specialist with perfectly manicured nails, painted red. She was new in-country, a librarian, a reservist, a mother, and most of her head was gone. Sweat beaded on my upper lip and there suddenly wasn't enough air in the room.

I heard the words, 'Reflect great credit on himself and the United States Air Force,' and snapped back into the here and now.

Following the script for these things, I turned, Wynngate turned, and we faced each other. A staff sergeant walked crisply from stage left to the general's shoulder, holding a dark blue velvet cushion, the decoration on it. Wynngate took it gently, almost tenderly, and pinned it to the front of my blouse. 'Good job, Vin,' he said. 'Try not to let it go to your head.' He smiled and I think I even detected a wink.

We shook on it and the photographer snapped one for posterity. The general and I exchanged salutes and I about-faced as applause rose from the auditorium. As I walked to the wings I glanced out, and in the front row I saw Alabama and Randy clapping. There was no wheelchair and Randy was standing on his own two feet. Yeah, lucky guy.

Acknowledgements

Writing this book was, if nothing else, a feat of collaboration. If I've made an error in some area of fact, the fault is mine. But if I've gotten it right, the credit goes to a list of folks who donated their time and expertise.

First of all there's Panda, aka Lieutenant Commander Michael Pandolfo (USAF ret.), who's a stickler for detail as well as being a good bloke. As I keep saying in these Acknowledgements pages, 'I really couldn't have written this novel without him,' and jotting a few short words of thanks up front really does feel quite inadequate in expressing my appreciation. (Thanks, Panda. Again!)

Assisting on the weapons side of things was Michael Jordan.

Tricia Owens kept me out of trouble in Vegas (is that possible?). And in Rio, Brent Sullivan got me into it. Alison Shot (a very talented singer) chaperoned me through the ranks of the topless talls at Bally's Jubilee. And Stephen Cake cast his eye over Cooper's mischief in Dar es Salaam.

Also, I'd like to thank Lt. Col. Gary P. Leeder, USAF, Operations Officer, Detachment 1, 53 EWG, Nellis AFB, Nevada, and all the others at Nellis: Lt. Col. Robert Dreyfus, USAF, Commander, Detachment 1, 53 EWG; Charles W Ramey, Director of Public Affairs, 99th Air Base Wing; AFOSI DET 206 and the office of the Staff Judge Advocate.

To Emma and Clara, who did the editing on this book – thanks, you made me look far better than I am.

And last but no means least, I'd like to thank my wife, Sam, who's always asking me where I am (even though I'm right beside her).